Dear Reader,

Happy Anniversary, Blaze! Ten years? How awesome is that? Time really does fly when you're having red-hot sex…er, I mean fun. Wait a minute, that's redundant. Anyway, we're thrilled this special 2-in-1 offers our first blazing story along with our latest!

In *Undeniable Pleasures,* the third and final book in our Pleasure Seekers miniseries, bad boy Jason Savage isn't used to mixing business with pleasure. But when he takes over a special case involving a difficult federal witness, he's all over it. Trouble is, sexy club owner Jordan Cosby has *pleasure* written all over her….

Our first book for Blaze, *You Sexy Thing!,* gives readers a glimpse into the lives of warring sex therapists who can't agree about anything…except how good the sex is between them.

We hope this special tenth anniversary visit to the past and present leaves you craving a smoke!

We'd love to hear what you think. Contact us at P.O. Box 12271, Toledo, OH 43612, or visit us on the web at www.toricarrington.net, or www.facebook.com/toricarrington where there's fun to be had every day.

Here's wishing you love, romance and *hot* reading.

Lori & Tony Karayianni

aka Tori Carrington

P.S. Check out the Blaze Authors' new Pet Project at blazeauthors.com.

Tori Carrington

UNDENIABLE PLEASURES
YOU SEXY THING!

TORONTO NEW YORK LONDON
AMSTERDAM PARIS SYDNEY HAMBURG
STOCKHOLM ATHENS TOKYO MILAN MADRID
PRAGUE WARSAW BUDAPEST AUCKLAND

ISBN-13: 978-0-373-79633-5

UNDENIABLE PLEASURES
Copyright © 2011 by Harlequin Books S.A.

The publisher acknowledges the
copyright holders of the individual works
as follows:

UNDENIABLE PLEASURES
Copyright © 2011 by Lori Karayianni &
Tony Karayianni

YOU SEXY THING!
Copyright © 2001 by Lori Karayianni &
Tony Karayianni

Recycling programs
for this product may
not exist in your area.

CONTENTS

ABOUT THE AUTHOR

RT Book Reviews Career Achievement Award-winning bestselling duo Lori Schlachter Karayianni and Tony Karayianni are the power behind the pen name Tori Carrington. Their more than forty-five titles include numerous Harlequin Blaze miniseries, as well as the ongoing Sofie Metropolis comedic mystery series with another publisher. Visit www.toricarrington.net and www.sofiemetro.com for more information on the duo and their titles.

Books by Tori Carrington

To get the inside scoop on Harlequin Blaze and its talented writers, be sure to check out blazeauthors.com.

UNDENIABLE PLEASURES

We dedicate this book to readers like us who like it HOT! You know who you are. And to editor extraordinaire Brenda Chin: Thank you for ten years of steamy sex and unforgettable love...strictly in the business sense, of course. Here's to the next ten: More, more more!

1

THIS KID WAS A GRADE-A, Top-Choice whack job whose only job at Lazarus was going to be to find his way back out the way he came in.

Jason Savage sat back in his office chair and closed the recruit candidate file in front of him. Finding new talent for Lazarus Security usually ranked as one of his favorite parts of his day. He enjoyed meeting kids fresh out of the military ready to use their training for civilian purposes.

But not today.

He rubbed his hands over his face and pushed the file tagged "Daryl Bennett" to the side of the desk.

He looked at the cell phone where he had it open and on speaker.

"Can you do it?" Partner and longtime friend Lincoln Williams asked.

While he'd been reviewing Daryl Bennett's résumé and test results, Lincoln had called him about a separate matter. Namely, Linc wanted him to take a security assignment off his hands so he could stay in Maine with the woman he'd followed there.

"I can do it. The question is, will I?"

He imagined Linc's stony stare on the other end of the connection and chuckled.

"What's in it for me?" Jason continued.

"A ticket out of town—just what you're looking for."

"The job is in Denver. Denver is a suburb."

It was a joke they liked to share because so many viewed Colorado Springs as an adjunct to Denver, the larger city to the north.

"I'll help get things moving on your bid to open the Baltimore office earlier," Linc added.

Jason sat up in his chair. "Now we're talking." He'd been angling to push ahead with Lazarus Security's plans to open satellite offices on either coast, Baltimore being the first because of its close proximity to D.C. And although those plans weren't scheduled for execution until next year at the earliest...well, he had his reasons for wanting to get out of town, stat. And they were very good ones. "Give me the job details."

He jotted down the information Linc gave him. His subject was witness for the prosecution in a high-profile federal case. The job was difficult (two teams of Marshals had been pulled because of undisclosed problems). And the trial was two weeks away.

"Walk in the park," Jason said.

"Maybe. If said park is in an active area of Waziristan," Linc chuckled, referring to the mountainous region between Afghanistan and Pakistan where they'd seen the worst action during their tours of duty...and where they and their Lazarus partners had gone through hell and come out the other side lifetime friends. "The accused is motivated—he has a high price on her head and word has it every contract wannabe within a five-hundred radius has his sites set on her."

Her?

Jason realized he hadn't gotten the witness's name and took it now: Jordan Cosby.

His chair springs groaned as he sat back again. "Shit. Is

this the case of that gun runner whose ex-girlfriend turned state's witness on him?"

"Rick Packard. The one and only."

"And Jordan is the ex-girlfriend…"

"That would be her."

He rubbed his face again thinking he needed a shave and more importantly, a good eight hours of uninterrupted sleep, something he hadn't seen in over a month. Which was the reason he wanted out of Colorado Springs. He had the sinking feeling nothing would ever go back to the way it was before. Not after what he'd done.

While he didn't particularly like the idea of watching over somebody's bimbo for two weeks, any excuse that got him out of town—and away from Lazarus—was a good one.

"When do I report?" he asked.

"Yesterday."

"Got it."

"Then what are you still doing on the phone with me?"

He stood up. "Funny, I was just asking myself the same question." He pressed Disconnect, closed the phone and then put it in his pocket, knowing that in some backwater town in Maine, Linc was grinning at least as wide as he was.

He checked his desk, picked up the files on the corner of it and then walked down the long corridor taking him to the front offices.

He explained the situation to Lisa Russo and Giulia Pawley, the two girls—pardon him, "women," as he was often reminded by female coworkers—that were the public face of the company along with receptionist Margie Hall. They were also the glue holding them together.

The front door opened and in walked the reason he needed to get out of there.

Hell.

Like Linc, he was friends with the other two partners,

Megan McGowan and Darius Folsom: tight friends. Hell, he'd grown up with Dari. But he'd made a very bad error in judgment—poor choice of words: he'd fucked up majorly—by sleeping with Meg while Dari was deployed overseas two months ago.

It had seemed rational at the time: no-ties sex that both of them needed while on a remote assignment. Then Dari had returned early and the shit had hit the fan.

That had been nearly nine weeks ago…and they still hadn't recovered from it. Not completely. Oh, on the surface it appeared everything was all right. But lightly scratch it, and fresh pus leached from the wound.

"Hey, Savage," Dari said as he accepted his messages from Margie.

Meg stepped up beside him. He immediately stiffened… in more ways than one.

And cursed himself for the involuntary reaction.

He grimaced as he handed the files he'd brought with him to Lisa.

"Mr. Bennett is waiting in the other room."

Jason raised a brow. He'd finished his interview with the never-would-be agent, if Jason had anything to say about it, an hour ago.

"He said he wanted to wait to have another word with you. I thought I'd make him wait a little longer before buzzing to let you know."

"Fine. I'll see to him on my way out. You know how to contact me."

"Jason?"

Megan's voice stopped him in his tracks.

"I spoke to Jax again yesterday. Any chance you'll reconsider your position?"

"Not in hell," he said.

He continued walking toward the waiting room off to the left.

His younger brother Jackson, or Jax as he was known, wanted to work for Lazarus so badly he could taste it. And for that reason alone Jason never intended to let him put it in his mouth.

That and he wished the kid would go back to school like he wanted. Learn something useful. Become a doctor or a lawyer. Anything that was completely different from what he was doing.

Jason hadn't been able to stop Jax from following him into the military. But he could stop him from working for Lazarus.

He opened the waiting-room door and crossed to where Daryl Bennett barely had time to get to his feet before he stopped in front of him and shook his hand. "Thank you for coming, Daryl, but this isn't going to work out."

The kid blinked at him, his thin, pale face going from open hopefulness to flushing to disappointment within a blink. "I don't understand, Mr. Savage. I did really well on all the tests."

Yes, he had aced all the physical tests. He was in amazing shape considering he topped six feet and likely didn't weight a pound over a buck-fifty.

The psychological tests on the other hand… "You neglected to mention what happened during your very brief stint in the military."

"Yes, but—"

"Like I said, thank you. And good luck with your job search."

"Mr. Savage!" The kid tried following him.

Jason closed the door behind him that locked automatically for security reasons, the room having a separate public exit so he wouldn't have to confront the guy again.

For God's sake, the kid had shot his commanding officer in the knee when he'd been ordered to drop and give a hundred. And for a screwup, Daryl had admitted responsibility for.

Whack job. Pure and simple. There was no place for him at Lazarus.

Just like there was no place for his brother Jax, albeit for different reasons.

Jason retraced his steps through the corridor to where his SUV was parked in the back, thinking about his younger brother. About how they always seemed to butt heads at every turn. How their grandmother doted on Jax and then turned around and gave Jason an earful every time he drove out to the farm for dinner.

He thought about the ways he might yet convince his brother to use the money their parents had left them to continue his education. It was enough to occupy his time and then some during the sixty-plus-mile drive north to Denver, where he then navigated the city to the address Linc had given him.

He still hadn't come up with a persuasive argument he hadn't already voiced a thousand times by the time he passed through the heightened building security and rode the elevator up to the apartment he was looking for.

"Hey." He flashed his ID to the two government stiffs flanking the front door of Jordan Cosby's apartment. "I'm your relief."

"It's about time," said the guy on the right while the agent on the left communicated with command via his earpiece and hidden transmitter. Then the two men gladly left their posts and headed toward the elevator. "Good luck. You're going to need it."

Jason knew they weren't going far. They would likely keep

post on a slightly more removed perimeter. But from here on in, he would be in charge of personal security.

He knocked on the door. A moment later it was opened… and he found himself staring at one of the most strikingly beautiful women he'd ever seen. And she was wearing next to nothing.

2

JORDAN COSBY WAS WET, rushed and fully prepared to give the morons outside her door what-for when she opened the door and found it saw not the two suits but a really hot guy in jeans and a black T-shirt. She stuck her head through the doorway finding neither of the U.S. Marshals there.

She finished buttoning the oversize white men's shirt she'd pulled on when she climbed from the shower to answer the door and then crossed her arms under her breasts.

"Either you're really good—in which case take your best shot—or you're the new guy Lincoln promised to send over."

"Bingo."

He walked inside without waiting for an invitation.

Jordan gave an eye roll and closed the door. Since her shirt didn't bear any bloodstains, she figured this was the associate Lincoln Williams had told her was on his way.

Raised as the only girl, not to mention the youngest, in a family full of guys, she'd always prided herself on being capable of holding her own and then some. But even she realized lately she was edging dangerously close to 'bitch' territory.

She stared at where she absently scratched her arm and stopped. The fact that she'd spent more time in her apartment in the past two weeks than she had in the past two years was half to blame. Responsibility for the rest went to the knowledge that she still had two weeks of what she was coming to describe as 'hell on earth' to endure. Then would come the trial she'd never wanted to be a part of in the first place to give damaging testimony against a man who had tattooed a very high price tag on her forehead.

And not only was she basically being held a prisoner in her own apartment—a place she was seldom in—but she was finding it impossible to talk anyone into coming over. The only visitors she seemed to get were like the man even now moving through her place as if he owned it. Her friends and associates were afraid of any contact that didn't include a cell phone for obvious reasons.

It didn't help that the reason she was in protective custody was because someone had shot through her car window while she was pulling out of the building's basement garage.

Memory of the incident even now caused her heart to beat harder and her palms to dampen. In that one moment she'd become all too aware that what she was facing was very real…and she'd finally agreed to the protective custody the Justice Department offered when they'd first asked her to testify.

As the owner of three successful clubs in Denver, New York and San Francisco, it might be her job to create excitement; but strictly the kind that left people with a hangover the next morning…not in the morgue being measured for a pine box.

Of course, being a people person meshed well with her club ownership. Unfortunately, the only people she saw lately were humorless, antisocial U.S. Marshals. She watched as the latest in the never-ending line of silent, alpha males made a tour through the two-bedroom town house apartment; she was waiting when he came back down the open, spiral staircase.

"Is it clear?" she asked.

She was impressed he hadn't drawn his gun as he made the rounds. The Marshals did it every time.

She sighed when he didn't respond. "Great. Another ape without a sense of humor."

"Might help if you didn't call them apes."

She cracked a smile, relief flooding her veins. Sure, she might act a little bitchy, but the truth was she horribly missed human interaction. "He speaks. Thank the Lord. Every other person they've sent over had zero personality, much less a sense of humor."

"Who said I had either?"

"By comparison? I think you've just won the Mr. America contest."

She watched as his gaze swept over her barely clad body. *Well*...

She was surprised by the flush of awareness that spread over her skin. While she was used to men appreciating her physical appearance, it had been two weeks since she'd enjoyed such open attention by an attractive male and her instant, nipple-hardening reaction was doubly intense than it otherwise might have been. That's what happened when you were locked away in your apartment by a bunch of cyborgs assigned to keep you safe.

That's what happened when you hadn't had sex in four months because the last guy you dated was a gunrunning criminal...

And when the same guy had no problem with the idea of not only seeing you dead, but being the power behind the trigger.

She shivered as the agent finished his perusal following a lingering look at her breasts and then met her gaze. "Aw, and we didn't even get to the swimsuit competition."

She gestured with her hand. "Be my guest."

His chuckle made the small hairs on her lower belly stand

up in a delicious wave. He crossed to her and held out his hand. "Jason Savage."

She took her time shaking the warm limb, marveling at his long, thick fingers. "Jordan Cosby."

He withdrew his hand. "Did I, um, interrupt something?"

"A little late for that question, isn't it?"

He had a grin as naughty as sin and twice as delectable. "I'm guessing shower."

"I'm guessing you're right."

"Feel free to return."

She wondered if it was too soon to ask a man she'd just met if he'd like to join her.

"You mind?" He walked toward the kitchen.

Jordan squinted, and then followed in his wake. "Do I mind what?"

He stepped to the counter where she'd made coffee a little while earlier, trying to maintain her regular hours which included not getting up before noon and massive amounts of caffeine in whatever form she could lay her hands on, beginning with—but certainly not limited to—coffee.

He took out the carafe, sniffed the contents and then checked the cupboards until he found a cup. He held it up to her to indicate that's what he'd been asking about.

"Well, I guess it doesn't matter if I mind then, does it?" she asked with a smile.

He poured himself a cup and then gave a mock toast before taking a sip. "How do you know Linc?"

"He handles security for one of my clubs."

He raised a brow. "Oh?"

Most people she met had the same reaction to her being a club owner. She wasn't entirely clear why, but to her the career step had been a natural one. She'd been taking double majors in business and finance at NYU when she met and fell in lust with Danny Leary. Their affair hadn't lasted long, but their friendship had. She hadn't blinked when he proposed they go into business together. And so was born Bridges NYC, her first club.

Friendships had played a large role in the opening of Bridges San Francisco and Bridges Denver, as well. And as such, she understood when to take part...and when to butt out and let her friends and managers see to things. Although she did like brainstorming events and bringing in national acts. And she thoroughly enjoyed partying at each of them.

She'd moved to Denver to help oversee the launch of the club a year ago along with manager and old friend Montana Sky. And at this point, didn't feel the desire to move on, finding a nice synchronicity to the city's groove that suited her.

"Mmm." She considered asking Jason to pour her a cup of coffee, too, but instead opened the refrigerator and reached for the milk, knowing full well as she did so that the hem of the shirt rode up, baring a healthy stretch of thigh. Enough to reveal she wore no panties. She closed the door and turned to smile at him...only to find he'd left the room.

Jordan made a face. Well, that didn't happen to her often enough for her to get used to.

She fixed herself a half a cup of coffee, put the milk back away and padded back into the living room where she found him standing before the wall of windows overlooking the busy street. He'd pulled back the curtains just enough to see out; curtains the other guards had insisted she keep closed.

She sipped her coffee and openly appreciated his form. His back was as hot as his front, with an ass made of granite and shoulders as wide as the doorway. His hair brushed the back of his collar and was in need of a cut. And what was it about men strapped with guns that always gave her a thrill?

Of course, it would be a good idea to remember the reason she'd ended up an inmate in her own life to begin with.

Savage didn't look in a hurry to go anywhere as he drank his coffee. Which was just fine with her. He could prove just the distraction this girl needed...

She only hoped that he didn't have any friends on the Top Ten F.B.I.'s Most Wanted List. Or that he wouldn't be having any conversations with them in her presence that she might be called to testify against...

WITHIN FIVE MINUTES, Jason noted ten holes in security.

He also sized up and dismissed the subject in need of it. He grimaced. Okay, he was trying to.

Jordan Cosby was a beautiful woman who knew how to use her sexuality to gain an advantage over the opposite sex. She was also a lady of means if her frou-frou apartment was anything to go by. He stared at an oversize, custom-made white leather couch the size of a bus, and guessed it was.

He'd certainly come across his fair share of women like her. And he'd slept with most of them. But considering the Middle-Eastern-size mess casual sex had placed him smack dab in the middle of, he wasn't going to have anything sexual to do with the likes of Jordan Cosby.

He glanced at where she was bent over a desk that served as a barrier between the open living and dining area, her back to him, the shirt riding up to reveal the tiniest, tantalizing peek of a perfectly shaped ass. He swallowed hard. Why did he have the feeling she wasn't going to make this easy for him?

"What are your plans for the day?" he asked, turning his attention back toward the window.

He heard the shuffling of papers. "The same as yesterday—nothing, nada, oh, and a whole lot of zilch."

"Good."

"For you, maybe."

"For you, too. Means you're safe."

"It means I'm about ready to jump out of my skin and through that window."

He saw her reflection in the window in question...and got the distinct impression she knew he was watching her, given her catlike smile. She'd turned back toward him and lifted herself to sit on the desk, her long, bare legs dangling over the side. She'd only done a few of the buttons on the shirt she wore so the inside curve of her breasts was clearly visible through the gaping material.

He rotated to face her, brow raised, challenging her to take it as far as she dared.

"Or…" she said in a low purr. "I could just jump out of this shirt and see what other ways we might occupy our time…"

She slowly uncrossed her legs.

Jason ordered himself not to look. Not to verify his suspicion that she wore no underwear.

Oh, boy…

Curiosity got the better of him and he dropped his gaze. The shirt blocked his view.

He told himself he was glad.

"Where are you going?" she asked when he headed back toward the kitchen.

"To make a few calls. In the meantime, I'd suggest you get out of that shirt…and put some clothes on. Because I don't mix business with pleasure."

"Where's the fun in that?"

He ignored her question as he closed the kitchen door behind him. He stopped and stood stock-still, trying to regain his bearings.

Why did he have the feeling this was a test?

More importantly, why did he have the feeling this was a test he was destined to fail?

<u>3</u>

ALTHOUGH SHE DIDN'T like it, Jordan did get dressed in a simple pair of black yoga pants and white tank top, and spent the next few hours on her laptop orchestrating club business. She didn't realize dusk was falling until the desktop lamp was the only light in the room. She looked around but didn't see Savage anywhere. In fact, she'd seen very little of him since he'd ordered her to get dressed. She knew he was still there somewhere, because every now and again he came into the room, checked the door and the windows…and then disappeared again.

The apartment wasn't that big, for God's sake.

Of course, if she really wanted to find him…

"Hello. Laptop to Jordan. Are you still there?"

She blinked at her screen and the live camera feed of Otto Fitch, the manager of Bridges San Francisco. She shifted in the chair she'd been sitting in for so long her ass had gone numb. The only saving grace of her predicament was her ability to keep in contact with others and on top of business via modern technology. In fact, two weeks into her isolation, she was probably beginning to wear on the nerves of the people she normally spoke to maybe once, twice a week at most. Now she was calling, texting and live-chatting with them several times a day. She was beginning to feel like a pest. But if she didn't do something, she would go absolutely bonkers in no time flat.

She caught herself scratching her arm and stopped, rubbing the raw skin instead, even as she looked around for the ghost that currently inhabited her apartment. She'd heard stories about Linc Williams's shadowy background. Hints at black ops and the F.B.I. and other business of a nefarious nature. And it looked like Jason Savage was cut from the same cloth. But that was the club hotline for you: she'd learned a long time ago the gossip about someone was usually much more interesting than the person in question.

She grimaced. Well, by and large that was the case. She'd believed the rumors circulating about Rick Packard had to be more hype than truth. She'd found out the hard way that wasn't the case.

Still, business was business, and his business had been none of her business.

Unfortunately the judge and the judicial system didn't share her viewpoint.

Essentially they had photographic proof she'd been present at two meetings Rick had with another notorious underworld figure, who appeared to be the true target of their investigation. And while she hadn't participated or even overheard either conversation, she had been asked to leave the table so they could discuss 'business' and then asked to return an hour later. Her own attorney was convinced the Justice Department was using her as a pawn to get Rick to turn on his 'business' partner, offer up testimony to put the bigger fish behind bars and save his own hide. And since he couldn't be sure what all she'd heard, or what testimony she might offer up...well, Rich had decided to go with Plan B instead.

Namely, to do away with her and any information she might have.

She shivered at the thought that her life was worth so little to another human, especially one she'd dated.

The truth was, she didn't have anything. Which left her feeling all the more vulnerable. A sensation she wasn't familiar with…and wasn't happy to become acquainted with now.

So what was the truth about Jason Savage?

Otto's dramatic sigh caught her attention. She blinked him back into focus and finally answered his question: "You can see I'm still here."

"No, honey, I can see you, but I'm not seeing you. Where's your head at?"

There was movement behind her as Savage came into the room from the kitchen and went to stand in his favorite spot in front of the windows. Her every cell went immediately on alert and she sat up a little straighter, which made her grimace harder.

"Donny Darko's holding me hostage," she muttered, half to herself.

Otto must have heard her because he said, "Ooh! I hope leather and hot oil is involved."

"I wish."

"Well, tell me he's hot, at least."

Jordan twisted her lips and then shifted the laptop until Jason Savage was caught in the camera shot. She pressed the zoom button until he stood in stark, handsome relief. One stroke of a key and Otto disappeared from view and Jason Savage filled the screen.

"Oh, honey, if his front is as yummy as his back… Tell him to turn around."

Jason must have heard Otto because he looked over his shoulder, seeming to stare straight at the camera. She pressed another key and captured the shot.

"Ohmygawd, girl, if you don't have the leather and oil, I'll send it to you. Express!" Otto said.

Jordan repositioned the laptop and refreshed the settings so she was once again chatting with Otto. She watched as the thirty-year-old Rutger Hauer look-alike leaned closer to his camera. "Pssst…if you don't want him, send him my way."

Jordan gave a wry smile, recalling the way Jason's face had darkened earlier as he watched her stretch suggestively on the desk. "Sorry, babe, but I don't think he swings your way."

Otto sighed. "Shame. He and I could have had fun together. A lot of fun."

Movement. She glanced over her shoulder to find Jason heading back toward the kitchen. The door closed a moment later.

"Please, please, please tell me you plan on putting your hands on that fine ass. At least once. For me. Please."

She sat back and crossed her arms over her chest. "He doesn't mix business with pleasure."

"Darlin', with that man I'd make his pleasure my business."

"Yeah, well, I don't know if I want to work that hard."

"Are you kidding me? You're the hardest working person I know. You're all about the job."

"Not when it comes to men."

Otto grinned at her. "Yes, well, maybe it's about time you put in a little elbow grease, girl. It ain't worth nothing if you don't have to work for it."

"Are you kidding me?" she repeated his earlier words to him. "Are you forgetting the small fact that my last relationship got me into the trouble I'm in now?"

"Honey, that wasn't a relationship…it was sex."

"Yes, well, that doubly proves my point."

"But he might be The One," Otto said.

"The one, what?"

He stared at her.

"And you base this on a three-second glimpse of his ass?"

He stuck his tongue out at her.

She laughed. "Come on, Otto, you know I don't buy into

all that fairy-tale crap. That's the cock-and-bull story they try to sell to little girls before they even make it out of the womb."

Jordan winced, wishing she hadn't said that. Not because it wasn't accurate. To the contrary, it was a little too close to the truth.

"Besides," she continued, before he could catch on to her hesitation, something he was amazingly adept at, and what had solidified an instant camaraderie when she'd interviewed him for the job over a year ago. "If I remember correctly, I think you're on your fifth One."

He sighed again, albeit this time for a different reason, she'd wager. "I've decided they were just practice. I'm still looking."

"Pierce and you are done already?"

"Ancient history, sweetie. We broke up last night."

Jordan leaned closer to the laptop. "I'm sorry."

He shrugged like it was of no concern to him, but she knew better. "Bygones. We weren't a good fit. We both knew it. He was 100-hundred thread count and I'm 1,000."

"Makes for a rough night's sleep."

"You ain't kidding. Still, I'm hopeful. I made eye contact with a handsome one at the open market today. I'm going back tomorrow to see if I can't catch his attention again. Speaking of getting someone's attention, you still have that little red number I bought you last Christmas…?"

She laughed. "You know, you're hopeless."

"Hopeless romantic, maybe."

"You say tomato…"

"Yeah, yeah."

"Anyway, enough of my *sex* life, or lack thereof. Let's get back to these numbers…"

She was glad he immediately returned to the business at hand, even as she considered his words…

THE WOMAN WAS PUT ON this earth solely to drive him mad, Jason was convinced.

Eighteen hours on the job, and he had the sinking sensation he'd never make it to twenty-four without taking what Jordan Cosby so temptingly offered.

He sat back in the chair and recrossed his legs at the ankles on the ottoman, fully dressed and fully alert. He'd made the rounds ten minutes ago and would make them again in another five. He illuminated the screen of his cell phone. It was just past 4:00 a.m. In three hours, Lazarus agent Dominic Falzone would come to relieve him so he could catch a few hours sleep. Not because he was tired, but because to stay at the top of his game, he needed to.

The apartment was dark and quiet. The better to nab any would-be assassins. So far, he hadn't spotted anything out of whack. But that didn't mean in the next moment someone wouldn't materialize from the dark with his and Jordan's names carved on his bullet casings. Jordan's for the massive amount of money her ex had put on her life, his because he stood in the way.

Still, despite the sexy distraction, he was happy to be away from Colorado Springs.

A hot, sweaty memory of what had happened two months ago in Florida between him and Megan McGowan slid through his mind. He sucked air in through his teeth, cursing himself and his mind for playing unfair tricks on him.

Okay, he admitted, maybe it had been about more than strictly sex when it came to his partner's girl. Not an easy thing to admit, considering he'd been the one to suggest the no-strings, one-night stand. Or that Darius Folsom had been his best friend since grade school.

He'd silently argued that the illicit nature of their liaison, as well as the fact that Megan was off-limits to him, were largely to blame. But it didn't explain everything.

He cursed under his breath. This was all new territory for

him, this thinking about relationships. He'd never betrayed a friend before, much less his best friend. And Megan...well, she'd been more than just a way to release the tension related to a case beyond frustrating.

He heard a sound behind him.

Jason slowly removed his feet from the stool and stood up, his .38 automatically in his palm, every thought from his head gone as he went on full alert. It sounded like it had come from the direction of the kitchen.

Just to be sure, he turned three-hundred-and-sixty degrees, scanning the shadows to verify no one had gotten the jump on him while he'd sat lost in his thoughts. Nothing. Jordan, herself, had gone up to her master bedroom—an entire apartment in and of itself—two hours ago, and during his round ten minutes ago, he'd cracked the door open to find her asleep in that mammoth, king-size thing she called a bed.

It had been all he could do not to climb into it with her...

He ousted the idea from his mind along with the other unwelcome thoughts and crept silently toward the closed kitchen door.

He'd thought he'd left it open the last time he'd gone in, but must have automatically closed it, as he'd done often during the day to cut himself off from temptation incarnate.

The conversation he'd overheard her having with Otto, the guy he knew managed her San Francisco club—reading up on Miss Jordan Cosby throughout the day had been an interesting endeavor to say the least—had only worsened his condition. Leather and oil? He couldn't seem to budge the image of her and both items from his mind whenever he saw her. It was definitely not where he wanted to be. It was his primary job to protect her, not entertain thoughts of mauling her.

He reached out and slowly pushed the swinging door inward.

There he found Miss August sitting on one of the stools at

her granite island, spotlighted perfectly by the soft, recessing ceiling lighting, wearing some sexy red number that left just enough to the imagination.

All things leather and oil loomed large in his mind...

4

DAMN, DAMN, DAMN...

Jason silently re-holstered his firearm and pushed the door the rest of the way open. Jordan didn't even look up from where she was pouring Cocoa Puffs into a bowl. Then she topped it off with whole milk from a carton.

"Sorry, did I wake you?" she asked.

He walked in to stand next to the island, picking up the box of cereal and looking at her with a raised brow. "Middle of the night munchies?"

She smiled, looking all too innocent...which told him she was anything but.

Keep the gaze above the neck, he ordered.

The more he tried, the more he failed.

The red number she had on was nothing short of amazing. Or, rather, the body wearing it rated that distinction. Jordan Cosby apparently took great pride in keeping in shape and it showed. Her breasts were high and tight, her waist long and toned, and her legs... He swallowed hard. Her legs went on and on and tempted his touch as surely as water drew a thirsty traveler.

If only he wasn't afraid he might drown...

"Want some?" she asked, reaching for the box.

The movement stretched her across the counter, her sweet ass nearly bare.

Jason blinked, sure he had to be dreaming. This couldn't be happening. He'd dozed off in the chair and his subconscious was providing this little peep show.

She climbed off the stool and rounded him, her bottom making contact with his already stiffening front.

Definitely not a dream…

He grasped her arm. "What do you think you're doing?"

She blinked up at him, trying to hold on to the innocent angle, although the widening of her pupils in her hazel eyes told him she was all too aware of his condition and the role she was playing in it. "Getting, um, a bowl. Of course."

Her scent teased his nose; not the spicy, citrus perfume she wore, but her own sweet musk. "Of course."

He released his hold. She not so innocently brushed up against him again as she passed.

God, this woman was going to be death of him.

She began pouring cereal into the bowl. He didn't think he was capable of swallowing a bite, but he didn't have it in him to refuse.

Grabbing a stool, he moved it so he was across the counter from her, a safe distance, even though being in the same room qualified as dangerous.

He realized music played softly. Mellow jazz. He'd spotted a console built into the wall in the front hall earlier. There must be another control somewhere, perhaps in her bedroom.

"Nature of the beast," she said, spooning the sugary cereal into her mouth, her lips curiously left bare of any color he could detect. In fact, he didn't think she had on a lick of makeup. Another woman might have gone full out. Jordan appeared to know how appealing she was regardless…and that attracted him on level he wasn't prepared to acknowledge.

"What beast?"

She'd pushed a bowl toward him along with the milk. He sat down and poured a healthy portion of cereal into it, and then some milk.

"Working late. Eating dinner at four in the morning."

"Dinner?"

She smiled at him around a mouthful of Cocoa Puffs. "Mmm. This is the time I usually get home from the club." She swallowed and then wiped a drop of milk from the side of her full mouth. "Dinner."

"Breakfast for dinner."

He dug into his own bowl, although it might as well have been cardboard for all he tasted of it. The only thing he wanted to have his tongue against was her.

She swung her hair back over her shoulder. "Not a cereal man?"

"Not for a long time."

She laughed. "So you cook, then."

"I cook."

She moved her cereal around in her bowl with her spoon. "A skill I never quite mastered."

"Only because you haven't tried. It's simple."

"Spoken like a man who was probably born knowing his way around a kitchen."

"Not quite. But close. My grandmother always insisted my younger brother Jackson and I be able to look after ourselves."

A shadow passed over her face. "Being raised with four older brothers and my father, I made a point of never learning how to cook."

"Ah."

"Ah, what?"

He shrugged. "Just ah."

"*Ah* always means something."

He slowed his movements. "Ah, one of those types. Don't

do anything a man might expect a woman to do. Bucking traditional conventions and all that."

"You disagree?"

He shook his head. "Nope. Not judging, merely remarking."

She looked at him for a long moment, as if trying to decipher if what he was saying was true. Apparently satisfied with what she found, she took another mouthful of cereal.

"I imagine you're used to late nights in your job, as well," she said.

"Comes with the territory."

They ate in silence for a moment and then she asked, "You know Linc well?"

"Well enough that he talked me into taking this gig."

She laughed. A quiet, husky sound that wrapped around him as surely as her fingers might.

"He's in Maine."

"Maine? What's going on there?"

"Nothing."

She squinted at him, but didn't follow up. He was glad, because he wasn't about to share his friend's personal business.

"How do you know each other?"

"We work together."

"You work for him?"

"No, we work together."

"So you're a partner at Lazarus, then."

A statement rather than a question.

"What? Don't look so surprised. I do my homework when it comes to anyone associated with any of my clubs."

He watched her put her spoon aside and pick up her bowl. Dear Lord, please tell him she wasn't about to...

He groaned deep in his throat as she lifted the bowl to her mouth and tipped it, drinking the chocolate milk.

She licked her lips leisurely, and he half expected her to

wet her paws and clean the sides of her mouth like a satisfied cat.

Oh, boy...

He pushed his own bowl aside, positive he couldn't take another bite.

"You know," Jordan said, leaning against the counter in a way that pressed her plump breasts together. "I've been considering ways you and I...um, might make this ordeal a lot more...pleasant for both of us."

He got up from the stool, picked up his bowl and hers and placed both in the sink.

He was surprised to find her in front of him when he turned back.

His breath froze in his lungs at the way she looked up at him coyly. She placed her right hand against his chest, as if plucking off a piece of lint on the black cotton.

"I didn't sign up for pleasant," he said, his voice sounding rough to his own ears.

She smiled. "That doesn't mean it can't be..."

The perfectly manicured hand dipped down on his stomach and then brushed against the most sensitive area of his anatomy.

Air hissed in through his teeth.

He got the distinct impression she was checking him for size.

Rather than be offended, or shocked, he chuckled, holding her gaze as he lifted a brow.

"Find what you're looking for?"

Her hazel eyes sparkled. "Mmm...I'm not sure yet."

She turned her hand around and boldly grasped the length of his cock through his jeans. He instantly stiffened further.

Her smile widened. "Oh, yeah. Definitely found it..."

Damn. He was going to kiss her.

As much as he told himself he shouldn't, it had been two months since he'd been with someone. He hadn't gone that long without since he was stationed overseas. And, damn it, Jordan was the hottest thing he'd seen in a good long while.

Even better, everything about her screamed 'temporary.' There, indeed, would be no strings attached…

He wasn't aware she'd undone three of the buttons on his jeans until he felt the heat of her fingers sliding into the waistband of his boxer briefs. Within moments, she had freed his length and weighed him in her palm.

"Impressive, Mr. Savage."

She tilted her head, holding his gaze, her tongue darting out to moisten her lips. "Tell me, do you live up to your name?"

"What do you think?"

He grasped her hips and hauled her to sit on the counter in front of him, parting her knees and then stepping between them. She swayed forward to kiss him, but he avoided the attempt, instead reaching for the skimpy straps on the naughty red bit of lingerie she wore.

"You're not the only one who needs to check the goods first," he said quietly.

He tugged the straps down over her arms until her breasts sprang from the front of the material. Her nipples were hard and rosy, the mounds as full and firm as he'd expected them to be.

"You approve?"

He rasped his thumbs over the stiff nubs, absorbing her shiver as he did so even as he hummed his approval.

Then his hand moved against her crotch…

The silky material was soaked straight through. He slid a fingertip inside the edge, finding her as bare and as soft and juicy as a ripe peach.

She began to say something, but gasped instead when he slid his finger inside her shallow channel and then farther still, until her hot, tight flesh squeezed him.

Nice…

He stared into her hooded eyes, taking in her flushed cheeks, her ragged breathing. Then he finally lowered his mouth to hers, fully intent on taking every last thing she offered...

5

THE GRANITE COUNTERTOP was cool against Jordan's bottom, but Jason was so very, very hot...

She shivered in anticipation of his kiss as he finally leaned into her.

Yes...

While she'd hoped her bid to gain his attention would work, she hadn't expected this degree of success. Well, she'd had a little help from Otto's Christmas gift. She knew first-hand there were few men who could refuse a little whisper of red nothing. Of course, she normally didn't have to rely on such measures. But as Jason's tongue tangled with hers, mmm, yes, the little bit of work she had to put into the seduction was definitely paying off.

The last man she'd slept with had been Rick. Over four months ago. Call her cautious, but after his arrest, she'd decided perhaps she should take a closer look at the men she dated. As a result, she hadn't been able to shut her mind down even when the sexual urge hit. She didn't want to find herself being subpoenaed to testify at another trial ever again.

If what Rick had been accused of creeped her out a little... well, that was between her and her journal.

Jason nudged her knees a little farther apart and stepped

closer still, until his long, hard length pressed against her moist softness. She shivered again.

Yes…

Normally it took a few glasses of wine and dancing and a night's worth of suggestive glances to get her this turned on. But as Jason stroked her breasts and kissed her deeply, a pool of dark need spread within her, growing deeper with each shallow breath she took.

His fingers worked down her trembling stomach to settle between her thighs. She wriggled a little closer, glad she'd waxed two days ago, something she usually didn't see to herself, but with so much time on her hands, and given the jungle that had been growing, she'd decided to do it…and had cursed herself for hours afterward.

Now she purred as he stroked her soft flesh with his index finger before dipping it inside her.

Sweet heaven, she was going to come…

She gasped as her muscles melted into a shimmering, rippling puddle, staring at him in shock and bliss as a moan reverberated against the back of her throat.

Wow. She must have been in a sorrier state than she'd thought.

She clenched her knees against his hips, wanting…needing to feel him deep inside her.

He moved away.

Jordan blinked, her shock burning into surprise at the abrupt response. She watched, speechless, as he turned and tucked himself back into his pants. He uttered a long line of curse words.

"What's going on?" she asked, restlessly licking her lips.

He slid her a look of pure want. "This…you and me… shouldn't happen. And it isn't going to. Not on my watch."

Her entire body throbbed with wanton desire. "Are you kidding?"

He stared at her. "Honey, there are two things I never joke about—sex and war."

She squinted at him. "And which category would you classify this as?"

He considered her for a long moment. "Both."

He strode from the room as if he were ducking live fire.

Jordan remained on the counter, gaping at the empty air he'd left in his wake, trying to wrap her head around what had just happened.

Seriously? Had he really just left her hanging like that?

Then again, she'd reached orgasm. If anyone had been left hanging, it had been him.

Which made no kind of sense at all.

She glanced down at the lingerie, which was little more than a belt around her waist at this point. She considered pulling the straps back up, but instead slid from the counter and allowed the scrap of silk to pool around her feet. Snatching it up, she headed for the stairs and her bedroom where she hoped she could find a toy up to handling unfinished business.

As for Mr. Savage, well, he had another think coming if he expected her to continue pursuing him after tonight. She might have been desperate enough to try to seduce him this time, but not even she was stupid enough to invite another rejection.

A damn shame. The preview she'd been given told her they would be very, very good together.

WHAT IN THE HELL HAD he been thinking?

Jason closed himself in the downstairs guest bathroom and ran ice-cold water in the sink, splashing handfuls over his face in a losing battle to regain control over himself. His cock was still painfully hard. His breathing still ragged. He stilled his hands against his face and took a deep breath. Hell, he even smelled like her, for Pete's sake.

He grabbed a towel and dried his face then turned to lean against the sink, sucked in a deep breath and searched for something guaranteed to make his dick go limp—namely, the other topic he never joked about.

In an instant, his mind's eye filled with a desert scene a half a world away. It had been hot as Hades and his team had been caught in a Waziristan valley with no cover and surrounded by hostiles.

He, Dari, Linc, Megan, Eli Stark and Barry Lazaro had been under heavy fire for more than an hour. Things didn't look good.

"God damn it, move move move!" Barry had ordered, spraying the surrounding hills with cover fire, allowing his fellow soldiers a chance at escape.

Jason had led the way, everyone following after.

How the enemy managed to sneak up on them was a mystery. They'd all been on high alert. Which meant they had been lying in wait.

Finally, they reached a rocky stand of trees. All of them ducked for cover, taking a moment to catch their breath.

"Plan!" Eli called.

They all shouted out different options. All except Lazaro…

Unfortunately, Lazaro wouldn't be calling out anything again…

Jason's cell phone vibrated, pulling him from his reverie.

He stretched his neck, finding his mental foray into the past having accomplished what he was after, and then some. Memories of that time always left him feeling raw and sober. And determined. He tossed the towel aside and answered the call.

"Dominic," he said.

"I'm downstairs. You may want to contact someone because these apes in monkey suits won't let me by."

Jason rubbed his face only to find Jordan's scent still on

his fingers. "It'd probably help if you didn't call them apes," he said, repeating what he'd said to Jordan earlier.

"Too late."

"Yeah. Let me do what I can. Oh, and remind me to sign you up for etiquette classes."

"Etiquette classes my ass."

Jason chuckled as he disconnected and walked back out into the hall to make the required call. He hesitated outside the kitchen door, then reached out and pushed it open. Jordan was gone, nothing but the cereal box on the counter to indicate she'd been there and the incident hadn't been a sexy figment of his imagination.

He lifted his fingers to his nose and inhaled her scent again, telling himself he was insane as he did so.

He only wished he could have tasted her…

He made the required call, put the cereal away and then paused next to the counter where Jordan had sat. He pressed his palm against the cool stone, almost feeling her warmth still.

He cursed under his breath and then headed for the living room and the front door where Dominic would be knocking any moment.

Of course, the last thing he expected to get was sleep. Not after what just happened. He was going to have a hard enough time stopping himself from going upstairs and joining Jordan in that mammoth bed of hers and picking up where they left off…

He opened the door and let Dominic in.

"You look happy," the recruit said.

"Ecstatic." He slammed the door. "I'll be upstairs in the guest bedroom. Call if you need anything."

"Will do."

6

By ONE O'CLOCK, JORDAN still hadn't emerged from her bedroom. Jason knew this because he'd been waiting for her, after catching a couple hours' rest, if not sleep, in the guest bedroom next to hers. He hadn't a choice but to leave without telling her Dominic would be in charge until his return from Lazarus. So he informed Dominic to introduce himself and provide his cell number if she asked for it.

And requested his stand-in be tactful while doing it.

It was Dom's parting words that left him pulling the collar of his T-shirt away from his neck even now, as he sat in his Lazarus office: "She as hot as her pictures?"

It hadn't occurred to him that Jordan might come on to Dominic...until the very single, very active recruit had said something. It wasn't that he believed himself so attractive that she wouldn't want anyone but him...but the idea of someone else taking what he so yearned to claim...

The pencil he held snapped in two.

"Whoa," Dari said from the doorway. "Shall I come back at a better time?"

Jason stared at the broken pencil, grimaced and then threw it out in the basket under his desk. "What's up?"

He'd come into Lazarus for a meeting set to begin in

twenty minutes and wanted to get some work out of the way first.

"I need to talk to you about something Linc said on the phone earlier."

Jason began to stand when the intercom buzzed. He held up a finger to ask Dari to wait a moment and told Lisa to go ahead.

"That interviewee from yesterday is back and would like to speak to you."

It took him a second to figure out who she was talking about. "That Daryl kid?"

"Yes, sir."

"I take it he's standing in front of you."

"Yes, sir."

"He won't be escorted to the other room?"

"No, sir."

Jason didn't ask who had given him access, since all visitors had to be buzzed in. There was no need for alarm. Yet.

"Tell him to make an appointment."

"I tried, sir."

Jason rubbed his closed eyelids. "Put him on the phone."

"Yes, sir."

A moment later, a strident, "Hello," sounded.

"Mr. Bennett, I suggest you do as Lisa suggests and make an appointment if you wish to speak to me."

"I won't take up much of your time, sir."

"I currently don't have any time to give you. Make an appointment."

He hung up the phone.

"Problems?"

Jason rounded the desk and leaned against the edge. "Nothing I can't handle. What's going on?"

Dari leaned against the doorjamb and crossed his arms. "Linc says you want to push up plans for the Baltimore satellite office."

Damn. While he'd hoped Linc would expedite the move as he'd promised, he had expected him to do so without mentioning him. "He did, did he?"

"Uh-huh."

Jason held his gaze. "Is there a question in there somewhere?"

"You know there is."

He crossed his own arms. "Well, then, you may want to rephrase it."

They stared at each other from across the room, the tension a clear indicator how much circumstances had changed between them no matter how much they all tried to act differently. He and Dari were no longer best friends: they were wary acquaintances and business partners. Which was exactly the reason why he needed to get out of Dodge. For good.

"Are you angling to leave Colorado City?" Dari asked.

"Yes."

"Why?"

Jason blinked.

Cursing himself, he turned back toward his desk, gathered up the papers there, and then offered, "You know me, I've never been good at staying in one place for long periods of time."

"Bullshit."

He faced his friend again. "When are you going to be cleared for return to service?" he asked, referring to the injuries Dari had sustained as a result of an IED. Injuries that had resulted in his coming back early, right on the heels of his and Megan's indiscretion.

"Soon."

"Yes, well, you can't say having me out of town will save you a whole lot of worry."

"Why?"

He narrowed his gaze. "Look, now's not the time to be

having this discussion. I have to go pluck this kid out of Lisa's hair before the meeting."

"Now's exactly the time we need to talk if the Baltimore office is going to be put on today's agenda."

"Blackmail?"

"No. I would prefer to have this conversation privately rather than in front of the others."

"I want to push up the opening date on the Baltimore office. You and the other partners either agree or disagree. Simple. Nothing more to discuss."

The intercom buzzed again. He leaned back and stabbed the button. "Yes?"

"Your grandmother on Line 1."

He paused for a moment. "Tell her I'll call her back."

He disconnected, figuring he was good for at least two more calls from Annie before he finally had to return it.

He pushed past his old friend. Dari caught his arm.

Jason looked at him for a long moment but said nothing.

He knew a stab of regret that things could never go back to the way they'd once been between them. Dari had been his best friend. The one guy he could turn to no matter what. Now, well, he'd screwed the pooch but good when it came to their friendship.

Finally, Dari seemed to realize he couldn't force the issue and released his grip. "Fine. I'll see you in the meeting."

Jason nodded and strode toward the front of the building and Daryl Bennett. He only hoped Dari didn't make good on his indirect threat to bring up the motivation behind the expedited Baltimore plans.

Still, either way, it needed to be done.

IT WAS PAST FOUR AND Jordan was ready to jump out of her skin. She'd gotten up just after one, had breakfast, worked out, caught a shower and was now faced with doing a whole lot of nothing for the next Lord only knew how long.

She was good at a lot of things, but being idle didn't rank among them. Her father liked to say she'd hit the ground running the instant she was born and she'd hadn't stopped for a breath since. This forced breather disturbed her in more ways than she cared to think about. In fact, one of her favorite physical activities was running. And she hadn't been able to do even that for two weeks. While the advanced aerobics DVDs she was using helped, she wondered if a personal trainer wouldn't challenge her more.

Her mind went blank again as she sat in front of her laptop at her desk, the screen taunting her. She had no rational reason to contact any of her three managers except to save herself from boredom. She could IM or call one of her four brothers or even her father, but she currently had zero appetite for their "I told you so" tones.

"I told you your lifestyle would land you in trouble," her older brother would offer.

Brad was fond of saying stuff like that. She supposed it came with the territory of being the oldest. And he took great pleasure in saying it to her, the youngest. But it made it no less irritating.

All of her friends were working, as she should be, so any type of meaningful conversation with them was out of the question. Besides, she swore most of them were afraid they would catch a bullet through the phone line, or somehow, someone might be interested in following the signal to their doorstep, and they would find themselves directly involved in a drama they had no interest in.

She sighed heavily and then glanced over at where the new guy Dominic cleaned his firearm. She made a face, not interested in interaction with him, either.

Plainly only one thing would work: she needed to get out of the apartment. Now!

She caught herself scratching her arm and stopped, growling low in her throat.

Okay, some of her pent-up frustration had to do with her brief, hot interaction with Jason in the kitchen last night. And even though she had found a toy or two to finish what he had started, the payoff had left her feeling empty...and hornier still. It was a new feeling for her since a climax in and of itself was usually enough.

Of course, it hadn't helped that she'd dreamed about Jason's kiss, his hands on her, his fingers inside her...only to have it stop and play again from the beginning.

The front door opened. She and Dominic got to their feet simultaneously.

"Thank God," they both said.

She and the sub stared at each other, then at Jason.

After looking at them both long and hard, he took the key from the door and slid it into his pocket. "Dom, you can head home. See you again in the morning."

"Sure thing."

Dominic holstered his gun, picked up a vest he'd laid over the back of a chair, and then headed out without a glance in her direction. Which was fine with her.

Jason closed the door. The apartment seemed smaller by half...and much warmer. "What happened?"

She squinted at him, reminded all over again how...*hot* he was. Commanding. As well as demanding. "How do you mean?"

"You two didn't hit it off?"

"I suppose you could say that." She sat back down at the computer, preferring not to discuss what had transpired between her and his replacement when she'd gotten up to discover Jason gone.

"You came on to him and he refused?"

"What?" She gaped at him, wondering where his mind was. "No. He came on to me and I refused."

He looked dubious.

"What, you think I hit on every guy that comes through that door?"

A brief pause and then, "Yeah. That's the impression you left me with."

"Well, change it, because that's not the case at all." She pretended to type something but it was little more than gibberish. "Call me fickle, but when a man refuses me, I don't make a habit out of jumping into the arms of the next available guy."

He held up a hand and strode across the room, probably for the kitchen again. "None of my business."

"My thoughts, exactly."

The kitchen door swung shut behind him.

Jordan sat for long moments at the laptop and drummed her fingers against the keys without hitting them hard enough to type.

This was ridiculous. You would think she was the one who'd left him hanging, rather than the other way around.

She got up and stalked to confront him.

She pushed the door open…and nearly hit him in the face with it. Luckily, he was quick on the draw and lifted a hand to stop it.

Problem was, the unexpected action caught her off guard. And he was closer than she wanted him to be.

She blinked into his coal-black eyes, noticing he was clean-shaven and smelled nice. Not for her, of course, but for the job.

"I'm going shopping," she announced.

7

DAMN, THIS WAS TURNING into the day from hell.

First he had to face off with Dari in his office, then again later during the meeting. And in between, he'd confronted Daryl, the whack job who'd convinced himself he was Lazarus material and refused to take no for an answer, no matter how insistently Jason told him there was no way in hell he would ever work there.

Now he stood face-to-face with a woman who drove him crazy in more ways than one.

"You're not going anywhere," he told her flatly. "You are not to step one foot out of this apartment."

He guessed Jordan Cosby wasn't used to being told what to do. He took some satisfaction in being the one person who could get away with it. But mostly he just wanted her to move away, not stand so close he could smell the scent of her shampoo on her pale blond hair.

"That's not part of the deal," she said. "Maybe you should read the protection contract."

Her spark was impossible to ignore. He'd bet not many men made it out alive when she set her sights on them. Which made him even more determined to be one of the exceptions.

"Ah, yes. You're referring to the one hour a day you arranged for outdoor activities."

"Even death-row inmates are entitled to that."

"Yes, well, that was before the price on your head included pot shots through car windows. The possibility of death—your death—spikes through the roof every time you're outside."

She lifted a brow. "I haven't been out of this apartment for two weeks."

"And the way I figure it, you have another two weeks to go."

Her stricken, albeit brief, expression struck a chord within him.

"Come on, Jason. I'm jumping out of my skin. If I don't get out of here, breathe some fresh air, I'm going to be certifiable. I've spent more time in this place in two weeks than I have in the past two years."

He crossed his arms, as much to put some sort of physical barrier between them as a mental one. "What are you suggesting?"

She thought for a moment, apparently not having given her plea that much consideration. The fact that she fully expected to be blocked from any outside activity struck a deeper chord.

"Shopping," she said.

Shit.

Just when he'd upgraded her status from bimbo to femme fatale, she had to go and stomp it back down to his original impression of her.

Shopping?

"Come on. I can go to places where I've never shopped before so it will be easier to protect me. You can come up with some unique way to get me out of here without anyone noticing..."

He was already on that part of the equation, even though he had yet to be fully sold on the idea. Going outside meant opening her up for anything and everything. It was his job to keep her alive long enough to testify at that trial and he was a stickler for not merely doing his job, but doing it well. Taking her out made that task infinitely more difficult.

At the same time, the need he saw on her beautiful face appealed to him on a level impossible to ignore.

"May I suggest you give me twenty-four hours advance notice?"

He hadn't realized her shoulders had squared and color had infused her face until she slumped and her skin paled again.

"I mean from here on out, I'd like twenty-four hours notice." He glanced at his watch. "As for now, I can get you out for a bit, say in an hour?"

It appeared to take her a moment to register what he'd said. But the instant she did, she threw herself into his arms and kissed his cheek. "Thank you, thank you, thank you! You have no idea what you've just done."

He mentally reeled from her unexpected attention, and fought his unwelcome physical reaction, even as he watched her rush from the room, presumably to get ready.

She was absolutely right: he had no idea what he'd just done.

And he had the feeling there were going to be a whole lot of similar moments in the days and weeks to come.

He turned back into the kitchen and took his cell out of his pocket, cursing himself as he went...

JORDAN PAUSED ON THE sidewalk and turned her face into the hot, summer sun, closing her eyes behind her large sunglasses and tilting back the big, floppy hat she wore so she could soak up as much of the rays as possible.

Heaven...

It was true what they said about the simplest things being the best. You never really understood how much you took for granted until it was denied you. On a typical, pre-captivity day, she'd likely have groaned at the heat and hurried to her next destination to keep from sweating. Now she wanted to savor every moment of her freedom, however brief.

"Keep moving." She instantly felt Jason's hand on her elbow. A little thrill rippled through her along with a ribbon of fear at the reminder that however free she felt, it was nothing but an illusion.

Jason proved as good as his word, ready to take her out within one hour as he'd said he would. Arrangements had been made for a decoy that looked stunningly similar to her with the help of a wig and real items out of her own wardrobe. In fact, the woman looked so much like Jordan, the U.S. Marshals assigned to protect her were tailing her instead… while she and Jason snuck out together with an elderly neighbor that lived two floors down.

They parted ways with Mrs. Zellman a couple of blocks north of their building and Jason had driven her exactly where she requested to be taken.

She looked at the man in question, readjusting her hat to cover her hair and sliding her sunglasses down her nose slightly to take him in. God, but the guy was hot. She had half convinced herself that a lack of options were to blame for the scorching chemistry they shared. But being outside, she understood she would have been wildly attracted to him in any environment.

He returned her gaze studiously.

"Thank you," she said simply.

To her surprise, he appeared uncomfortable with her gratitude. "You planning on moving anytime soon? Not a good idea to be standing in the middle of a public area in plain sight. The words *stationary target* come to mind."

She smiled, deciding she wasn't going to let anything or anybody spoil this hour for her.

"This way…" she said.

IT WAS OFFICIAL: HE NEEDED to have his head examined.

What in the hell was thinking, letting Jordan out of the apartment? Oh, he wasn't worried that she was in any more danger (he was positive the decoy had worked and hadn't seen one thing out of the ordinary since he'd left to get a taxi from a company Lazarus sometimes used just for similar occasions), but because he was having a hard time keeping his mind on the job at hand instead of watching her for the mere pleasure of doing so.

He'd known, from the moment he met her, that Miss Jordan Cosby was drop-dead gorgeous. But out here, with her exuding happiness and sexiness like an irresistible scent...

"Now, let's go shopping!"

Jason winced. Great. Now he had to watch her browse through shops, trying on clothes and doing all that female stuff he made a point of never doing with any of the women he'd known, dated or with whom he was otherwise acquainted.

He walked a half step behind her, his left hand ready to push her down, his right near his gun in case he spotted anything suspicious. The day was hot and the Denver sun burned the back of his neck. At this point, he'd be glad for air-conditioning. But the heat didn't appear to affect Jordan as she strutted down the street looking like a woman who'd just escaped captivity. And, he supposed, she was exactly that.

But shopping?

She turned left into an open area...and he realized she wasn't taking him to a boutique that catered to the ridiculously rich and issued large, boxy bags emblazoned with a gold name to tote around as some sort of sign letting others know the holder had shopped there.

No, she'd taken him to an outdoor fresh produce market. He blinked several times. Huh. Wonders never ceased...

SHE'D SURPRISED HIM. Good. Jordan experienced a sense of satisfaction at dashing Jason's expectations as she stepped up to a tomato stand and picked up a plump, red one, sniffing it at leisure.

"What?" she asked. "Certainly you didn't think I'd take you shopping for clothes?"

He glanced around the market that was some fifty stalls long. "I would have preferred it if you had."

"Oh?"

She filled a small paper bag with a few selections and then handed it to the attendant to be weighed and priced.

"It would have made protecting you easier."

Jordan paid for her purchase and accepted a larger bag she could use to carry additional items. "What? You don't really think someone is hiding out here on the off chance I might need something to eat?"

He glowered at her. "No, but I am thinking if someone did pick up your scent, this place would give them ample opportunity to squeeze off a shot."

"So all you have to do is keep your eye on the entrance, then." She nodded toward the place they'd come in.

"And the exit." He nodded toward the back. "As well as the surrounding balconies."

"I'll stay under the umbrellas."

"It helps."

She moved on to the next stall, picking over peaches and pears. She hummed as she sniffed the fruit, fully aware of how closely Jason was watching her instead of looking for possible hitmen lurking in the shadows. It was all she could do to stop herself from licking a peach just to see his reaction.

Okay, she admitted his being by her side might, just might, have something to do with her almost giddy mood. Ever since meeting him, her life looked a little brighter, a bit more expansive...and a hell of a lot sexier.

As she considered other produce options, purchasing a few, she was aware of her bag getting a little heavier. She glanced to see Jason had placed a couple of items he'd purchased inside.

She raised a brow.

"A guy's gotta eat."

She smiled. "Just don't expect me to fix anything for you."

His dark eyes smiled back at her. "Wouldn't dream of it."

"Okay, then. Just so we're clear." Then she held out the bag toward him.

"What? Surely your feminist sensibility bristles at the thought of a man carrying a bag for you?"

"Nope."

He took it, his chuckle tickling the back of her knees as she led the way to the next stall and the goodies waiting there to be touched, sniffed and consumed…

8

As much as Jason had dreaded the outing, the hour had sped by quickly, and surprisingly he'd enjoyed himself. Not as much as Jordan apparently had—he suspected that was physically impossible—but he'd smiled more than he probably should have. And it was a sensation that lasted throughout the day, despite the hellacious beginning that morning. Jordan hadn't posed a single problem, and they got back to the apartment nearly an hour after they left it, meeting back up with her downstairs neighbor before returning. Then he'd called Dominic with the decoy, arranging for them to bring the scheme full circle.

Now, hours later, long after Jordan had called it a night—or pretended to—and gone upstairs to her suite, he was in the kitchen preparing peach crepes with fresh cream.

He'd made sure all the doors were open so the scent could waft upstairs, but so far there wasn't any sign she smelled anything. He checked his watch. Just after three. Dinnertime, as she'd called it. Surely she would come drifting down for her bowl of cereal any moment.

Unless, like his "innocent" tinkering around in her kitchen, her cereal eating had been merely a ploy to get him into bed.

He absently rubbed the back of his neck as he switched off the flame and then tilted the final crepe from the pan onto a plate. Is that what he was doing? Trying to get her into bed?

No, he told himself. He merely enjoyed her company. And he wanted a chance to show off his cooking skills.

Liar.

He'd learned the crepe bit from his younger brother a few years ago after he'd taken a cooking class in high school. Jason had ribbed him, but he'd been happy Jax was taking an interest in something that didn't require he carry a gun. He considered his own handiwork; his brother still made better crepes.

Jason leaned back and looked through the open door toward the stairs. Still nothing.

Damn.

He turned toward the laptop he'd left open on the counter and accessed his Lazarus account. It showed Jordan was online. He smiled…

JORDAN SAT CROSS-LEGGED in the middle of her bed, chatting with Otto via IM. She'd told him about her outing earlier and he was begging for another video shot of Mr. Savage Hottie, as he'd taken to referring to Jason.

She caught a whiff of something sweet.

I think he's cooking something, she told Otto.

All that AND he knows his way around a kitchen? Girl, what are you waiting for?

Jordan twisted her lips. You forget, he turned me down flat.

No, babe, he left you flapping in the breeze.

Like I needed the reminder. Thanks.

Don't mention it. But before you go sending off the cowboy with the horse, I think you should give it another shot.

You can't be serious?

Dead serious.

You can't tell me you want me to put on that red number again?

Oh, hell no. I think you should wear your rattiest robe and Minnie Mouse slippers and put your hair up in a ponytail. Make it look like sex is the last thing on your mind.

Jordan stared at his words.

But, of course, you will have the red number on underneath.

She laughed. You're impossible.

Impossibly irresistible, you mean.

That, too.

Another IM box popped up on the screen. Who was SAVAGEBEAST?

Her mouth went dry. She quickly accessed Jason's message. Hungry?

She sat for several minutes staring at the one word.

Hey, you still there? Otto asked. Or did you take my advice and go down for some more of that yummy dish?

He just IM'd me.

And?

Her fingers hovered above the keyboard.

What did he say?

She told him.

Well, honey, if that isn't close to an engraved invitation, I don't know what is.

What should I say?

Say? Nothing. I think you should go straight down.

She chewed on the inside of her lip.

At the very least, respond to him. He obviously knows you're online.

What should I say?

Jordan, would you like me to come put the condom on for you, too?

She laughed.

Go on, get your hot little ass down there. Besides, I've wasted enough time with you tonight already.

Yeah, what am I paying for you, anyway?

You mean outside entertaining you?

Goodbye, Otto.

Nighty-night, sweetie. I expect to hear EVERYTHING in the morning.

Fat chance.

Especially if it's FAT.

She shook her head, watching as the chat box told her Otto had gone offline.

Which left her staring at Jason's IM box.

What to say, what to say...

She smiled as she typed...

HE WAS GOING TO BE STUCK eating the crepes himself.

Jason stared at the two plates he'd fixed, complete with sifted powdered sugar and drummed his fingers against the countertop. Served him right. Wasn't he the one who'd had rebuffed her advances last night? Rebuffed? He remembered walking away, leaving her sitting on the edge of this very island looking like sex incarnate.

Shit.

He was in the middle of closing the laptop when the chime sounded indicating an IM message. He quickly lifted the screen.

Do you deliver? was Jordan's response.

He squinted at her words.

He hadn't anticipated her suggesting he bring the food up to her room. He glanced at the plates then at the stairs through the open doorway behind him. There really was no sense in pretending. While he'd spent the past hour prepping the meal, this was about sex, pure and simple. And him wanting it from her.

Damn.

What should he say?

The perfect response occurred to him and he began typing...

Depends on how well you tip...

JORDAN READ JASON'S response and smiled. Then it dawned on her that he might be heading up to her room now.

She quickly typed, Come on up and find out... and then closed the laptop, scooting to put it on the bedside table before springing up to do exactly as Otto suggested, although she questioned following his advice again after the disastrous results last time.

She stuffed her feet into the pair of hideous pink slippers one of her brothers had gotten her for Christmas one year, and yanked on the matching robe. She wasn't wearing the red number underneath, but since she was a lady who liked lingerie, she was wearing something comparable, albeit it in icy-blue.

She was pulling her hair back into a messy ponytail when she heard a knock at her bedroom door.

She rushed to it, then rubbed both of her damp palms against the thick chenille of her robe before opening the door. Her palms were instantly wet again—along with other, more strategic areas—as she stared at him balancing a tray.

"Room service," he said quietly.

She wanted to ask him what was on the menu, but his potently suggestive expression jammed the words in the middle of her throat.

She opened the door wider.

"Where do you want it?" he asked, looking around.

She cleared her throat, able to speak now that he wasn't

looking at her like he wanted her on a plate. "On the bed... of course."

She swore she heard him clear his own throat before saying, "Of course," and then moving toward the king-size bed to put the tray down on top of it.

He turned to face her, taking in her attire.

Her smile widened. "What? Disappointed?"

"To the contrary. I like the effort you went to."

She stepped to the bed and took in the contents. It looked even better than it smelled, which was saying a lot. "I'm not sure I'm following you."

"I don't believe for a minute that's what you normally wear. Which means you purposely dressed like that for me."

She nearly choked on a piece of crepe she'd pulled from the plate. She pressed two fingertips to her lips and swallowed. "Touché."

She sucked on the pad of her thumb.

"Did you, um, really make this?" she asked, watching as his eyes darkened.

"Mmm. You planning on eating it? Or just standing there with something else in your mouth?"

His words brought back last night—was that really only twenty-four hours ago?—and she smiled. "Depends."

"On what?"

"On what you'd like to serve me."

He held her heated gaze for a long heartbeat. "Why don't we begin with the crepes..."

He moved to get the two high-backed chairs situated on either side of a small table near the windows while she climbed on top of the bed and settled in cross-legged again, arranging the hideous robe so it covered enough, but not too much. She picked up one of the plates and a fork and dug in.

"Wow," she said, taking a bite. "This is really good..."

"I could teach you how to make them. It's not rocket science."

She took two more forkfuls before answering. "Why would I want to do that? You can make them for me."

At least for the next two weeks, anyway.

She openly considered him, for the first time wondering what might happen after that. Which made no sense, since they really didn't know each other anyway. At least not outside their current crazy situation.

Still, somehow she wondered if he might be interested in seeing her again...outside of work, that is.

"So," he said, handing her a tall glass of orange juice. "How did you meet Packard?"

She took a sip of the liquid, realizing he'd added champagne to it. "Trying to get me drunk, Mr. Savage?"

A grin flickered around the edges of his sexy mouth. "I think it would take a great deal more than the little bit of bubbly I poured in there." He pointed at her glass with his fork and then took another bite. "Answer my question."

"Why? It doesn't matter."

He stared at her unblinkingly.

"All right then, if you want the boring story, you can have it." She popped a bit of peach into her mouth that had likely been flambéed with some sort of delicious liqueur. "I met Rick at my New York club."

He appeared to be waiting for more.

She shrugged. "That's it."

"Not the chatty type, are you?"

She laughed. "I could say the same of you."

"I'm not the one who's been subpoenaed to testify at my ex's trial."

"Fair enough." She'd give him that. "But I bet you could share some interesting details about your love life just the same."

He dropped his gaze to his food. Interesting. "Sex life. I don't have a love life."

She raised her brows. "Never?"

"Quit trying to change the subject."

"But I do it so well."

"Probably with others, but it's not going to work with me. How long did you date?"

She made a face, really not in the mood to discuss Rick Packard just then. He served as a reminder why she should lay low not only to avoid half-cocked hitmen, but to stay away from men who were more trouble than they were worth.

She looked at Jason a little more closely. He wouldn't prove to be one of them, would he?

Then again, it wasn't that long ago she'd decided she should put all men into that category. At least for the time being.

"What do you want me to tell you?" She shrugged. "He was good in bed. It was as simple and as complicated as that..."

9

JASON NEARLY CHOKED ON a piece of peach while Jordan smiled cheekily across the tray from him.

Damn, but he'd believed himself beyond surprise when it came to anything, much less the opposite sex. He frowned, remembering a similar surprise he'd experienced recently... and questioned his sanity.

If he retained an ounce of sense, he'd finish his crepes and head back downstairs.

His gaze caught on the top of Jordan's robe where it bowed open, revealing a light blue scrap of something sexy beneath—something sexy covering something even sexier. His hand slowed where he cut off another bite.

"We didn't date all that long. Because of our travel schedules, we maybe saw each other a handful of times over a two-month period."

"Exclusive?"

She didn't answer for a long moment, appearing infatuated with the contents of her plate. He found himself wanting her to look at him that way. And then she did just that and he wished she hadn't.

She said, "On my side, yes, I guess it was. Although not purposely. I must have been busy. On his, I couldn't say."

"What does the federal prosecutor want you to testify to?"

"On who I'd seen Rick with. And about a certain conversation I didn't overhear with one of the individuals." She reached up and took her hair out of that ridiculous band. Her golden curls cascaded down over her shoulders. Shoulders now left bare as the robe slid down over her arms.

It took sheer effort for him to keep his mind on the conversation as he marveled at her smooth skin.

"Not that I plan on giving them anything they can use," she said. "I don't rat out friends."

"Even if the friends in question have put a contract out on you?"

Her smile was decidedly sexy. "*Especially* if the friends in question have put out a contract on me."

"So you're not sharing out of fear."

"I'm not sharing because I'm not a rat, pure and simple. I was raised with four older brothers. I learned fairly quickly what happens to a girl when she tattles."

"Or doesn't."

"I think when it comes to women, men always expect them to give up the goods fairly quickly."

He remembered Megan telling Dari about their one night together and grimaced.

"Uh-oh. What's that look mean?"

Jason squinted at her. "What look?"

"That look. Just then."

"It means I may have squeezed a little too much lemon on the peaches."

"I don't think so. It means there might be a little too much lemon in one of your relationships."

Okay, if anything was a sign he should hightail it back downstairs, that was it.

"For what it's worth?" she said quietly. "I don't have anything to rat out. My attorney and I figured out fairly quickly that I'm being used as a pawn in some sort of Justice Department game to get Rick to turn against one of his associates..."

She laughed without humor. "So you see, my life is in jeopardy not because of what I know, but because of who I knew. Or thought I did, anyway…"

The last part was said so softly, he had to strain to hear it.

He reached for her plate.

"I'm not done," She fought him for it.

"There's nothing left."

She refused to release the plate so he let go. "Yes, there is. The best part." She dragged her fingertip through the cream and syrup and then stuck the digit into her decadent mouth.

Jason wasn't sure he was successful at completely muffling his groan at the pornographic sight. If she licked the plate, he would be a goner…

Instead, she held it up for him to take, her robe shifting lower still as she did so.

He took the plate, put it on top of his own and then picked up the tray.

"You're leaving?"

Jason froze halfway to the door.

"But you haven't collected your tip yet…"

He closed his eyes and said a little prayer as he listened to her moving around on the bed behind him.

Somehow he didn't think getting out of there was going to be so easy…

LYING BACK AGAINST HER elbows staring at Jason's back, Jordan knew a moment of fear he might reject her again.

Her heart thud an erratic rhythm against her ribcage as her robe slid to the bed on either side of her, belt tied around her waist the only part effectively on her.

Turn around, she silently whispered. Please turn back around…

He did.

Her heart dipped low into her pelvis and then boomeranged back up again. She shook her head so her hair flowed back behind her then bent her legs at the knees, rubbing one against the other. The friction hardened her nipples under the thin fabric of her teddy as she considered him under lowered lashes, speaking without saying a word.

Stay or go. Those were his choices. But, oh, how she wished he'd choose to stay...

At this point, he appeared incapable of movement.

"You need help with that?" she asked, gesturing toward the tray even as she continued rubbing her legs leisurely against one another.

Given the intense expression on his face, she half expected him to drop the tray and its contents and launch himself onto the bed. Instead, he put it down on the bedside table next to her laptop and then sat down beside her. Before she could blink, his mouth was on hers and his hand was sliding up her waist.

Oh, yes...

DAMN, BUT SHE TASTED even better than he remembered. And that was saying one hell of a lot.

Jason wasn't completely clear on what happened. All he knew was one minute he was walking through the door and the next, he was kissing her like there was no tomorrow. Which, of course, could very well be the case if he didn't keep his wits about him and an armed idiot on a mission caught him unawares.

He groaned inwardly, sliding his tongue against hers. At that moment he was aware of nothing but the desire to stake his claim on her. All over.

The silk of her sexy something was cool against his fingers, the skin underneath hot and soft. He stripped the fabric from her in no time, leaving her bare to his gaze and touch, nothing but a small, dim lamp on a side table lighting the room. He already knew she was bare all over, but just seeing the swollen folds of flesh between her long legs was enough to make his mouth water all over again.

She was beautiful. And she knew it. Which made her even more beautiful.

He took a deep breath when he felt her fingers dip inside the front waist of his jeans, seeking and finding what she was looking for with easy effort. Jason grit his back teeth together as she squeezed his pulsing hard-on and then hurried to unbutton the fly to give her better access.

Damn, but it felt good to have her holding him like that.

She lay in the middle of her robe, the sight enough to make any man take pause. He'd seen hundreds of women, had them this close, breathed in their scent, enjoyed their company and bodies, but for reasons he couldn't quite define, the heat in his groin burned hotter and extended beyond to encompass his chest.

He kissed her deeply and then trailed a path to her breasts, laving the stiff peaks before pulling each deep into his mouth. Her breathless approval made him harder still. He blindly reached for the tray on the table then glanced to make sure he was getting what he wanted: one of the two glasses.

"Thirsty?" she whispered.

He held her gaze as he positioned the flute above her and poured it over her engorged nipple. She gasped and her back arched. Jason leisurely licked the liquid from her, squeezing the soft mound so he could pull the tip deep into his mouth. Then he followed the trickle down under the generous curve, lapping up the sweet, tangy concoction that tasted even better against her skin.

He pulled back and poured some more over her stomach, relishing her intake of breath at the contact. Rivulets moved with the trembling of her belly and he took his time following each of them, lapping them up.

He moved even lower, lifting his head to take in the needy

expression on her beautiful face. It was all he could do not to throw the glass aside and take her right then…

JORDAN COULDN'T SEEM to catch her breath. The manufacturer of the high-end car she'd recently bought had boasted it could go from 1-to-infinity in 2.3 seconds. Jason had taken her to that speed within a blink.

God, the guy was hot. His thick, roped arms rippled as he moved, tempting her touch. His eyes were as dark as a moonless night. His mouth…

He dipped his tongue into her navel and she gasped.

His mouth had to rank as one of the undiscovered wonders of the world.

She didn't realize she'd closed her eyes until his movements stopped. She cracked her eyelids open to take him and his suggestive grin in. She swallowed hard, watching as he worked his free hand down her thigh, sliding to the inside… and then spread it, following with the other. The cool air on her heated privates felt good. The cold mimosa he poured on her brought her back up off the bed. The liquid ran down between her folds, coating her. Jason held her hips still and then followed with his hot, skillful mouth.

Jordan moaned, twisting her hands into the robe on either side of her, her eyes drifting back closed, her body filled with sweet, shimmering warmth. Ripples of sensation surged upward with every lap of his tongue. Then he parted her folds and fastened his mouth on the throbbing core of her and those ripples coalesced into an ever-growing ball of pure fire. She couldn't seem to draw a breath and every muscle seized.

Then the ball exploded into a million sparkling stars, expanding to fill her to overflowing. She felt suspended in time and space, on the bed yet above it, yet not there at all. All the tension of the past two weeks melted away, leaving just her…and the hot man between her legs.

Slowly, the tide ebbed more than flowed and her breathing

started to return to normal. Still Jason remained where he was, lapping up the proof of her orgasm.

Jordan stretched her neck, her smile feeling permanently attached as she blindly threaded her fingers through his hair.

"Wow," she whispered.

Moments later, he pulled back, blowing on her overheated flesh. "Baby, we're just getting started..."

10

MARK ONE FOR THE RECORD books: Jason nearly came with Jordan when she hit the big 'O.' A first for him. While he enjoyed giving pleasure, and knew he was good at it, he'd never experienced the same connection he had while performing oral on a woman.

Her open responsiveness might be to credit. Or the sheer bliss she exuded like a scent.

Whatever the reason, he'd needed the time afterward as much as she did to recompose himself. The last thing he wanted was to blow his wad before he'd even started.

He leisurely laved her engorged flesh, enjoying the taste of her on his tongue, paying close attention to the pink, shiny bud. Her body still trembled, as much from pleasure as anticipation he guessed. He put the empty glass down on the floor and slowly made his way back up her abdomen, lingering at points he'd missed before and then held his body aloft from hers, kissing her deeply.

She moaned deep in her throat and wrapped her arms around him, pulling him close, the arches of her feet rubbing against the back of his calves as she wordlessly invited him for a closer meeting. He took his time kissing her, it having been a good, long time since he'd so thoroughly relished the simple contact. One of the most notable aspects of his brief affair with Megan was their agreement they not share the intimacy of a kiss.

It wasn't until now he realized how potently intimate a kiss could be.

Or was it just Jordan?

She moved her hands along his back, down to grasp his ass, eager for the next move. Then her fingers were encircling his pulsing erection. He broke their kiss and stretched his neck at her knowing touch.

"Condom," she whispered.

"Back pocket."

"Side drawer."

He reached over to the bedside table—closer than his jeans where they lay on the floor—and extracted a rubber. A rip of foil and they both slid the lubricated latex over his length. But despite her eagerness for him to do so, he didn't enter her. Instead, he resumed their kiss, awareness and need pulsing through him from every flick of her tongue, graze of her nipples against his chest, feel of her wet folds pressing against his hardness attempting to force penetration.

Finally, he positioned the tip against her slick portal, entering her ever so slightly. He ground his back teeth together at the tight, hot feel of her surrounding him.

Then he breathed in her gasp as he slid all the way in to the hilt.

Sweet heaven…

He went still, noting she did the same. His heart beat forcibly against his ribcage. Blood rushed past his ears. Pure, unadulterated need pooled in his groin, spreading and spreading until he was drowning in it.

He knew nothing but this one moment, this single second, his gaze bonded to hers, their bodies joined.

He slowly eased out and then slid in again. Jordan moaned, her back coming up off the bed, her ankles tightening against his calves, her muscles contracting around his erection.

Then his mind shut down and he was no longer in control

of his movements, his thoughts. Everything went on automatic as he stroked her inside and out, freeing him to wonder at the myriad, red-hot sensations rising within him, allowing him to take in her beautiful face as she openly watched him through half-lidded eyes. His arms shook and sweat beaded on his brow. But he didn't quicken his strokes. If anything, he slowed them, savoring the sex, in no hurry to reach the destination.

But just as all roads led to somewhere, he felt his climax building—slowly, ever so slowly—until it lapped against the shore as if from a distant origin, flowing in, ever in…

Jordan's soft, raw moan further fueled the tide and they came together for what had to be one of the sweetest orgasms he'd ever achieved.

LATER, JORDAN COLLAPSED against the bare mattress. Somewhere over the past three hours, they'd managed to strip even the sheets from the bed, the euphoric first climax followed by more, harder, rougher, sweeter…

"Wow," she whispered, feeling boneless.

"Yeah. Wow," Jason agreed, lying next to her, their hips, arms and feet touching.

She was drenched in sweat, and sunlight was beginning to indirectly brighten the room since her bedroom faced the west to catch the sunset rather than the sunrise. At some point, he'd taken a brief call, from Dominic she assumed. The thought that someone else was inside the apartment had slightly freaked her out until Jason touched her again and everything else fled from her mind.

It had been a good, long time since she'd enjoyed a nice, long marathon session. Her every muscle was relaxed, her labia throbbed and she felt so thoroughly sated a shooter could enter the room right that minute and she would die a happy woman.

Of course, she hoped that wouldn't happen.

"Dom's downstairs."

She smiled and turned her head to look at him. "How'd you explain…"

"I didn't. I told him we would both be asleep—in separate rooms—and asked him not to disturb either of us."

"Do you think he suspects?"

He turned his head toward her. "Would it bother you if he did?"

She slowly smiled. "No."

"It doesn't matter, then."

"I guess it doesn't."

She held his gaze for a long moment and then stared back up at the ceiling, swallowing hard.

"To think, we could have been doing this since yesterday."

His chuckle was so genuine she couldn't help laughing with him.

To her surprise, her eyes began drifting closed. She caught herself.

Wow. When was the last time she'd actually slept with a man?

Jason pushed to a sitting position and swung his legs over the side of the bed. She marveled at the sight of him.

"I think I better get downstairs."

"No sleep?"

He slid her a suggestive look. "If I stay here, I don't think there'll be much sleeping involved. Do you?"

She rolled to her side, using her arm as a pillow. "I don't know."

He ran the back of his fingers down over her side. She shivered from head to toe.

"Point made."

He chuckled as he got up, grabbed his clothes, then headed for the connecting master bath.

Jordan lay listening to him shower, thinking she would like to join him, but unable to move a muscle. She should at least pull a sheet up over herself, but she couldn't even seem to scare up the motivation for that simple maneuver which involved reaching over to the side of the bed.

Her eyes began drifting closed again...

JASON EMERGED FROM THE bathroom, pulling on his T-shirt as he went. He began to say something then stopped, taking in Jordan's stillness. She was sleeping.

He rubbed his chin, allowing his gaze to drift over her beautifully naked body. From her almost white-blond hair to her long legs, she was a looker if ever there was one. And he had just spent the most incredible three hours with her. It was all he could do not to climb back into that bed with her and take up where they'd left off.

If she hadn't been sleeping, he would have.

He stood silently for a long moment, taking her in. She didn't strike him as the type to let her guard down easily. She reminded him a lot of himself in that regard. So he found it oddly endearing she'd done it with him.

Of course, the fact that he was a guard—a glorified body-guard, as one of Lazarus's biggest clients jokingly called him whenever his services were required—might have something to do with it. He ordered himself not to read too much into it.

He picked up a pillow and sheet from the floor, placing the former near her head and then gently covering her. She made a soft sound that might have been a 'thank you' as she tugged the pillow under her head and snuggled deeper under the sheet.

Damn, but she was making it hard not to climb back into that bed and curve himself around her again.

His cell vibrated on the side table. He snatched it up before it could wake her and opened it, not answering until he had closed the bedroom door after himself.

"Dominic," he said.

"Just got a call from downstairs—looks like we got our-selves a genuine, bona fide bogey..."

11

"WHAT'VE WE GOT?" JASON asked as he joined Dominic at the front window.

"Gorillas just called with an alert. Two guys casing the place over the past hour." Dominic handed him the binoculars.

"See anything?"

"Two o'clock, rooftop two blocks up."

Jason trained the glasses on the area in question, immediately spotting the gunman. He seemed to be having a problem connecting the scope to a rifle.

Damn amateurs.

"Where's the other one?"

"Nobody knows."

Jason dropped the glasses. "Five will get you ten he's parked outside that building waiting for his buddy to finish."

"That's what I'm thinking."

He looked again. The idiot finally attached the scope.

He took his cell out and called Ben Mason. "Be on the lookout. The guy's about to make a run for it."

"Roger. Got the other one out front."

"Shocker."

He disconnected.

"Give him something to look at," he said.

Dominic reached for the scope-equipped M107 .50-caliber sniper rifle leaning against the wall and then trained his own gun on the gunman. Jason watched as the would-be shooter took a while to find the apartment. Then he jerked back, squinted into the sunlight in his eyes and looked again. Jason waved.

He could practically hear the shooter say, "Shit," as he scrambled to his feet and ran to the access door in a half squat that told him he was in no way attached to the military.

Dominic propped the weapon back against the wall and a minute later Jason got the call that both men had been taken into custody.

He handed the binoculars back to Dominic. "Genuine bogey, my ass."

The younger man offered up a toothy grin. "He was armed."

"And was more likely to hurt himself with the weapon than anyone else."

A shrug. "More excitement than I've seen in two days."

"Yeah, well, a pro is the one we need to look for. Give a good sweep and then close the curtains."

Jason headed for the kitchen and coffee. It was true what he said, one lucky shot was all it took to get the job done. And even though an amateur was more likely to be caught, that wouldn't make the target any less dead.

As he poured himself a large mug from the pot Dominic had made, he glanced toward the stairs, thinking of the target in question even now sleeping off the effects of their sexy activities. The thought of her innocently walking in front of the windows and having an asshole like the one they'd just encountered bothered him no end.

Of course, having a pro take her out didn't sit any better with him. But at least there was some honor in that.

After half a cup and a check of his email, he called Ben to

get the all clear and then told Dominic he was going to grab a couple more hours of sleep and went up to the guest bedroom. He had a lot to get done today and it would be better if he didn't have to do it without any sleep...

JORDAN WOKE UP SMILING. She stretched, feeling better than she had in a good, long time and looked at the clock: twelve-thirty. She lay still for a moment, letting the past twelve hours roll through her mind, her smile growing wider.

Wow.

The one word was still all her mind was capable of conjuring. Sex with Jason had been...mind-blowing...incredible... hot, hot, hot.

And she intended to have more of it with him as soon as humanly possible.

She stripped the sheet off and headed for the shower. A half hour later she was blow-dried and dressed in white drawstring linen pants and tank, hot pink underwear underneath, ready to seek out Jason and see when they might continue their sack session. But first food. She was starving.

Maybe he'd consider making her another one of those delicious crepes. Hell, they were so good, she might be interested in learning how to cook them herself.

She ran into Dominic at the foot of the stairs. "Hey. Where's Jason?" she asked.

"Out for the day."

She raised her brows. "Day?"

"Yeah. What do you need?"

The way he looked at her made her want to say, "Not you," but she refrained. "Nothing that can't wait until he gets back."

Actually, what she had in mind required she wait until he got back.

She sighed and headed for the kitchen, making a fresh pot of coffee and grabbing a peach from a bowl in the middle of the island. She fetched her laptop from her desk in the other room, ignoring where Dominic stood in front of the windows, and went back into the kitchen. She perched on a stool and logged on to the computer where she found eight emails waiting for her. She opened the first when her cell phone rang.

Her brother Brad.

She really wasn't up to talking to him until she had at least one cup of coffee. She let it forward to voice mail.

The message bubble popped up. "I know you're up. Pick up."

Her cell began ringing again.

She sighed and answered. "I hate technology," she said by way of hello.

"Given how much you use it, I'm thinking you're having a love affair with it."

She grimaced. "Then it would be a threesome."

"That's sick."

"Oh, stop. You know what I mean." She accessed the first email. "What do you want?"

"That's some hello."

"I thought we already did that."

"Isn't it enough for me to want to call and see how my baby sister's doing?"

She gave an eye roll and sat back. Bradley Cosby lived in San Francisco and owned a very successful construction company. And as the oldest, he was also the biggest pain in the ass. "No."

"I take it you're still locked up."

"Yes. For the next twelve days, eighteen hours and thirty-six minutes. But you knew that already, didn't you?"

"Yeah. I just like hearing you say it."

"You would."

"It would have saved us all a lot of trouble had we been able to lock you up from ages fifteen to thirty."

"Ha-ha. You talk to Dad lately?"

"Yesterday. He's in Nova Scotia with his latest squeeze."

Considering that their father was sixty-three and the women he dated were the same age, she didn't think squeeze entered anywhere into the occasion.

Well, except for the one time when he saw a woman in her fifties for a while who'd obviously had her breasts done. It had been all Jordan could do to not ask her to put something on to cover her revealing tank top. With her luck, she'd have made a tart response only to learn the woman had had a double mastectomy and the implants were necessary.

She read the email from her Denver club manager Montana Sky. Apparently Montana thought Jordan needed company and told her she was stopping by at three with company. An arrow told her to click on a link. She clicked.

"Is there anything else you wanted? Or did you just call to torture me?"

"No. Pretty much just called to torture you."

"Figured as much. You could have done that via IM."

"Yeah, but it wouldn't have been nearly as much fun."

"Mmm." She watched as a picture of what had to be the tiniest kitten she'd ever seen popped up on the screen, apparently a fostered pet through Pals Forever Animal Rescue. She sat back and stared at the black ball of fur with bright green eyes.

"Jordan? Just say the word and I'm on the next plane out."

"Huh? What?" Montana was bringing her a cat? Oh, hell. "No, no. I'm fine. Thanks, though. Talk to you soon."

She hung up the cell and immediately dialed Montana's number only to get her voice mail.

Shocker.

Blasted employees. Where did they get the idea they were her friends, welcome to drop by at any time to give her critters?

From her, that's who.

She left a message, but she didn't expect Montana would acknowledge it. No, she fully anticipated the black-haired ex-model would pop up at her door, pet carrier in hand.

Damn...

"Drop it, Jax. It ain't gonna happen."

Jason sat back in the wooden chair at the Denver BBQ restaurant his younger brother had chosen when he'd called inviting him to lunch.

Their grandmother liked to remark that if she hadn't witnessed both births herself, she'd have sworn they'd come from different mothers. Where Jason bore the black hair and eyes of their father, Jax was the spitting image of their mother with hazel eyes and light brown hair.

Jackson considered him with a level gaze. "You'd rather I work at a bar?"

"I'd rather you open your own restaurant."

"I'm not interested in opening my own restaurant. I want to work at Lazarus."

Only three years separated them in age, but sometimes Jason felt like it was twenty. Why wouldn't the kid listen to him?

He looked at his watch and then through the window overlooking the street. Jordan would be up by now. He wondered what she was doing. His cell buzzed. He plucked it from his belt and looked at the display. A call from his grandmother.

Great.

He let it slide to voice mail, not up to listening to her argue Jax's point for him. A text message popped up. It was from Lisa at Lazarus.

You were missed at today's meeting. Megan wants to talk to you. Oh, and that creepy guy showed up again. A couple of the guys escorted him out.

Jason rubbed the back of his neck and put the phone on the table.

"I've been offered a position at a competing company."

He stared at his brother.

Jackson shrugged. "That's why I invited you out. Not to ask you—again—to hire me at Lazarus, but to say I'm seriously considering Pegasus's offer."

"Pegasus? They're run by a half-wit who shot himself in the foot when he served. Literally."

Jax smiled. "I know. It appears to be a great source of amusement around the place."

"Yeah, well, do they think it's funny that two of his recruits have been killed over the past two years because the dumbass doesn't know his security from his asshole?"

Jax stared at him. "It won't happen to me."

"It might if you work for him."

"It might if I work anywhere."

"Including Lazarus."

His brother sighed and pushed his plate back although he'd only eaten half his ribs. "Look, I just thought you should know."

"You know he probably only wanted to hire you because you're my brother and you'd be a feather in his peacock coat."

Jax's eyes narrowed. "I'll let you get the bill." He got up and left the table without saying another word.

Jason cursed under his breath as he peeled off enough bills to cover their meals plus a generous tip and got up himself. As far as wrong words went, he knew beyond a shadow that his last one rated among the worst. His brother was a more than capable warrior. Hell, you only had to look at the good stock he came from and all he'd accomplished on the battlefield and off, despite Jordan's best efforts to keep him off. But he'd be damned if he'd let him put his ass on the line any more than he had to. Look what it had done to him. He had absolutely no life outside his job. As for women…

He thought of Jordan and was surprised to find himself frowning instead of smiling, thinking of the shooter this morning and the danger her life was in, made all the greater by his momentary loss of focus.

As for women, he'd be much better off sticking to his job…

12

JORDAN SAT ON A STOOL at the kitchen island considering the scrap of black fluff Montana had guilted her into accepting.

She'd faced her Denver nightclub manager after Dominic had given the okay and let the leggy brunette inside the apartment along with her two paper bags with handles. One held a litter box and food. The other a mewling black kitten no bigger than the length of her hand.

"No way," she'd said, refusing to take either bag.

"The way I see it, you two need each other." Montana had flipped her long black hair over one shoulder and smiled at her.

Now, an hour and a lost argument later, she sat staring at the unwanted gift.

Single with a cat. Ugh.

And weren't black cats bad luck? Something about never crossing their paths or some like thing.

She made a face. The feline named Cleo seemed to catch her grimace and stopped playing with the sink sprayer long enough to scamper over to bat at her hand where it propped up her chin.

Jordan smiled and scratched the kitten behind the ears. She did have to say it was impossible to stay mad with the little munchkin around. But what in the hell was she going to do with a cat?

A sound came from behind her. She caught Jason's gaze as he entered the room. He looked as perplexed as she felt. But she got the distinct impression it was for a completely different reason.

"What is that?" he asked.

Cleo took advantage of her distracted state and batted and bit on her hair. "What does it look like?"

He met her gaze, a thousand unsaid words seeming to pass between them, much of it making perfect sense, some of it not at all. "A cat."

"Smart man."

"Smart ass. Where'd you get it?"

"A friend brought it over."

He arched a brow. "A friend."

"I'm surprised Dominic didn't fill you in on it."

"I am, too." She scooped the kitten up and went to stand in front of him. "What's the matter? You afraid someone is trying to sneak an explosive device inside of a kitten?"

"Stranger things have been known to happen."

She held the scrap up to him. "Jason Savage, meet Cleo. Cleo, this is the big, mean man protecting me."

He grimaced at Cleo and Cleo stared back at him. If Jordan wasn't mistaken, the kitten was growling.

She laughed. "Looks like she doesn't like you."

"Impossible. All females like me."

She tucked the kitten against her chest. "There's always a first time for everything."

"It's a cat."

"It's a kitten."

He wrinkled his nose and then rubbed it with the back of his wrist, looking about to sneeze.

"You're not allergic?" she asked.

"Don't be ridiculous."

She watched as he walked across the kitchen to his laptop. Then it struck her. She could have gotten out of accepting the gift by feigning an allergy.

Was it too late? she wondered.

The kitten rubbed her downy head against her arm and a burst of protectiveness ballooned in her.

"We need to talk," Jason said from where he'd set up his laptop on the island directly across from the stools.

"Funny, I was thinking the same thing." She smiled as she sat down and set Cleo free. The kitten made a beeline straight for the laptop. Jason ignored her.

"There were three attempts made this morning."

Jordan's smile slowly faded. "Attempts? As in against my life?"

He met her gaze. "Are there any other kind?"

She tried to come up with a sarcastic comeback but found the words stuck in the back of her throat. Had she really managed to forget for a precious moment why she was stuck in her apartment? And the true reason for Jason's presence?

Yes, she realized, she had. And the man directly opposite her was to credit and to blame...

JASON HATED THE EXPRESSION on Jordan's beautiful face. When she smiled, well, she did funny things to his insides, things that manifested themselves in a growing physical need for her that leapt off the charts.

He rubbed the back of his neck and referred to his laptop, anything to keep from looking at her.

After lunch, he'd met with the Marshals office contact and discovered that in addition to the rank amateurs on the rooftop, they'd apprehended two other, unconnected, armed individuals attempting to gain access to the building who had no business being anywhere near it.

"We're going to be ramping up security. From here on in...I'm sorry, but no more outings."

When she didn't say anything right away, he looked up. She wore the same expression she had a moment ago, indicating she either hadn't heard him or had and was good at pretending the information didn't matter. He guessed the former.

"Jordan?"

He noticed the softness in his tone and the way she responded to it. He cleared his throat.

"Did you hear what I said?"

She nodded slowly. "Yes. Right. No more outings."

The piece of fluff she'd unleashed on the counter darted across the keyboard of his laptop. He scooped it up, surprised by how little it weighed, and then let it loose on the other side of the screen where she zoomed away and toward safety… right against Jordan's chest.

A place he wouldn't mind being tucked against just then, albeit for different reasons.

"What did you want to talk to me about?"

"Internet shopping."

Her words made no sense at all.

"Jordan?"

"Huh?" She blinked at him and then at the cat trying to gain access to the front of her tank top. He couldn't help his smile, wondering if it were a male instead of a female. When they were that young, it was sometimes difficult to tell. He watched as she placed the feline in front of her and scratched its ears. Hell, she already had the cat eating out of her hand.

He absently rubbed the back of his neck again.

"Internet shopping?" he reminded her.

"Oh. Yes." The cat lost interest and ran toward the faucet, her tiny legs not stopping in time so she toppled into the sink. He winced at the sound and was about to check to see if she was all right when a playful head popped up, gave a shake and then batted at the faucet.

"I ordered a couple of things last week and the online tracker says they've been delivered, but I haven't seen them."

"The Marshals probably intercepted the delivery."

She stared at him. "Really."

It was more of a sarcastic statement than a question.

"Well, I hope they're enjoying themselves."

"Should I ask?"

She smiled saucily. "If you get the packages for me, you can see."

The suggestion made his jeans instantly tighten across the groin. "I'm on it."

She laughed throatily.

"So, getting hungry?" she asked.

He swore he just popped a button altogether on his jeans. He was starving. For her.

Which is exactly the reason why he couldn't give in to it.

Although Dominic was still on duty for another hour...

"Meet you in the bathroom in two minutes," he said.

"One."

"Lose the scrap of fur first."

"Got it."

He blinked and she was gone.

And he followed right after her...

WHAT SEEMED LIKE AN EON later, but was only minutes, Jordan devoured Jason's mouth, breaking contact only so she could tug off his T-shirt and he could strip her of her tank. The downstairs bathroom was as big as a master, with a Jacuzzi tub and large, tiled shower. She pushed him against the wall and worked his button fly while he rid her of her bra and pulled the tie on her drawstring linen pants so that they pooled around her ankles where she stepped out of them. His jeans and both their undergarments followed suit until they were flush, flesh to flesh, heat to heat. He muttered under his breath and then reached for his jeans, extracting a condom from the back pocket. She took it from him and sheathed his hot, hard length, loving the feel of him in her fingers.

Dear heaven he was even hotter than she remembered. Which was saying a lot, because she'd already ranked him well within her Top Five when it came to sex. He backed her up until she was against the tile. She lifted her leg to hug his hip and she instantly wrapped both legs around him until his sex was sandwiched between her swollen folds. She couldn't seem to catch her breath as she braced her hands against his shoulders and thrust her hips against his. He entered her in one long sigh.

Oh, yes…

Fire flittered and flicked and burned until it consumed her every part. She held his intense gaze, watching as his jaw tensed and the muscles across his chest and arms tightened, his flat, washboard abs expanding and contracting as his breathing grew more ragged. Evidence of his being affected as powerfully as she was by their forbidden liaison inched her turn-on factor even higher.

She tilted her hips, taking even more of him in. He muttered something under his breath and then thrust into her deeply. Then again and again…

Jordan moaned, flattening her arms against the tile to give her greater leverage as she held her hips away from the wall. His hands grasped her bottom, parting her farther.

She couldn't believe she was so close to orgasm. Without a drink. Without foreplay. Without so much as a *hello, howdoyoudo.* Just like that, she was about to topple over the edge.

And at Jason's low groan, she did exactly that…

13

HELL AND DAMNATION.

Jason was sure he'd just broken some sort of land speed record. He prided himself on control, but when Jordan's slick muscles contracted around him, he was rendered powerless and came with her.

The sound of their labored breathing echoed in the tiled room, amplified by the stark walls. He was vaguely aware that the kitten she'd placed in the large hot tub meowed, trying but failing to gain a footing against the glazed sides.

"Wow," Jordan whispered, her pink tongue dipping out to moisten her well-kissed lips.

He leaned in to kiss her again, in complete agreement. She draped her arms over his shoulders, her nipples grazing his chest. Damn, but she was hot. Hotter than any woman had a right to be.

"How much time do we have left?" he asked, his erection growing hard again.

She smiled. "If we had an hour, then I'd say fifty-nine minutes, thirty seconds."

He chuckled against her sensual mouth. "You tell anybody I came that fast, I'll deny it."

"Whoever would I tell?"

Who, indeed?

He reached between them and stroked her breasts. He couldn't seem to get enough of touching her. Her legs were still wrapped around his waist, his cock deep inside her. She tilted her hips and even her hair seemed to shiver in after-shock.

He groaned and withdrew from her heat, helping her to her feet.

"Done?" she whispered, continuing to kiss him.

"Oh, baby, we're just getting started…"

He put on a fresh condom, then swiveled her around. She gasped and arched her back, pressing her bare bottom more closely against him and putting her head against his shoulder. He tilted her chin so they could continue kissing and then trailed his fingers to her right breast even as his other hand slid around her hip to caress her sex. So hot, so wet, so sweet…

He parted her swollen flesh and stroked her tight bud. He swallowed her low moan even as he positioned his once again rock-hard erection between her soft folds, not entering. She writhed in his arms, trying to force penetration. He felt her hand against his erection, pressing him harder against her.

Jason gritted his back teeth together, determined not to come so fast this time. Why did he have the feeling he might not have much of a say in that?

THERE WAS SOMETHING decadently delicious about stealing a few sexy moments in the bathroom while the world continued to turn as usual outside the closed door. Jordan sucked her bottom lip between her teeth as Jason ran his long, hard length between her legs. Damn, he felt good. And after the first orgasm, her body was relaxed and flowing, wondrously open to the myriad sensations washing over her.

Reluctantly she hauled her mouth from his so she could bend ever so slightly forward to encourage penetration. She shivered all over as he entered her.

Her knees melted and she reached to support herself against the wall, sliding back against him until he was deep inside.

Yes...

He grasped her hips, positioning her just so and began slowly stroking her, inside and out. Her breasts swayed, her breathing grew more shallow, and her very skin seemed to quiver. So, so good...

A soft fog of sensation buffeted her. All she felt was him moving in and out of her. The thickening of her own blood. The sweet pressure building in her lower abdomen. He slid his fingers between her legs from the front and stroked her externally and she moaned, covering his hand with hers and then reaching beyond, feeling him surge forward and withdraw.

There came a point when she could no longer tell where she ended and he began. And when she reached crisis point, she knew he was right there with her.

It was all she could do not to dissolve into a puddle right there on the tile around his feet.

And if it wasn't for the knock on the door, she very well might have...

JASON DIDN'T BOTHER trying to hide anything. If Dominic was knocking, that meant something was up. He dressed, giving Jordan the chance to do the same, and checked his cell. Three calls from Dominic he didn't even hear.

Damn.

He hurried outside, pulling the door closed behind him.

"What's up?"

To his credit, Dom didn't try getting a look inside. "Bad news, boss."

They walked together to the front room.

"Word just came in—Miss Cosby's San Francisco club caught fire. Loss is expected to be complete."

"Foul play?"

"Preliminary report says 'cause suspicious.'"

There had been threats made against all three clubs, but none had yet to be followed through on. Until now.

He went to the kitchen where he accessed his laptop even as he dialed Lazarus and told Dominic to get the Marshals' contact on the line.

He could only imagine what Jordan's reaction to the news was going to be.

"It gets worse," Dominic said as he dialed his own cell. "Someone was severely injured in the fire."

JORDAN WONDERED WHY she hadn't considered having more bathroom sex before now. There was easy access and with the shower right there, it was convenient. She hung up the towel she'd used to dry and got dressed, her movements slow and lethargic. Of course, there was also no bed around to stretch out on, which was a definite drawback. Then again, there was always the bathtub to fill and crawl into.

She looked into the tub and the kitten was there staring up at her with big, hopeful eyes. She smiled.

"Well, guess you got an eyeful, huh?" she said, plucking up the ball of fur.

Cleo purred loudly against her, igniting feelings that went nicely with the sensations still flowing through her body. She opened the door and walked into the hall, checking her cell as she went. There were six missed calls, all but one of them from San Francisco friends and employees. The other was from her brother.

She frowned as she accessed her voice mail.

At the sound of the assistant manager's weepy voice, her steps slowed. Then stopped altogether right outside the kitchen door as she listened to the other messages, all telling her the same thing: there'd been a fire. And Otto was in critical condition in the hospital.

She met Jason's gaze across the room and knew immediately that he knew.

She slowly dropped her arm to her side. "I've got to go."

He advanced on her. "Not a good idea."

"I don't give a shit if it's a good idea, or the worst one I've ever had. One of my best friends is lying in a hospital ICU. I'm going."

She turned to go upstairs and he grasped her arms. She shivered at his touch.

"Let me get some information first, Jordan. Please."

The pleading look on his face touched something deep within her.

"Call your friends. Talk to them. But don't do anything without checking with me first. Okay?"

She noticed Dominic looking at them oddly, but couldn't care less what their conversation might be giving away.

Her instinct was to grab her purse and catch the next flight out. She didn't even need to pack.

Jason's grasp became more of a caress and then he dropped his hands to his sides. "There's a good chance this might have been done on purpose for the sole intention of getting you to go there."

She squinted at him, trying to follow his logic. "Why not come after me here?"

"Because we have you covered here. Out there—traveling, moving around—you're an easier target."

She wasn't sure she liked being referred to as a target, easy or otherwise. No, she despised it.

"You mean I'm to blame for Otto getting hurt?"

He shook his head. "No. Otto is. From what I've been able to find out so far, he ran back into the club to try to save something."

"His precious collection of Batman figures," she whispered, hurting for her friend and what he must have been feeling in that moment. A moment that had nearly cost him his life.

And might still.

She felt suddenly cold.

"I think you better sit down," Jason said.

Rather than lead her farther into the kitchen, he guided her to the living room instead where she sank into a chair. Cleo meowed and nudged her head against Jordan's neck. She was happy for the soft gesture but could barely acknowledge it.

"I'll have Dominic bring you something to drink. What do you want?"

"Nothing. Thanks."

He looked toward the kitchen.

"It's okay. Go do what you need to do. It's your job."

But being a good friend and a good boss was hers.

"Are you all right?" he asked.

She stared at him.

"Right. Stupid question." He drew in a deep breath. "I'll just be in the other room if you need anything."

She nodded her thanks, watching as he went.

Was it possible that mere minutes ago they were enjoying hot sex in the bathroom?

Cleo meowed and perched on her shoulder, rubbing her nose against Jordan's jaw. She smiled sadly and then lifted the kitten to the side of her face, reveling in her sweet softness. Then she put her down on the floor and lifted her cell phone, pressing the first name she came to, her gaze drawn to the front door.

How far would she get before Jason was on her heels?

Her brother answered on the second ring and she was gratefully distracted from thoughts of finding out.

14

TWO HOURS LATER, THE plan was set.

Jason considered the outline he'd drawn up on his laptop. After watching Jordan overcome her original shock—pacing the living room floor, her cell phone superglued to her ear, the kitten chasing after her the whole time—he knew she was closer to, how had she put it when he first met her? Oh, yes. Jumping out of her skin. She was closer to doing that than at any time before.

He might prefer her jumping out of her clothes, but her skin was another matter altogether.

While keeping a subject happy in a case of this nature shouldn't be his first priority, in Jordan's he found it almost critical. Spending years in the field drawing up contingency plans told him that even when conditions weren't optimal, there were always ways around, through or under a bad situation. So he'd decided he'd get her to San Francisco come hell or high water.

He'd yet to tell her that, though.

He clicked on the next page on his laptop and glanced at his watch. Once his decision was made, his mind had easily switched gears in both support and implementation of the plan. Anyone who asked would be hard fought to find anything but solid reasoning behind his actions. When they'd gone out, he'd realized that using a decoy while holing Jordan away elsewhere might not be a bad idea at all, and he'd considered it an option before now should things heat up further. It might not be something the Justice Department had the resources to do, outside of taking her to a safe house, but Lazarus could easily swing it with little difficulty.

The way he saw it, Jordan would be much safer away from this place. There had been another attempt at access since this morning, and sources on the ground told him the bounty on her head had increased substantially since yesterday, meaning the pros would be getting in on the act, if they hadn't already.

In fact, he was afraid a pro was already working it and the San Francisco club fire was part of the plan.

But so long as he worked with that in mind, he should be okay.

His cell phone rang. Megan McGowan's name popped up in the display.

Shit. The last person he wanted to talk to just then.

"Meg," he said simply when he answered.

"What's up, Savage? There's a team over here ignoring their assigned tasks and dedicated to working on something for you. They even refused to let me in on what was going on until I insisted."

Jason grinned, imagining the scene. He'd asked the gang he'd remotely assembled to hold their cards close to their vest. That they'd tried to keep Megan out of it was highly amusing. That she made them tell her was even more so.

"Tell me you're really not thinking about going to San Francisco?"

His smile vanished.

"Because if you are, I think it's a very, very bad idea. Keeping an eye out for professionals in Denver is slightly easier because there are few around. They have to come in from outside which makes them more visible. The west coast, on the other hand…"

Jason knew his reasoning would hold up under scrutiny to everyone. Everyone but Megan.

He hated to think what personal insight he'd given her during their brief affair down in Florida. But now he was being forced to.

"Got it covered, Meg," he said.

"I know you do. But wouldn't it be best to stay put? Perimeters are already in place, the territory's familiar. Changing the game plan now puts the target in significantly greater danger."

He recalled Jordan saying she hated being called that. Now he understood why.

Although he didn't dare indicate that. Hell, Megan wasn't beyond calling the other partners and suggesting he be pulled off the case. And he sure as hell wasn't going to allow that to happen.

Surprisingly, he'd received little resistance from either the Justice Department or the U.S. Marshal's Office. So long as they were kept in the loop and Jordan was delivered to the courthouse on time, they didn't care what he did. If boredom had anything to do with their easy agreement, they weren't saying.

"That's exactly the reason I think it's important to shake things up. The pros like predictability—it gives them a chance to find the chink in the armor. By moving around, that armor is no longer visible."

"And less effective."

"Depending on if they know where the subject is. Which they won't."

"If you fly commercial—"

"Not going to. All ready have private transportation lined up."

"A charter?"

"Yes."

"How much is this going to cost us?"

"Nothing. The subject is going to cover expenses." Jordan had both the resources and the motivation to do just that.

"I haven't seen an expense slip of that nature cross my desk."

"Good." He grinned, not about to give her anything else.

The payment had come out of dummy accounts, ten times removed from Jordan, him and Lazarus. There would be no tracing it back. If anyone looked, they would see a small family visiting the area from Marin County had chartered the private plane and that the reservation had existed for months.

Megan's sigh crackled over the line. "Can you at least come in so we can talk about it?"

"Sorry. The plan is already in motion."

Silence. And then, "Okay. You know you have my full backing. Call if you need anything, you hear?" Another heartbeat of silence, then, "And I mean anything."

"Thanks, Meg. I will."

He disconnected the line and stood for a moment regaining his bearings.

Damn. If anyone were capable of pointing out the holes in his logic, it was Megan.

Yet all he had to do was look through that doorway and see Jordan pacing the floor, her beautiful face pale and drawn, and he knew he had to make this happen for her...

JORDAN TURNED QUICKLY to pace in the other direction and nearly squashed Cleo. She picked up the kitten, who easily forgave her, and focused her attention on the assistant manager of Bridges, who filled her in on Otto's condition.

"I'm sitting in the waiting room now. The nurse says there's been no change."

"What about his family? Have you heard anything from his sister yet?"

Silence and then, "She called a little while ago. She won't be coming."

Jordan stopped pacing and briefly closed her eyes. Otto wasn't given to talking much about his family, but over a couple bottles of Bordeaux one night after the club closed, he spilled that he came from an *über*conservative family that wasn't very happy with the choices he was making in his personal life. He hadn't spoken to his parents in nearly a decade and his sister…well, they kept in contact via periodic phone calls. But he hadn't really seen her since last year.

He had no one but what he called his 'family by choice,' meaning his friends. And she considered herself to be one of them.

Cleo batted at her hand where she still held the phone even as Cissy said, "Jordan? You still there?"

"Yes. Yes, I am." Unfortunately. Where she should be was on a plane to San Francisco. She needed to be there for Otto.

The doorbell rang. She blinked, staring at the wooden barrier. No one ever just rang the doorbell. Even before her forced isolation, there was a process you had to go through to gain access to her floor.

She told Cissy she'd call her back as Dominic strode by on his way to answer the door.

Jordan slid her cell into her pocket and sat down on the padded arm of the closest chair, watching.

She recognized the woman almost immediately, even though she looked different from the last time she saw her—she was the one who had acted as her decoy when Jason had taken her out. While there were some similarities in build and weight, that's where they ended. The other woman was a redhead and looked nothing like her so far as she could see. Of course, a wig and similar clothes helped…

She squinted. What was the woman doing there now? And

why was she with two other guys who obviously worked at the same company as Jason and Dominic?

"Jordan?"

She looked over her shoulder to find Jason standing in the kitchen doorway. A nod of his head indicated he wanted her to join him.

Placing Cleo on the chair, she moved in his direction, her gaze glued to the four talking quietly on the other side of the room.

"What's going on?" she asked.

She watched as he closed the door after her, her heart dipping low into her stomach. It wasn't so long ago he'd closed the bathroom door for other reasons...

But his squared stance told her he didn't want to talk about sex. Not that they'd done a whole lot of talking in the bathroom...

She gestured over her shoulder. "Isn't that the girl you used as a decoy the other day?"

"It is," he answered.

She dipped her head closer. "And?"

"And what?"

"And what is she doing here now?"

He stared at her for a moment and then pulled out a stool. "Sit down. There's something I want to go over with you."

"What's going on?" she asked again, sitting.

He moved his laptop in front of her and began talking. She lost the gist of his words though after the first few sentences, nor did she understand what he was pointing to on the screen. She didn't know if it was a result of what he was saying or because of his nearness. He leaned a hand against the back of the stool, his arm skimming her back, his chest pressing into her shoulder, his manly scent filling her senses. Heat filled her inside and out and her gaze caught on his strong profile rather than the computer screen. Damn, but he had a great mouth. Not just great-looking, but great-feeling...

"Jordan? Are you listening?"

She blinked up into his beautiful dark eyes. "No."

His pupils dilated and he looked wonderfully close to kissing her. "Why?"

"Because you're taking me to San Francisco, aren't you? This is what all this is about?"

He appeared determined not to smile, but she knew he wanted to. "It's not going to happen unless you listen to—"

She kissed him. Full on, full in and fully, touching the side of his face, wondering if it were physically possible to inhale someone, because that's exactly what she wanted to do in that one moment.

"I love you," she said.

He looked startled…and she felt startled.

She licked her lips several times and squirmed on the stool. "I mean, I love that you're doing this." She gestured. "Of course, I don't love you. That's just ridiculous. Ludicrous, really. I don't even know you…"

What was she doing? Aside from the fact that she'd said words that she'd rarely uttered in her life, she seemed to be digging herself into an even bigger hole.

Even as she tried to argue her way out of it, a part of her pondered her true, core motivation. Was it possible she was falling for Jason? That somewhere she had crossed the line between sex and love?

The idea both exhilarated her…and scared her to death.

She awkwardly cleared her throat and pointed toward the laptop. "So, what were you saying?"

15

TWO HOURS LATER, JASON sat across from Jordan on the private jet, oblivious to everything but her. He didn't register the oversize white leather chairs, or the fresh fruits and vegetables a flight attendant had placed on the table between them, or Dominic sitting across the aisle typing on his laptop, or the clouds outside the window that buffeted them from the ground below. All he could see was her curled up on the chair, a fluffy brown blanket pulled up to her chin, her blond hair tousled, fast asleep.

"I love you."

The words seemed to reverberate throughout his entire body.

He could count the times he'd heard the words on one finger: once. From his mother, the night she and his father had left home that fateful winter night. She hadn't said it before, so he'd been just as surprised then as he was now.

Oh, he'd heard the words from various women over the years. Usually in the heat of passion. Nothing he'd ever taken seriously.

And he told himself he shouldn't take Jordan's words seriously now.

But there had been something about the way she'd looked

at him where she said it. For one instant, the world had shifted on its axis.

Jason ran his hand over his hair, popped his seat belt and got up to go to the bathroom at the back of the plane. He closed the door and then splashed water over his face, staring at himself in the mirror. The room was as outrageously appointed as the rest of the aircraft, but he barely saw it as he considered his reflection. He wasn't a bad-looking guy, he supposed. A little rough around the edges. He liked to say he was good-looking enough to get laid as often as he wanted, but not so good-looking that women wanted to keep him indefinitely.

He certainly wasn't the type of guy to obsess over a few carelessly said words inspired by…what? Surprise? Gratitude?

And he positively wasn't the type of guy who wanted to hear them.

Aw, hell…

He yanked a folded towel off the counter and mopped his face with it, considering the toiletries lined up in a rack. He wasn't this…guy. The kind that belonged in these surroundings. While Jordan looked right at home snuggled up in the front cabin, he was little more than a raggedy-ass wet dog in a roomful of well-groomed cats.

Sex. That's all it was supposed to be about between them. Awesome, mind-blowing sex.

He didn't want anything more than that. Never saw himself settling down. Starting a family.

For what it was worth, the Jordan he'd first met and was coming to know didn't seem like the kind of woman who wanted any of that, either.

Then why was her expression etched into his retinas?

He turned and leaned against the counter, crossing his arms over his chest. Of course, it wasn't so long ago that simple sex had ended up turning into something more.

Still, not even his experience with Megan in Florida, and the ugly aftermath, compared to this.

"Stop obsessing, Savage. You don't obsess."

He recognized that being stuck in such close confines with Jordan was partially to blame. Once they were in San Francisco...

There was a soft knock on the door.

For a moment he thought it might be Jordan. He quickly opened it to find the flight attendant smiling.

"The pilot's just informed me we're about to begin our final descent. Please take your seat and fasten your seat belt."

She walked away.

He stood staring after her and then his gaze caught on Jordan where she was now fully awake, using one of those hand mirrors to straighten her hair and check her makeup. She seemed to sense his gaze and looked up at him, smiling. His gut squeezed, thinking that the flight attendant's words could easily apply to his current predicament: he was about to begin his final descent. Straight into some sort of man-made hell...

JORDAN WASN'T COMPLETELY clear on how Jason had made it happen, but before she could blink, she was entering Otto's private hospital room. He'd regained consciousness while they were somewhere over Nevada and despite his obvious pain, his face lit up like a Christmas tree when she walked in clad in scrubs, her hair hidden under a cap, thick, goggle-like glasses obscuring her features.

"You look hideous," he said as she took off the glasses but left the cap in place.

"Gee, thanks. If you had any idea what it took to get here, you'd be a little more gracious."

"Jordan, gracious went out with spandex."

He laughed and then grabbed his stomach with bandaged hands.

"God, how badly does it hurt?" she asked, coming to sit next to him. She reached out, then hesitated. "Where can I touch you? Is it safe anywhere?"

"Honey, it's safe for you to touch me anywhere." She smiled and put her hand on his knee, giving it a squeeze that didn't seem to put him in any pain. "How bad is it?"

"I'm told it's not as bad as it looks. Third-degree burns on my hands and wrists. And second-degree down my right side from neck to hip." He grimaced. "Do you think the scars will give me a little cache?"

"You don't need any more cache."

"Sweet. Of course, I could have done without the bump on the head. I have the mother of all headaches. Then there's the time it's going to take for my eyebrows and hair to grow back."

"Priorities."

He looked down. "Yeah." He remained quiet for a few moments and then said, "I'm sorry about the club, Jordan."

"What? You're kidding, right? The club can be replaced. But you—" she squeezed his knee "—cannot. There's only one you. And if it's all the same to you, I'd like to keep you around for a while."

"But I got a note warning me to get out—"

"That absolutely no one in law enforcement would have paid a lick of attention to." Considering her status as a protected federal witness with a bounty on her head, that wasn't entirely accurate. But the truth wasn't going to help her friend any.

And it wasn't going to bring back her club.

She briefly closed her eyes, cursing the day she ever met Rick Packard and wishing him dead with all the vehemence that he apparently wished her.

"Yes, but…"

Otto fell silent. She thought about admonishing him again,

but realized how worthless it would be just then. Instead, she thought of something that might distract him.

"Hey, guess what I got?" she asked.

He looked at her.

She fished her cell out of the inside pocket of the scrubs and opened it. She flashed him a picture of Cleo.

"A cat?" He stared at the phone and then at her. "Oh, baby girl, tell me you didn't."

She laughed. "Montana brought her to me. She's some sort of rescue. Her name's Cleo."

"Well, I suppose if you're going to have a cat, she should be named after the Queen of Denial. Especially since you're named after a river in one of those other Middle Eastern countries."

Jordan laughed.

He shook his head. "Single female...with a cat. Have I taught you nothing?"

"I know, right?" She put the cell back in her pocket. "You know what's even more desperate? I miss her already. I had to leave her back in Denver with the decoy."

He stared at her. "How did you manage to get here, anyway? I thought Mr. Savage Hottie was holding you hostage in your apartment?"

"Yes, well, he's the one who made this happen."

Otto's eyes narrowed. "Uh-oh. Please tell me it ain't so..."

"What?"

"You're not falling for the glorified ape in a suit, are you?"

"He doesn't wear suits. And, no. Of course not." Her smile widened. "But I do think it's safe to tell you he is a complete animal in the bedroom."

He looked around. "Where is he? Oh, tell me you brought him with you?"

"I did. He's outside."

"Well, what are you waiting for? Get him in here already!"

"In a minute. I want to spend some time alone with you first."

He made a face. "Spoilsport. Get me a mirror, will you?"

She produced one along with a tube of concealer, having come prepared. After long moments trying to repair himself with his limited mobility and bandaged hands, he gave up and sighed. "There's no hope."

She laughed. "Here, let me…"

He considered her handiwork when she was done. "It's the lighting. No one looks good. Not even you."

"Oh, shut up." She moved to switch off the overhead light and turned the lamp behind his bed on instead. "Better?"

"Dark is always better."

There was a knock, then the door that connected to the next room rather than the hallway, opened. "Jordan? Time's up."

"Well, that must be the nice Mr. Savage. Come in here so I can meet the man responsible for bringing my best girl to me."

Jordan tucked her chin into her chest to keep from laughing out loud at Otto's outrageous request.

Jason hesitated. He began to extend his hand, then saw Otto's bandaged limbs and awkwardly retracted it. "Sorry to hear what happened."

Otto's once-over was so blatant, Jordan was nearly embarrassed.

Jason cleared his throat and looked at her. "You ready?"

"Are we going to be able to come back?" she asked.

"I'll try to get you over in the morning. But no guarantees."

She smiled at him.

He cleared his throat again. "I'll wait in the next room while you say goodbye. Don't forget the glasses. And leave via the hall."

"Okay."

The door closed behind him and she sighed before looking back at Otto.

"Uh-oh. Girl, you got it bad."

"Oh, be quiet. You're incorrigible."

"That I am. But I'm also right."

Jordan leaned in and kissed him lingeringly on the cheek before drawing slightly back to gaze into his dear face. "Get well, my friend."

"It's not like I have anything else to do at the moment."

She smiled.

"Jordan?"

She stopped near the door. "What?"

"Promise me you'll be careful?"

Somehow she got the feeling he wasn't talking about the innumerable contract killers on her tail.

"I will."

"Promise."

Her throat nearly closed on the words. "I promise..."

16

THIS WAS ALL WRONG...

Jason paced the length of one of the three hotel suites he'd booked and back again. Dominic was in a room across the hall, his orders to keep his eye glued to the peephole. A plainclothes Marshal was posted in the lobby, another in a coffee shop across the street. No one knew they were there. He had no reason to feel on edge.

Yet he did.

He was experiencing the same uneasy feeling he'd had on the battlefield when their team had been surrounded and Lazaro had been hit.

He moved toward the bathroom and knocked on the door. "Get dressed. Now! We're getting out of here."

He dialed Dominic on his cell as Jordan opened the bathroom door, a cloud of steam following her towel-clad form out.

"What's happening? What's going on?"

He grasped her arm and moved her toward the bed where her clothes lay. "Get dressed. As quickly as you can."

He cursed when Dominic didn't pick up.

He dialed the Marshal in the lobby just as a knock sounded. Fuck.

He pushed a startled Jordan toward the door to his right.

The room was connected to the suites on either side of them: he had a fifty-fifty chance of getting it right.

He pocketed his cell, palmed his .38 and swung the door open.

"You son of a bitch," a man he'd never seen before in his life said, taking a swing at him and missing....

JORDAN GASPED AS JASON twisted the familiar man's arm behind his back and pressed his gun against his temple. "Don't shoot!"

She stood frozen, her mind refusing to register the scene beyond surface details as she clutched the towel between her breasts.

"You know this man?"

She could do little more than swallow, positioned halfway between their suite and the next.

"Jordan, do you know him?"

"Of course, she knows me. I'm her brother."

Dominic rushed up from behind the pair, his own gun drawn and pointed at Brad's head. Jordan gasped.

"Where in the hell were you?" Jason asked him.

"John. Sorry, boss."

Brad stepped out of the hold and stood staring at Jason as if he was going to take another swipe at him.

She rushed forward. "Yes, he's my brother."

Jason dropped his gun arm to his side and told Dominic to stand down.

"You sure?"

Jason stared at him. "Go back to your post. And next time take your phone with you."

Dominic backed from the room, closing the door after himself.

"What are you doing here?" Jordan asked her brother, coming to stand between him and Jason.

Brad's gaze took in her semi-clothed state. "Funny, I was

just going to ask the same of you." He glared at Jason. "Or you. What in hell were you thinking bringing my sister to San Francisco? Even I got wind of the increasing price on her head and I'm as far removed from the ground as can be."

"Increasing?" She turned so she could look at Jason while keeping her brother in sight.

Jason grimaced as he slid his gun back into his shoulder holster but didn't secure it. "I asked you not to tell anyone you were here."

"He's not anyone. He's my brother."

"And who is this guy?" her brother asked.

Jason was considering him. "Stupid move, your coming here."

"He could have shot you," Jordan agreed.

Jason's gaze lingered on hers for a moment. "No, he probably led them here."

"Them?"

He gently grasped her arm and urged her in the direction of the bed again. "Get dressed."

Brad puffed his chest out. "I want to know what she's doing undressed in the first place."

Jordan gave an eye roll and then gathered her clothes from the bed and stepped toward the bathroom. "I was taking a shower, you moron. Not that it matters. My sex life is none of your business and hasn't been for a long, long time. Just like yours is none of mine."

She disappeared into the bathroom and slammed the door, cursing stupid, trigger-happy men.

JASON'S ADRENAL SYSTEM was on fire. He'd been half a breath away from emptying the chamber of his .38 into Jordan's brother's temple. He wasn't in any condition to wrap his head entirely around the idea.

"I wasn't followed," Brad said.

"Sure, you weren't."

Leaving his holster open, he called the Marshals posted downstairs and across the street and then called Dominic.

"We're out of here in three," he told him. "Get the car."

"Where to?"

"We'll figure that out on the way."

He hung up.

He stared at the other man, who openly stared back. They were about the same age and same height, but that's where the similarities ended. Brad and Jordan were very obviously siblings, sharing their blond hair and hazel eyes. He recognized the guy had skills, and he might not have been so easy to stop had he not been blinded by anger. As for his getting by the Marshals posted downstairs, it was obvious from his golf shirt and chinos he wasn't armed, and he'd probably just walked right where he wanted to go.

Of course, he should have been stopped, which meant the support Marshals weren't being very supportive.

Which made it doubly important he get Jordan out of there but quick…

"I'm still waiting to hear why in the hell you brought her here," Brad demanded.

Jason crossed the room and rapped on the bathroom door. It opened and Jordan came out fully dressed and toting the one small carry-on bag she'd brought with her on the impromptu trip.

"I'd really like to answer you, but right now it's imperative I get her out of here."

The hair at his nape stood on end. He placed his hand on the back of Jordan's neck and pushed her down even as he shouted for Brad to do the same. A split second later, glass shattered, the closed curtains bowed inward as if from a strong breeze, and the stuffing exploded from a pillow on the bed.

Shit!

"Go, go, go!"

Keeping his hand on Jordan to keep her bent down as far as possible, he slid his gun out with his other and took out the two lights in the room, then urged her toward the door where he pushed a stunned Brad through, hurrying them both down the hall.

Elevator or exit stairs?

Service elevator. There might be someone posted either above or below them on the stairs, making it a veritable gauntlet, whereas on the service elevator, he could stop on any floor, with the kitchen being his safest bet. Even this late at night it would be staffed, making outside access difficult.

Damn it. Any access, period, should have been impossible. What in the hell was going on?

A spray of bullets hit the regular elevator doors from the windows positioned opposite designed to allow in plenty of daylight…or a hitman's bullets. He held both Jordan and Brad back, counting. Then, when he estimated the gunman was reloading, he hurried them both across the open area to the narrow hall beyond that held the service elevator. As he followed, he practically felt the breeze from the next round of gunfire aimed in their direction.

Since there were no buildings directly opposite the hotel, that meant the shooter had to be positioned farther away, probably from the office building he observed some stories higher than the hotel a block away, which meant the gunman had had to break out a window. If the guy was a pro, he'd have carved the needed hole without any fuss. And he was guessing the guy was. Possibly even the one who had set the club ablaze in the hope of drawing Jordan to San Francisco.

Besides, only a pro would have figured out they were there and put a tail on her brother on the off chance she'd call him.

The shooter had probably sent up a prayer of thanks when the idiot had led him directly to her.

He ushered them both into the service elevator when the

doors opened and they all stood upright, the silence echoing against the plain walls.

"I don't understand," Brad said. "I know I wasn't followed."

"A tail doesn't have to be behind you to follow you," Jason said. "He could have easily used your cell phone to trace your movements." He looked at Jordan. "What did you use to call him? Your own cell? Or the hotel phone?"

She blinked as if she didn't understand the question, then said, "The hotel phone…"

They all fell silent again.

The service doors opened on the kitchen. He held Jordan back as he checked out the immediate area, spotting nothing out of the ordinary. He'd already mapped out the hotel and knew exactly how to access the outside.

"Now what the hell do we do?" Brad asked.

"Now you're going to have to travel with us to the private airstrip outside town. From there, I recommend you fly somewhere outside the city until this shit dies down."

Holding Jordan close to his side, Jason led the way through the maze of the kitchen, carefully gauging the expressions of the staff. One of the younger guys working prep nodded ever so slightly to his left. He nodded his thanks, already knowing the outside exit was that way.

Within minutes they were on the street, Dominic pulled up in the car they'd rented, and they were off with no further drama.

He'd made a grave error in underestimating his opponents.

It was a mistake he wouldn't be making again…

17

JORDAN HAD NO IDEA WHERE she was. She blinked her eyes open and then closed them against the bright sunlight streaming in through a window to her left. When they'd arrived at their destination in the dead of night, she'd barely gotten a look around before being hurried upstairs to one of the bedrooms. Jason had asked her not to turn on the light and she hadn't. She'd been so spent she'd barely managed to strip out of her clothes and climb into the narrow twin bed where she'd instantly dropped off to sleep.

She couldn't be sure what time it was. And she couldn't consult her cell phone because Jason had confiscated it before they boarded the private plane. He'd said he'd arrange to have it mailed back to her apartment. She'd been miffed, but hadn't put up an argument. Not after someone had tried to turn her into human Swiss cheese.

She shuddered and huddled under the light blanket, the scene so vivid she swore she could still hear the gunshots.

How had a simple phone call resulted in all of that? One minute she'd been in the shower, so immensely relieved Otto was going to be okay that she'd actually felt something other than panic since learning of his injuries. And that something was sweet anticipation at the prospect of spending some primo alone time with the man who had made her visit happen.

Then, the next minute, she'd been terrified her heart would beat through the wall of her chest. Or, worse, a bullet or two or a hundred might find the adrenaline soaked organ and leave nothing but a memory of where it should have been.

When someone had taken a pot shot at her car a few days ago, she hadn't even been sure it was bullet. Tonight, there was no doubting. She was still fishing wood splinters from the door out of her right arm where she'd caught flying debris.

She shuddered again, her mind going blank.

What seemed like a long time later, she looked around for a clock. There was an old windup on a faded nightstand next to the bed. She picked it up to find it had been a while since it had been used. The hands were stuck on three-thirty-three. She idly turned the key, taking some comfort in the quiet ticking. It served as a reminder she was still there.

She stripped the blanket back and swung her legs over the side of the bed. There were simple pink slippers on the floor and a plaid robe draped across the foot of the bed. Jason's? She stroked the soft flannel and then buried her face in it, smelling him on it. She smiled, picking up the faint tang of his lime aftershave. Yes, it was definitely Jason's.

Where were they? At his place? If so, why was she sleeping in a twin bed and not some king-size monstrosity?

More importantly, why wasn't he in it with her?

She got up and pulled the robe on, nearly wrapping it around her twice before securing the belt. She walked to the window and looked out at a whole lot of nothing.

She blinked, sure she had to be seeing things. They'd returned to Denver, hadn't they? Then where were the buildings? And were those…cornfields?

She squinted. They sure looked like cornfields.

She heard a sound in the hall. She hurried to open the door to let Jason know she was awake. But instead, she found herself face-to-face with a woman who could have been fifty or seventy dressed in jeans and a checked shirt.

"Good, you're up. If you want lunch, you'll need to be downstairs in five minutes. If you don't, you'll have to wait till supper…"

"I WANT YOU TO GO BACK into town."

Jason stared down his younger brother Jax from across the kitchen.

"You can't be serious?"

"I am. And I want you to take Gram with you."

"Gram ain't going nowhere but to the cupboard to get an extra plate out. Your girlfriend's up," the older woman said as she walked into the room.

Jason switched his stare to his grandmother. "She's not my girlfriend. And you didn't talk to her, did you? I specifically asked you to let me know if you heard her get up."

"The girl opened the door and nearly bumped into me. I was required to be polite. Haven't I taught you any manners at all?"

He should have known better to challenge Annie Savage. His gran was as ornery as they got. Which was a good thing considering she'd had to raise her two headstrong grandsons after her own son died in that accident just up the road. Jason's father had been her only child, the one she had raised alone after Grandpa Jim left the tractor in the middle of a field during harvest time one year and never looked back. It was rumored that Annie had received a postcard from Boston years later, wishing her well. But Jason had never had the guts to actually ask if that was the case.

Annie had reclaimed her maiden name, gave it to her son and never looked back. Sometimes, though, Jason got the impression she'd never really started moving forward, either.

"Look, things may get a little hairy around here. I'd just

as soon neither one of you was anywhere near here if things get out of hand."

Gram had already turned her back on him and got the plate she was after out of the cupboard.

Jason grimaced and walked toward the hall, nearly tripping over the kitten Dominic had delivered to the house a little while ago. Gram had balked at keeping a strange animal inside the house, but he'd ignored her, setting Cleo's litter box up in the laundry room off the kitchen and her food and water bowls next to the back door. Now, if he could keep Gram from throwing the kitten out into the barn, they'd be fine.

He looked up to find Jordan coming down the stairs. He stopped dead in his tracks. She had on the same thing she'd worn yesterday, tan linen pants and a white tank top. And her attention wasn't on him, but her surroundings. His grimace deepened. He could only imagine what she made of the simple, hundred-year-old farmhouse he'd grown up in. The unpolished wood floor at her feet sloped due to settling, the walls were in dire need of painting, and he didn't think any of the furniture in the house was without a nick or a scratch.

Funny, it had never much mattered to him before. Why should it matter now?

He doubted Miss Jordan Cosby had ever been inside a house like this before, much less slept in one. He watched as she wrapped her arms around herself and wondered if the place made her itch.

Oh, despite the similar way in which they approached life, he'd known they were from different worlds. She was penthouse living, he was down home. He had a drawer full of jeans and she had closets full of designer duds. But it hadn't really registered with him. Before now.

She turned her head and their gazes met. She smiled.

Jason cleared his throat, watching as the darned cat ran in her direction. If he didn't know better, he'd think the scrap of black fur already knew who she belonged to, even though they'd only spent a brief time together yesterday.

"Cleo!" Jordan scooped the kitten up and rubbed her against her cheek. He could hear the animal's purr from across the room.

And he could practically hear his own bottomless hunger for the beautiful blonde rumble in his stomach.

She moved slowly closer to him, her attention on the kitten. "Where are we?"

He slid his hands into his jeans pockets. "The house I grew up in."

"And the woman I ran into?"

"My grandmother."

"The name's Annie," Gram said over his shoulder.

Jason moved to the side. Gram wiped her hands on the kitchen towel she held and then extended her right.

"And you are?" she prompted while they were shaking.

"Jordan. Jordan Cosby. Nice to meet you."

Gram looked at the kitten she held. "I hope you're not planning on bringing the cat to the table?"

"Oh, no. Of course not." Jordan put the kitten down then looked at her own hands.

"Sink," Gram said.

"Thanks."

Jordan slid between them and into the kitchen. Jason stared at his grandmother.

"What?" she said innocently.

He shook his head and entered the kitchen as well, finding Jordan exchanging greetings with his brother.

He'd brought her here to keep her safe, not introduce her to the family. Why, then, did he feel like he'd just got caught sneaking a girl up to his room?

He'd been working to get Jax and Gram out of the house since this morning—actually since the instant he'd shown up and ushered Jordan upstairs. He should have known better.

At the first hint of danger, Jax had planted his feet. And, of course, Gram wasn't about to go anywhere and leave her beloved farm unprotected.

Now there were six Lazarus employees surrounding the property and Jason had firearms tucked away within easy reach of every door and window. He had the unsettling feeling that whatever was going to happen, it was going to happen here.

Sources told him the price on Jordan's pretty head had tripled in the past twenty-four hours, with a bonus to be paid the quicker it was done. Rick Packard must be getting very antsy indeed, smelling the prison Pine Sol every time he took a breath.

"Well, come on, then," Gram said, ladling freshly made tomato soup into bowls at the stove. "You know how I feel about eating meals on time."

Jordan had just washed her hands and turned to meet his gaze, a smile in her eyes. He frowned as he neared the table and pulled out a chair for her. Gram raised her brows. He scowled at her.

"Thank you," Jordan said.

Gram put a bowl of soup in front of her and then handed her a clean kitchen towel. "Here. You don't want to get any soup on that pretty white outfit. It'll be hell to get out."

"I'll be careful."

"Suit yourself."

Jason put the plate of grilled cheese sandwiches on the table and got the milk out of the fridge.

"I made a pitcher of sweet tea," Gram said.

It was his turn to raise his brows. Annie raised hers back and then got the pitcher from the fridge herself, pouring Jordan a glass and giving it to her.

His grandmother never catered to visitors. She staunchly believed that guests shouldn't expect special treatment. Why, then, was she being so polite to this particular visitor?

Hell. She wasn't trying to play matchmaker?

His scowl deepened.

Gram and Jax took their places at the table.

"Aren't you going to sit down?" Gram asked.

"No," he said. "I'll catch leftovers."

"You'll eat now or you won't eat."

He picked up a grilled cheese sandwich and waved at it at her. "Satisfied."

He began walking from the room.

"So, Jordan, tell me. How long you been sleeping with my grandson?"

Jason nearly tripped over his own feet in his hurry to get as far away as fast as he could...

18

JORDAN WAS USED TO BEING the ballsy female, not being the focus of one. There was no game-playing with Annie Savage. She was direct and fresh and as forthright as they came. And Jordan liked her immediately.

The same applied to Jason's younger brother Jackson, but for other reasons. He and Jason might look nothing alike, but there was a calm certainty and strength about both of them that made a person feel safe. A quality she really hadn't given much thought to, until she'd had a thousand bullets racing toward her, all of them with her name etched on them.

Yes, she was strong. But the kind of strength she had held zero effectiveness against live ammo.

After Annie shooed her from the kitchen, refusing to allow Jordan to even take the dishes to the sink much less wash them, she reluctantly left the room and went in search of Jason. She found him standing in the open front doorway, the scene beyond blurred by the screen door. Cleo was batting at his left boot and then climbed his left leg, her tiny nails gaining leverage on the thick denim of his jeans. He neither flinched nor moved, merely looked down at the kitten. Then he plucked her up by the scruff of the neck and held her in front of his face, staring at her.

He sneezed.

Jordan smiled and went to take her from him.

"I'm telling you, you're allergic."

He made a face at her. "I don't have allergies. And if I did, they certainly wouldn't be to a harmless animal like that."

"Uh-huh." She scratched Cleo behind the ears and then put her down. The kitten scampered toward the throw rug in the hall behind them, diving under the corner.

Jordan stepped next to Jason, mimicking him by crossing her arms over her chest and staring through the door. The long, gravel driveway led to a quiet, two-lane road beyond.

"Anything?" she asked.

She felt his gaze on her profile. "Old man Thompson just went up the road in his tractor. It must be time for him to turn the south 200 in preparation to plant soybeans. Other than that, nothing."

She looked at him. "That's good, right?"

"That's expected. I don't anticipate anything to happen until after dark."

She swallowed hard.

"Looks like you should have worn the towel after all."

She glanced down at the two tiny soup splatters on her tank. "Yeah."

"I'm sure you have twenty more just like it at home."

"Two."

He stared at her.

"Okay, probably more like five. Maybe."

"Maybe more."

Why did she feel like that was an indictment?

"Sorry about Gram."

"Why? I think she's delightful."

"What, like something out of painting? Or some novel that you've read?"

"No, she reminds me of my Nana. She owned a farm in Nebraska. I used to visit her every summer and help out."

If he was surprised, he didn't show it. His stoic expression refocused on the scene outside.

"I'm no snob, Jason."

He blinked.

"That's what you thought, isn't it? That I'd find your family, this wonderfully warm house, lacking? Wrinkle my snooty nose, thinking it all beneath me?"

He didn't say anything for a long moment and then finally looked at her. "Yeah. Yeah, I did."

She smiled. "But you don't anymore?"

"There are slightly bigger fish to fry."

A shiver ran up her arm, both from the heat of his gaze as well as the insinuation of his words. "Before someone throws me from the frying pan into the fire, you mean?"

He didn't say anything.

"Right. Okay. Yes…"

She stood next to him for a few minutes more, staring outside. She wasn't sure if she felt reassured by their change in surroundings or more intimidated, if simply because she wasn't really familiar with them. While she'd spent a couple of weeks at her own grandmother's Nebraska farm for a few summers in her early teens, the visits had always emerged as time outside of time because it was nothing like her everyday life.

"My family wasn't always well-off," she said quietly, half to herself. "Dad and his partners didn't really start making good money until I was about nine or ten. I was young enough that I really didn't remember the rough times, but my four older brothers do." She smiled in warm remembrance. "They always called me a spoiled brat because I'd always had much more than they had when they were younger."

"New, high-end car at sixteen. Ivy-league education. A monthly allowance larger than some people's annual income…"

She looked down, feeling her cheeks heat. "Yeah…"

"Could you live like this, do you think?"

"Like how?"

"Here. On a farm like this."

"Now?" She squinted at him, trying to figure out where he was going with this. Was he still trying to pinpoint her as a snob? Was he the type of guy who would want his woman to allow him to be the breadwinner? The head of the household?

What was she talking about? Jason was the type of guy who would never settle down. Just like she was that type of girl.

Her brow furrowed in thought.

"Do you live here?" she asked. "Do you still farm?"

He looked away, a perplexed expression on his handsome face. She wondered if she was wearing a similar one.

"No."

"Do you want to?"

He lifted his right hand and rubbed the back of his neck. She noted he did this from time to time, and that it was an unconscious gesture of...what? Uncertainty? Anxiety?

"No."

"Well, then, I guess my answer isn't important then, is it?"

He looked at her.

"Or is it?"

Their entire conversation seemed strange to her, somehow.

She cleared her throat. "So, um, Annie's your paternal grandmother, then?"

He nodded.

"And your grandfather?"

"Savage is Gram's maiden name."

His sentence trailed off somewhere into the distance, where, she was afraid, it was going to remain.

His cell phone buzzed. He looked so thoroughly relieved at the interruption, she was almost relieved for him.

"Savage," he said without looking at the display.

He opened the screen door and walked outside. She wanted to follow but stopped herself, taking that as her cue to leave him be.

She turned back toward the kitchen, wondering if Annie or Jackson would be willing to answer her questions. And asking herself if it was wise to travel down that path…

HOURS LATER, JASON STOOD just inside the open barn doors looking out, considering the farmhouse and surrounding acres for the third time that day. Dusk was a little over an hour away and so far, there had been no activity. But that didn't mean anything. Out there, somewhere, loomed a threat he was determined to prepare himself against.

Jax came up next to him. "Quiet."

He nodded. "Too quiet."

"I agree."

Silence fell between them as they considered the threatening clouds hanging low on the western horizon. The calm before the storm. Jason didn't need a meteorologist to tell him that bad weather was on the way. The wind had already picked up, bringing with it the distant scent of rain. It wasn't unusual on hot days like today. But whereas he might normally welcome the reprieve, take comfort in the storm, now he worried about it. It would make detecting any oncoming attack more difficult. Wind could mask a stranger's footsteps, a clap of thunder might disguise the report of gunfire.

Jason had given up on trying to convince his family to go into the city some time ago. And he had even begun to accept that they'd probably be more of a help than a hindrance. He'd caught Annie cleaning her trusty old shotgun named Etta a little earlier, along with two handguns he remembered always being around the house. He had little doubt she had plenty of ammo for all three. After all, she'd been the one who taught both him and Jax how to shoot when they'd been little older than five, and she'd made sure they kept up on their skills throughout high school. Hell, occasionally the three of them still spent Sunday afternoons taking target practice at the homemade range out back.

Annie had taught them well. He looked at his brother. Both of them.

As for Jordan, she appeared to be holding up remarkably well. From time to time, he caught her rubbing her arms as if warding off a chill, although the evening hadn't cooled down any. It was still hot as Hades.

He'd half expected her to complain about needing her cell phone or laptop, but she hadn't uttered a word. Instead, she seemed content to pump Gram and Jax for information he'd been reluctant to give her. Just watching her interact so easily with them both had touched a place inside of him that he hadn't been aware existed.

And made him hotter for her than ever. It was all he could do not to corner her somewhere out of eyeshot, slip his hand up her snug tank and claim her sexy mouth with his.

He cleared his throat, remembering present company.

Speaking of expectations…

"I'm surprised you aren't bending my ear trying to convince me to hire you on at Lazarus," he said.

Jax looked at him. "I think there's something slightly more important happening right now."

Jason grinned and then rested his hand against his shoulder, squeezing. "Yes. I guess there is."

The stood in companionable, alert silence. Jason was proud of and impressed with his little brother.

"One thing I could never figure out," he said quietly. "Is why you'd want to follow in my footsteps."

Jax didn't answer immediately. Instead, he appeared to weigh his words. Jason took note of the intense expression on his brother's face. "You were my role model. The one I wanted to most be like."

He grimaced. "That's because I was your only model."

"No. It's because you were the best one."

Impossible. In high school, Jason had always been in hot water. He could never hold down a job and got into trouble with girls and guys equally, albeit for different reasons. It wasn't until he followed his high school best friend, Dari Folsom, into the Marines that Jason had finally found his calling, discovered what he'd been put on this earth to do.

Jackson had never had those problems. He excelled at everything he did. He wouldn't have said *shit* if he had a mouth full of it. And while his brother was younger than him, he wasn't that young that he wouldn't have noticed the trouble Jason had gotten into.

"Yeah," Jax nodded. "I remember. But I also remember you were always there for your friends and family. If anybody needed anything, you were always Johnny on the spot, ready to lend a hand or give an ass-whipping…"

Jason chuckled at the description.

"You were never bad for the sake of being bad. At the heart of everything you did was…well, a heart of gold." He grinned. "And that, big brother, is what makes you my role model."

Jason stared at Jax as if he were seeing him for the first time. As if he were seeing himself.

Still, the memory of what had gone down in those distant, hostile mountains of Waziristan, when Barry Lazaro had bought it, leaving the rest of them with holes bigger than the ones he'd suffered by gunfire, only served to remind him of why he wanted his brother to choose another path.

The thought of something happening to Jax…

The side screen door slapped shut. "You two just going to stand out there all day shooting the breeze or you are going to come in here at some point and let us poor gals in on the plan?"

They both chuckled.

"Pity the fool who thinks they can get a leg up on Gram," Jax said.

"Pity the fool, indeed..."

19

JORDAN SAT AT THE FOOT of the second staircase leading into the kitchen rubbing an oilcloth over the smooth gun. Annie had taught her how to use it, even taking her out back and having her get used to the kick. The older woman had given Jason an earful for not having taught Jordan how to protect herself before now.

Then Jordan received a similar earful. Annie informed her a woman of her obvious grit had no business not knowing how to defend herself. Of course, Jordan really hadn't had reason to worry about it until now. Hey, shoot her, she wasn't used to having people eager to kill her.

She grimaced at her choice of words.

The sun was setting through the dense clouds to the west, filling the room with an eerie orange-red glow. She stuck her hand out into the beam and flipped it over, thinking it looked like blood. She drew her hand back and wiped it on her pant leg, as if the limb was coated in it.

She got up to go upstairs to the bedroom and ran into Jason in the hall. She stopped, staring at him in the same strange light.

They hadn't been alone all day. Now that they were, a sigh seemed to wash through her.

"How are you holding up?" he asked quietly.

She looked at the gun in her hand and smiled. "Okay, I guess. Is every night going to be like this until the trial?"

He took the gun from her and examined it. "I've already made arrangements to get you out of here first thing in the morning."

If he had told her that the sun was rising instead of setting, she couldn't have been more surprised. She stood there, not quite knowing what to say, or if she could even force any words out.

"Me?" she practically croaked.

He squinted at her and then nodded almost imperceptibly, his handsome features half in shadow, giving him an even sexier, darker look.

"As in alone?"

He hesitated. "Yes."

Her stomach tightened. What was he saying?

It only now struck her as odd that she'd gotten used to their arrangement. It didn't matter where they were—her apartment in Denver, the hotel in San Francisco, or here—as long as he was by her side, she was okay. Even when she wasn't.

He cleared his throat. "They've obviously got a line on me. That makes it more dangerous for you. I've arranged for another firm to take up where I'm leaving off. And the U.S. Marshal's Office is stepping up their protection."

She swallowed hard. "Don't you think it might have been a good idea to ask if that was okay with me?"

He didn't say anything for a moment, his gaze moving over her and then back up to her eyes. "Do you trust me?"

She realized that she did. Implicitly. "Yes."

"Then trust that I'm convinced this is the only way to keep you safe."

"For the trial."

His gaze raked her face. "No, for you."

She believed him. And the admission made her feel as

if the last dying rays of the sun penetrated her everywhere, filling her to overflowing.

"This wouldn't have anything to do with us, I mean you and me..." she asked.

"Becoming personally involved?" He held the gun out. She reached to take it and he pressed her hand between his and the cold steel. "I'd be lying if I said it wasn't part of the reason."

Her fingers warmed under his.

"Hell, Jordan, I brought you to my grandmother's place. I would never have done that for any other client."

The warmth spread throughout her.

Their hands and the gun still between them, she stepped forward, and pressed her mouth against his.

It seemed like forever since they'd last kissed and she took her time about it. She loved his mouth. Loved the way his tongue dipped out and teased her lips. Loved the ragged catch of his breathing as if surprised by his reaction to the simple display of affection.

He tucked the gun into the back waist of his jeans and drew her closer. She touched the side of his face and deepened the kiss, keeping her eyes open to watch him watch her. Had she ever felt this connected to another human being? She swore her heart was beating in rhythm with his.

A small voice in the back of her head tried to sound a warning, but as her tongue slid against his, and her breasts rubbed ever so slightly against his chest, it grew softer and softer until she no longer heard it at all.

He worked his hands up under the hem of her tank. When the rough pads of his thumbs met with the skin of her lower stomach, she sucked in a breath. He tugged her closer, pressing the hard evidence of his arousal against her belly. She snaked her hands under his arms and up over his shoulders as if she needed to secure herself, sheer need sweeping through her.

She wanted to feel him inside her. Now. In that one moment, she didn't care what was going on around them or how many gunmen might be hiding in the surrounding fields looking for the chance to take a potshot. All she wanted to do was strip off his clothes and lay herself bare before him, inviting him to stroke her body inside and out.

"Criminy. There's a bedroom right behind you," Annie said, shifting sideways to pass them. "But you better be quick about it. It's going to be pitch-black in twenty minutes and you won't have time for any such shenanigans."

Jordan froze, staring at Jason through wide eyes. She saw a mixture of amusement and exasperation on his face as they listened to Annie descend the stairs.

"Does she do that often?"

"What? Sneak up on me when I'm kissing a pretty girl?"

"Yeah."

"Not since the twelfth grade. Which is probably the last time I kissed a pretty girl in the house."

"Oh?" She swallowed hard, trying to tamp down her runaway emotions, but failing. Her mind kept thinking about the bedroom just steps away. "What was her name?"

"Jenny McMillan. Her family owns the farm next to Gram's."

"When's the last time you saw her?"

"Probably back when I kissed her. I heard she got married and has three kids now."

Why that should cause relief, she wasn't sure, but Jordan was glad the little hussy wasn't competition.

She laughed at herself.

"What?" Jason asked.

"Nothing." She cleared her throat. "So…do you want to?"

His eyes darkened.

She knew they shouldn't, that they needed to keep their wits about them with the coming night. But it affected her need for him not at all.

And as he took her hand and opened the door to what she now knew was his old bedroom, she guessed it didn't affect his, either.

They stripped out of their clothes quickly, disconnecting their kiss only to take off her shirt. By the time they reached the bed, they were naked and he was sheathed. And once they fell across the bed, they were full connected.

Jordan shivered, experiencing a completion she'd never felt before.

He slowly withdrew and then slid in again and her shiver turned into a shudder. Dear, sweet heaven, he felt so good. He bent in to kiss her again even as he stroked her, long and deep. She curved her ankles around his calves and he grasped her bottom, parting her for an even deeper meeting. She moaned into his mouth and sweat formed on his brow.

He stared into her eyes. "We don't have much time."

She kissed him. "Ready when you are."

His groan told her it was then. Merely knowing she caused him to lose control so quickly sent her spiraling right over the edge with him…

JASON GRIT HIS BACK TEETH and his hips locked as he climaxed. He felt boneless, thoroughly sated. But he knew the feeling wouldn't last. Just then, his cell phone rang, a ruckus sounded somewhere outside and Jackson called up to him.

"Damn."

He rolled off Jordan and into his jeans. He was halfway into his boots when he reached the door and opened his cell.

"Undefined movement on the northeast corner of the property," Dominic reported.

"Jason?"

He faced Jordan where she was getting dressed behind him. "Stay here. Follow the plans exactly as I outlined them. Okay?"

She hesitated and then nodded.

He closed the door after himself and barreled down the stairs, his mind racing as fast as his pulse. He'd left Gram's handgun on the nightstand. He hoped Jordan saw it and acted accordingly.

"What is it?" he asked, entering the kitchen and accepting a shotgun from Jax as he went.

"We're not sure yet."

He went to the front door, even though the back door was closer to the area where there was movement.

"Where are you going?" Jax wanted to know.

"It's a diversion."

"How can you be so sure?"

He gave Jax a long look as he picked up his radio from the hall table, instructing the fifteen men—a mix of Lazarus personnel and U.S. Marshals—on the perimeter to remain where they were.

Unfortunately, it appeared half the group was already on their way to said disturbance.

Jason emerged onto the front porch, shotgun ready and scanned his surroundings. The sun had set but it was still light enough to see. But it wouldn't be for long.

He lifted the radio. "Report."

"Hold in, boss. What in the hell is that? It's a...wild pig, I think," Dominic said. The words were followed by a swear word. Jason agreed completely.

If he had any doubt the movement had been a diversionary tactic, he didn't now. There were no pigs, wild or otherwise, within a five-mile radius of the farm.

"I see something on the SE corner," came a separate report from Jonathon Reece.

Jason smiled grimly. It was time.

20

AFTER TEN LONG MINUTES in the bedroom, Jordan couldn't handle another second. She quietly opened the door and peered out. The house was pitch-black, no moon shining through the windows to illuminate the way. She edged out and crept down the hall toward the stairs, her hands sweaty on Annie's revolver. She decided to go down the back way to the kitchen rather than the front, feeling somewhat more secure since the stairwell was slightly concealed. She emerged into the kitchen and was immediately grabbed from behind.

"Shh," a man said into her ear.

It wasn't Jason, of that much she was sure. Her heart thud an irregular rhythm as she berated herself for being so stupid. She should have remained in the bedroom.

Her hands had dropped down so she held the gun pointed at the floor. Her mind raced with a way to try to use it against her assailant.

She was turned around and found herself staring at Jax.

"Oh, thank God…" Her entire body shuddered in relief.

"Sorry, didn't mean to scare you. But we have a situation."

"And your means of not scaring me necessitated you covering my mouth?"

He chuckled softly. "Yeah."

Annie sidled up next to her smelling like gun oil. "You should have shot him."

"Gram," Jax said in a hushed voice.

"What? Grab me like that and find yourself a couple grams heavier with lead."

The radio crackled quietly. The three of them leaned in to listen. Jordan made out Jason's voice immediately.

"Report," he said.

"Wild boar here, as well," came the response from Jonathan.

"You're right, Savage," added Dominic. "Found a cage. This baby didn't just wander here from points outside, he was purposely let loose." Silence and then, "And Shockley has disappeared from his post and any attempts to raise him get no response."

Jordan squinted at Jax. "What's going on?"

Annie answered, "Someone's playing us for a bunch of damn fools, that's what's going on."

Jax added, "Two wild pigs have been found running the property from two different directions. Diversionary tactics."

Jordan looked around at the two windows, the open hall door and the closed back door, feeling suddenly overexposed.

"Maybe I should have stayed in the bedroom."

"No, you need to stay right here with us," Annie said. "Jason'll handle this. He may be thickheaded when it comes to family and matters of the heart, but he'll look after you. Better soldiers you won't find when it comes to either of my boys."

Jordan tried to be reassured by her words, but all she could think about was how slick her palms were and, after what had happened with Jax, whether she'd have the strength needed to fight back, should someone grab her again.

Then again, it occurred to her that such a person wouldn't grab her. They'd just shoot her and get it over with.

She squeezed her eyes briefly shut. Please, please let this night be over.

Problem was, it had just begun...

TWO HOURS LATER, JASON stood near the NW corner of the house. Nothing more had happened after the two incidents earlier in the evening. Both pigs had been taken away. Then he'd crossed paths with Jonathon Reece during his rounds, the recruit had joked they should have kept them. They could have had one hell of a roast once all this was over.

Jason scanned the grounds around him, thinking they were a long way from that. He still hadn't figured out what had happened to Jerry Shockley. Whether a faulty radio was to blame. Or if someone had taken him out...

He glanced toward the house, wondering what they were doing inside. Had Jordan stayed in the room as he'd instructed? He doubted it. She probably sat tight for five minutes before venturing downstairs. Good thing Gram and Jax were in there to keep her from doing anything stupid.

He remembered their brief time together before everything went down earlier. He raised his right hand to his nose. He could still smell her. Fresh need washed through him.

He swore a blue streak and then crept to the SW corner of the house.

His distracted state was at the heart of everything that had gone wrong so far. If he'd had half a functioning brain, he would have handed off the assignment to someone more objective than he was capable of being after they'd slept together. Why hadn't he? Her safety was first...and not only when it came to the job. Her safety was important to him, period.

He caught the crackle of a radio transmission from his earpiece, but no words. He stopped and listened. Nothing.

Damn.

He rounded the corner and ran into Jax.

"What in the hell are you doing out here?" he demanded quietly.

"Thought I heard a sound and came out to investigate."

"Yeah, well, that would be me..."

"I figured that one out on my own. I also think I'll be of better use out here. The girls have things covered inside."

Jason remembered his brother's words earlier. He was coming to view Jax in a different light.

He still wanted to protect him. But he was also coming to understand his brother might no longer be in need of that protection.

There was static over his earpiece again.

"I've got something."

Silence.

He and Jax stared at each other. There was no telling who had made the transmission or where they were when they'd made it.

JORDAN AND ANNIE HEARD the same transmission.

"You know what to do," Annie said.

"I'm not leaving you alone."

"Missy, it's not my narrow behind they're after. Now get going."

They'd worked it out that if things got sticky, she was to head for the storm cellar and barricade herself in.

A sound echoed in the room.

They both froze where they stood in the middle of the kitchen, the darkness allowing for sight only when there was movement. And neither of them were about to move.

Through the window she saw the outline of someone shift by. But she was positive the sound had come from inside the house. Jackson had gone out a few minutes ago. Had he come back in? But if it was him, why wasn't he saying anything?

She turned her head ever so slightly, trying to make something out in the darkness. The old floorboards creaked under her weight.

Damn!

Her palms instantly grew wet where she held the revolver.

"Go, now!" Annie whispered urgently.

It took a millisecond for her to register the command, but the instant she did, she crouched and ran for the cellar door.

Gunfire exploded in the small room. Jordan felt something slam into her back then she fell face-first to the floor...

JASON SAW THE FLASH inside the house before he heard the report of gunfire. His legs seemed mired in mud as he rushed the back door. He emerged into the kitchen just as the overhead light switched on. He stared at the motionless body stretched across the middle of the floor, a pool of blood trickling down the slight slope toward the cupboards.

Missing recruit Jerry Shockley.

"Holy shit," Jordan said from where she sat on the floor near the cellar door. The door in question bore two bullet holes about where her head would have been had she been standing.

Gram stood near her, smoke emitting from the barrel of her twelve-gauge.

Jordan blinked at her. "Thanks."

"Don't mention it."

Jason swore under his breath as he checked for a pulse: definitely dead.

He didn't question Gram's decision to shoot. There was no viable reason for Shockley to have been anywhere near the house unless it was for corrupt purposes.

He spoke into his radio, telling Jax everything was under control inside, but to keep his eyes peeled outside. Just because they'd gotten this one didn't mean Jerry was working alone. In fact, it was better for them to assume he wasn't.

He stared into the face of the forty-something man with

dark hair and stocky build. He knew he was an ex-Army grunt, but wondered how the guy had made it that far even wearing the Lazarus Security uniform without notice.

Damn. He needed to move on Plan B and quick. They were only two hours in and if his own men were turning on him, what would the rest of the night bring?

He grabbed a couple of kitchen towels from a drawer and put them on the floor to keep the blood from spreading.

"Hey, those are my good towels," Gram objected.

"I'm happy for any suggestions."

"Yeah, I've got a suggestion for you—get out of my kitchen and get back to work. Jordan and I can handle this."

Jason raised a brow.

"We've handled it to this point, haven't we? I fully expect you to take care of any additional business that needs to be seen to."

He chuckled, watching as his grandmother salvaged her towels and then kicked the body over to slow the flow of blood.

It appeared she did have things under control.

As for Jordan...

He was surprised to find she'd gotten to her feet. While she looked a little shaky, she was getting a bucket and a mop from a closet, intent on making the best of the situation.

He rubbed his chin and smiled. "You okay?"

She smiled back. "I'm alive. So, yeah. I'm more than okay."

Her beautiful face was the color of rice paper and even her blond hair seemed to quiver. But he saw the determined strength in her eyes.

It was an awesome sight, one he wanted to guarantee he'd see again.

He pulled out his cell phone to make the necessary arrangements. "All right, then. I will be just outside if you need anything."

"What we need is for you to keep these dumb sons of bitches out of my house," Annie said.

"I'll see what I can do about that, Gram."

"You better. Don't want to be wasting any more ammo on the likes of this one." She prodded the dead man with the toe of her boot.

Jason moved toward the door when he heard another gunshot come from somewhere outside.

Damn. All hell was breaking loose.

21

JORDAN HURRIED TO SWITCH off the light as Jason rushed back outside. Her heart had barely slowed before it was racing again. What was going on? She wasn't good with not knowing what was happening around her.

She moved across the room and nearly tripped over the body. She shuddered as she felt around for her gun on the floor near the cellar door. Finding it, she jerked upright, her sight readjusting to the darkness.

This was insane. She felt like she was caught in some bad, old-time Western movie. Problem was, she wasn't watching the TV screen—she was caught in it.

She noticed Annie moving around.

"What are you doing?" she whispered.

"Trying to clean up this mess."

It took some effort for Jordan not to laugh out loud.

She moved toward the window, staying off to the side, her gun raised, trying to make out the situation outside.

Where had the gunfire come from? And how close was it?

Someone ran past the window. She gasped and lay flat against the wall, only to be pulled away from it by Annie.

"You won't want to be doing that, child. Any stray bullets of a good caliber will shoot clean through that wall."

Well, so much for feeling safer...

JASON SHOUTED INTO THE phone as he ran toward the direction of the gunfire near the barn. "Plan B!"

He barely made out Megan's response before hanging up and pulling his gun out of its holster.

Damn it!

He hadn't spotted Jax outside the house, so he was reasonably sure his brother had been at one or the other end of the gunfire. He only hoped it was on the right end.

He neared the open barn doors and flanked the left side, holding his gun upright. He listened for one, two heartbeats and then swung around the side, his gun leading the way.

He made out familiar shapes: hay bales, stalls for the goats, tractor. But nothing to indicate anyone was in there.

He spoke quietly into his radio. "Jax? Report."

Nothing.

He set his jaw and then moved toward the back of the barn, not stopping until he reached his destination and fresh cover.

He radioed for his brother again.

"Southwest corner of the house," was the response.

Shit...

He was in the wrong place.

He hurried outside and headed back toward the old farmhouse, wondering how he could have mistaken the direction of the gunfire. He'd been convinced it came from the barn.

He rounded the corner of the house and found...nothing. No Jax. No radio.

What in the hell was going on?

It stood to reason that as he was moving, so was his brother. But in which direction? Since he hadn't seen him during his advance, he decided he must have gone up the other side of the house. Rather than follow, though, he backtracked and moved along the other side toward the front.

The minute he turned the corner, he was relieved he'd followed his gut instincts. Because a few feet off, someone stood with his back to Jason. And his gun against Jax's temple.

ONCE ANNIE WAS SATISFIED the floor was clean enough, she stood on the other side of the window, looking outside much the same Jordan was. Jordan found comfort in that. Comfort in the soft hush of the other woman's breathing. Comfort in her being so near, she could smell the detergent on her clothes.

Comfort in that she wouldn't be alone when…if something happened.

It was an almost relaxed, female comfort she'd rarely felt outside the visits to her own grandmother's house.

If she found it odd she was thinking along those lines just now, she didn't question it. She'd believed she'd known what stress was—until she was faced with her current situation.

"Look, here's Jason now," Annie said quietly.

Jordan's gaze had dropped to outline the intricate lace of the white sheer curtain between her and the window and lifted to follow Jason's progress from the barn back to the house, knowing immediately it was him, the way he moved. She felt something entirely different than she felt a moment ago.

Jason passed by directly outside the window on his way to the front of the house and she jumped.

Exactly how much adrenaline was the human body designed to produce in a twenty-four hour period? She didn't have a clue, but she figured she was using more than she had in the past decade. Was it possible to run out?

"Come on," Annie whispered urgently.

Her heart skipped a beat. "Where?"

She was half afraid Annie was going to try pushing her down into the cellar again, and started to object. Then she realized she was being led toward the hall.

Good. She couldn't imagine being downstairs, self-barricaded in the musty, closed-in confines with no way of knowing what was going on outside and no way of finding out.

She followed Annie into the front room and then to the door, which was closed tightly. They took up either side and then slowly moved to look out.

Jordan understood what was going on immediately. Right in front stood Jason, his gun held out in front of him, obviously trained on something. She shifted toward that object and saw Jax being held at gunpoint, he and his captor with their backs to Jason, apparently expecting him to emerge from the other side of the house.

"He's got the jump on him," Annie said.

Jordan absently rubbed her arms, not so sure. How could Jason have the jump on the guy if the gunman had Jax hostage?

She closed her eyes tightly, sending up a silent prayer...

JASON'S PALMS DAMPENED.

Damn. It had been a good, long while since he'd displayed any outward symptoms of fear. He'd been well trained not to betray any of the signs.

Then again, he had never been directly responsible for his brother's safety, either.

A small voice told him that wasn't true. And with startling clarity, he remembered his father's words the night he and his mother had headed out, never to come back again:

"Take care of your little brother, Jason."

And he had. He'd lived with those words nearly every moment of every day. Heard them every time Jax came to him wanting to work for Lazarus. Been deafened by them the day Jax shipped overseas for his first deployment.

And now he was directly responsible for his little brother's safety. He'd put him in harm's way. And was now paying the price...

He squinted at the man holding Jax hostage, thinking he looked vaguely familiar. Did he know him?

He edged closer to get a better look and to do what he planned, which was to disarm him before he even knew what had happened.

Dam. It was that kid from Lazarus! The one with the questionable military record that had refused to take no for an answer.

He was a foot away.

"You may have got the jump on me, but it won't happen with my brother. Of that you can rest assured," Jax said with quiet certainty.

"I told you to shut up," Daryl Bennett hissed.

His words chased the surprise and emotion from Jason's mind and he reacted with the smooth efficiency granted by his training. Noting Bennett's finger was on the trigger guard and not the trigger, he smacked his elbow up, bringing the arm and gun away from his brother, then grabbed his wrist, twisting him away from his hostage.

Within two seconds, the hostage-taker was the hostage.

Jax moved to face them, but not as quickly as he should have. "I have no idea how he jumped me."

Jason realized why he was moving slower: there was a stain spreading on his jeans leg.

Jax followed his gaze as if he'd forgotten about the wound. "Yeah, I took one."

He pulled off his T-shirt and tied it off around the top of his thigh in a makeshift tourniquet.

Jason tightened his arm around Bennett's neck and he made a choking sound.

"Don't worry," Jax said. "It's just a flesh wound." He laughed without humor. "If it weren't, I'd have bled out by now."

Jason loosened his arm tension a hair, understanding it

would take little to crush Bennett's windpipe and make sure he never breathed again.

"What are you after?" he asked Bennett. "What are you doing here?"

He swallowed thickly. "I came here to prove I was up to the job, any job, I wanted."

"By shooting my brother?"

"You think I was looking to prove it to you? No, I needed to prove it to myself. You wouldn't even give me a chance when I came into Lazarus, man…" He swallowed again, apparently with difficulty.

"When did you meet Shockley?"

Jason knew it was a shot in the dark. But at this point, any shot was.

"When I was testing." He chuckled and then coughed. "Couldn't believe my luck when he told me about your girlfriend and the price on her head. It didn't take much to convince him we should throw in together. Not only could I get back at you and prove myself capable, I'd make a shitload of money to boot."

The shot in the dark had hit the target head on. Daryl Bennett had been Shockley's second. And it explained how Jason's location had been blown.

Who else knew where he was holding Jordan?

At this point, one person was one too many.

The front door of the house opened. He watched as Gram came outside, Jordan following after.

"Let him go so I can shoot him," Annie said, lifting her shotgun.

Jason understood the urge too well. Hell, he wanted to do the same. It amused him not at all to discover he'd been right about the kid and his unfit psychological state.

"Go back inside," he told his grandmother even as Jax limped to the porch to lean against it.

The distant whoop-whoop of a helicopter sounded. He didn't look up, but everyone else did.

If there was anyone else in the proverbial bushes waiting to make a move, now would be the time. Jordan stood on the porch as clear as a neon-red X.

"Damn it, get back inside!"

He began to turn Bennett in the direction of the barn where he intended to tie him up. Bennett moved suddenly and he felt something sharp pierce his upper thigh.

Son of a bitch.

22

JORDAN WATCHED IN HORROR as the guy Jason was holding buried a knife the size of machete in Jason's leg. She rushed forward, but Annie held her back, gun raised. She'd never felt so helpless as he stumbled a few steps backward and the guy broke free, diving for the gun that had been knocked from his grip.

Gunfire ripped through the night, the sound competing with the helicopter flying somewhere above them.

It wasn't Annie who'd shot the guy. It was Jackson.

The instant the man dropped to his knees, staring at the telltale stain spreading across his chest, Jordan broke free from Annie and rushed to Jason's side. She tried to keep him from falling over and reached for the knife.

"Don't touch it!" Jackson said over the sound of the helicopter, coming to Jason's other side. "It's best to leave it where it is until we know differently. If it hit the femoral artery…"

She stumbled at the idea.

If the knife hit an artery…

The deafening chop-chop of the helicopter's blades grew closer. She looked up to see it right above them.

"It's for you!" Jason shouted.

She squinted at him, her hair whipping around her face.

"Go!" he said. "They're going to take you someplace safe!"

"I'm not going anywhere!" she shouted back.

She and Jackson moved him to sit gingerly on the stairs. His wince sent a shock of fear running through her.

The copter landed and a guy wearing a Lazarus Security T-shirt ducked out and ran in their direction.

Jackson shook hands with him. "This is the subject— Jordan Cosby. Jordan this is Darius Folsom."

He nodded in her direction and she nodded back. He took in the situation.

"Take her!" Jason ordered.

"I will, but she's not the only one!" Darius said. "You're all coming with me."

He waved toward the helicopter and a woman came out. As Darius helped Jason, the woman, who introduced herself as Megan to Jordan and Annie, directed them to follow her.

Jordan didn't let out the breath she was holding until they were all inside the helicopter and it had left the ground.

23

"SHE WANTS TO SPEAK with you."

Thirty-six hours had passed since the moment Jason had last seen Jordan's beautiful face. It seemed like thirty-six years.

When the helicopter took off from the hospital helipad where it left him, Jax and Gram, and then moved on to take Jordan to meet up with Lazarus partner Lincoln Williams in Cheyenne, Wyoming, he'd watched her watching him until he could do so no longer. And he would have continued, had he not been forced away for medical attention. He'd experienced a profound relief knowing she was not only okay, but would continue to be okay, along with a mysterious ache so acute you would have thought he'd taken the jagged hunting knife to the chest instead of the leg.

He looked down at the bandage that lay under his jeans. Thankfully the knife hadn't hit the femoral, although it had come darn close. The same applied to Jackson's gunshot wound, but his brother had agreed to take the doctor's advice and remain in the hospital for observation, while he had walked out almost as soon as the knife had been removed.

"Jason?"

Lisa's voice over the speaker intruded on his thoughts. Jordan must be calling.

"Tell her I'm not here."

"She says Linc wants to move her. And she refuses to budge until she talks to you."

He scrubbed his face with his hands. "Linc will figure it out."

Lord knows he'd done that often enough during their time together. Besides, he knew if he took the call, and she asked to see him, he'd be on the next transport out.

And he couldn't do that. Not only because it wasn't smart, but because it wasn't smart.

"Tell her I'm not here," he repeated, then punched disconnect.

He pushed away from the chair and went to stand near the window overlooking the training grounds. Fresh recruits were being put through their paces by Megan McGowan. He could already tell who would make the grade and who wouldn't.

He grimaced. He only wished he had seen the threat Daryl Bennett had represented in its entirety...

Megan shouted orders and pressed her boot against a recruit's back where he did push-ups. He smiled and shook his head.

He had never been one to live with regrets...until recently. His affair with Megan was something he regretted completely. If he could take it back, he would. Their one night together had wreaked havoc with their friendship, not to mention what it had done to him and Dari.

The rifts were the motivating factor behind his taking Jordan's case off of Lincoln's hands to begin with. Something, anything, to get him out of Dodge and away from Lazarus.

And then he'd met Jordan...

As he continued to watch Megan, he recognized similarities between the two women. Oh, not physically. Not even in background. But their strength...

Well, they were the closest any two women had come to equaling his grandmother.

He squinted, his attention turning inward.

That was odd. You would think he'd be more attracted to women like his mother, who had been ultrafeminine and accommodating. And he was. Or he had been, anyway.

Unfortunately, those were the women he'd found easiest to dismiss.

He didn't believe he was unconsciously passing judgment on his mother. Far from it. Perhaps he'd sought out women like her in the past, believing it would be one of them for whom he'd fall.

Instead, it had taken a woman more like his grandmother to push him over the edge.

He caught himself grinning wryly and turned from the window. Annie would be highly amused by the observation, he thought. Hell, she'd probably tell him she'd known it all along. But he was so thickheaded, it had taken a knife to the leg for him to figure it out.

He hadn't planned to fall for Megan. But he had. Or, rather, he'd come close to falling for her and likely would have all the way had Dari not returned to take his rightful place in her heart.

But he had fallen completely for Jordan.

He found himself standing in front of the wall calendar, noting the date of her scheduled court appearance mere days from now. Would he go to her then, he wondered. Did he dare?

Of course, there were no guarantees she would be free from custody even after the hearing. In high-profile cases such as this with high-profile defendants, it wasn't over until it was over. Which meant her life might be in danger for much longer than anyone expected.

The idea didn't sit well with him. And he would never say the words to her, no matter how truthful.

He realized the circuitous path of his thoughts.

Would he look her up? If only to see if what had developed between them during their time together was still there? If how he felt was real?

And when he found out they were?

Truth was, he hadn't really envisioned this route for himself…the whole wife and kids thing.

His brain froze at the words.

It took a moment for him to jar himself out of it.

Wife and kids? Who was he kidding?

Neither had any place in his future. He wasn't husband material. He wouldn't know the first thing about being one, if only because he had no role model.

But it was more than that. Far more. Everything had happened so quickly, he couldn't allow himself to trust it…trust himself. He'd rationally talked himself into what had happened with Megan. He couldn't rush into something irrationally now.

God, he couldn't remember ever feeling this outside himself, out of sorts, at any other time in history. And he didn't like feeling that way now. There was so much he needed to do to clear up the last mess he'd made before he could even think about getting into the next one.

He winced at putting the word *mess* anywhere in the vicinity of Jordan.

At any rate, he already had his road mapped out. He was going to open the field office in Baltimore, cultivate his contacts, and shoot for international assignments that would not only take him away from Colorado Springs, but out of the country, period. That was the best thing for him.

The thought that he might not ever see Jordan again caused something raw to burrow under his skin and not only stay there, but dig deeper with every breath he took.

He cursed loudly and left the office, heading for the back

and the training grounds where he hoped recruit abuse would help clear his mind and force his sorry ass back on track…

JORDAN LOOKED OUT OVER the Savannah garden square from her third-floor bedroom window. It was the third city she'd been in in three days since Lincoln Williams had relocated her every eighteen hours whether there was any threat or not. And insofar as she could tell, there hadn't been. First there was Cheyenne, Wyoming, then southern Arizona, and now they were in coastal Georgia.

This was her favorite place so far. She wasn't sure how Linc was connected to the owner of the house in which they were staying the night, but it was a posh place that embodied so much of what the old city was about. She had her own well-appointed room which overlooked a lush garden square that looked both eerie and romantic in the golden light from the setting sun, the rays reflecting off the droplets of rain that remained after an earlier downpour.

More than that, though, the thick summer heat reflected the heaviness she'd felt inside ever since leaving Jason on that hospital helipad.

All attempts to contact him, by hook or by crook, had failed. He refused to speak to her.

Her chest felt suddenly, unbearably tight.

She turned from the window and looked at the items on the antique table positioned in front of the tall windows. She picked up the day's newspaper. Even the Savannah Morning News had a piece on the ongoing case against Rick.

She barely registered the words as she read about other witnesses and the brief mention of an incident outside Colorado Springs rumored to be connected to the notorious gunrunner. She felt so far removed from all of it she could easily be reading about someone else. Someone she didn't know. Or care to know.

She'd never been one to wish she could turn back the hands

of time. She'd learned early on that it did you no good. She'd never wished for anything more than for her mother to have survived her delivery. She'd desperately yearned to have her there with her: her first day of school, her first crush, the day she got her period, her first boyfriend. No matter how much she'd cried closed up in her room, her mother had never materialized to comfort her. And her father and brothers had been so overwhelmed by her utterly female tears, their reactions had been nearly comical. Mostly, though, they had left her alone.

But now she found herself wishing she could go back to the night she'd met Rick Packard. And this time, she'd turn him down flat. Not because of the bounty on her head. But because it meant she would never have met Jason...

And she found herself wishing again her mother were there to confide in...

She drew in a ragged breath and put the paper back down, dragging her finger along the tabletop as she walked toward the bed and grasped a thick bedpost. She should be tired. But she knew if she laid down, she wouldn't be able to sleep, so there was little point. She'd been unable to do much of anything for the past three days. Even Otto had commented during the one Skpe chat Linc had allowed her right before leaving Arizona that she looked like shit.

That brought a ghost of a smile to her face as she lifted a hand to her messy hair. She probably still looked a sight.

How much her life had changed in just a short time. How much she had changed. She didn't even feel like herself.

A rap at the door, silence, then a triple knock: code for Lincoln.

She turned the key and opened it to find the dark, hulking security expert filling the hall.

"Grab your stuff—we're leaving."

24

JASON WAS IN HIS TRUCK driving out to Gram's place when the news came down: Rick Packard had died of an unfortunate accident. Apparently he had slipped and hit his head in the bathtub...

He pulled over to the side of the empty road, squinting at the way the setting sun hit the swaying cornfields. Was Jordan watching the sunset? Was she seeing the same sight he was? Or something completely different?

"Did you hear what I said?" Lincoln asked.

He leaned back in his chair. "I heard."

Silence and then, "Where are you?"

He smiled. "In Colorado Springs."

"Where were you today?"

"Here and there."

Linc paused a moment. "You wouldn't happen to have been anywhere near Westchester, New York, would you?" he said darkly.

Jason didn't answer.

"Never mind. I don't want to know."

Jason scratched his thumbnail against his right brow. He hadn't been anywhere near New York...but that didn't mean he hadn't made a few calls, made it known to a few people in that area who owed him a favor or two that he wouldn't mind if Packard were involved in an 'unfortunate accident.'

The fact that he had been? Not his fault.

"How is she?" Jason asked quietly.

It seemed to take Linc a moment to process his question. "I think she might be sick."

He sat up straighter. "At the news?"

He felt sick himself at the idea she'd mourn the son of a bitch who had placed a price on her head.

"No. The past three days."

Relief relaxed his muscles. He watched in the rearview mirror as a car approached from behind and then passed him. Old man Johnson waved and he waved back.

"How so?" he asked. "Cold? Flu?"

"I don't know. She's not eating. And I don't think she's sleeping. If you saw her…"

Jason closed his eyes wishing he could see her.

"If you saw her, you wouldn't recognize her."

"Oh?"

"I don't think she's combed her hair since we left Cheyenne."

Jason chuckled, unable to picture Jordan anything other than perfect.

"Have you taken her to the doc?"

"No. I'm taking her home."

"To Denver?"

"Yes."

"Where is she now?"

"Sleeping in the front cabin of the chartered plane."

It hadn't been that long ago when she'd been sleeping across from him on a plane. She'd looked so beautiful. So vulnerable. So sexy.

Linc cleared his throat. "What happened between you two?"

He glanced toward where the sun had slid halfway over the horizon. "What do you mean?"

"If I didn't know better, I'd say she was suffering from a sickness no doc can cure."

He didn't answer.

"You know, heartsickness."

Jason lifted a brow. Had that word just left Linc's mouth? There was a time when the powerful man wouldn't have even broached this subject. Now he was giving advice to the love-lorn.

"I'm sure I don't know what you mean."

"Right. That's why she asks to talk to you every five minutes."

Jason cleared his throat, both embarrassed and happy at the information.

"At any rate, I just wanted to keep you posted."

"Are you sure it's a good idea to bring her back here?"

"With Packard's death, there's no longer a threat."

"It will take a while for that kind of news to circulate."

"Not when there's money involved. No pay, no hit. Period. And that kind of news has a way of getting around faster than the price placed on her head to begin with."

"Yeah, you're probably right."

He heard rustling on Linc's end. "She's awake and moving around so I better get off the phone before she figures out I'm talking to you and rips the cell from my hand."

Jason smiled, easily imagining her doing just that.

And knowing he would be rendered helpless if she did.

"Thanks for the heads-up, friend."

"You're welcome. Even though I get the feeling that it wasn't exactly news to you…"

"Later, Linc."

"Yeah. Later."

He disconnected and continued sitting for a minute,

thinking about the day behind him…and of Jordan in an airplane in the sky somewhere, returning home.

A truck pulled up and stopped beside him. A horn beeped. He looked over to find Gram staring at him.

"Engine trouble?" she asked.

"No." He showed her the phone.

"You stopped to take a call?" She shook her gray head and put her truck back in gear. "Soft in the head. That's what the new generation is. Pulling over to take a phone call. I'm amazed you all can tell your heads from your assholes…"

The last part he filled in because he couldn't actually hear her words; she'd already driven on, heading in the same direction he was, bags of feed in the truck bed.

He had no choice but to follow…

RICK PACKARD WAS DEAD…

Two days later, Jordan stood among the boxes strewn across the living room floor of her Denver apartment, staring through the front window, taking in a view she wouldn't be seeing again after today. That was probably just as well, because where before, she might have looked beyond the rooftops to the overall skyscape, now all she saw were opportunities for people who meant her harm to hide.

She shivered. It wasn't that she mourned Rick's death. At least no more than she would anyone's passing, despite the hell he'd been directly responsible for putting her through these past weeks. Mostly, she guessed she mourned the loss of her innocence.

What layers of life existed out there that she had blithely been unaware of until now? *Unaware* probably wasn't the word she was looking for—you couldn't be a club owner and not know about the shadowy underworld. But she hadn't directly experienced the unrelenting bite until now. She hadn't understood that there were consequences to even the most casual of contacts.

What surprised her is that she had actually found excitement living on the fringes. She'd thought she could dally around, skip around the criminal element, without ever being affected in a negative way.

Boy, had she learned her lesson the hard way.

Now?

Well, now that Otto had been released from the hospital and was well on his way to recovery, the San Francisco club site razed and ready to be rebuilt, better than before, and the price tag tacked to her forehead removed, she'd been unceremoniously returned home and wished good luck with the rest of her life.

Unfortunately, one painful truth rang clear after her first night back: her Denver 'home' had never really been a home.

Jason...

She quickly removed his name from her mind and turned from the windows to survey how the move was progressing. After spending so much time avoiding thoughts of him, she would have expected it would get easier instead of harder. The more she tried not to think of him, the more she did.

But permitting herself to think of him only allowed the dark cloud forever clinging to her like a shadow to engulf her. And she couldn't do that. Not now.

Maybe after she figured out what she wanted to do, where she wanted to go, she'd give herself over to the confounding, painful emotions.

Once the memory of his kiss didn't make her lips tingle...

The thought of his arms around her didn't cause her heart to contract...

The sting of his rejection began to ease...

She tugged on the open ear of one of the boxes and peered inside. She'd wrapped the items she thought she might like to keep in bubble wrap and carefully stowed them inside, while the other boxes were destined for the Salvation Army, storage or to be given to friends. The largest number of these boxes were destined for Otto, who she thought would at least be amused by the unexpected delivery. She could hear his response even now.

"Fondue forks? The least you could have done was given me the mini-Gerkins to go with them."

The idea made her smile. Maybe she'd go out for a prolonged visit with him in San Francisco. That her brother Brad also lived nearby was an added bonus.

Her cell phone rang. She pulled it out and looked at the display, never aware she was hopeful Jason might call until she saw someone else's name featured.

She answered. "Hi, Dad."

"Hi, sweet pea. How goes the move?"

She'd been allowed so little interaction with him over the past week, his attention now seemed doubly important. He called at least twice a day to see how she was, always beginning the call in the same way. He hadn't called her 'sweet pea' since she was sixteen and stridently insisted she was no longer a kid.

"It's going…"

She wove among the boxes, talking to him about everything and nothing, the dark cloud dissipating slightly.

"So have you made a decision about where you're going to end up?"

"No. Not yet. I'm thinking maybe San Francisco for a visit, but I'm not sure yet…"

A few moments later they hung up and she sat on the lower stairs, listening to the silence in the apartment. Maybe it would help if she retraced her steps to the beginning of her career, to New York City to visit her first club and club manager Danny Leary.

There was one place she needed to go before she proceeded with anything, though. And she really should get it over with so she could move forward.

She went upstairs to shower and dress.

25

JASON SAT AT GRAM'S KITCHEN table, having finished the chores she'd given him, and was now nursing a glass of iced tea.

"I swear, you're so down in the mouth, I'm surprised you're not tripping over it."

He didn't need to look up from the glass to know Gram had returned from whatever errands she'd run. He hadn't heard the truck pull into the drive, but that was no surprise. Cleo the kitten had nearly been into his glass before he'd realized she'd jumped on the table.

"I have no idea what you're talking about." He scooted the black fluff of fur away before his grandmother saw her.

"Uh-huh."

Jax came in the back door carrying bags of groceries. "Good, you're not doing anything," he said. "You can unload the two bags of feed on your way out."

He eyed his brother. "Who said I was going anywhere?"

Jax and Gram shared a look.

Sometimes he felt like the odd man out when it came to the two of them. There always seemed to be a secret they shared, or a thought only they understood. Something he wasn't privy to and never would be.

He pushed from the table. "I'm going outside…"

He felt Gram's hand on his shoulder pushing him back

down. He was surprised by the strength she still possessed. Neither he nor Jax had ever been a match against her while growing up. It was a good thing in his case, because he'd always seemed to be in some kind of trouble or another. "You're not going anywhere. Jax is."

"Where am I going?"

"To get those feed bags out of the truck."

His brother grimaced, but didn't say another word as he trudged back outside with only the slightest traces of a limp from his injury, leaving them alone.

Annie poured herself a glass of iced tea and sat down.

The last place Jason wanted to be just then was facing his grandmother across the table. He'd come out to the farm for some peace. Instead, he was afraid he was about to get a whole different kind of peace…a piece of her mind.

This trying-to-forget-Jordan bit wasn't working out quite the way he'd planned. He'd fully expected she would be part of the long-forgotten past by now. A blip, a spike, a happy memory, but a memory just the same. Instead, she was the first damn thing he thought about when he woke up every morning and the last damn thing he thought about every night. And sleep, well, the more he tried to empty his mind of visions of her, the more they crowded in, her eyes, her smile, her soft moans haunting him.

Even Megan had noticed and had approached him about it at The Barracks, the night before. That she was probably the last person he wanted to talk to about his feelings for another woman hadn't seemed to faze her.

"Okay, since you won't talk to me, I'll tell you what I believe," she'd finally said after verbally poking and prodding at him for a solid, torturous half hour. "You're in love."

In love.

What in the hell did that mean, exactly? And if he had fallen in to it, how in the hell did one go about falling *out* of it?

He shifted in his chair, aware Annie was watching him a little too closely.

She sure was taking her sweet time about speaking her piece. She sipped her tea, her gaze never leaving his face.

"Don't you think it's time you stopped moping?" she finally asked.

"I'm not moping."

"You're moping."

He took a deep breath. "Okay, I'm moping."

She lifted a brow.

He offered a wry smile.

Yeah, he'd admit it was probably the first time he'd agreed with his grandmother. Well, maybe not the first, but definitely the fastest. And she'd apparently noticed.

Of course she did; she noticed everything.

"So what do you plan to do about it?" she asked.

He sat back in his chair. Cleo seemed to think that was her cue to leap into his lap. "How do you mean?"

"Well, the way I see it, you have two choices. You can either stop and get on with your life, or you can do something about it."

He didn't say anything for a long moment, choosing to stare at the condensation running down the side of his glass instead.

"Well?"

"There's nothing I can do about it." The kitten's needle-sharp claws pierced his stomach as she began climbing to whatever godforsaken destination she had in mind. He plucked her up by the scruff, stared at her for a long moment, and then put her on the floor again.

"So move on then," Annie said.

"I can't do that, either."

She tapped her short fingernails against the table. "You really are a sad sack, aren't you?"

He chuckled without humor.

"The girl has you in quite a state, doesn't she?"

It was the first time Jordan had been introduced in any of their conversations as the reason behind his foul mood as of late. He was surprised Gram had mentioned her before now. Although, really, it was no secret. They all knew Jordan Cosby was the cause of it.

"No, I have me in a state. The girl's fine."

"Oh?"

He knew better to open the door that wide. Hell, a crack was all Annie needed to force it all the way open.

"So you're the one who ended it?"

He grumbled under his breath, downed what little iced tea remained in his glass, then got up to walk to the sink. "Something has to have started in order for it to end."

"Looked to me like things had more than started while she was here. In fact, it appeared you two were deep in it."

He stared at her over his shoulder as he washed his glass. "Shows what you know."

"You think I'm talking about sex."

He nearly dropped the glass in the sink.

"What? I may be old but I'm not dead. You guys made enough noise to be heard the next county over."

Holy hell…

"So let me get this straight," she continued. "What you're trying to tell me is that you're moping over the loss of great sex?"

"Who said it was great?"

He gave him a long look.

"Sorry."

"Don't apologize to me, boy. Apologize to your damn self. Because the only one you're fooling is you."

She got up and handed him her glass.

"Here, do this one, too, while you're at it."

The sound of tires crunching gravel caused both of them

to glance toward the window. He didn't recognize the car, but he recognized the driver.

His chest tightened as he watched Jordan climb out, her white-blond hair pulled back into a ponytail. Expensive shades were perched on her perfect nose. Her hot body was clad in her favored white linen.

"Huh," Annie said. "Imagine that."

Jason stared at her. "You didn't have anything to do with this?"

"Nope. Not a thing."

He wasn't sure he believed her.

Jordan was talking to Jax.

"It's the God's honest truth." She pushed him away from the sink. "Now you go on and get out of here. I think Jordan and I need to have a talk."

"No way in hell am I leaving you alone with her."

"No way in hell are you staying in my kitchen when you're not welcome. Now scat."

She pushed him toward the front of the house, apparently not wanting him to cross paths with Jordan. And that was more than all right with him. He wasn't sure he could trust himself to speak just then.

The front screen door slapped closed behind him even as he heard Jordan greet his grandmother in the kitchen.

Damn, what had he gotten himself into?

JORDAN SMILED WARMLY at Annie Savage as she gave her a brief hug. The older woman stiffened, as if unfamiliar with the casual greeting. Jordan hugged her all the harder and then stood back.

"I hope you don't mind my dropping in like this unannounced."

"Nonsense. You feel free to stop by anytime you like. Can I get you some iced tea?"

Jordan looked around, certain she could smell Jason's

aftershave in the room. And she knew his truck was parked in the driveway. Seeing it had nearly sent her into Reverse and back down to the road.

"He's not here."

She glanced at Annie.

"Jason. He's not in the house."

She relaxed a little. "Good."

Annie poured two glasses of iced tea and then put cookies on a plate. They both took seats at the table. "Is it?"

"Is it what?"

"Good that Jason isn't in here?"

Jordan felt her cheeks warm, happy for the distraction when Cleo barreled straight for her legs, not stopping until she'd climbed into her lap. She gathered the kitten close and rubbed her cheek against her, absorbing her happy purr.

"Both of you are dumb as doorknobs."

Jordan stared at her. "Cleo's not dumb."

Annie returned her stare for a long moment then burst out laughing. "You're right, she's not. But you and that boy of mine aren't too bright if you think you're hiding what you think you are."

Jordan cleared her throat and put Cleo in her lap, holding her there with a tummy tickle in case she made another attempt for her shoulders. "I'm not hiding anything."

"Oh? You seemed awful relieved when I told you Jason wasn't in the house."

"That's because I was."

"Uh-huh. Like I said—hiding."

Jordan looked down, wondering if Cleo had any idea how uncomfortable this conversation had become. Luckily, she didn't seem to care.

The kitten, obviously looking for total adoration, launched herself off Jordan's lap and made a beeline for Annie, climbing up to sit on her shoulder. Jordan looked on in surprise. The older woman didn't so much as blink. You would think she hadn't even noticed the feline attack…if not for the slight way she inclined her head toward the demon seed.

"I just stopped by to thank you," Jordan said quietly. "And to ask for a favor."

"Uh-huh." Annie looked skeptical. "You're welcome. And what is it?"

"I'm hoping you won't mind keeping Cleo a little longer…"

JASON PACED ONE WAY, then the other, in front of the barn, staring at the house and imagining what the two women inside it could be talking about.

He turned around and nearly slammed straight into Jax who was coming through the doors.

"Hey, what did I do?"

Jason rocked back on his heels and grimaced. "Sorry. Didn't see you."

"Gathered that."

They stood looking at each other.

They hadn't spoken a great deal since the night of the shooting. Not because they didn't have anything to say, Jason guessed, but because there was too much to say. Everything was too new, too raw, to sort out just then, on top of everything else going on in his head.

"Why don't you just go in there?" his brother asked.

"Gram kicked me out."

"Uh-oh."

"Yeah."

Jax leaned against the barn and crossed his arms. "I'm thinking about taking that position with the competing company."

"Pegasus?" Jason blinked at him. He wanted to ask his brother to reconsider. To take some time to think it out. But he said nothing. Mostly because just then he didn't know what was right for himself, much less for anyone else. Which was strange in and of itself, because he was accustomed to being straight on everything.

"Yeah. I just thought you should know."

Jason grimaced, knowing there was some appropriate response, but didn't have a clue what it was.

Jax cleared his throat and nodded toward the house. "Mind my asking what's going on between you two?"

"Who? Me and Gram?"

"No. That I know about. Remember?"

"Then, yes, I do mind."

The sound of screen door slapping shut turned their attention back toward the house.

Jason nearly vibrated right out of his boots at the sight of Jordan walking in his direction.

"I think that's my cue to leave," Jax said.

Jason turned to object, but his brother had already disappeared back into the barn. He wondered if it was too late for him to do the same.

"Hi."

He slowly angled himself to look at Jordan.

Damn, but the woman was even more beautiful than he remembered. And that was saying a lot, because in his memory, he had practically elevated her to goddess status.

"Hey."

She'd pushed the sunglasses back on her head, leaving her vibrant hazel eyes free to unleash whatever power it was she had over him.

"Can we talk for a minute?" she asked.

His gaze dropped to her lush mouth. He rubbed the back of his hand against his own and swallowed the sudden desire to kiss her.

Sudden? He woke with it, went to sleep with it and thought about it every damn minute of every damn day.

"Yeah, okay."

"You sure?"

He squinted at her. "Yeah. Why?"

"Well, you seem to be going out of your way not to talk to me lately."

That was before he blinked and found her standing right in front of him.

Now he couldn't imagine wanting to do anything *but* talk to her.

"I'm moving out of Denver."

Her words caught him short. "To where?"

She looked down. "I don't know yet."

He couldn't seem to wrap his head around the idea. Which was odd, considering five minutes ago he'd convinced himself he didn't want to see her again.

"When?"

"I leave tonight."

"That soon?"

She smiled and looked back up into his face. "Yeah."

There was a sound behind in the barn. He caught sight of Jax just a little too close to the doors to be discreet.

He grimaced and said, "Walk with me?"

She shrugged. "Sure. But only for a few minutes. I have some things to finish up before I go."

He felt both ridiculously light that she was there…and inexplicably heavy by her news. He couldn't figure it out. How could he possibly be two things at once?

"I'm going to be leaving soon myself," he found himself saying.

She looked at him as they walked. He kept his gaze steadfastly trained forward, leading the way back behind the house, to the firing range.

"Where to?"

"Baltimore."

"Baltimore?"

"Yeah." He rubbed the back of his neck. "I hope to be open-

ing a satellite office for Lazarus there. The project wasn't
scheduled until some unspecified point in the future, but…"

"But you want to get it started now."

He squinted at her. "Yeah."

They stood for long moments in silence. A light westerly
breeze brought hints of autumn their way. After the intense
heat of recent days, it was both a blessing and a curse.

The breeze also delivered Jordan's unforgettable scent to
him. He told himself to move so he was no longer downwind,
but he couldn't seem to help himself. He wanted to smell her.
Damn it, he wanted to do a hell of a lot more than that…

"May I ask you a question?" she said quietly, strands of
her blond hair trailing over her beautiful face.

He didn't answer.

"What happened between us?"

The question made him stiffen in more ways than one.

"I'm not sure I know what you mean."

She laughed without humor as she drew her finger across
her cheek, removing strands of hair from the corner of her
mouth. "I'm sure you do."

"Sex."

The word was out before he knew he was going to say it.
And he both sighed in relief and cringed as a result.

"Ouch," she said.

Hell…

He found himself grasping her upper arms and pulling
her close so she was forced to look at nothing but him.

"What do you want me to say, Jordan?" He searched her
eyes, which emerged more green with emotion now. "That I
fell in love with you?"

His heart beat so hard in his chest, he was surprised she
couldn't see it.

"Are you ready to hear that? Hell, am I ready to say it?"

She appeared speechless.

"And even if the answer to both questions is yes, where

does that leave us?" He told himself to release her before he said something even dumber. But he couldn't.

"You and I, we come from the same mold," he said. "Oh, except for certain body parts. But you know what I mean. Neither of us has needed anyone before now. We're as far from the marrying kind as you can get..."

She nodded. "I know."

"Good."

He forced himself to drop his hands, satisfied she understood what he was trying to say.

She seemed to be having a hard time swallowing. "What I also know is this..."

She stepped into him and pressed her mouth so delicately against his, he could almost convince himself she wasn't kissing him at all. Except that everything inside him wouldn't allow him the denial.

He groaned and wrapped his arms around her, drawing her body in close to his.

Long minutes later, they broke apart, breathless.

"Sex," he ground out.

"No," she said. "Maybe that's how it started. But our time apart has proved there's much more there. Much, much more. Somewhere between sex and love lies the truth."

"The truth?"

"That we're both in love." He watched her tongue flick out to moisten her incredible lips. "So now, the question is what, if anything, are we going to do about it?"

He began to open his mouth and she pressed a finger against it.

"Don't you dare say 'it's just sex' or I'll have to put my new-found gun skills to the test..."

He chuckled and crowded her close again, breathing in everything that was her.

"Come to Baltimore with me."

The instant the words were out, he knew they were the right ones.

He couldn't imagine the future without her in it. Not only would he spend undue amounts of time tripping over his mouth, as Gram said, he would always regret not having done something about…this. About her. About how he felt about her. He understood that now.

He had never been one for regrets. He wasn't going to change that now.

"How's the club market?" she whispered.

He ground his hips against hers. "Hot."

She made a sound deep in her throat. "So when do we go…?"

There was a loud rap on the window behind them. They looked to see Annie shaking her head. Then she gave them the thumbs-up.

Jason looked at Jordan again. "Ever do it in a hayloft?"

Her smile touched him in places hands never could. "Can't say as I have."

He picked her up and tossed her over his shoulder. "I have the feeling we're going to be trying a whole lot of things neither of us have done before."

She gasped. "I say bring…it…on…"

* * * * *

YOU SEXY THING!

1

New York City

"GEE, THANKS, BUD, you're a regular Donald Trump."

Dylan Fairbanks folded back the magazine he was reading and frowned at the hygienically challenged cabby. Did that mean he had tipped the driver too much or too little? Hard to tell. That was the problem with New Yorkers. Their sarcasm cut both ways. He shrugged, deciding a two-dollar tip was more than generous. Especially considering that they'd left his stomach—and his notes for today's appearance—somewhere on the Queensboro Bridge. The autumn breeze had snatched the notes out of his hand and carried them through the half-open window. Unfortunately, the breeze had left behind the stench he'd been trying to clear out in the first place.

A valet opened the door and Dylan climbed out, looking over the fifth hotel he was scheduled to stay at in as many days. It was certainly larger than the one he'd stayed at in Harrisburg, Pennsylvania, the night before. Good. He could use the basic creature comforts like a laptop connection and virtual anonymity to catch up on his correspondence and see to work that he'd fallen criminally behind on since leaving San Francisco last week.

But first he had to find his publisher's PR rep, Tanja Berry. She had disappeared sometime last night with little more than a brief note saying she'd meet him here this morning. He scanned the people bustling in and out of the revolving brass-framed door, wondering exactly when she had planned to meet him. Since no one sported her purple-tipped short black hair, he guessed it wasn't now.

Where was she? He glanced at his watch. She had better show up soon or else they'd never make it to the radio station in time for his interview.

"Dr. Fairbanks?"

Dylan freed his overstuffed suitcase from the revolving monster that doubled as a door then grimaced at a uniformed young man with bad acne. "It depends on what you want."

The guy looked puzzled, Dylan's halfhearted attempt at humor skimming right over his head.

He sighed. "Yeah, that would be me." A prospect that usually left him pretty satisfied with himself and his life, but right now made him want to trade his doctorate for a teamsters membership card.

"You're already checked in, sir." The concierge-in-training handed him a room key, then wrestled him for his one suitcase. "It's Room 1715. Miss, um, Berry suggested you go on up. She's already there."

"Very good." He tugged on the handle of his suitcase, battling the youth for control. "And I can see to this. Thank you." He finally gained possession and nearly fell over backward for his effort.

Miss Berry had likely already given the kid a generous tip for scouting him out. He wasn't about to pay him any more. He brushed away the pang of guilt and told himself he was being savvy. But the simple truth was that he had grown up with very little money of his own, and now that he had money, he was hesitant to part ways with it. You never knew what the future held. And over the course of the promotional tour he was coming to think he was in the wrong business. He was convinced hotel employees made more per annum than he did. He headed for the glass-encased elevators. This was one less entry he'd have to make on his expense sheet. And that was always a plus.

Dylan punched the up button next to the elevators and stood back to wait. And wait. And wait. He ran his hand over his face. Only five days into his three-week promotional book tour and he wanted to change his name and move to someplace where nobody knew his name. Where no one called him "the world's greatest sex expert." Where people didn't know he'd written a book, much less two—the latest one bearing the misleading title *Reaching New Heights—Advice on How to Obtain Ultimate Sexual Pleasure*. Having men sidle up to him at book signings to ask what tips he could give them to drive the opposite sex wild—wink-wink—had lost its patina long ago. And so had the women of all ages and socioeconomic backgrounds who slipped him hotel room keys that he immediately threw into the wastebasket he always kept under the signing table.

If his "fans" had bothered to look beyond the racy cover copy, they would have already had the answers to their bawdy questions. No, he couldn't give anyone tips on how to drive women wild. However, if they were looking to satisfy their spouses, then maybe he could give them advice. As for the hotel keys…well, anyone who'd actually read his bio would know that he had been celibate by choice since his divorce four years ago. Any woman who openly propositioned him, no matter how lovely or innocent-looking, immediately forfeited a spot on his very short list of prospects for "the next and last Mrs. Fairbanks." In fact, the list was so short it held only one person.

Speaking of which…

He released the handle of his suitcase then fumbled in his inside jacket pocket for his cell phone. A glance at his watch told him it was not only too early to reach Diana at work on the West Coast, but that he was running seriously late. If this damn elevator—

Ding.

Sighing, he slipped his cell phone back into his pocket and stepped inside the empty, moving fishbowl that served as an elevator. Staring at the unmarked plastic key, he tried to remember the room number. Seventeen-fifteen. He punched the button for the seventeenth floor, only vaguely noticing that the button for the sixteenth was already lit though the elevator was empty. He stepped to the glass and watched as the lobby grew farther and farther away. People milled around the large open area as he grasped his cell phone again. He hit a preprogrammed number then glanced at the magazine he still held, listening to the line ring.

Sex Doctor Grace Mattias Leads the Way into a Brave New Sexual Frontier.

Dylan stared at the headline. "'Brave new sexual frontier,' my narrow behind." It looked like she was recycling the same old line of BS carried over from the sixties. The left sidebar held a cartoon of a redhead in a tight, short dress holding condoms in one hand, a monstrous vibrator in the other. His gaze drifted to the other page. The caricature there—presumably of him—showed a dark-haired guy holding his hands in front of his crotch with a horrified expression on his face like some male virgin from the Regency period. What the caricature didn't say, the headline did. Doctor Fairbanks Declares Monogamous Marriage Only Path to Sexual Fulfillment.

If he had known the features editor had planned to pit him against someone else, much less this apparently graceless Grace Mattias, he never would have agreed to the interview. Sure, his message was there. Couched between below-the-belt jabs at his conservatism and purposely provocative counterpoints provided by Mattias. Not exactly his most stellar appearance.

The line stopped ringing. "Hello—"

"Diana. I'm glad I caught you. I've—"

"You've reached the residence of Diana Evans..."

Dylan stared at the phone then grimaced. He'd gotten her answering machine enough times in the past two days, he should have been ready for the deceptive pause between Diana's greeting and her regrets. But he'd been fooled every time. Which made him feel like an even bigger fool.

Pressing the disconnect key, he distantly wondered where she was so early in the morning. It was only five in the morning in San Francisco. Much too early to have left for her job as junior partner at Coulter, Connor and Caplain, Attorneys-at-Law. He'd been hoping to make contact with her to share the decision he'd made before leaving for his trip. Well, not *share* it share it. He wanted to arrange for her to meet him in Miami later next week. It was late enough in the year for the north to be chilly and he'd thought balmy Florida would be the perfect place for him to propose to her.

He frowned, looking down at his naked ring finger. Sometimes he swore he could still make out the tan line where his last wedding ring had been. His imagination, of course. It had to be, because he hadn't worn the ring for four years. And then it had only been for a meager four months.

Well, okay, maybe he'd kept it on for a year. He'd been so shocked when Julie had filed divorce papers he hadn't thought to take the blasted thing off for at least eight months. It had taken his mother's threat to sandblast the sucker off in his sleep to make him twist the simple gold band down the length of his finger. Of course his mother, Sharon—who preferred to be called Moonbeam—had objected to the visual symbol of possession, even during the short time he and Julie had been married. She'd had her own wedding rings melted down to a charm in the shape of an eagle over thirty years ago, shortly after she and his father had married. She wore it on a clinking bracelet that bore other mutilated remnants of what she called her "formal, materialistic life."

Dylan didn't even want to think about what his father had done with his ring. Especially since his latest interest included body piercings.

Thirty-six years of marriage and his parents still acted like flower children left over from some long-forgotten era. Hell, he hadn't even introduced Diana to them yet. A niggling part of him still thought his parents had played a role in Julie's sudden defection. It was awfully coincidental that five days after he and Julie had gone for an overnight visit to El Rancho, his parents' communelike spread in northern California, she'd packed her bags and left.

He absently rubbed the back of his neck. He couldn't really blame his parents for what had clearly been his fault. No matter how tempting. Or how easy. He and he alone had been responsible for that fiasco. He'd let his libido dictate a lifetime decision, one that was better made over time. Like the amount of time he'd taken to develop his relationship with Diana.

Sure, he'd known the moment he met Diana sixteen months ago that she was the perfect matrimonial choice. For one thing, she was the complete opposite of Julie. In place of Julie's wild brunette good looks Diana was sleekly blonde. Where Julie had preferred tight-fitting primary colors, Diana chose loose-fitting earth tones. Where Julie had wanted to run off and get married in Vegas within hours of their first meeting, Diana seemed to prefer to allow him to take his time to make decisions, never breathing a word about matrimony unless he broached the subject.

Dylan straightened. This time when he uttered the words *till death do us part,* he intended to see them through to the utter end.

Of course it would help if he could actually get Diana on the line.

The elevator doors behind him finally slid open. Grasping the handle of his suitcase, he exited, then followed the arrows toward room 1715...no, 1615. There. He slid his card key in, waited for the red light to turn green, then turned the handle. Nothing.

Damn. What else could possibly go wrong on this trip?

He tried again more slowly. Then again, more rapidly. The door refused to give.

He stepped back in exasperation. The bellboy obviously had given him the wrong card.

He stared down the long hall that would take him back to the elevator, then down at his watch. He was really running late. The faint sound of Latino music caught his attention. He spotted a maid's cart a couple of doors down. Without thinking twice, he started toward it, reaching for the cash in his pocket. He wondered how much it would take to get the maid to let him into his own room.

Surprisingly, it didn't take much doing. The young woman opened the door for him, then actually held her hand up and said something in Spanish. She walked away without taking his money.

Dylan slowly tucked the cash back into his pocket. *I'll be damned.* Maybe his day was starting to look up.

He stepped into the room to find steam billowing from the bathroom on his left. Probably as-immodest-as-they-came Tanja was catching a quick shower before the interview. He turned the corner, intent on knocking on the door and reminding her of the time, only to find the door wide-open. And a woman he'd never seen in his entire life taking a shower, the curtain thrown all the way open.

Dylan went completely, utterly, speechlessly still.

Mere feet away from him, a very...tall...very...well-developed woman stood under the oscillating spray. Water clung to perfectly rounded breasts then cascaded over dusky, erect nipples, to slide down a wonderfully toned stomach. He swallowed hard, powerless to stop his gaze from venturing even further. Crystalline droplets clung to the red-gold, curly thatch of hair between her slender thighs.

Dylan dug his fingers into his palms, vaguely aware of the way they suddenly itched. To his surprise, he found himself jealous of the water. He wanted to be the one to explore every inch of flawless skin the water touched.

His mind finally kicking back into gear, he brought his gaze up to her face.

She was watching him.

"Imagine that. My own personal Peeping Tom." A smile flitted across her lips. "You don't mind locking the door on your way back out, do you, Tom? I mean, after you've looked your fill."

Dylan felt his skin grow hotter than the steam coating him. "I can't believe… I have no idea… I am so very sorry. I must have the wrong room."

He somehow backtracked his way to the hall, his feet moving though he didn't recall sending them the order to do just that. He stood staring at the room that looked like any other as the automatic locking door slowly began closing. What in the hell had just happened? A scant second before the door could close completely, he stuck a hand out to stop it, then reached in to tug his suitcase out.

He collapsed against the door and closed his eyes, dragging in deep breaths to even out the hammering of his heartbeat.

He supposed this was the way kids felt after they walked in on their parents having sex for the first time.

He groaned at the comparison, then moved away from the door, as if just touching it was somehow…immoral.

He'd made an honest mistake. That's all. He'd gotten into the elevator. Got distracted thinking about the lack of sex in his life. He swallowed again. No, no, the limbo status of his life. Then got out on the floor that had already been pressed before he even entered the damn thing.

He'd never been so embarrassed…so humiliated in his entire life.

Well, okay, there was that one incident when he was twelve when his mother had stripped him of his swim trunks in the pool, trying to teach him the finer points of nudism. But this ranked a very, very close second.

GRACIE MATTIAS TUCKED a thick white towel around her body then padded quickly toward the door. A cautious glance around and down the hall outside told her that her uninvited guest was long gone.

She closed the door then stared at the locks. There was the automatic one. The double bolt. The security chain. One by one she locked and checked all of them, not surprised that her fingers were trembling. It wasn't every day that one got surprised in the shower like that. She realized the logic of her statement, and the unlikely chance that it would happen again in this lifetime, then sighed and undid all the locks again. She forced herself to turn and stalk into the living area of the sumptuous suite. She refused to live her life in fear of what might happen. Or spend every spare moment looking over her shoulder for lurking degenerates. Or check the backseat every time she got into her car. For heaven's sake, she counseled people on how to overcome such emotional fears. She couldn't begin to cater to them herself.

She swiveled on her heel, then secured every damn lock again.

There was fearless and there was stupid. And no matter how adorably dumbfounded the man was who had turned her normal shower experience into something to remember, the simple fact was she didn't know him from Jack the Ripper.

She stepped back into the living area, picked up the phone and dialed a room number.

"Very funny, Rick," she said when her personal assistant answered. Suddenly she wondered why he had a room three floors away from her. Shouldn't he be next door? Ready to protect her honor should some Peeping Tom burst into her room for an eyeful while she was in the shower?

She grimaced. Give her a minute and her subconscious would recreate the infamous shower scene from *Psycho*. She really needed to get a grip.

Something thudded on the other end of the line. "What's funny?" he said.

Gracie sank into the king-size mattress and switched the receiver to her other ear. She'd chosen her assistant for his organizational skills, not for his sense of humor. It didn't hurt that he was five years younger than she was and could double for Leonardo DiCaprio. Of course, she'd have to nip his comedic tendencies in the bud right now if she was to remain sane during the next two weeks of her promotional tour. "I know I said I was getting bored with this trip. But did you have to send me a Peeping Tom to liven things up? Certainly even you are more imaginative than that."

Rick's long-suffering sigh sounded over the line. "Grace, what are you blathering on about now? Peeping Tom? You're sixteen floors up. Unless you're talking about someone looking at you through binoculars from the building across the street—"

"I'm talking about the guy who just walked into my room while I was taking a shower."

"Aah."

"So you did have something to do with it," she said with relief, picking up a copy of her book, which lay on the bed next to her.

"Nope."

"Rick, I'm going to hang up now."

"I think you're losing it, Dr. Mattias."

"You're just catching on now? Rick, I lost it way back when you were still calling your penis a pee-pee."

His laugh tickled her ear. "You know, this sex-talk stuff is taking some getting used to."

"This from someone who hears it every day. Anyway, we're not anywhere near indulging in sex talk, Rick. I merely called an important part of your anatomy by its proper name. I could ask you what you call it." Grace fanned her thumb against the three hundred and some pages of her hardcover book. Sometimes it was difficult to believe that she had had the discipline to sit down and write such a tome on human sexuality. Other times, she remembered every single word in there and flushed, horrified that she'd actually said one thing or another.

As long as the media never found out she was a fraud.

Well, she wasn't really a fraud. Exactly. It was just that all of her advice was based on 812 case studies rather than personal experience. Which was as it should be. Still, she couldn't help thinking that putting her theories into practice would have allowed her a more...intimate insight into what she was suggesting others do with their love lives.

She flipped the book over to gaze at the back of the dust jacket. She hadn't wanted to include a picture of herself. But there one was. Funny, the woman smiling into the camera appeared *very* sexually experienced.

She tossed the book onto the floor then curled her toes around the edges.

Another muffled sound filtered through the telephone line, reminding her that she was still talking to her assistant. "Rick, what are you doing?"

"Would you believe me if I said your Peeping Tom just paid me a visit?"

"Nope."

"Didn't think so." He chuckled, though somehow Grace got the distinct impression it wasn't meant for her.

Crossing her legs, she switched the receiver to her other ear. "Are you messing around on company time, Rick?" she asked curiously.

She realized she knew very little about her assistant's private life. Not that she wanted to, mind you. But it suddenly struck her as odd that he would have one. And so soon after their arrival in New York.

She glanced over her shoulder, toward the monumental view out her window, and wondered what life would be like if she had someone in her room with her right now. Preferably a tall, dark and sexy someone who could fool around with her while she was on the phone. Take a long, breathtaking walk with through Central Park. Go see a Broadway play with. Someone to sip cappuccino with at one of those cozy coffeehouses all over the place.

A shiver shimmied down her spine, reminding her just how long it was since she'd been with someone.

Her stomach growled, reminding her she hadn't had breakfast.

Let's see, a tall, dark and nameless man, or her kitchen with all her shiny appliances and her refrigerator full of food? She twisted her lips. Tough call. Then again, there was no plausible reason she couldn't have both....

"Has there been a time I haven't been there for you, Gracie?" Rick said, offering up a nonanswer sort of answer that made her smile. "Look, how serious was this incident? Do you want me to contact security and report the guy? Have them change your key card code?"

Her fingers tightened around the receiver. "No, I really don't want to go through all the hassle. My mind may be telling me I just survived a close call with death, but my gut says the poor jerk just got the wrong room. Anyway, reporting the incident will only distract me from the interview."

"Speaking of which, I hope this call means you're ready, because my phone message light is blinking. It's probably the car the station sent to pick us up."

Grace yelped and jumped up. She wasn't anywhere near ready. She eyed the daring, bright pink number she and Rick had settled on for the outrageous radio talk-show host, then lifted a hand to her still wet hair. "See you downstairs in five."

More like twenty, but he didn't have to know that.

"You're late." The junior producer of WDRT's morning radio show descended on Dylan and Tanja like a swooping crow complete with curved nose and clipboard. Through speakers set up in every corner, a clip of seemingly unending commercials poured over the airwaves. Dylan felt hands on his shoulders. He tensed.

"Sheesh, Doc, I'm just trying to take your coat," Tanja said.

"Oh." He allowed her to tug the tan overcoat down the length of his arms, then grasped the new set of notes he'd put together in the cab on the way over.

Tanja leaned closer, one of the spiked, purple tips of her hair nearly taking out an eyeball. She lowered her voice. "Are you okay? You're wound up tighter than a seventeen-year-old virgin on prom night."

He grimaced. "Thanks for the comparison, Tanja."

The instant he'd met the young PR rep his publisher had sent to accompany him on his tour, he was convinced his editor had gone out of his way to make sure he found someone the total opposite of Dylan's character. Dylan could see Charlie Hasseldorf getting quite a chuckle out of the situation. Then Dylan had landed in New York and discovered that here, nearly every professional Tanja's age...well, looked like Tanja.

The producer clapped his hands impatiently. "Look, I don't

have time for any prep so you're just going to have to play it by ear, Doc. The other doc's already in there."

"Other doctor?" Dylan choked, looking at Tanja.

She shrugged and smiled, but it was hard for her to look innocent when she appeared to have just stepped out of a tattoo parlor. "I haven't a clue."

"Well, isn't it your job to find out?"

"We don't have time for this now." The producer fairly shoved him toward the door. "After you, Dr. Fairbanks."

Dylan righted himself. What other doctor? And why hadn't he been told of this beforehand so he could adequately prepare? By now he was used to having his theories challenged by local whackos, but at least he'd been able to do a bit of research before he actually faced the smirking individuals he guessed were chosen more for their disbeliefs than their beliefs.

He was led down a long white hall with various doors leading off it. Dylan straightened his suit jacket and eyed the jeans the other guy was wearing. Perhaps he should have taken Tanja's advice and dressed down for the occasion. It didn't matter that it was radio and the listeners couldn't see him, Tanja had told him. The shock jock could see him. And absolutely nobody wore suits to radio shows.

"Just seat yourself to the right," the producer said, opening a glass door. "Headphones will be on the counter in front of you."

The first thing Dylan spotted in the dimly lit room was a camera.

Damn.

Obviously Tanja had also forgotten to tell him they were being filmed.

He grasped the producer's sleeve before he could vanish along with the PR rep. "Is this being televised?"

"Haven't you seen the show before, Dr. Fairbanks?"

Dylan frowned. "Seen? I thought this was a radio show."

"It is. But snippets of celebrity interviews are put together for a nightly half-hour show on a cable access channel. Yours will probably air in a week or two, depending on our schedule."

Dylan stiffened. He didn't like the way he came across on the small screen. An image of that magazine caricature came to mind. He immediately unclasped his hands where they rested in front of his groin.

For Pete's sake, it was an entertainment show. Certainly he could handle it. Anyway, it was too late to back out now.

He stepped into the room, bringing into view the radio host, his blond head bent over something an assistant held out to him. Then he spotted the table he was supposed to seat himself at. Eyes focused on the padded headphones, he seated himself then slid them over his head, his gaze constantly flitting back to the camera perched in the corner like an all-seeing, critical beast.

"Hi," a female voice spoke into his ears. "I've heard a lot about you, but I don't believe we've actually met."

Dylan's eyebrows popped up as he listened to the low, positively humming voice. He glanced toward a glass enclosure, but the brunette inside—the show's cohost, he guessed—appeared engrossed in her notes and knocking back coffee.

"I'm Gracie Mattias."

An odd, swirling sensation began in the pit of his stomach.

"Here. I'm right next to you. The other side."

Dylan swiveled to his right. Indeed, she was right next to him. And the odd sensation in his stomach pulled into a complicated, inexplicable knot.

The cartoon rendition of her he'd seen in the magazine earlier did absolutely no justice to Dr. Grace Mattias, sex therapist, live and in the flesh. *Flesh* being the operative word. Generously endowed, alluring flesh. And hair. Fiery, coppery red hair that curled all over the place. He couldn't fathom why, but he thought of her hair wet. Probably because he had showers on the brain since his unfortunate encounter earlier. Or maybe because when wet, the red mass would likely skim down her back to tickle the dimples just above her bottom. And she would indeed have dimples. Decadent, deep indentations that would perfectly complement her perfect body and would beg to be explored by a man's tongue.

Dylan swallowed...hard.

Then he silently berated himself for such a completely physical reaction to the woman sitting next to him. His adversary. His opposite in every way.

He didn't know what was with him. It wasn't as if he hadn't seen an attractive woman before, much less an attractive female colleague. But attractive didn't begin to cover Grace Mattias. In fact, nothing much seemed to be covering Grace Mattias. His gaze slid over the hot-pink clingy material of her deep-veed jacket, down, down, to where her skirt barely skimmed the tops of her delicious thighs. Legs that could rival a model's went on and on until he found himself staring at the highest, strappiest sandals he'd ever seen in his life.

Catching himself, he snapped his gaze back to her face. Her pink, pink lips pursed as she gave him the same thorough once-over. "Actually, I think we have met, Dr. Fairbanks."

Dylan managed to shake his head, not trusting himself to speak for fear it would come out sounding like a preadolescent squeak.

She tapped a pink-tipped fingernail against her full, luscious mouth. "Uh-huh. In fact, I'm sure of it." She smiled, revealing nicely ridged teeth that hadn't fallen prey to a dentist's sander. "Though I believe I know you as Tom."

Dylan chuckled, relaxing a bit. "Now I know we haven't met before. I'd never have misrepresented myself as someone else...." Even as he said the words, a low alarm went off in a part of his brain that still worked.

Her smile widened as she folded her arms under her

breasts, causing them to pop up even further. "Yes. As in Peeping Tom," she finished.

Oh, shit.

It couldn't be.

It wasn't possible he'd blundered into another situation with the same woman twice in one day. The law of averages completely went against such an improbability.

Yet here he was. Staring at the water nymph from the shower earlier that morning.

2

Dylan watched as Grace Mattias pulled her hair back, revealing the lightly freckled, even planes of her face. "Picture me without makeup…and clothes."

He closed his eyes tightly and uttered a pungent curse.

"Dr. Fairbanks?" A male voice said into his earphones. "The FCC frowns on the use of such language."

He grimaced and forced himself to face forward, well away from the provocative woman next to him and toward the radio host. How bad could it get? This was a morning show, right? Certainly there were guidelines the show had to follow. "Are we on the air?"

"Not yet." This time it was the radio host who spoke. And Dylan didn't like the width of his predatory grin. "But we will be in three, two, one… Welcome back everybody. This is Baxter Berning on WDRT and you're listening to America's most popular syndicated talk show. Boy, are you ever in store for a tasty treat today. If you've just tuned in, don't worry about what you've missed. If you've stuck around, then you're about to hit pay dirt. I'd like to begin this segment by introducing two of the foremost experts in the area of *sex*." He drew out the word with suggestive flair then picked up a book Dylan didn't recognize because it wasn't his own. Baxter introduced Grace. Then he homed in on

Dylan, ignoring the copy of his book at his elbow as he leaned forward.

Bad news. Whenever they overlooked his book, it meant they were about to go off on a tangent, outside the list of acceptable interview questions Tanja had provided the producer. Worse news.

"Now let's see if I can get this straight, Dr. Fairbanks. Am I to gather from your conversation with Gracie—can I call you Gracie?"

The redhead next to him nodded, causing all that red hair to shimmer under a warm spotlight. Then she leaned closer to her mic, almost as if about to kiss it, and said, "You can call me anything you'd like, Baxter. Just don't call me late for bed."

Dylan cringed. *This* was a doctor? He didn't know any doctors who spoke like that. Okay, there were his parents, but for all intents and purposes, they weren't *real* doctors anymore.

The host reacted. "Ooh. For my listeners, I'd like to point out that Gracie is every bit the sex kitten she sounds like. This is one interview you'll want to check out when it airs on TV." He leaned forward. "Anyway, back to you Dr. Fairbanks."

"Call me Dylan, please," he said, uncomfortably tugging on the lapels of his jacket.

"Right. Anyway, am I correct in assuming that you, um, played Peeping Tom to Gracie's sexy victim this morning?"

Oh, God. It was one thing to have suffered through the unfortunate event in the first place. To be humiliated before a national audience was altogether different. "Not by design, I assure you," he said, then cleared the high-pitched panic from his voice. "It was a simple misunderstanding. I mistook Dr. Mattias's hotel room for my own, and by innocent accident let myself into her room."

"I was in the shower," Grace clarified.

Dylan jerked to gape at her. She didn't have to share that. He cringed and prayed Diana wasn't listening to the show in San Francisco.

"Uh-huh. I've heard of wanting to get a peek at the competition, Doc, but this is fantastic." The host sat back, dragging his mic with him. "So tell us, does the female sex doc look as good out of her clothes as in?"

Dylan's collar felt like a tightening noose as he slanted another gaze Grace's way. *Oh, boy, did she,* his own body responded. But to Baxter he said, "I'm afraid I didn't get a good look."

"Didn't get a good look," the host repeated. "Now that's the biggest load I've ever heard. Are you human, man? I mean, just look at her. That's a piece even the Pope would look twice at. You can't tell me you didn't take advantage of the prime opportunity and devour that tight little body with your eyes."

"If that was a compliment, thank you, Baxter." Grace's voice practically purred in Dylan's ears.

He hit his chin on the mic. "I'll be the first to admit that Dr. Mattias is…attractive."

"Trust me, you're not the first, and you won't be the last, Doc."

Grace laughed, a throaty sound that made the swirling in Dylan's stomach slink lower. "I'm afraid you're making Dylan uncomfortable, Bax. If you'd read his book, and believe me, I have, then you'd know that he doesn't buy into the whole chemistry theory. He believes the human anatomy was designed solely for reproduction purposes and that only within the confines of a monogamous relationship—"

"Marriage," Dylan corrected, regaining his bearings, and unendingly grateful his colleague had shifted the conversation back to solid ground. If they stuck to their books and medical terminology, he'd be fine.

She smiled at him. "All right, then, marriage. As I was

saying, Dr. Dylan believes only within the bonds of marriage should sexual, um, attraction be explored."

The host's gaze bore into Dylan. "Does that mean you're still a virgin, Doc?"

He nearly choked. "No. No, of course not."

The shock jock snapped his fingers in front of his microphone. "Then you're one of those, oh, what's the term they're throwing around like yesterday's paper? I got it. A born-again virgin. Are you a born-again virgin, then?"

Dylan hated the term, though by the host's definition, he suspected his situation fit within the wide parameters. "No comment."

"Come on, Doc, just look at her. Are you telling me that you don't just totally want to bang her brains out? Whip out ol' George and get down to introductions? For crying out loud, Gracie is a walking wet dream."

Explicit images flashed through Dylan's mind. Visions of Grace standing under the shower stream, the water sluicing over her womanly curves, her nipples hard and begging for attention, her thighs warm and wet with an altogether different moisture.

Get it together, Dylan. Now was not the time or the place to explore his most untoward thoughts of the woman next to him.

He cleared his throat. "Don't get me wrong. As I point out in Chapter Four of my latest book, *Reaching New Heights— Advice on How to Obtain Ultimate Sexual Pleasure,* attraction between a man and a woman plays an important role when they first meet. But it's a mere pebble in the foundation of a solid, fulfilling relationship."

The host made a face, obviously not getting the response he wanted. He opened Grace's book and flipped through the pages. "Seems yours and the sex doctor's beliefs are completely contrary then." He grinned at Grace. "It says here that you suggest your patients go out on sexual safaris."

"Some patients," Grace said, straightening her head-phones, then fluffing all that red hair back around them. "Those without a dark, painful sexual past who are merely in need of finding themselves...sexually. An awakening of sorts, if you will."

Sexual safari? Dylan thought. It was only when the voices in his headphones went silent that he realized he'd made the remark aloud.

"You were saying?" the host asked.

Yeah, he was saying. Dylan sat up a little straighter, speaking into the mic at an angle as he looked at Grace. "Define sexual safari, Dr. Mattias."

"I'm crushed you haven't read my book," she said, giving him a playfully sexy little pout that made that...feeling slide even lower. "A sexual safari is where I recommend the patient respond to basic, fundamental human need. No asset-probing, spouse-hunting, car-perusing behavior allowed. Rather, the patient is encouraged to act on urges society has taught us to ignore or suppress in the name of pseudomorality and human decency." She smiled. "In essence, I tell these particular patients to act with their hearts rather than their heads."

The host emitted a low whistle. "Baby, let me go get my camouflage underwear and oil my elephant gun."

Dylan ignored him, instead locking gazes with the woman next to him. "So you counsel your patients to have one-night stands. Promote promiscuity. Is that what you're saying, Dr. Mattias?"

"No. I encourage these particular patients to cut loose at least once in their lives so there are no relationship-ruining 'what ifs' and 'what could have beens' later on in life. I counsel them to connect with their sexual selves, learn what pleases them without the heavy complications serious rela-tionships entail. You know, the whole, 'will he think I'm too fat,' 'am I pleasing her' scenario. If you set out to please your-self and yourself alone, then you're in a much better position to know what pleases others, either in that relationship, or in the one that will stand the test of 'until death do you part.' And even you have to admit, Dr. Dylan, that sexual satisfaction is an important element in any healthy marriage."

"Yes, but *only* within the bonds of matrimony. As for the other, growing sexually aware of yourself, there are better, more…principled ways to go about achieving that goal. And abstinence, or delaying acting on that purely physical, animal attraction makes for an even sweeter, more satisfying experience, wouldn't you agree…Gracie?"

The host fanned himself with Grace's book. "And tell me, Dr. Hottie, do you go…man-hunting often?"

For a long moment Grace held Dylan's gaze as if she was unable to look away. He noticed the look of pure, undiluted sensuality in the velvety brown depths of her eyes. The telling dilation of her pupils. Finally she smiled, then slowly looked toward their host. "I think I'll follow my colleague's lead and answer a demure 'no comment.'"

"Oh, don't go coy on me now, baby," Baxter crowed. "We have a caller on line four. John, you're on. Do you have a question you'd like to ask one of our guests?"

"Am I on the air?"

"Yes, sir, you are. Shoot away."

"Okay, um…I'm having a problem and I was, you know, hoping one or both of your guests might be able to help me with it."

The host sighed heavily into the mic. "John, if it takes you this long to get to the point, no wonder you're having problems."

Dylan leaned toward his own mic. "Go ahead, John."

"Yes, well, um, my wife and I have been married for five years now and…"

A long silence ensued.

"And," the host prompted.

"And, well, I'm lucky if we have sex once a month. There, I said it. What can I do about it?"

Dylan opened his mouth to ask for more details, but Gracie's voice, sounding infinitely less like a porn star's and more like a professional, filled his ears. "Were you two sexually active before you were married, John?"

Dylan grimaced. "With all due respect, Dr. Mattias, I don't see what that's got to do with anything. The fact is that they are married, and they're currently experiencing…marital difficulties."

The host laughed. "Yeah, I'd say not getting any is a marital difficulty."

Grace looked at him, a flash of something he couldn't identify lighting her eyes. "I wasn't going to suggest that the couple regress back to the time before their marriage, Dr. Dylan. I was merely trying to ascertain whether or not they'd found themselves individually, sexually, before they took their business in front of a priest or a pastor or a rabbi." She turned her head away from him. "John, do you and your wife have any kids?"

"Um, no."

"So there's no reason you can't turn your entire house into a sexual playground then, is there?"

"Sexual playground?"

"Yes, John. This is what I suggest you do. First of all, you'll want to talk to your wife. Find out what her secret fantasy is. If she hasn't shared it with you in the five years you've been married, this may take some time. But once you do find out, act on it. Transform your house to reflect this fantasy. Cater to her every whim. Let her know that her emotional and sexual happiness mean as much to you as your own desire to, in our honorable host's words, get some."

Chuckles filled Dylan's ears as he sat back, grudgingly impressed with the advice, though her immediate rejection of his own opinion stung like a son of a bitch. While he wouldn't have suggested the construction of a "playground," sexual communication was always important, making her basic advice sound.

Baxter came back, "Sounds like good advice to me. Thanks for calling, John. And good luck with the old lady." There was a tiny click. "We're going to break for a minute or two to let the sex doctor's advice sink in. We'll be right back to ask our guests where they stand on masturbation. You won't want to miss that. I sure don't."

The sound of commercials filtered through the headphones and Dylan followed everyone's lead in taking his off. The host, so tuned in to him and Grace only moments before, was conversing with the producer, leading him to believe his entire interplay with Grace was for entertainment purposes only.

"So where *do* you stand on the topic of masturbation, Dr. Dylan?"

He shifted to find Grace Mattias crossing her long, long legs and smiling at him suggestively.

Despite his best intentions, Dylan couldn't help grinning at her. He pushed the microphone away to make sure this little encounter wasn't used for ammunition when the commercials were over. "Oh, beyond a doubt, it leads to blindness."

Her instant laughter was spontaneous, warm and contagious. He laughed along with her, his muscles relaxing at the release of some of the tension between them. But he recognized that a whole different kind of tension had just shot up a notch.

"You probably already know where I stand, anyway, seeing as you read my book."

She nodded. "So long as it's not used instead of sex, your marital partner doesn't know about your extracurricular activities and it doesn't involve sex toys, you're all for it."

"In moderation," he added.

"And with the ultimate amount of discretion."

"Very important."

"So you don't think the act of, um, watching…your significant other bring herself to climax can be…sexual stimulating?"

Dylan stared at her. An image of one amazingly sexy and gloriously naked Gracie Mattias stretched across a king-size bed, her thighs open, her engorged womanhood clearly in view, flashed across his mind. Her pink-tipped fingers first cupped her breasts, plucking at her erect nipples, then slid down the toned length of her stomach, toward—

He shook his head, banishing the erotic thought from his mind. "I think masturbation is an intimate matter best kept between one's hands…and oneself."

"Okay, guys, we're back in ten seconds," the producer said, indicating their headphones.

Dylan carefully readied himself and repositioned the mic in front of his mouth, wondering if he'd be able to even think of the word *masturbation* again without connecting it to one wildly sexy Gracie Mattias.

GRACIE STEPPED OUTSIDE and took a deep, satisfying breath of the polluted New York City air. The smell of car exhaust mingled with the scents emanating from a nearby diner and the crisp scent of fallen leaves. If she tried hard enough, she imagined she could make out the slight tang of the ocean not far away.

A drop of water landed on her upturned forehead. Another on her chin. She opened her eyes to realize that it wasn't the ocean she smelled, but an impending rainstorm. Ah, an unseasonably warm autumn day in New York City. In a matter of seconds, it would probably start pouring. But she couldn't bring herself to care. She felt…electrified somehow. So vividly alive. Her skin tingled with excitement. She was gloriously aware of every sweet nuance that made her human. The feel of her breasts pressing against the thin tank top under her jacket, the skirt hugging her hips and bottom, made her feel every inch a woman.

The downpour began.

She hailed a taxi then climbed in, laughing when she found herself soaked straight through.

She shrugged out of her jacket, told the driver which hotel, then settled back in the seat. "Take the scenic route through the park. I've always loved the park."

"Lady, do you know what kind of traffic we're going to run into this time of day?"

She smiled at him in the rearview mirror. "Yeah."

Right now she couldn't care less if it took her two hours to get back to her hotel room. Rick was out running errands for her, the radio talk-show host had asked her for her phone number and she'd just experienced one of the more stimulating challenges of her life in the shape of one super-sexy Dr. Dylan Fairbanks.

An image of Dr. Dylan crowded out all other thought and she smiled. Just thinking about him made her hungry for an unnamable something. She didn't try to name the feeling. She didn't want to. Not yet. She wanted to enjoy the curious warmth spreading through her belly and settling between her tingling thighs.

She stuck her hand into her purse and fished out an extra-large packet of peanuts, compliments of the hotel. While the salty morsels couldn't hope to satisfy her recently awakened hunger, they could at least satisfy her stomach.

She absently crunched on the nuts. Professionally speaking, she couldn't have asked for a better setup. Rick had agreed, telling her postinterview that her choice of attire had worked wonders on the host, distracting him even while she drove each of her points home with a solid rubber mallet. No, she hadn't expected Dr. Fairbanks to be there. But given his expression when he first spotted her sitting next to him, she

guessed that he hadn't, either. And when she realized he'd
been the one to accidentally walk in on her in the shower
that morning…well, suddenly this tour wasn't half as boring
as it had been.

Of course, a few of her racier comments later on in the
show would have singed her mother's eyebrows. Had her
mother been listening. Which Gracie doubted. But Dylan's
choked reactions somehow had been more satisfying.

She couldn't have asked for a better way to prove her theories than going nose-to-nose with one of the country's pre-
mier masters of sexual inhibition.

A delicious shiver began just below her earlobes and traveled down to her toes. She stretched her feet out as far as they
could go, then reached into her monster bag and fished out
Dr. Dylan's book. Nowhere to be found was a photo of him.
Only a very brief bio outlining his professional experience.
Which was impressive indeed. She had expected him to be
a fiftyish, balding, overweight guy in glasses who got into
spouting off about morality because he didn't have a chance
in hell of leading a more interesting life. But the real Dr.
Dylan Fairbanks…well, he had turned out to be sexier than
sin.

She remembered the way he had looked at her. Both this
morning at the hotel, then at the station when they had indulged in off-air conversation. Something about him seemed
to sizzle. He had an almost visible red aura that tempted her
closer, made her want to see if all his professional doctrines
could be put to better use with sexual expertise.

Her chewing slowed.

Was he a hypocrite? She'd run into her share of alpha
males who preached to her about values with their mouths,
while seeking her leg under the table with their hands. Behavior that always earned the offending male a meeting with
the sharp prongs of her fork. She stuffed the book back into
her bag next to a copy of her own. She didn't think Dr. Dylan

was that type. To the contrary, he appeared to adamantly believe every last word he'd written in his sexually repressed
book. She leaned her head against the seat and stared up at
the skyscrapers through the back window. Looking at the rain
coming down that way seemed somehow surreal, magical.

Her cell phone chirped in her purse. She let it ring.

"Hey, lady, you gonna get that or what?"

"I was thinking 'or what.'" Despite her response, she
brushed the salt from her hands, then fished the noisy piece
of plastic out. *Rick,* the display read. She punched the talk
button. "I'm paying an arm and leg for a taxi drive through
the park, Rick. This had better be good."

"You should have told me you wanted to see the city. I
could have gotten you on one of those Grayline Tours, or
whatever they're called. Anyway, this is good. More than
good. I just got a call from the radio station. You're not going
to believe this. The number of callers was through the roof.
Among the highest they've ever received."

She slipped her shoes off, indulging in a wide smile.
"Really?"

He laughed. "All that education and that's the best you
can do? You disappoint me, Dr. Mattias."

"Hey, I'm enjoying the moment."

"As well you should. I, of course, took the liberty of passing on the news to your publisher. They're very happy."

"Sure they are. More money for them."

"More money for you."

Grace's smile slipped. The rain clouds soaking the city
seemed to descend from the skies and settle around her shoulders.

Money had dictated so much of her life. Which were the
best schools for her to attend? What latest designer was the
most fashionable? Whose children were the best to be seen
with? Her parents had tried to drill into her from a young age
that money and success were all that mattered in life. She

had spent much of that same life determined to prove them wrong. She'd dyed her hair green when she was eleven. Hung around with the "out" crowd. Majored in courses designed to make her mother's lips disappear with disapproval.

She was well into her teens before she realized she was behaving like a spoiled little rich girl. Worse, she was committing a sin as bad as her parents' by practicing reverse discrimination.

Since then, she had striven to base her judgments solely on the individual or the situation, not the balance of his or her bank account.

And she'd discovered that her major in human sexuality was something she enjoyed purely for the sake of enjoyment. Not because her parents choked whenever she discussed her studies at the dinner table.

She cleared her throat. "This isn't about money, Rick. It never was."

A heartbeat of a silence. "Then increase my salary. I won't mind."

She laughed and ran her toes along the sensitive bottom of her other foot.

"Enjoy your ride through the park, Gracie."

"I fully intend to."

She pressed the disconnect button and started to slip the phone back into her bag. Then she changed her mind and dialed her mother's number. A glance at her watch told her it was past eleven. After brunch with the church ladies. Before lunch at whatever auxiliary meeting.

"Mattias residence."

"*Hõla,* Consuela. It's Grace. Is Mom around terrorizing the place?"

A soft giggle, then, "Just this morning she sez to me, 'Consuela, I found wrinkle in bedspread. Completely unacceptable behavior. From now on make beds twice.'"

"Sounds like Mom all right." All too much like Mom. A

woman with a formidable education who had traded a career for her husband and daughter…and counting wrinkles in bedspreads. Gracie had never needed to look beyond her own mother for the reasons why she never wanted to marry. Her identity was too high a price to pay for a pair of warm feet to cuddle up to in bed at night. She'd always told herself she'd get a dog if she felt the need for constant companionship. Her parents' marriage was proof positive that men asked for too much and gave up too little. It was enough to pick up her own socks. She didn't want to have to pick up a husband's, as well.

She leaned back and smiled, watching the vivid colors of autumn in Central Park sweep by as Consuela filled her in on a punctuation-challenged litany of her mother's recent complaints. All of them nitpicky issues that probably would never have entered her mind if she looked beyond her house and husband and had a career of her own.

Consuela finally sighed, indicating she'd vented as much as she was going to that day. "You want you should talk to her?"

Gracie hesitated then bit her bottom lip. Not because she didn't want to talk to her mother. But because the view outside her window was absolutely breathtaking. Only in New York could you blink your eyes like Samantha on *Bewitched* and move from city chic to abundant nature so quickly. She sighed. "Yeah, put her on. I haven't done my bad deed for the day yet. I figure making her late for lunch should do it."

Consuela told her to hold the line.

Grace trailed a finger down the steamed inside of the taxi window. Once, when she'd been home for spring break in her second year of college, she'd had the temerity to ask her mother if she'd ever achieved an orgasm. Despite her ongoing attempts to shock both her parents to the point of sputtering, she'd asked the question out of curiosity. Her parents had never seemed to share a physical closeness. They spent more time apart than together. And when they were together, they seemed occupied talking about which party to attend and who they should be seen with. The only time Gracie saw her mother actually touch her father was when she was picking invisible lint off his jacket before they left for social events. Even then, she did it in such a way so that no more than her fingertips brushed the material. When Gracie's course material had concentrated on sexual frigidity, it was only natural that Gracie thought of her mother. Only natural that Gracie would want to apply her recently acquired knowledge to everyday life.

Her mother's answer to the orgasm question had been the only time Grace had been slapped.

"Good heavens, Consuela, can't you even see to the simple task of asking who it is?" Gracie heard her mother's voice come over the line, followed by, "Hello?"

"Hi, Mom."

"Gracie!" A fumbling of the phone. "Consuela, it's Gracie."

Gracie didn't want to cause any more trouble for the good-humored housekeeper by pointing out to her mother that Consuela and she had already spoken, but it took mammoth effort.

"Hi, darling. What a surprise it is hearing from you. You're never up this early."

"I'm working, Mom. I'm on that promotional tour, remember? I did a radio interview this morning in New York."

"Oh! Yes, of course. I must have forgotten."

Gracie tucked her chin into her chest and bit her lip. She wasn't sure if her mother actually did forget half the details of her only child's life, or whether she preferred to ignore them.

"So are you nervous? No, pretend I didn't ask that. I don't think I've ever seen you nervous. Besides, you have that radio show you do every week. Why would you be nervous?"

"Actually, Mom, this was a different format, so I was a bit

nervous. It's over though, so I'm feeling pretty pleased with myself." Gracie turned her head, watching as a young mother fastened the hood of a child's raincoat. She smiled wistfully. Had her mother ever stood out in the middle of a downpour completely unprotected to make sure she had *her* coat fastened securely? Not that she could remember. Sounded like something she'd have the nanny or housekeeper see to.

She blindly reached again into her monster purse. Bypassing the bag of peanuts, she instead slid out a copy of her book. "Have you received the book yet?"

"The book…oh, right! I'm sure we have. In fact, I'm positive that we have. It must be around here somewhere. Why just this morning I'm sure I saw Consuela sneaking a peek between the covers."

Ah, the self-protective reversion to "we" that her mother fell back on when she couldn't quite face things on her own. Gracie wondered exactly who "we" encompassed. Her mother and her father? The entire household? Or the entire city of Baltimore? Gracie slowly ran her finger over the raised lettering, wondering at the hypersensitivity of her fingertip. "And you? Have you read it, Mom?"

A pause. Then a sigh. "No, dear, I'm afraid I haven't. And I don't think I will, either, if it's all the same to you."

"It isn't all the same to me, Mom. I sent that copy especially for you. Not Dad. Not Consuela. It…" She sat up then straightened her skirt. An impossible task given its shortness. "It would mean a lot to me, Mom. I'd really like your input."

"Don't be ridiculous, Grace. What good would my input do now? You couldn't possibly change anything."

"I don't want to change anything. I just want you to read it. Can you do that for me?" Grace leaned her forehead against the glass, then rolled the window down and took a deep breath of the cool, damp air. Finally she laughed, then said,

"Never mind, Mom. I wouldn't want to make you do anything you're uncomfortable with."

"That's my girl. I knew you'd come around if we talked about it, dear."

But we haven't talked about it. I've talked, you've stonewalled. Just another day in the life and times of Grace and Priscilla Mattias.

At any rate, she supposed she should be grateful she hadn't gotten the usual "Grace, your biological clock's ticking… there's only a small number of suitable men out there and they're all being snatched up by other women…are you ever going to settle down and give me grandkids" speech that punctuated most of her conversations with her mother.

"If it makes any difference, I'm glad your interview went well, Grace. And I'm happy that things are going the way… well, the way that you want them."

What went unsaid was that "things" weren't going the way her mother wanted them. "Thanks, Mom. I appreciate you saying that." She leaned back into the seat and grabbed for her peanuts. Things *were* going just the way she wanted them. Her first book was taking off. She had her new bayside condo in Baltimore that was now being renovated. And she was enjoying every moment of making her own decisions without someone constantly breathing down her neck and asking her just what in the hell she thought she was doing.

She smiled to herself. Yes, she was very happy with her life, indeed. She popped a few peanuts into her mouth. "So tell me, Mom. Which problem do you hope to throw money at during lunch today?"

3

CHOPPED LIVER. THAT'S what he felt like after his bout with Dr. Gracie Mattias, pure and simple and bloody raw. Dylan cast a glance around the lobby. Tanja wasn't even around for him to vent at. She'd abandoned him outside the radio station, claiming she had family in the area and had scheduled to meet a friend for lunch, did he mind? He'd wanted to tell her yes, he did mind, but hadn't. He was afraid he'd sound too…demanding? Unbending? Whiny?

He cringed at the last description, realizing that's exactly what he was doing. He was whining. Just like a five-year-old who had his bike stolen, training wheels and all.

It was ridiculous, really. Overall the interview had gone well. Toward the end he had even begun to enjoy himself, giving as good as he got when it came to trading digs with the sex doctor.

Jesus, had he really just thought of her as the sex doctor? If so, what did that make him? The anti-sex doctor?

He didn't want to begin to analyze that bizarre train of thought.

Dylan poked at the elevator button again, somehow managing a half-assed smile in the general direction of a young couple who had just stepped in from the rain to stand next to him. Their cheerful, attentive-to-each-other disposition made his disposition even darker.

"This is the first day of the rest of our lives."

Dylan grimaced, then nodded at the young woman to show he had heard.

"We just got married." The man looped his arms around the woman and tugged her closer. "This is the first day of our honeymoon."

"Congratulations." Dylan forced a closemouthed smile then turned back toward the elevator.

Kissing noises sounded beside him. He rubbed the back of his neck, wondering where the stairs were, and whether he was up to climbing seventeen floors. "Uh," he began, interrupting the couple from their amorous pursuits. "A word of warning. When the elevator stops, you may want to make sure it's actually on the floor you want."

The couple looked at him, then each other, sporting quizzical expressions he had been sorely tempted to bestow on a few of his more…interesting patients. Like the one who got into wearing women's silk stockings under his Brooks Brothers business suits when he appeared in Superior Court.

He cleared his throat. "I found out the hard way that they don't always do that. The elevators. You know, stop on the floor you want. Creates a bit of a…mess." Although he really couldn't call what had happened this morning a mess. An unfortunate mishap, maybe. A wild accident. But definitely not a mess. Not when a man got to take a peek at a woman of Gracie Mattias's caliber.

"Um, thanks."

"Don't mention it."

Finally, a ding. The elevator doors opened. Dylan stepped in and to the back, automatically making room for the couple. He reached around them and pushed the button for his floor.

"Hold that elevator!"

Dylan clenched his jaw and covertly reached around the

couple to punch the close button. All he wanted was to get back to his room, shrug out of his damp clothes, then review his schedule for the next two weeks. Make a list of things to have Tanja see to. First and foremost, making sure that he knew exactly who he was going to be up against in coming interviews.

"Thanks." A breathless someone stuck her hand between the closing doors, then slid in between them.

Dylan stood a little straighter, willing the doors to close before someone else could delay his ascension to his room and sweet peace.

"It's you."

Dylan jerked to stare at the late arrival. And nearly dropped to his knees. Which wouldn't have been an inappropriate response given the woman he was staring at. He hadn't noticed at the radio station, but Dr. Grace Mattias was tall. Nearly as tall as he was at six foot. A goddess. No, no, Galatea in the Pygmalion tale. Galatea, the statue Pygmalion had crafted of the perfect mate. Aphrodite had taken pity on the poor guy and brought the statue to life because of Pygmalion's deep love for the inanimate object. That's who Grace reminded him of. Even more with her damp hair curving against the skin of her cheeks and neck. Tiny droplets plopped against her soaked white tank, drawing his gaze to the hardened tips of her breasts.

Heat, sure and swift, swept through his groin and he fought the urge to groan aloud. Gracie Mattias wasn't destined for wife and motherhood as Galatea had been. No, she was put on earth solely to torture men like him with her oozing sensuality and provocative ways.

She cocked her head slightly to the side and gave him a hesitant smile, as though trying to analyze what was going on in his head. He'd be better off remembering that Gracie was completely capable of doing just that. He immediately snapped straighter.

"Don't look so shocked," she said. "I think we've already, um, established that we're staying at the same hotel."

The couple with their arms wrapped around each other looked their way. "In separate rooms," Dylan pointed out.

"Of course in separate rooms. We don't even know each other."

Dylan grimaced. "From the sound of it, that's not necessarily something that would stop you."

"Ooh, that was a low blow, Dr. Dylan. We're not on the radio show anymore. You can put the jabs away now."

He dipped his chin and managed a wry grin. "Sorry. That was kind of a cheap shot, wasn't it?"

"Bargain basement."

He slanted her a gaze from the corner of his eye. She seemed completely unconcerned with her disheveled appearance. This was at odds with her carefully put together front for the radio host. She didn't make apologies and utter some inane comment about how she must look. She didn't move to get a hairbrush from the depths of the huge handbag slung over her shoulder. And she didn't try to repair her makeup. He wondered exactly how long she had been out in the rain.

He took a deep breath, pulling in a subtle, tangy scent that hovered somewhere between juicy, overripe oranges and tart, green apples. Her shampoo, maybe. Though it wasn't beyond the realm of possibility that she, herself, naturally smelled like the succulent fruit.

"Excuse me, do you mind if I take a look?"

Dylan blinked at the young woman standing in front of him. The bride was gesturing toward the window behind him that overlooked the vast lobby as they moved upward.

"Sorry. Sure, go ahead."

She did. And took her new husband with her.

Dylan stood ramrod straight in front of the closed elevator doors. Gracie joined him.

"Newlyweds," he said quietly.

"Ah."

A dull thump sounded from behind him. Dylan looked over his shoulder to find that the newlyweds had apparently taken in enough of the view and were now taking in each other. His eyes widened as the woman practically climbed up on the man. The man's hand skimmed her side then cupped her behind the knee. In a smooth move, he lifted her leg then thrust his body against her softness.

Dylan jerked back to face the elevator doors.

"Exhibitionists," Gracie whispered.

He looked at her blankly. "Rude."

She tossed her head back and laughed. "Come on, Dr. Dylan, I should think that since they're married almost anything should go in your book."

He jabbed a thumb over his shoulder. "Nowhere did I write that this was acceptable behavior."

Gracie's deep, deep brown eyes held amusement. "I meant figuratively, not literally."

"Oh."

She held up a finger. "Speaking of which." She began rummaging through her bulging bag, then tugged something out with a little resistance. "Here."

He stared at the book she held as if he was afraid it might bite. Seeing as it was her book, he wasn't taking any chances.

"I had one left over from the stack my publisher sent to the station. Go on, take it."

He did.

"I figure that you were caught at a bit of a disadvantage this morning. You know, having not reviewed my theories and all."

He held up the magazine tucked under his arm still opened to the page focusing on her. "I wasn't as uninformed as you think."

"Oh, my God! Can I see that? How did you get ahold of a

copy so quickly? Rick, that's my assistant, hasn't said a word about its release."

Dylan reluctantly let the magazine go. He stood silently wishing the elevator would get to his floor already as Gracie silently read the piece. He tensed at her little bursts of laughter, trying to ignore the low moans coming from the couple behind them. Then she flipped the magazine over to where he was featured. Dylan gave in to the urge to work his finger inside his overtight collar.

"Says here you're married."

"Divorced."

"Oh, baby," the bride moaned.

Dylan noticed that Gracie sneaked a glance at the couple, her brows jumping high on her forehead. She turned forward again, color touching her cheeks. Dylan didn't even want to think of what it would take to shock the shocking sex doctor. She leaned closer to him, giving him another whiff of her fruity scent. "Um, I wouldn't look back there if I were you."

"I wasn't planning to."

The elevator finally drew to a stop. *There is a God.* The doors slid open and Dylan immediately began to step out. Away from the groping newlyweds. Far, far away from the enticing Dr. Mattias.

Gracie slapped the magazine against his chest. "This is how you got yourself in trouble the last time. This is my stop, remember?" Her smile held mischief and amusement as she got out then held the doors open with her hand. "Would you like to know what my recommended course for therapy would be for you, Dr. Dylan?"

His gaze drifted to where her breasts pressed against the flimsy material of her tank, the lace of her bra clearly visible beneath the damp fabric.

"I mean, given what I know about you so far, which isn't a whole lot outside of your book."

He jerked his gaze back to her face. "I'm not sure I want to hear this."

"Good, because I'm going to tell you anyway." She flipped her wet hair over a mostly bare shoulder. "What you need is a nice, traditional wild turn in the sack. And I'd recommend you see to it posthaste."

Dylan nearly choked on whatever response he would have made as she waggled her fingers at him then sashayed down the hall. And *sashay* was the word for it. Finally the doors slid shut. He closed his eyes and swallowed as an article of clothing he didn't even want to try to identify landed next to his left foot, no doubt compliments of the couple behind him.

WILD TURN IN THE SACK, INDEED. Dylan set about the nerve-calming, erotic-image-banishing task of unpacking his solitary suitcase. Something he would have had a chance to do earlier had he not accidentally interrupted Gracie Mattias's shower that morning. Something he would be doing efficiently now if not for her inflammatory words. With quick, irritated movements, he rehung his blue shirt next to his navy slacks, well away from his tan jacket. Not that it mattered. He was scheduled to be in New York for only another day anyway. Tomorrow afternoon he was scheduled for a brief interview with a reporter from a top psychology magazine, then he was flying to St. Louis.

He decisively closed the closet doors then sat down to take off his shoes. Only then did he grow aware of his semi-aroused state. He closed his eyes, determined to ignore the physical messages his body was sending him. He stripped out of his damp clothes and put on the hotel robe. There. He felt better already.

His sexual reaction to Gracie didn't surprise him. He was only human after all. And she was one hundred percent female in heat. It's how he acted on that basic, fundamental response that differentiated him from a mindless animal. Humans, in general, had the ability to make conscious decisions. While many still subscribed to the "I couldn't help myself, it was an accident" philosophy when it came to extramarital affairs, the argument had never held much water for him. A man could always help himself. There was nothing accidental about falling into bed with a woman. In fact, whenever one of his patients tried using the excuse on him, he usually came back with something along the lines of "Right. So what you're telling me is that you just tripped and fell right into her vagina."

He carefully hung his suit on the towel warmer in the bathroom, smoothed out the wrinkles, then walked back into the other room. He sat down at the desk, eyed his laptop, the phone, then settled his gaze on Gracie's book. *Sex is Not a Four-Letter Word—Smashing Sexual Conventions.* The title was spelled across a glossy white cover in pink and gold raised lettering. He pushed it aside and picked up the telephone receiver instead. Maybe he'd be able to get through to Diana.

A brief knock sounded at the door, then Tanja breezed right in. "Can you believe this rain? Isn't it awesome?"

"My words, exactly." Dylan grimaced at her. "You know you might want to think twice about just walking in here like that. You never know when you might catch me…in various stages of undress."

"I should be so lucky." She stopped in the middle of the room, hands on slender hips, even the purple spikes of her hair seeming to radiate energy. "Come on, Doc, you're not the type to walk around your own apartment in your birthday suit, so there's no real danger there, is there?"

"Coulter, Connor and Caplain, Attorneys-at-Law."

Dylan stopped glowering at Tanja then asked to be put through to Diana. He drummed his fingers against the desktop, then slid Gracie's book into the drawer before the PR rep could spot it. Four rings, then he was put through to Diana's voice mail.

Tanja pried the receiver from his hand and soundly hung it up. "You can call whoever that was back when we get to Chicago."

"Hey! I was just about to leave the number where I could be contacted."

"It's changing so what's the point?" She swung the closet doors open, eyed the contents, then took out his suitcase and launched it toward the bed. Moments later, his clothes followed.

"What do you mean Chicago? We're supposed to be going to St. Louis next. And that's not until tomorrow."

"Change in plans."

"Change in plans?" He caught another launch of his neatly pressed clothes and tried to save them further wrinkling. "Don't I have a say in that?"

Tanja stared at him, tapping her black-painted nail against her lips. "Nope." She chose a couple of items from the pile and thrust them against his chest. "Get dressed. Our plane leaves in an hour."

"What about the interview tomorrow?"

"Small-time."

Feeling stupid, he turned to follow her thorough and completely shameless invasion of his privacy. "What's in Chicago?"

Tanja stopped hooking his toiletries into his bag and grinned at him. "Only the most popular televised talk show in the country."

"I thought that was Rosie."

"Yeah, but Rosie wouldn't give us the entire hour." She stuffed the shaving bag into his arms. "With one condition."

He frowned, clutching his things for dear life. "What condition?"

"That you share the spotlight with one very controversial Dr. Grace Mattias."

For the second time in an hour, Dylan found himself sputtering for a response. "No way...not a chance in hell...over my dead body..." The objections tumbled from his mouth one right after the other, having little or no impact on Tanja as she put his laptop away.

"Come on, Dylan, you guys made quite the team this morning. Everyone loved you. You pulled in some of the highest ratings the show has ever seen."

His brows shot up. "We did?" He'd never gotten high ratings in any of his promotional efforts before. Hell, he hadn't been able to give away his first book, and it had never gone to a second printing. The thought that he may have reached not just someone but a wide range of someones today...well, that was what this was all about, wasn't it? It might mean a turning of the tides. Instead of days filled juggling patients with teaching, he could reach a nationwide audience. Command impressive fees for speaking appearances. Prove once and for all that his parents were wrong and he was right.

Tanja smiled at him and added his briefcase to his overloaded arms. "You did." She turned him around, then patted his bottom. "Now get a move on, Doc. We've got a plane to catch."

4

Chicago

A KITCHEN.

Well, maybe not a kitchen, but definitely a kitchenette. One of those kinds that you could barely move around in but held all the basic necessities, like a new microwave, an old stove and an empty refrigerator. Gracie was vaguely aware of the door closing after the bellboy as she stood staring at the cramped space immediately to the left in the enormous Chicago hotel room. She'd come across a place like this once before, in Fort Lauderdale. Likely this wing used to be an apartment complex that had been converted to a hotel. A quick glance around the spacious living-dining area, and the bedroom and bath to the right, fueled her speculation.

The strap to her laptop-carrying case slid off her shoulder. She allowed the case to drop slowly to the floor, enraptured with her new find. She hadn't had grains of salt under her fingernails since she began this crazy promotional tour. She opened and closed cabinet doors, peered into the empty but cold refrigerator, eyed the limited number of pots and pans, all with a ridiculous grin on her face. Someone watching might have thought she'd unearthed Atlantis instead of a chipped old stove, but she was beyond caring. She'd been in dire straits ever since she and Rick had caught dinner at a poor excuse for a Thai restaurant last night in New York and she had itched to get back into the restaurant kitchen to show the clueless Greek owner how it should be done. Instead, Rick had guided her out of there before she irreversibly embarrassed someone. Like herself.

Gracie ran her hand across the clean counter then straightened the miniature coffeemaker. Okay, so the place didn't even come close to resembling her own state-of-the-art kitchen in Baltimore, but it was workable. Truth be told, she'd done a lot with much less in her first apartment, right after she'd graduated from college. Back when she had been determined to strike out on her own, pull her own weight and ignore the checks from her father's accountant that piled up, unopened, on the scratched desk near the door that bore at least three dead bolts and countless chains and security devices. She'd never been prouder than when she'd made that little one-room place home. And she'd learned the finer points of making do with what one had. A trying but immensely gratifying experience. Especially when all her hard work had landed her a spot with a midlevel psychiatric practice before branching out on her own four years later.

She leaned against the wall and tapped a finger against her lips. A list. She had to make a list of what she needed from the store. The essentials were here. She wouldn't have to invest in salt and pepper or sugar. The hotel had provided coffee and a small selection of teas, though she always traveled with her own supply ordered specially from Arizona.

What should she make? Something simple, requiring the fewest ingredients. But something that would fill the small place with a delectable aroma and would go with a good bottle of red wine. No, white. Fish. She was in Chicago, wasn't she? Surely they would have a good selection of fish. Waking up to the smell of fish would remind her of home if not endear her to her neighbors.

A brief call to the concierge gave her directions to a small family-owned grocer a couple of blocks away. She hung up the phone on his offer to have an order placed on her behalf, then grabbed her purse and headed for the elevators.

A small cowbell above the advertisement-covered door announced her arrival at the grocer. No larger than the hotel room she had just left, the neat grocer had a good selection nonetheless. And plenty of fresh produce. As she happily made her selections, she allowed her mind to wander at will. Although only after 5:00 p.m. central time, darkness enveloped the street, weaving a web of billowed intimacy Gracie embraced. Chicago's climate was similar to New York's, albeit windier, earning the architecturally rich city its name, but it had an altogether different atmosphere. The unique, laid-back flavor of the Midwest was laced throughout despite the city's valiant efforts to shrug it off. And the people weren't as cynical, the lapping waves of Lake Michigan against the coast seeming to lull them into a feeling of peace.

"Can I see the trout, please? Yes, that one. To the left." Grace accepted the paper-protected fish from the woman behind the counter and examined the clear condition of the eyes and the pinkness of the gills. She stared down into the open mouth, the sight comically reminding her of Dr. Dylan Fairbanks's reaction when she'd told him he needed to get laid.

She handed the fish back. "I'll take it."

She added the item to her basket and turned toward the produce section. While Dr. Dylan's facial expression had resembled that of the trout, she had the distinct impression that he was anything but a cold fish. Something elemental lurked in his green eyes. A maturity, an intensity, an innate sexuality that made it difficult to meet his gaze head-on initially, yet held you captive thereafter. An intriguing paradox that reminded her how her skin had tingled after their meeting at the radio station. How verbally sparring with him had made her wonder what going a couple of rounds with him in bed might be like.

He *was* a sex therapist, so she didn't doubt he'd know all the exciting little details. But there was a difference between knowing and practicing. And she suspected that Dr. Dylan would put into practice everything he'd learned.

A shiver shimmied down the length of her spine, making her feel suddenly warm in her light raincoat.

Absently adding a couple of lemons to her basket, she moved on to pick through lettuce. An idea danced along the fringes of her thoughts and she unsuccessfully tried to grasp it. She envisioned her book. No, no, it didn't have anything to do with her mother's refusal to read it. She made a face, banishing the image of Priscilla's tight-lipped face before it could spring roots. She moved to the tomatoes, testing them and adding a couple to her groceries. Rick? Did it have anything to do with her assistant and his mysterious company that morning in his New York hotel room? No, that wasn't it, either. Although the idea of a couple struggling against twisted sheets did ring a distant bell. Either that, or someone else had just entered the grocery store.

She edged along peppers and mushrooms then came to a halt before a large display of cucumbers. She slowly picked one up.

The bell rang louder. And along with it came a vivid image of Dr. Dylan Fairbanks's grinning face when they'd discussed masturbation.

Stumbling right in on the heels of the image was her sheer terror when the radio shock jock had asked Dr. Dylan whether or not he was a born-again virgin. She'd barely registered his response, so afraid that the host would shine that "virginal" light on her. Thankfully, he hadn't. But that did nothing to assuage her longstanding fear that someday, someone *would* ask her the question, despite her carefully made-up appearance of being one hundred percent hot tamale who practiced the very advice she preached. And then where would she be? Not that she was a virgin by any stretch of the imagination. But she wasn't what she pretended to be, either.

Leading up to the promotional tour, she'd been petrified of being fingered for a fraud. Her theory on the need for sexual safaris was the greatest of her unpracticed advice. She remembered seeing an interview once with a marriage counselor who had never been married. The host had virtually thrown the psychologist's advice right out the window, despite her years of backbreaking field research. Of course it had been one of those late-night, openly televised forums where the host made a point of going for the cheap shots. But the fact remained that if her limited sexual experience were to come to light, her hope of getting her word out would be little more than a car left abandoned at the side of the road with its hood up.

She absently ran the pad of her thumb over the prickly exterior of the cucumber, the innocuous movement sending a thrill of awareness over her skin. There was no denying that she was attracted to Dr. Dylan, though she firmly limited her attraction to him to physical attributes. What other reasons were there for being attracted to him? She didn't know him. She knew some of his stuffy opinions, but that was a far cry from knowing the full man.

Who wouldn't be attracted to him physically? He was tall, enigmatic, handsome as all get-out and downright sexy.

And the concept of a sexual safari with him posed a decadently intriguing challenge, indeed....

She stood stock-still for a full minute, staring blindly at the cucumber she still held, her mind growing sluggish as it put two and two together. Then everything snapped together. Her heart did an erratic flip in her chest as she tripped straight over the path her subconscious had been trying to lead her down for the past few minutes.

That was it! She needed to put on her safari gear and bag one sexy prey in the shape of Dr. Dylan Fairbanks. Mussing some bed sheets with him would put an end to her feelings of being a fraud.

The earth began rotating again, and along with it a show of thigh-quivering mental images. A bare, sculpted torso. Strong, hair-covered legs. Ragged breathing. Soft, needy cries. Slick, sweat-covered skin. A pulse-throbbing erection pressed against soft flesh, preparing to enter.

Gracie's breath caught as she swallowed against the saliva gathering at the back of her throat. She shakily patted her hair. Okay, the prospect of sleeping with Dylan clearly wasn't offensive. She gave a feeble laugh. Who was she kidding? She was practically wetting herself just thinking about it.

Trying to get a grip on herself, she considered that sleeping with Dr. Dylan could have some drawbacks. After all, he wasn't a nameless, handsome face picked out at random in a neutral gaming zone.

She put back the cucumber she held and picked up one of the larger ones.

She would get the once-in-a-lifetime chance to prove beyond a shadow of a doubt that Dr. Dylan Fairbanks and his ancient, out-of-whack philosophies were way off base.

She added the cucumber to her basket, and couldn't help noticing the suddenly rubbery condition of her knees, and the anticipatory searing heat that rushed through her bloodstream.

Yes. Hunting Dr. Dylan was exactly what she needed to do…

DYLAN OPENED THE DOOR to the small grocer's, grimacing at the sound of the cowbell announcing his arrival. Right now he just wanted to blend in with the background. Carve out a little privacy so he could start thinking straight again. Not that the hokey cowbell prevented that. Rather the bright yellow V-necked sweater and olive-green cargo pants he had on pretty much ruled out blending in with the background.

He tugged at the too-snug shirt material, telling himself for the fifth time since leaving the hotel that he should have left his suit on. But after the soaking it had taken in New York, then the wrinkling on the plane, he wasn't sure it was salvageable, much less wearable. The morning's mishaps had slid into a day full of disasters—the latest debacle being the loss of his luggage—and he had little choice but to allow Tanja to go shopping for him. Why didn't it surprise him that the PR rep had completely ignored his express instructions to find something suitable, something he would buy for himself and instead bought him a temporary wardrobe more suited for a teenager than a responsible adult?

He felt like a…break-dancer.

He cringed. Boy, he'd just dated himself there, hadn't he? In all honesty, he had no idea what a kid on the cutting edge of fashion was called nowadays. And he'd had no idea what to do when Tanja had given him a tart little wave and disappeared on him…again.

At least one thing was going in his favor. The instant he'd discovered the kitchen in his hotel room, he found the perfect opportunity to temporarily place his budget and himself on a diet. Though it had been years since he'd had to worry about money, and weight had never been a problem, waste was something he'd never been very good at. A habit that stemmed directly from his parents.

Finally freeing a pint-size cart from the one it was attached to, he turned the corner and promptly bumped into an older gentleman. He was rerouting a path around him when he realized the guy was eyeing the prophylactics section. He did a double take, not wanting to see the man who was old enough to be his grandfather read the back of a package that touted the words *colored, ribbed*.

"Sorry," Dylan said under his breath, and headed down the next aisle.

He reminded himself that his foul mood wasn't the result of what he'd just seen—although it hadn't helped any. His foul mood had gotten worse when he'd taken his seat on the plane to Chicago and found himself sitting across the aisle and one row back from one Miss Hottie. A woman who not only hadn't seemed to notice him, but kept crossing her long, long legs in a way that had been…well, downright distracting. He hadn't checked, but he was certain he had a bruise from where the businessman sitting next to him kept elbowing him in order to get a better look.

He checked the price for a box of shredded wheat, frowned, then put the box back. He pushed the crippled cart down the aisle, idly wondering what the sex doctor had on tap for tonight. And who those plans included.

He slowed in front of the frozen food section. Only two freezers, but the essentials for the single professional on the move were all there. And a good deal more affordable than the box of cereal he'd just placed back on the shelf. Not that he didn't have money. But given the way he was raised… well, he wanted to be frugal. On occasion that meant forgoing his favorite cereal for a cheap TV dinner.

He reached in and grabbed the brand on sale and tossed it into his cart, telling himself he'd only succumb to buying it if nothing else popped out at him.

He resumed warring with the uncooperative cart. It didn't help matters that every time he moved, the metal thingies on the side pockets of the unfamiliar pants clinked. He glanced down, wondering how much damage he would do if he just ripped them off. Who wanted to make so much noise? A young woman with a small boy watched him as he passed. He managed a polite smile. Just barely. He wished something else would hurry up and grab his attention before he gave up and went back to the hotel to nuke the frozen dinner.

He had turned the corner to the produce section when something grabbed his attention all right. More accurately, *someone.*

He tried to pull the cart to a halt, only to have the front wheels fight him and end up crashing against a display for canned beans. Dylan hardly noticed. Despite the fact that Grace Mattias had her back turned to him, there was no mistaking all that red hair. Did the woman always dress like that when going to the market? While he couldn't make out much of her legs, he'd recognize those shoes anywhere. And her white raincoat was cinched tightly at the waist, emphasizing her trim figure.

He glanced around, trying to determine if she was alone. Judging by the basket she carried, and the absence of any hovering, panting male, he surmised she probably was.

Though why he should care, he didn't want to begin to explore. Lord knows, he was the last man who wanted to be hovering or panting over a woman like Gracie.

Still, he found himself watching her as she picked up a pear, running her fingertips along the odd-shaped fruit, then lifting it to her nose. He swallowed hard at the thorough, thoughtful inspection, then opened his mouth, as if about to take a bite of the fruit she held himself. He caught himself and snapped his teeth together. She put the pear back on the display, then began to turn. Dylan quickly pretended interest in the items next to him. *Peaches.* Figured.

There was no reason to think Grace would recognize him. Hell, *he* didn't even recognize him. He couldn't have looked more different from this morning had he tried. Which, of course, he hadn't. But maybe Tanja's bad taste had its advantages. The last thing he wanted was to engage in conversation with Gracie Mattias so soon. It was bad enough he'd have to appear with her tomorrow after what she'd said to him before leaving the elevator in New York. To have her see him here, alone…well, he could only imagine what she'd have to say about *that*.

"Why, if it isn't the world's most prominent sex expert."

Dylan nearly crushed the overripe peach in his hand at the sound of Gracie's voice. He fought the desire to play it off, glance around as if to question who she was talking to. But the way she'd addressed him left no doubt to whom she was speaking. And pretending otherwise would only make him look…more desperate.

He turned his head, managing surprise. Which wasn't difficult because a scene from an Al Pacino movie suddenly sprang to mind. Pacino had met the heroine-slash-suspected-serial-killer at a small market just like this one. She'd also been wearing a raincoat…and had nothing on underneath it.

Something warm and wet dripped between his fingers. He glanced down to find he'd pulverized the peach.

To his chagrin, Grace's smile widened. "Don't tell me. You have a kitchen, too."

"Kitchen?" he repeated dumbly, reaching for a handkerchief that wasn't there. What good were so many pockets if they didn't hold anything?

She handed him a paper towel she'd torn from an overhead holder. "Yes. My hotel room has a kitchen. Well, a kitchenette really, and I decided to cook. I naturally assumed that was the reason you were here, as well. We must be in the same…hotel. Again. Which only makes sense if the show's putting us up."

She made a production of looking into his cart. Which made the fact that the only item in there was a frozen dinner that much worse.

"Sense. Yes." Dylan wondered if sleep was going to be anywhere on his itinerary of things to do now that he knew Gracie would be showering…er, sleeping under the same roof.

She straightened, shifting her full basket from one hand to

the other. "You know, since you're obviously eating alone—" she gestured toward the cart "—and I have plans to…eat alone, why don't we eat alone together?" Her smile had the strangest effect on him. "I'll even let you get the wine. After all, it's not like either of us has to drive home or anything."

"Wine…"

It suddenly slammed into him that Gracie Mattias was actually inviting him to her place, her room, for dinner.

It also occurred to him that she was coming on to him stronger than Limburger cheese.

But why would she be coming on to him? Yes, there had been a certain provocative quality about their conversations thus far, but they'd seemed harmless enough. And when she'd suggested in the elevator that he needed a wild turn in the sack, she hadn't indicated she saw herself as a player in that particular scenario.

She reached around him to sample the peaches, giving him an undiluted whiff of her subtle perfume. He found himself fighting a groan.

"Um, I don't think that would be a very good idea."

She turned her head to glance at him, putting her enticing mouth mere inches away from his. "What wouldn't?"

He gestured helplessly, his words lost somewhere between his chest and his mouth. "The peaches," he said finally. "They're never as good as when they're in season."

Well, that didn't make much sense. He'd meant to say he didn't think it would be a good idea if they had dinner together. Alone. In one or the other of their hotel rooms.

He stood straighter. And why wouldn't it be a good idea? Because Gracie was wildly attractive? Certainly even he was adult enough to keep his libido in check during something as innocent as dinner. He hadn't been looking forward to spending the night alone. Over the past five days, he'd had his fill of alone. He could do with a little company. And if there was one thing he'd learned, it was that keeping company with Gracie Mattias was anything but boring.

Wasn't this what he had signed on for when he'd decided to write his latest book? To sway people to his way of thinking? What better method to do that than by having dinner with his leading adversary? He'd certainly had his share of tough sells. She couldn't be any tougher than those he'd encountered thus far. He'd tried to prove Gracie wrong on the public front. Perhaps a more private one would do the trick.

"My place," he said, giving her a room number. "You bring the food, and I'll supply the wine."

"Isn't it usually the other way around?"

He gave her a grin of his own. "Yes, well, I got the impression that you don't like to do anything the old-fashioned way, Dr. Mattias."

"Then your powers of observation are better than I thought." She nodded. "Okay. But that means you have to supply dessert."

Dylan's stomach dropped to his groin. The way she said the word made him think all sorts of decadent thoughts that included—but certainly weren't limited to—licking whipped cream off sexy Gracie's mouth…and other more sensitive places.

Maybe this wasn't such a good idea.…

Grace began walking away. "See you in an hour, Dr. Dylan. Oh, and make that white wine, will you?"

DYLAN TORE OPEN THE PACKAGE of assorted cookies, cursing when they flung to the far corners of the counter, everywhere but on the plate he had put out to hold them. Cookies and milk, he'd decided, was as wholesome a dessert as ever there was. Gracie didn't have to know it had taken him longer to chose the dessert than it had to find a decent bottle of wine. Anything involving strawberries, sticky chocolate, or that had a smooth consistency, he'd instantly ruled out. Day-old, crunchy cookies were the only thing that had fit the bill.

He piled the cookies onto a plate then angled into the dining area. He'd set the small table a little earlier but now stood staring at it. The whole setting looked somehow too intimate, too…suggestive. Too much like a scene for seduction.

Wrong.

He'd agreed to this little meeting solely to try to bring her around to his way of thinking. Placing the cookies on the table, he decided the overhead light wasn't bright enough. He circled around the room, flicking on every lamp in the place, then flicked on the television and tuned in CNN. A quick trip into the kitchen found the wine he'd been letting breathe on the table resting instead on the counter. After he'd propped his briefcase along with his laptop onto the dining table next to the place settings, he stood back. There. Everything looked more casual. More businesslike. More like the last thing on his mind was sampling Gracie Mattias instead of her food.

He grimaced and rubbed his stubble-covered chin. If that was the last thing on his mind, then why did it spring forth so quickly?

The phone rang on the table in the corner, breaking his thought cleanly in two. He glanced at his watch, then stepped to pluck up the receiver.

"Dylan, it's Tanja."

He frowned, wondering at the sound of pulsating music in the background. "She lives." And apparently better than he did, if the music was any indication.

"Look, I just got a call from your editor. Is your cell phone switched on?"

Dylan glanced toward his briefcase where the instrument in question lay silent on top of some papers. "I don't think I turned it on after the flight. Why?"

"Because that Diana you've been trying to contact has been trying to call you, that's why."

"Oh, shit." Dylan glanced again at the time. He firmly told himself that he hadn't forgotten Diana. After all the day's disasters, and last-minute change in plans, he'd just been... distracted, that's all. And his state of mind had absolutely nothing to do with Grace Mattias. At least not on a personal level. His interest in her was strictly professional.

The sound of a brass horn through the receiver nearly deafened him. "Tanja, where are you?"

"At a jazz joint, of course. Have you never been to Chicago before, Dylan?"

Oh, he'd been to Chicago. Several times. But he'd never even thought about going to a jazz joint.

He found the idea strangely appealing now.

He raked his hand through his hair. "Shouldn't you be preparing for tomorrow? Seeing as all this sprang up at the last minute—"

"Everything's taken care of, Dylan. Leave it to me."

He grimaced. He'd left more to her than he should have and look where that had gotten him. Holed up in a Chicago hotel room in clothes that made him want to turn on rap music. "Tell me why I'm not reassured."

"Because you're a control freak, that's why." Her laugh took some of the sting out of her words. "Have a good night, Doc. I'll see you in the morning."

Dylan began to tell her not to hang up, but couldn't get the words out before the dial tone buzzed in his ear. Slowly he replaced the receiver in its cradle. A jazz joint? Any hardworking PR person would be mapping out a list of approved questions for tomorrow's host to ask. Working on a briefing strategy so that he would come away from the interview looking his best. Oh, but not his PR rep. Tanja was too busy hanging out at a jazz joint to do something as tedious as her job.

Stepping to the dining table, he took his cell phone from his briefcase. He had, indeed, neglected to turn it back on after the flight. He pressed the auto dial for Diana's number in San Francisco at the same time a knock sounded at the front door. Listening to the line ring, he pulled open the door to find Gracie standing in the hall smiling at him.

"Room service," she said, breezing past him into the room.

Clutching the phone to his ear, he turned to watch her walk by. Her formfitting white tank top skimmed over generous breasts. And her very short skirt fit across her pert little bottom.

Dylan nearly dropped the cell phone when it stopped ringing. "Hello."

"Hi—"

"You've reached the residence of…"

He yanked the phone away from his ear and stared at it. He'd fallen for it again. Turning from where Grace watched him curiously, he finished listening to Diana's directives, then left a brief message outlining where he was and where she could get ahold of him. When he glanced back at the table, he found Grace had unpacked the food she'd brought along and sat inelegantly munching on a chunk of fresh French bread. "Phone tag, huh?"

Dylan stepped to the table and tossed his cell phone back into his open briefcase. "Yeah."

She tucked her long, curly red hair behind her ear and smiled up at him. "Always fun."

Dylan's gaze was still plastered to her ear and the hair she had tucked behind it. Diana's hair was blond and short and neat. Gracie's was red, curly and…wild. Still, he'd never stared at Diana's hair this way. "Yeah…fun."

She didn't seem to notice his inattention and her smile took on a decidedly teasing quality. "Hope it's not anything important."

"Huh?"

She gestured toward the phone he'd put down. "The call."

"Oh. No. Not really." Just the rest of his life, that's all.

"Well, come and get it while it's hot."

Dylan nearly swallowed his tongue whole. "Huh?" he finally managed to squeeze out after much, too much, time had gone by.

She laughed. An unspeakably sexy sound that would be right at home at that jazz joint Tanja was at. "The food. It's best if eaten hot."

"Ah." He sat down, trying to hide the reduction of his vocabulary down to sounds rather than words. That proved one of the points he made in his book. "Steer well away from women who leave you tongue-tied. It's during those encounters that you begin thinking with parts of your body not related to your brain." He nearly laughed aloud.

Gracie speared a piece of fish and slid it into her mouth. After swallowing, she asked, "Are you going to share the joke? Or am I the joke?"

"It's nothing. Just thinking about what someone said. Not related to you, I assure you." He found himself putting his paper napkin in his lap and stopped himself. "This looks good."

As a single male who didn't often make the effort for himself, he appreciated a nicely prepared meal. And this one was indeed well prepared. The items were so well put together, had he not seen the fish and vegetables in her basket at the market he would have suspected she'd ordered it in. He squinted at her. Which, of course, was still a possibility.

He then realized he'd forgotten the wine in the kitchen. Excusing himself, he went to retrieve it. She apparently recognized the vintage and she hummed with appreciation. He filled her glass, then his own, then reseated himself.

After her ceaseless repartee earlier in the day, her sudden silence proved unnerving to him. So much so that when she reached across him for the bread by his arm, he nearly jumped out of his cargo pants.

She laughed quietly. "Boy, you're wound up, aren't you?"

He rubbed the back of his neck. "It's been a long day."

"I don't know. I've had worse."

He'd had, too, but he thought it best to leave the conversation there lest she discover his behavior had nothing to do with the day and more to do with her nearness.

He watched her fork a sprig of asparagus then nibble on the end. The fish in his mouth turned to sandpaper and he was suddenly incapable of swallowing it.

Sure sign number one that his interest in her was taking a seriously wrong turn.

He forced his gaze back to his plate, wishing he'd turned up the sound on the television. The silence that stretched between them left too much room for thought. And chased away every last argument he'd hoped to make tonight.

Gracie's appearance wasn't helping matters much. Though he suspected that no matter what she was wearing, Gracie Mattias would ooze enough sex appeal to start World War III. That appeal wound its way around him, cocooning him in some sort of sensual haze that almost made him dizzy.

She quietly cleared her throat. A sound that should have been normal, but was somehow low and suggestive coming from her. Almost like a feline purr. "So, Dr. Dylan, how long has it been for you?"

He nearly choked on his wine. "Pardon me?"

Grace motioned toward the food on the table. "How long has it been since you've had a home-cooked meal?" Her brown eyes sparkled. "Why? What did you think I meant?"

He decided to come straight out with it. He might feel dumb, but he was a little sick of playing it. "Sex."

He was satisfied by her sudden coughing fit. He handed her her water glass. When that didn't seem to work, he gave her a soft, then a harder thump on the back. She finally spat out into her napkin whatever was lodged in her throat. "Gad, talk about bad table manners. Martha Stewart would be crushed." She fanned her reddened cheeks with one hand, took a drink of water with her other. She smiled. "Thanks."

"Don't mention it." The incident should have served as a bucket of ice-cold water to his libido, but instead the heat generated from the brief, innocuous touch of his hand to her back was nearly stinging in intensity. "I do have to question the timing of the…episode, however." He gave her a teasing grin.

She cautiously tested another bite of food. "You mean what kind of sex therapist in her right mind would choke at the mention of the word *sex?*"

He nodded. "Something like that."

"Let's just say I didn't expect the word to come from your mouth, Dr. Dylan."

"Just Dylan. Please."

"I'll try. But you have to admit, Dr. Dylan does have a certain ring to it." She sat back, wineglass in hand, and openly pondered him. "So how long has it been?" She smiled. "And this time I do mean sex."

Four years, six months and twenty-five days, his subconscious offered silently. An answer he had been proud of only a short time ago. A fact he wanted to change posthaste when sitting next to Grace.

"Touché," he said. He wasn't about to share the very personal details of his sex life with her. To do so would only invite further temptation. Hell, just looking at her made him remember how exciting it was to trap a woman's moan in her throat by covering her mouth with his. Brought vividly to mind the sweet arch of a woman's back as she strained to get closer. Filled his nose with the musky smell of a woman's heated sex.

His chest tightened and he suddenly couldn't get enough air.

Sure sign number two of his growing attraction toward her.

He found himself on the verge of groaning and fought to refocus on the meal. He was surprised to find the food on his plate nearly gone. Funny, he could barely recall having eaten a single bite of it.

"Is that the type of question you advise your patients to ask?" he said, counseling himself to work through his uncomfortable condition. Find common ground, stand firmly on it, and maybe he just might get around to making at least one point tonight. "The sex thing?"

She tucked her hair behind her ear again. "Depends on the patient. You?"

"Never."

"Never?" The arch of her brow fascinated him. "Oh, wait. Yes, I remember. Sex shouldn't even enter the equation conversation-wise until well after the third date, right? Chapter One, Section Four, if I'm not mistaken."

"Chapter Two, Section One, but I'm flattered."

Her smile made him wonder if she'd purposely quoted the wrong passage. "And in the case of STDs, sexually transmitted diseases? Say genital herpes? Don't you think it's important a person know up front whether or not the person they're dating is in a position to pass on a lifelong disease to them?"

He wiped his mouth with the napkin. "I suppose you suggest they provide a recent HIV test the moment the guy picks the girl up."

"Or when the girl picks the guy up. If they want to have unprotected sex…yes, I do."

He grimaced. "A relationship has to do with more than just sex, Gracie."

"Granted, but you can't ignore that sex does play an important role. If two people aren't sexually compatible, then they may be setting themselves up for a lifetime of misery if they don't find that out up front."

"Ah, a new twist on the process of elimination." He leaned his elbow on the table. "If they build their relationship solely on how good the initial sex is, they're destined to keep that divorce rate right up there at fifty percent."

She began to say something, then snapped her mouth closed. Dylan gazed at her lips, moist from where she'd just sipped her wine. "How's your track record on the STD issue, Dr. Dylan?"

He couldn't have answered her if he'd tried. His throat had just completely closed up.

She held up her hands and gave a small laugh. "Okay. Why don't we just say that on this issue we agree to disagree?"

He nodded. "Good idea."

She leaned forward and resumed eating, apparently happy to continue on as if their exchange had never occurred.

But after long minutes ticked by with no sound other than the suddenly far too intimate sounds of her eating, Dylan felt the desire to prod her back to life. Something, anything to snap his acute concentration on her nearness.

Why didn't she say anything more? Prod him to answer her questions about sex and STDs? Make one of her barbed, well-aimed remarks? Tell him he was all wet? Something, anything, to break this surreal spell their silence was putting on him.

"This your first book?" he forced out, the words sounding unnaturally loud in the quiet room.

She sipped her wine, then nodded. "You?"

"Second."

Well, that attempt at jump-starting the conversation had succeeded with flying colors, hadn't it? He knew his inability to speak in coherent sentences was another sign, but he refused to acknowledge it. If he ignored the signs, maybe they would just go away.

Oh, great advice, Doctor.

Gracie's hand on his wrist nearly made him vault from his chair.

Sure sign number four. The rush of desire so strong he swore he had a hard-on.

"Could you pass the wine, please?"

Dylan stared at her for a long moment. Either her pupils were dilated, or he was projecting his own circumstances onto her. "Oh. Sure." He poured her more wine, then topped off his own glass, though it was still full.

She smiled at him. He smiled back, then cleared his throat.

So he'd made a huge mistake in inviting her here. Humongous. Phenomenal. But the meal was almost over. And he hadn't made a fool of himself, or betrayed his beliefs once. Good. Very good.

He hurriedly finished what was on his plate, then wiped his hands on his napkin. "Well, that was certainly enjoyable. Thanks so much for bringing it."

There was that laugh again. He'd have to make a note to himself: never make Gracie Mattias laugh.

"But we haven't even had dessert yet," she said.

Every last damn image he'd had of her since seeing her in the shower that morning slid provocatively through his mind. And in every single one she was naked, hot and needy.

"Do you have milk?"

She could have been speaking a foreign language for all the sense he made out of her words.

"For the cookies."

He practically leaped from the chair. "Oh. Yes. I'll...go get it."

In the privacy of the kitchen, he propped his hands against the counter and took huge, silent, calming breaths. *Get it together, man. She's only a woman. Just like any other woman.*

Who was he kidding? She was temptation incarnate.

A year or two ago he'd had a married male patient who had been hopelessly attracted to a next-door neighbor. His advice to him was to envision a matronly aunt whenever he crossed paths with her.

Dylan tried to envision his old Aunt Reggie, who had always seemed ancient to him, wore support socks with her flowered housecoats, and always smelled like cabbage.

He closed his eyes, realizing the imagery wasn't working. Funny, he couldn't remember if his advice had worked for his patient, either. Shortly after that session, the guy had never come back.

"Do you need some help?"

Dylan turned around in the cramped confines of the kitchen, putting him nearly nose to nose with his own personal temptation.

"Do I ever."

Then he did the very thing he counseled his patients against. The last thing an almost-engaged man should even entertain doing. He thrust his hands into all that glorious red hair and brought his mouth down on hers like a man on death row being offered his last meal.

5

SWEET MERCY. GRACIE THREW her eyes open wide, rendered completely speechless by Dylan's unexpected, all-out fiery assault on her mouth. Halfway through her fish she'd begun to wonder if she had what it took to bag one Dr. Dylan Fairbanks. Aside from his apparent initial awkwardness, he hadn't been the one to end up choking.

She'd used nearly every weapon in her sexual arsenal. Lingered over her food as though she found it unbearably delicious. Found a reason to touch him by asking him to pass the wine. Crossed and recrossed her legs. Sent him little signals with a flip of her hair here, a slant of a suggestive glance there, not to mention the repeated licking of her lips. And he'd ignored every single last one of them, sitting adjacent from her as cool as you please, completely composed, his integrity intact.

Then there was that damnable silence. It seemed to amplify the sound of her own heartbeat in her ears, her one-sided flirting making her all the hotter for him. With every click of an invisible clock, she'd wanted him more and more, until she was afraid she was going to shove his laptop to the floor and crawl across their plates to kiss him.

Oh, God but he had an incredible mouth.

Gracie returned his assault with equal fervor, pulling at his firm lips, nipping at his tongue, and delving her own tongue deep into his mouth. She felt like a hungry child who had been denied an edible gift then found it waiting for her on her bed pillow. Her lips molded so perfectly against his that she thought for a ridiculous moment that they had been made to kiss his. Far from the awkwardness usually experienced during first kisses, this one shot way beyond fumbled positioning, teeth knocking and tongue sparring. They shared something that made her thighs quiver. It was almost as if she'd been kissing him all of her life. Well, maybe not all of her life, but certainly a helluva lot longer than a half minute. And she thought she wouldn't be able to get enough of him even if she took a deep breath and inhaled him whole.

She curled her fingers in his sweater. She'd been ready to pack it all in when he hadn't even glanced at the cleavage she'd worked so hard to display during dinner. Not once. And he'd appeared in such a hurry to get her out of there, she was sure the last thing on his mind had been her.

Then she'd stepped into the kitchen and he was on her like a Velcro suit.

She felt his hand on her outer thigh and whimpered, his skin seeming to brand hers with fire. She tugged him closer by his sweater, his hand skimming over her flesh, setting nerve endings aflame in its wake. He curved his fingers over her silk-covered bottom and gave a squeeze so torturously possessive she shuddered. As she tugged, he pulled, bringing her softness against his hard arousal. Gracie's breathing grew so ragged she was afraid there wasn't enough air in the room to satisfy her need for the necessary element. She shoved her hands deep into his back pockets and squeezed his tight rear end, wanting to feel him even closer.

He tugged his mouth from hers and trailed a hot, wet path to her ear. "God, I've been itching to touch you since I saw you in that damn shower this morning all naked and lathered up."

His words sent a shiver skittering along the surface of her skin, leaving her tiny hairs standing on end. Tugging on the hem of his sweater, she bunched the soft fabric in her hands and shoved it up as she slid down. With fingers she couldn't seem to move fast enough, she popped the snap to his pants and drew the zipper down, immensely satisfied with his quick indrawn breath. His hands tightened in her hair, apparently torn between wanting to push her away and yank her closer but settling for just touching her.

A tug on the open material and his erection sprang free from both his pants and briefs. She laughed. "My, my. Careful there…you could put an eye out with that thing."

He groaned and before she could get a chance to fit her lips around the tip of his erection he yanked her back to her feet with one hand, tugged his pants back up with the other. "Do that and I'll finish before we even get a chance to begin."

Then his mouth was on hers again, his hot hand on her bare thigh, and all thought of protest instantly scattered to the corners of her mind. He slid his hand from beneath her sinfully short skirt and grasped her hips, turning her until she was against the counter, then lifting her on top of it. Her quiet laugh told of her surprise, but it didn't stop her from spreading her legs and wantonly yanking him between them. When the hard length of him nestled against her swollen folds through her panties, she nearly cried out in exquisite pleasure.

She'd known the sexy doc would be good, but for God's sake, they hadn't really even done anything yet and she was a tongue flick away from orgasm. He bent to her right breast, forcing her to grope for a supporting grip against the counter behind her. Her fingers touched something and she glanced to see that it was a cookie. She pushed it out of the way, arching her back as he fastened his mouth over her engorged nipple right through the material of her tank and bra.

Dear God…

Her womb contracted so violently she nearly catapulted from the counter. Sensing her crisis, Dylan ground against her, his hold tightening, his mouth breathing hot air through her tank and onto her damp nipple. Gracie heard a low, gut-tightening moan fill the room and realized only distantly that it was her own as she succumbed to the delicious shivers racking her body.

Dylan pulled his mouth from her breast and lay his head against her shoulder. "Oh, God, if I don't take you now, Gracie, I swear I'm going to burst."

She began impatiently pushing his pants out of the way. "So take me."

He caught her wrists in his hands, his green eyes intense. "I can't."

Her heart dipped low in her stomach then rebounded to lodge in her thick throat. "What?"

"I…I don't have anything to protect you, damn it."

She nearly collapsed in a mixture of relief and unbearable pleasure. Freeing one of her wrists from his, she dipped her fingers into the V of her tank, sliding out a brightly colored foil packet. His brows drew slightly, almost comically, together as he looked from her to it, and she knew that protection hadn't been the only thing stopping him from taking things between them all the way. But she'd be damned if she was going to let him wriggle out of it now.

She slid her legs around his waist, pulling him tightly against her. "Now…where were we?"

She slanted her mouth against his, feeling all powerful when, after a brief hesitation, he groaned and kissed her back with double the intensity he had earlier.

She wasn't sure if it was him or her, but somehow they managed not only to free her of her panties, but him of his pants, and finally he was cradled between her legs, his hot, throbbing, latex-covered erection sandwiched between her slick, swollen flesh. The coolness of the tile under her bottom, and his heat between her legs, snatched away her breath. When he fit the tip of his arousal into her opening, she was certain she'd never be able to breathe again.

After the mad upward spiral of her desire and her climax only moments before, she thought herself more than ready for him. But the hesitant stretching of her muscles told her it was better if they took it slow.

Until he slid himself in to the hilt, filling her in one long stroke, making her shiver.

She could no longer hold herself upright. She collapsed back onto her hands as she tightened her legs around his waist, bracing her hips for his next delicious stroke. Then his next.

Every cell of Gracie's body felt brilliantly, vividly alive. The tiny hair on her arms and at the back of her neck stood up on end, her legs ached, and her muscles contracted, trying to pull him in farther even as he withdrew to thrust into her again. She moved her hips to grind against him, barely aware of his throwing his head back and groaning at the unexpected move. Then he snapped upright, a needy expression contorting his handsome face. A lock of hair fell over his right brow as he grasped her hips and thrust into her harder...faster, chasing every coherent thought straight from Gracie's mind. Driving her insane with desire.

Her breath coming in rapid gasps, she felt him tense, sensing him on the verge of climax. She tilted her hips forward more, taking him deeper, biting hard on her bottom lip as his fingers bit into the flesh of her thighs. She couldn't help noticing how magnificent it was, to view a man as delectably attractive as Dr. Dylan Fairbanks in the throes of pleasure. His entire body tensed, the veins in his neck stood out in stark release, his teeth were clenched tightly together as he gave himself over to emotions he had no control over.

Finally he collapsed, his temple against hers, his arms

shaking as he propped his hands against the counter mere millimeters away from hers, his thumbs covering hers.

She swallowed hard, fighting to catch her breath. Amazingly, she could still feel him filling her. Completely erect. She was just about to shimmy her hips, to let him know she was up for more if he was, when the shrill ring of the phone in the other room tore through the thick film of intimacy weaving them together.

For long moments, Gracie questioned whether or not he even heard the ringing. She smiled and rubbed her temple against his. "It could be the concierge telling us the hotel is on fire."

She heard him swallow, only then realizing he had yet to look at her.

"I wish it was the concierge. But I'm afraid it's someone else. Somebody I don't think I really want to talk to just now."

Gracie's grip against the counter slipped as he pulled away. Before she could ease her feet to the floor, he was already buttoning his pants and heading toward the kitchen door. He stopped, turned, then ran his hand through his tousled hair. "Don't, um, go anywhere. Stay right here. In the kitchen."

Gracie smiled at his obviously agitated demeanor, reluctant to shrug off the astounding feelings they'd just shared even as she put herself back together. Ignoring his directive, she rounded the corner into the main room, watching as Dylan paced, the receiver held closely to his ear.

"I've been trying to contact you for three straight days," he said, an edge to his voice she wondered would be there if not for her. "I see. Sure." He caught sight of where Gracie stood smiling after him and completely froze, his eyes larger than the dinner plates they had just eaten from. "Can you hold on a minute? No, no, don't hang up. Lord knows when I'll be able to get you on the line again."

He dropped the receiver to his side, his palm covering the mouthpiece. "Sorry, I have to take this call."

Gracie shrugged, as if to indicate that he should go ahead. Then the serious, weighty way he stared at her slowly began to sink in. He had to take the call and wanted to do so without her presence.

"Oh."

She reached down and put her shoes back on as he stood in the same, unmoving position.

Was the person on the other end of the line a woman? His ex-wife? Girlfriend? She didn't know. And tried to ignore her curiosity to find out.

She stood straight, glancing toward the table.

"I'll have the maid take care of that," he told her.

She flicked her gaze back to his face. "All right." She tugged at the straps of her tank, as if she could somehow make them conceal her better. "Well, I guess I'll see you tomorrow then."

She pretended to ignore his grimace as she gathered what little was left of the pride he'd just shot to hell around her feet and headed for the door. "Sweet dreams," she called out, waggling her fingers in a teasing way before the barrier clicked closed.

She leaned against the door and swallowed.

Wow…

What in the hell had just happened in there? She wasn't completely sure. What was worse was that she wasn't sure she wanted to find out.

What she did know was that her nerve endings sang a tune full of life and energy. That her thigh muscles ached just the tiniest bit. And that her womanhood throbbed with a sensation she wasn't sure she had experienced before.

She also knew that she just had been dropped like yesterday's newspaper.

Well, not dropped, exactly. How could you be dropped if you'd never been picked up? She'd set out to have a sexual tryst with one handsome Dr. Dylan Fairbanks, and she'd accomplished that task. In spades. What she hadn't been prepared for was what came afterward. How…abruptly it would end.

She twisted her lips. She certainly hadn't expected any long-term commitment. In fact, she'd been against that scenario from the outset. This had been her shot at her own personal sexual safari. And, oh, boy, cutting loose sure did have its benefits. She'd never felt so uninhibited, sexy, wild. She supposed Dylan's own aversion to such…provocative behavior merely added another edgy dimension to the entire encounter. There had been something…challenging and dangerous about enticing Dr. Dylan to step from his conservative restraints and give himself over to temptation. And knowing that she had been the one to make him do it was doubly intriguing.

Still, something flitted along the outskirts of her immediate thoughts to tease her, taunt her, dare her to name it. This was ridiculous really. She and Dylan were grown adults, secure in their own identities, established in their respective careers and lives. Add to that that they'd just shared some incredible sex, and well, they had it all. Didn't they?

Of course they did.

The sound of Dylan's muted voice drifted through the wood as he continued talking to whoever was on the phone. Pushing from the door, Gracie stuck her chin out and moved toward the elevator and her own room where she could take notes on her experience and compare it to the case studies she had used in her book.

DYLAN SAT FROZEN ON THE couch, the telephone receiver dangling from his hand. He stared at it, unable to recall why he was holding it. Then his broken conversation with Diana came back to him in bits and pieces. Lame segments that still didn't make sense because his ears were roaring and his body felt as if he were covered in lava.

He glanced toward the door. The same door Grace Mattias had just walked out of minutes before. His mind went completely blank, making him forget about Diana and the phone call all over again. The shrill beep-beep indicating that the receiver was off the hook nearly catapulted him from the cushion.

It took him three tries before he fit the shrieking instrument into its cradle.

What in the hell had just happened? One minute he'd been a glass of milk and a cookie away from showing Grace the door. The next he was showing her something else entirely. A side of himself that he hadn't seen in a long, long time.

Had he really shoved her onto the counter, pushed her skirt up and had at her like a teen having a go at the stacked babysitter?

Dylan dropped his head into his hands and groaned. Loudly.

What had he been thinking? He grit his teeth. Obviously he hadn't been thinking. At least not with any part of his body that mattered.

For God's sake, he was a civilized male who not only knew civilized behavior, he wrote about it.

Bits of fragmented memories taunted him. How many times when an adulterer patient told him "it just happened" had he loftily responded with "oh, you just happened to trip and fall into her vagina."

Only in his case, he hadn't fallen into Gracie's slick, tight flesh…he'd thrust into it again and again.

He threw himself back on the sofa and groaned.

Of course, he and Diana weren't married. But that didn't alleviate his guilt. In his mind, he was just as dirty as those two-timing slouches he used to chastise. What did it matter that he and Diana hadn't even had sex yet? That's what made his relationship with her special. He'd made a conscious decision to wait. To pursue his commitment to her with total and complete chivalry. To prove that men did not live by sex alone. That they were driven by more than their sex drive. Capable of celibacy until their wedding night.

How had one hour alone with Gracie Mattias shot the past four years to hell?

Pulling away the pillow he had crammed down over his face, he glanced at the front of his pants. Despite everything, he got rock-hard all over again just thinking about her.

He pushed off of the sofa, put a call in to the concierge to arrange for color- and style-specific clothes to be delivered to him, then headed for the shower.

Only his actions refused to allow him freedom from his tormented thoughts. He remembered the way Gracie's face had fallen when he'd essentially booted her out of the room. Until that moment he never would have thought Gracie capable of that expression. In that one instant she looked like spurned teenager and hurt lover all rolled up into one.

Of course, that expression had lasted only an instant, after which she'd smiled the familiar sassy smile of hers and waggled her fingers at him as she said goodbye. But the fact remained, he had seen the expression. It hit him like a fist to the gut.

He switched the water in the shower to ice-cold, then stepped into it, clothes and all. His breath whooshed from his lungs and every thought rushed from his mind other than to force himself to stand under the punishing spray until every last sign of arousal vanished. And until he could figure out what he was going to do to right this wrong.

Which, despite the frigid cold, took a full three minutes.

Gasping for air, and shivering, he finally switched the stream off and stripped out of his clothes. First thing he needed to do was apologize to Grace. While she had been an equal and willing participant in the evening's events, he still felt the need to apologize for his behavior. He'd been an animal, a greedy horny toad. He'd thought nothing of shoving her skirt up her smooth thighs and taking his pleasure, with absolutely no thought of her and her needs. Hell, he hadn't even made a stab at foreplay. He didn't even know if she'd gotten any enjoyment out of the experience.

Not that he intended to remedy it if she hadn't. Oh, no. From here on out, rule number one was to stay as far away from Miss Hottie Grace Mattias as possible. And never, ever be in the same room alone with her again.

Just because he'd fallen off the horse didn't mean he couldn't get right back on it again. What had happened tonight was no more than a missed hurdle. A momentary blip on the screen. A crack on the sidewalk of his path. There was no reason to think he couldn't continue right on as though it had never happened.

Except, of course, that he needed to tell Diana.

He cringed, thinking the cold shower hadn't been necessary at all. The mere prospect of divulging what had happened between him and Gracie to Diana was enough to chase every hot, seductive thought from his mind.

But tell her, he would. Honesty was always the best policy.

He only wished he knew when that moment would come. He'd been so distracted during their brief conversation, he'd completely forgotten the reason he'd wanted to talk to her. To invite her down to Miami where he planned to propose.

Shrugging into the hotel robe, he made his way into the other room to begin the long process of cleaning up the mess, both on the table and of his life.

6

IT WASN'T POSSIBLE THAT he looked even better today than he had yesterday.

That was the only thought that sprang forth and refused to budge from Gracie's mind when she bumped into Dylan Fairbanks in the syndicated television talk show's green room, which wasn't green at all, but purple. Overwhelmingly purple, from the walls to the carpet and everything in between. Even the appetizers set out on a tray seemed to have a purple tinge to them.

"Want to take a guess as to the host's favorite color?" her assistant Rick asked, giving her one of his lopsided smiles.

Gracie pried her gaze away from Dylan and absently considered the finger food. "Oh, I don't know…green?"

When Rick didn't respond with a laugh or other wisecrack, she looked at him.

"What is it?" she asked, suddenly alarmed.

"Nothing. It's just that I think you're looking a little green right about now."

"Very funny." Gracie felt like whacking him in the arm. But he looked good in his nifty new suit and she didn't want to wrinkle it. She returned her attention to the food.

No, no crackers. They tended to gravitate straight to her front teeth. Something crunchy. Ah, a carrot! As usual, she got up late this morning—awakened by a phone call from Rick—and hadn't had time to even make herself a cup of tea, much less breakfast. It was just as well, because the lingering scent of the fish she'd cooked the night before had robbed her of her appetite.

"If I didn't know better, I'd say you're nervous."

Unfortunately Rick appeared to know her better than she was comfortable with. Hmm…maybe she should advertise for a new assistant when she got back to Baltimore. She sighed, knowing she'd never do that. Rick was the best assistant a woman could ask for. Like a wife, minus the emotional debris. "But you do know better."

His grin made a comeback. "Yep." He glanced at the open notepad he held. "Do you want to go over the format again?"

She shook her head. "No. I think I have it straight. I go one-on-one with the host first. Then Dr. Dy—Fairbanks gets his shot. Then the host will put us together for the remaining half hour."

He turned the page. "And remember, the host is pretty conservative."

Giving in to temptation, she popped a piece of cheese into her mouth, careful to chew with only her back teeth. "With an audience that's majority female." She waved off his warning. "Don't worry, I already have a strategy all worked out."

"The 'feminine mystique' angle?"

She hummed. "God, is this cheese good or am I just enormously hungry?"

"You're enormously hungry."

She swallowed and smiled at him wryly. "Oh, before I forget, my answering service took three calls last night—"

Rick closed his notepad. "The Decateurs had a bad episode with the body oil you recommended, a possible referral from Dr. Moss and an inquiry from a potential new patient. Got them."

She wagged a finger at him. "I knew there was a reason I keep you around."

He feigned shock. "You mean beyond my dashing good looks?"

She laughed. "I'm more of the tall, dark and handsome type myself."

Movement caught her attention from the corner of her eye as she popped another cheese square into her mouth. Speaking of tall, dark and handsome, a particular one in question was bearing down on her.

"Excuse me a moment, won't you." Dylan urgently grasped her arm, pulling her away from where she had been talking to Rick. She gaped at him, nearly tottering off her heels.

"I need to speak to you," he said quietly.

Gracie tried to ignore where his touch felt like pure fire against her skin as she straightened her skirt and quickly tried to finish chewing her cheese. She swallowed hard. "You can speak to me all you want. On the show in five minutes."

"Now."

Something inside Gracie rankled. She glanced to where Rick was looking on with a raised brow from one side of the room, while Dylan's publicity rep peeked around the show's producer from the other side. The purple streaks in the PR rep's hair went nicely with the decor, Gracie thought wryly.

She looked back at Dylan. Well, not directly at him, at him, but at a mole on his forehead, near the edge of his right brow. A particularly delectable-looking mole. "So talk."

He suddenly looked altogether agitated, making her feel the same. Until she figured out what he was about to do. She finally met his gaze straight on, refusing to acknowledge the sexy green of his eyes. "Oh, no, don't tell me you're about to apologize, Dylan."

His instant stiffening told her that's exactly what he was about to do. "Why not?"

"Because that would be the worst possible thing you could

do right now, that's why not." She lowered her voice. Was it her imagination, or were Rick and Tanja covertly edging their way closer? "I don't know, Dylan. There might be some in need of your apology, but I'm not one of them. We're adults, right?"

"And what we did last night was purely adult," he said before she could continue.

"And completely consensual. I have absolutely no regrets. If you do…well, I don't want to know about them." She crossed her arms under her breasts. Today she had on a royal-navy suit and white silk blouse, in recognition of the daytime televised venue, but her skirt was still short short, her heels high high. "I may be a psychologist, but I'm not about to let you ease your mind by confessing all to me. I'm not interested in what happened beyond I had a damn good time. That's it. Got it?"

"You had a good time?"

Her stomach dipped at the surprise in his voice. "I think I said 'damn good time.'" She uncrossed her arms at the admission and pretended to pick lint from the sleeve of her jacket. Only when she had her emotions back under control did she dare meet his gaze again. She smiled. "Do I strike you as the doormat type, Dylan? The type who would have sex merely to satisfy someone else?"

He stood for a long moment, apparently not breathing if his resulting whoosh of an exhale was any indication. "No."

She tried not to notice how relieved he looked, and how much she wished she could plaster her mouth right on top of his. "And I don't think you are, either."

"Me? Oh, no. No, of course not."

She bit discreetly on her bottom lip. "Then last night was all about fundamental urges and spontaneous combustion. Two adults having consensual sex, pure and simple. There's no reason for either of us to apologize. At least not to each other."

"It's not going to happen again," he said. More like blurted. "I wasn't planning on it."

He suddenly frowned. "Why not?"

She couldn't help laughing. She'd been about to say last night hadn't been planned, either. But she couldn't say that, could she? Because she had set out to seduce him. If only she had planned down the line a little further, things might have looked better right now.

She sighed, all trace of amusement gone. "Look, Dylan, last night I had a great time, all right? But let's face it. You and I...well, we'd end up maiming each other if left in a room alone together for prolonged periods of time. That doesn't bode well for either a relationship, or a serial case of one-night stands, does it?"

He looked genuinely perplexed. "Relationship? One-night stands?" He scratched the area over his ear, drawing her attention to his well-shaped hand and long fingers. She remembered all too vividly what his hand had felt like molded around her breasts.

The fabric of her blouse and jacket seemed to rasp against her hardening nipples and she caught herself licking her lips in anticipation of something that couldn't be again. Or could it?

Dylan's face went completely white. "I'm engaged."

No, it most definitely couldn't.

Gracie nearly choked. "Did you just say you were engaged?"

He averted his gaze, his hand moving from his ear to the back of his neck. "I meant to say something last night...that's why what happened shouldn't have...and it's for that reason I need to apologize."

"You're engaged?" she found herself repeating again, and wished it were physically possible to kick herself in the rear. Well, she supposed it was possible, but not in the way she needed to be kicked. One good boot that would send her flying was in order. Something that equaled the virtual punch she had just taken to the stomach.

Okay, Gracie, you can handle this. You even address this scenario in your book, remember?

While that was the case, and her advice to any unsuspecting women—or men—was to get as far away from the cheating slime as fast as possible, to have it happen to her…well, that was different. Wasn't it?

She took a deep, even breath. Control. She needed to regain control over this situation.

"Gracie?"

She nearly hit the ceiling at the sound of Rick's voice so close to her back. She turned.

"It's time."

Gracie gave Dylan one last smile, deciding to overlook the thoughtful expression on his face at what she had probably just given away.

"Well, I guess you do need to do some apologizing. As I said, however, it's not to me."

Good. That was good. Right? She'd handled herself like the pro she was. Cool, calm and collected. Even managed to score a couple of points, if she was a good judge.

But as the show's producer led her out of the room first, she thought it would take the jaws of life to extricate her nails from the palms of her hands.

He's engaged.

She didn't really understand the enormity of her upset. Her heart literally felt as if one of those hokey medicine men had slipped his hand into her chest and was taking great pleasure in squeezing the life from the all-important organ.

Okay, so maybe she didn't feel as blasé as she'd pretended about what had happened in Dylan's kitchen last night. Maybe the fact that she had spent half the night scribbling notes that didn't always make any sense was a good indicator. When she'd finally drifted off to sleep, her dreams had been filled

with images of him gripped between her thighs, his face con-
torted in pleasure. But she was pretty confident that Dylan's
abrupt dismissal of her was more to blame for her reaction
than any delusions of attraction that went beyond sex. Pride
was a funny thing. It made people do stupid things. She was
confident that pride was behind her sleeplessness and her
continued sexual interest in the sexy sex doctor. No woman
liked to be forgotten so quickly, even if she never intended
a relationship to go beyond the one-night-stand stage. In a
shadowy, unexplored corner of her mind, she liked to think
the man in question was questioning whether he'd ever be
the same again, and whether he'd ever find another woman
to better the experience. Panting after her, so to speak.

The woman in question certainly never expected to find
out the man not only wasn't panting after her, but that he
planned to marry someone else.

"Stop talking in the third person, Gracie," she murmured
to herself as she straightened her skirt.

The producer she followed through the mazelike, narrow
hallways to the soundstage gave her a strange look, then
turned back around.

In the end, however, did it really matter if he was engaged
or not? At least he wasn't married.

The line of reasoning wasn't working.

Okay, then, since she'd certainly had no plans to pursue
a relationship after last night, because she'd genuinely been
in the dark as to Dylan's…lack of freedom, and the fact that
the fiancée was unknown to her, she hadn't really broken
any of her own rules. Had she?

*Note to self: write an addendum to include in reprints of
my book. When indulging in sexual safaris, make sure you
and the prey in question never cross paths again.*

There! That was it. The reason why her own personal
sexual safari was a bust. She hadn't stopped to consider the
impact to her and Dylan's professional relationship. Well, that

was easily remedied, because after this show there was absolutely no reason to expect their paths to cross again anytime soon. Indeed, given his disclosure, never would be a good estimation of when that would happen again.

"Take the seat to the left," the producer instructed.

Gracie did as she was told.

She sat still as a microphone was strategically placed on her lapel. She frowned. Why was she labeling last night a bust? It might be a lot of things, but a failure was not one of them. She had been highly successful in bagging her prey. She'd gotten exactly what she wanted. Sex on the kitchen counter with one sexy Dylan Fairbanks.

But if she had been so successful, why had she wanted to press her mouth against that adorable mole at the corner of Dylan's brow just now? And why was she sitting in front of a live audience of two hundred, on a soundstage, picking her brain over what had happened with Dylan. Rather than focusing on what she would say to the popular host?

The producer handed her a copy of her book and a crowd warmer stepped out to address everyone. She cleared her throat and focused her attention on the young woman, thinking it just as well that she didn't have time to answer the questions she had just posed to herself, because she wasn't sure she would like the answers.

DYLAN TUGGED AT HIS too-tight tie, a tie that had been perfectly adjusted a mere hour ago but now threatened to choke him. Checking the number on the door, making doubly sure he was on the right floor, he gained access to his hotel room and slammed the door after himself.

Dog food. That's what one sexy, frustrating Dr. Gracie Mattias had just made of his life and his philosophies on national TV. And not even the choice brand, either. The generic stuff. The kind that made you want to heave the instant you opened the can.

He absently rubbed the back of his neck and dropped into a dining room chair, his laptop open in front of him. He knew what the generic variety smelled like because he'd had a dog once. A mutt of questionable pedigree from a local animal shelter. It had been a gift from his mother, Moonbeam, when he'd finally scrounged enough cash together to move off the El Rancho compound and into his own apartment in San Fran.

"It'll help keep you human," she told him, the pup tucked under her arm as she stood outside his apartment. An apartment he'd been in for a mere twenty-four hours. He'd battled between closing the door on her and making room in his book-laden arms so he could take the panting canine. He'd wanted to stage a protest that would put to shame those his parents were well-known for…then she'd given him that smile. That one he'd never been able to argue with.

He punched at the button that would boot his laptop. Human. Right. The mangy mutt had set out to make his life a living hell from the get-go. He'd begun with his furniture, scratching and gnawing the scant secondhand pieces during the day while Dylan was away at Stanford teaching basic psych. The destruction continued on into the night, when often were the times he'd been awakened by rancid doggie breath. He recalled midnight trips to the bathroom interrupted by strategically placed doggie mines.

Finally, after everything in the apartment bore evidence of his canine roommate—destroyed or otherwise deemed unusable—Dylan had feigned a long-scheduled trip for a seminar in Chicago and dumped the mutt at his parents'. There the unfondly named Killer had stayed.

The hound was at least ten years old now. Amazing. There were times when he entered his trendy house in Pacific Heights and tensed, waiting for a secret attack from the twenty-pound beast. Strange, because Killer had never sunk his teeth into a single piece of Dylan's rich brown swanky

Italian leather furniture. Regardless, Dylan swore he could make out battle scars around his ankles.

Not unlike the battle scars he wore after today's bout with Gracie Mattias on the syndicated TV show.

He cringed, the memory bringing him full circle to the dog food the frustratingly sexy sex doc had made out of his arguments on self-restraint in front of a nationwide audience.

He ignored that after last night he was probably the last person to be speaking on the merits of self-restraint. Especially to Grace Mattias, who had spent that same night shooting every last inch of his self-restraint to bits, then following it up by incinerating the remaining fragments on today's show.

He covered his face with his hands, all too easily conjuring up the image of her sitting across from him, choosing to cross her long, long legs at the exact moment he opened his mouth to respond to one of her loaded remarks. But it was one exchange in particular that made him groan aloud even now.

Interrupting the host of the show, Gracie had leaned forward and asked, "Tell me, Dr. Fairbanks, would you have me and everyone else believe that you haven't given in to your most basic, fundamental urges since your own admitted vow of celibacy?"

Feeling as though Gracie had just placed her hands around his neck and commenced choking him, he'd looked to the host for help. But she appeared as interested in the answer to the loaded question as Gracie was.

He'd cleared his throat, silently reciting ten of the many dead-sure, giveaway signs of lying as he considered his answer. He wasn't overly concerned about how far Grace intended to take the topic, though he supposed in retrospect he should have been. To flat-out lie wasn't the way he operated. "Dr. Mattias, as a psychotherapist, you're familiar with the advice given to patients trying to break self-defeating behavior, are you not? For the sake of argument, let's say we're talking about a smoker."

"Ah, burning. Good analogy."

Actually, it was the best he could come up with and it sucked dead toads, but he'd needed to put out the fire before his entire professional—and personal—life went up in smoke. "So tell me, Doctor, what do you say to a patient who has gone without a cigarette for four solid years, then one day lights up?"

"To explore the interesting things you might do with a cigar?" she'd said with a suggestive smile.

He'd winced but ignored her aside. "Do you shrug your shoulders and tell him he might as well take up smoking again? No. You encourage him to crack the whip and get right back up on that wagon, don't you?"

"Well, so long as it involves a whip…"

Thankfully the host chose that moment to jump in, expressing an interest in discussing the various sex toys Dr. Mattias would suggest a couple use to make their love lives more interesting, then broke for commercial.

He'd survived with all his body parts intact. Just barely.

For the past ten minutes he'd sat in front of his running laptop without really seeing it. He clicked open a couple files, not wanting to mull over something that had been bothering him ever since that exchange. A question weightier than the exchange itself.

More specifically, why Gracie hadn't revealed that he… she…they…

Oh, for God's sake, he couldn't even think the word.

"We had hot, wild, irresponsible sex," he said between clenched teeth.

He poked agitatedly at the keyboard until he'd spat out every possible adjective he could type to describe his feelings about his own behavior, then leaned back in the chair and rubbed his thumbs over his closed eyelids.

Well, why hadn't she?

It stood to reason that she had nothing to lose and every-thing to gain by letting that ferocious cat out of the bag. Es-pecially after he'd virtually blurted that he was engaged. Well, not officially engaged yet, but he soon would be. Still, strangely, she'd held the bag closed and out of sight…except, of course, when he'd heard the sucker growling during her one and only reference to his celibacy. Or, more accurately, the breaking of that celibacy.

Then, of course, there was the whole issue of faithfulness she could have delved into but hadn't.

"It doesn't make any sense."

He snapped his eyes open, realizing he'd said the words aloud, emphasizing just how significant it was.

He realized that it just might be a question that would for-ever go unanswered.

"Thank God."

The predominant thought that had seen him through the remainder of the show was that at its end he and one inexpli-cably sexy Gracie Mattias would never have to cross paths again. In fact, he was so anxious to hurry that prospect along, he'd made it a point after the live show to hightail it out of there, relying on Tanja's considerable talents as she led the way through the backstage maze then out the door and into the chauffeured Lincoln at a near run.

Last night was an aberration. A one-time mistake. A night-mare he had the choice to wake up from. And he was doing exactly that. From here on out he was back to being the guy with whom he was familiar. The one he knew. The man he looked at in the mirror every morning confident that he was living his life exactly the way he intended. The guy who planned to marry Diana Evans.

From now on there would be no tart-mouthed sex doc to mince his philosophies into dog food. No long legs and provocative behavior to tempt him. No kitchen counters and overactive libido.

He glanced at his watch. He had an hour to get ready for his afternoon flight. The last thing he wanted was to be late and have Tanja trek in here and do his packing for him.

Shutting off his laptop, he slid it back into its carrying case, then turned toward the bedroom. Not that he had much to pack, just what he had on, the few clothes he'd ordered and a few toiletries he'd bought downstairs. The clothes from last night he'd thrown in the garbage and was pleased to see the maid had taken them away.

He stepped into the bedroom and stopped. On top of his bed was his luggage. The same luggage the airline had lost the day before.

He grinned.

In more ways than one, things were definitely looking up.

7

HOT. SO INCREDIBLY HOT. It only went with the territory that she should get the one room in the Houston hotel whose air conditioner was on the fritz.

Careful not to mar her freshly painted nails, Gracie bent over to consider the locking gadgets on her balcony door. She was seven floors up for God's sake, what kind of security risk could there possibly be? You'd have to be a rock climber or a sky diver in order to gain access to the tiny sitting area much less break into the room itself. Maneuvering some kind of slide mechanism, releasing the bar on the floor, then flipping the ordinary lock, she pulled. A speaker in the corner of her room broadcast an earsplitting siren. She squealed.

A woman's voice sounded over the system. "Security alert. Security alert. It has been determined that the breach action is noncautionary. Sorry for the inconvenience."

Gracie quickly closed the door and leaned against it, staring at the speaker. Had she done that? All she'd wanted was a breath of fresh air, not the onset of World War III.

The telephone rang. Her gaze slid to the instrument, then back to the screeching speaker.

"Hello?"

Silence. Or at least what she thought was silence. Who could tell with all the racket?

She covered her other ear and tried again. "Hello? This is the occupant of Room 6732. If this is security, please shut that damn siren off."

"Gracie?"

She slapped her hand to her head. "Mom. How did you find me here?" Sure, her mother had her cell phone number, but half the time the instrument sat in her bag switched to off. Who needed emergency sexual advice? Her opinion was that her cell phone was strictly for the convenience of her calling others. If there was some sort of emergency, Rick's phone was on 24/7.

Which is probably where her mother got the number.

"Is everyone all right?" she asked, realizing that this just might be a family emergency.

"Everyone's fine on this end, dear. What is that infernal noise? Have you gotten yourself into trouble again?"

Gracie stalked to the corner of the room and examined the speaker, searching for some sort of shut-off switch. "No, Mom, I haven't gotten myself into trouble…again." She rolled her eyes heavenward. One time. One lousy time when she was sixteen she got pulled into the police station for making out in the backseat with her teenage boyfriend and her mother made it sound like an everyday occurrence. "It's the room's emergency system. I'm trying to shut it off now."

"Well, it doesn't sound like you're doing a very good job of it. Just what type of hotel are you staying at? Has there been a raid?"

"Raid?" Gracie couldn't help her bark of laughter. "No, Mom, I don't think your run-of-the-mill prostitutes could afford this place." Still, having Priscilla think the alarm was the result of some sort of drug bust was more exciting than the truth that she'd merely tried to gain access to the balcony of her unair-conditioned room.

"Prostitutes? For God's sake, Grace, who said anything

about prostitutes? I was referring to something more of a military nature."

"I'm in Texas, Mom, not a Third World country."

"Same difference."

She rolled her eyes then paced toward the balcony door again, wondering if slipping the locking mechanisms back into place would do the trick. The phone cord stretched across the bed, dumping the contents of her nail polish remover all over the paisley comforter. She groaned in increasing agitation.

"What? What's happening now?" her mother prodded as Gracie swiped at the mess seeping across the spread with the towel she'd wrapped around her wet hair. Of course it only stood to reason that not a single nail escaped contact with the acetone, ruining her manicure with only a half hour to go before her book signing at a local mall.

"Grace Marie, answer me."

"Nothing's happening, Mom. Nothing that a gunshot to the head wouldn't solve."

Giving up, she flopped down on the bed, pushed the acetone-laden towel away and covered her other ear with her hand. "Oh, well, they'll have to turn the alarm off eventually, won't they? So tell me, Mom, how are you doing?"

Priscilla sighed then said, "Not very well, if you want to know the truth."

Anyone else might find her sitting on a stained bedspread in a sweltering hotel room with a squealing alarm going off and simultaneously talking on the phone bizarre. But given the two days since Chicago, strange events were becoming par for the course for Gracie. Only she could have accidentally boarded a plane bound for Vancouver rather than Houston and ended up sitting in an airport for five hours until she could get on the next open flight out. Fate dictated that she be the one to find out the hard way that you really shouldn't be drinking coffee when the pilot warned of severe turbulence ahead. And only she could order a hamburger and fries from room service and get some sort of green wrapped sandwich she wasn't sure she should eat or use as a doorstop.

And only she would be sitting in the middle of the current mess asking her mother what could possibly be wrong in the land of Baltimore suburbia.

God, please don't ever let her turn into her mother.

"Well, you know how I am about…private matters, Gracie. Do you plan to be home soon?"

Private matters? Her mother wanted to talk to her about private matters? She shook her head, concerned something had jarred loose. Of course, she reminded herself that "private matters" could include almost anything on her mother's list, such as her foot massager had gone postal. "No, Mom, I won't be home soon. I'm on tour, you know, to promote that book I wrote, for at least the next ten days, remember?"

"Oh."

Yes, "oh" about summed it up.

Silence reigned. Well, at least over the phone line. Gracie vaguely registered a pounding on the wall next to her. Obviously her neighbor wasn't as accustomed to such weird occurrences.

She focused again on her mother. "Mom? Look, I'm sure whatever it is can be discussed over the phone." Still, nothing. "You know, you'd be surprised by how many people I counsel over the phone rather than in person. They tend to like the anonymity."

"I'm not one of your…patients, Grace."

She smiled. She knew that would get her. "Good, you're still there."

"Of course I'm still here. I wouldn't hang up without saying goodbye."

She was right there. Gracie couldn't count the times her mother had hung up on her out of frustration or anger. And every time she had warned her in advance. Something along the lines of, "I'm hanging up on you now, Grace. Goodbye," or "I'll talk to you again when you're more reasonable. Goodbye."

She racked her brain trying to come up with a reason to get her to do so now. She didn't have the time for this. Really, she didn't. She needed to be getting ready for her book signing.

"Your father and I haven't…shared a bed in over three months."

Gracie had been in the process of crossing her leg under her. The declaration caught her midmove and she instead slid onto the floor with a thud. Abruptly the alarm cut off, though an odd ringing kept on in her ears. "What…what did you just say, Mom?"

She wanted to emphasize the word *Mom.* Wanted Priscilla to remember that it was her daughter she was talking to. What happened to the wacky foot massager? *That* she could deal with. She scrunched her eyes closed. She really wasn't sure she wanted to hear this. Which was funny, because she'd taken a wicked sort of pleasure in questioning her mother about her sex life up until now. Mostly because Gracie had known her mother would never respond.

She snapped her eyes open. Well, guess what? Never just came up on deadline.

"You heard me." Priscilla cleared her throat. "Your father and I…haven't shared a bed for—"

"Three months." *Yeah, yeah, I heard you. I was just hoping you would lose your nerve and take the words back.* Say something that sounded similar and play the whole thing off. Like "shared a beer," or "pared a bear," something, anything but what she'd just said.

"Uh-huh." Oh, but that was good. She had virtually just flushed six years of higher education down the toilet, and probably proved her mother's skepticism of her aptitude with that two-syllable response.

Let's see…how exactly did one respond to a question of this nature from their own mother? "Um, you and Dad have always shared the same room. Did one of you move into a guest room?"

Her mother's sigh was both exasperated and exasperating. "Of course not. We're still *sleeping* together. You know, in the same bed."

"Good. That's good. That indicates at least a measure of intimacy."

"How? I turn in at ten. He comes in after midnight after I'm asleep. And when I get up in the morning, he's already gone. We might as well be sleeping in separate beds for all I see of him."

That's exactly how she saw her parents, so why shouldn't that be the reality?

"Gracie?"

"What?" She pushed herself up from the floor and sat on the bed. "Oh, sorry. Just lost in thought there for a moment."

"I tried waiting up for him once."

Seeing as that would have been her next question if this had been a regular patient, Grace nodded. But this wasn't a regular patient. This was her mother, for Pete's sake! She bit hard on her bottom lip to keep herself from saying that this…lull in her parents' love live was quite all right, normal in fact. That it wasn't unheard-of for married couples to go years without sexual intimacy. But that would go completely against her proactive philosophy.

Speaking of which… "Mom, have you read my book yet?"

Silence.

Someone knocked at the door. Gracie tamped down the desire to tell whoever it was that the alarm was off already, and couldn't they see she was dealing with a family crisis, then she looked at her watch. Oh, God! She only had ten minutes to get ready for the book signing!

Another knock. "Gracie?" Rick's voice filtered through the door. "The cab's waiting."

Of course it was. Was it too much to ask to have someone else running late?

"Look, Mom, I'm really, really sorry—" *no, she wasn't* "—but I have to go. I'm already way behind schedule and I'm not even dressed yet."

"But—"

"I'll call you later, okay?"

She began to tug the receiver away from her ear, ignoring her mother's protests, then she pulled it back. "Goodbye."

She returned the receiver to its cradle with more force than necessary and stood staring at the offensive instrument for a long, quiet moment. With any luck, by tonight her mother would have completely forgotten about this rip in parallel worlds and everything would go back to being normal.

Another knock, this time more insistent. "Gracie, I can hear you. Chop-chop, Dr. Hottie, we've got a book signing to do."

She wanted to tell her assistant to go ahead, do it without her. She'd give him complete control over the signing, he could even sign his own name for all she cared. All she wanted to do was crawl into bed, draw the covers over her head and pretend the past twenty minutes hadn't happened.

Instead, she yanked open the door and stared at Rick. "All right, already."

A HALF HOUR LATER GRACIE tottered into the bookstore with Rick shaking his head behind her. "One of these days you're going to break your neck, wearing those things."

She glanced back at him, then scanned the huge atrium of the shopping mall behind him. "Well, if I do, it'll be all your fault. If I recall correctly, it was you who took one look at my button-down blazers, which are completely in style by the way, and told me I needed a sexier image. In fact, you were the one who picked out these very shoes."

"Yes, well, I thought you would know how to walk in them."

"Contrary to popular male belief, Rick, women are not born with the innate ability to walk in heels."

"Boy, we're in rare form today, aren't we? What's eating you?"

"Aside from an air-raid siren going off in my room, my thong underwear being wedged in my butt and a phone call from my mother wanting sexual advice...nothing. Everything's just peachy." She lifted a finger. "By the way, make a note. I never want to get married."

She caught his wince, though she couldn't say exactly what he was wincing about. If he could sympathize with the thong bikini thing, she'd prefer not to know about that right now.

She turned around to lead the way to the manager's office and ran smack dab straight into someone. "I'm sorry. I wasn't watching where I was going."

"No apology necessary. I wasn't paying attention, either."

Gracie stumbled back a couple steps to gape at her anonymous cobumper. She blinked once. Then twice. Then thought she didn't need to be walking in order to fall off her heels. She stared into the not-so-anonymous shocked face of one far too sexy Dr. Dylan Fairbanks. Her favorite mistake.

But it wasn't until she looked beyond him, to his PR rep Tanja and her cute purple-tipped hair that she knew she wasn't hallucinating. Judging by the way Tanja averted her gaze and smiled in amusement, she also had the sinking sensation that of the four of them, she and Dylan were the only ones who hadn't known about the possibility of their running into each other again.

Dylan regained control over his tongue first. "What are *you* doing here?"

Well, that was certainly a greeting a girl looked forward to after the morning she had just experienced. Especially from a two-timing faithless groom whom she never would have slept with had she known he was engaged. "Well, hello, how are you doing, long time no see to you, too, Dr. Dylan."

Rick cleared his throat and put a hand on her arm. "Dr. Mattias is here for a book signing."

Tanja's exotic dark eyes widened…a little too wide, Gracie thought. "Really? So is Dr. Dy…er Fairbanks."

Rick's grin at the petite, pretty PR rep made Gracie want to fire him. "You don't say?"

"Well, someone had better say something that makes sense and quick," Dylan said, his wide chest puffed out in that way that made Gracie want to plant her hands against it.

Instead, she shifted her briefcase from one of those same itchy hands to the other. "What time is your signing?"

"Two to five."

"Really?" she asked, drawing the word out and slanting a gaze at Rick. "What a coincidence. So is mine."

Rick cleared his throat. "Sorry, Grace, I meant to tell you, but there just wasn't time. The store manager caught the TV show the other day, and when she heard you two were going to be in town together, she thought it would be a good idea to schedule you together."

"And how would she know we were both scheduled to be in town?"

Dylan looked at Tanja. "I wasn't even supposed to be in Houston. I was in Dallas for a seminar this morning."

Tanja smiled. "Okay, same state, then. And, um, Rick and I compared schedules the other day in New York."

Gracie covertly rubbed behind her ear, two and two clicking into place a little too neatly. She remembered that day all too well, mostly because that's the morning she had met Dylan…in her shower. She'd called Rick immediately afterward and recalled getting the impression he wasn't alone.

Hmm…why did she suspect that promotional schedules weren't the only things that had passed between the two traitors?

Grace trained her best evil eye on Rick.

"Come on, Grace," Rick said, grimacing. "I told you about the phenomenal response our polling agency pulled on the show. Then there was the radio appearance before then. Even your publisher agreed that scheduling you with Dr. Fairbanks was a good idea."

Tanja piped in, "Dylan's publisher, as well."

Gracie couldn't help noticing that Dylan gave the pretty pixie a glare to equal hers.

She said to Rick, "I'm not upset because I'm scheduled with Dylan. I'm ticked that you didn't tell me before now."

"I didn't…"

Gracie pointed at the sign nearby clearly showcasing the two of them, along with a clipping of a newspaper piece. A piece that had to be days in the planning. "Don't even try it, buster."

Dylan leaned closer to Tanja. "You're fired."

She laughed, then caught herself and cleared her throat. "You can't fire me. I work for the publisher."

He tugged at his tie. "Well, then, you're dismissed."

Gracie rolled her eyes. "Aren't you overreacting just a bit?"

"Overreacting? No, I wouldn't say I'm overreacting. I've just been told that I'm to spend the next three hours with a woman whose belief system goes completely against mine. I'd say my reaction is dead-on."

Oh, yeah, well, those belief systems weren't all that different the other night, were they?

For a second Gracie was afraid she'd said the words aloud given the way everyone was looking at her. Then she realized they were waiting for a regular response from her. She nearly leaned against the display to her right in relief. "Trust me, Dr. Dylan, this isn't going to be a picnic for me, either."

"Is everything all right?"

Dylan looked a breath away from telling the interloper to butt out, but clamped his mouth closed as he apparently noticed her badge identifying her as the manager.

Gracie smiled and extended her hand, giving Rick a quiet aside. "You and me, later." To the manager she said, "Everything's fine. Just a little mix-up is all. It's nice to meet you."

Introductions were made, idle conversation indulged in for the next few minutes as customers navigated around them in the store's entrance. Then they were shown to the back where two armchairs were positioned in front of a mock fireplace. A long table, which she and Dylan were obviously to share, stretched out before them.

Gracie rounded the table from one side, Dylan the other. She didn't know for sure, but she guessed he was going as out of his way to avoid her gaze as she was his. He smacked what looked like a laptop case down on the table; she followed suit with her briefcase. He pulled his chair a little farther to the other side; she did the same with hers.

Rick appeared at her side. "The stockperson is collecting the books from the back now."

Gracie's heart skipped a beat. She grasped his arm before he could walk away. A completely devious plan was taking shape in her head. "Wait a minute…"

"Uh-oh. I don't know if I like that look."

"After what you just did, I don't particularly care what you like," she said with a generous smile. "Besides, do this and I just might think about forgiving you."

During the past few weeks she'd become very acquainted with the back rooms of bookstores, mostly because the bathroom was located there. While the odd store kept their stock neatly organized, the vast majority of them were lucky to find the day's shipment in the chaos. A glance around the monstrous, busy, shorthanded store told her that this particular one undoubtedly fell into the chaos category. "I don't know what's going on between you and Tanja, but you can't breathe a word of this to her. This is what I want you to do…"

A half hour later, Gracie sat happily greeting readers on her side of the table, signing dozens of copies of her book… while Dylan sat glowering on the other side, the manager repeatedly apologizing for the loss of his books.

"I put them near the door myself, ready to be set out, Dr. Dylan—"

"It's Fairbanks."

"Yes, of course. Sorry. Dr. Fairbanks." Gracie would have felt bad for the poor woman, except that she appeared a veteran of the signing wars and already looked a little put out by Dylan's pouty behavior. "My staff is going through the stock now. I'm sure your books will turn up very soon."

He waved her away.

Gracie handed a signed copy of her book to an elderly woman who needed the help of a cane to walk. "I hope you enjoy it."

"Oh, I'm sure I will, dear."

Gracie's smile froze in place as she thought of this morning. While the reader could have been her mother's mother, the dynamics were the same. *If you don't like the book, whatever you do, please don't call me.*

Dylan leaned closer to her, his clean, fresh aftershave giving him away before he spoke. Gracie nearly jumped out of her skin.

"I'd love to see her expression when she gets to the part about sexual safaris."

Gracie hiked a brow. "What? You don't think the older generation is entitled to a healthy sex life?"

The hardening of his jaw drew her attention to the enticing stretch of flesh. "Of course I do, but what you're prescribing is more liable to give them heart failure."

She leaned closer to whisper into his ear, nearly closing her eyes and enjoying the smell of him. "Ah, but what a way to go, huh?"

His cringe was exactly what she'd been after, but it also chased him back to his own side of the table. A shame, indeed, because she felt much better with him closer.

She smiled as a reader approached the table, glanced Dylan's way, then picked up one of her books. "You'd better be careful, Dylan, or I might think you're jealous."

"Jealous? Of what?" He gestured toward her stacks. "Except, of course, that you have your books and I don't."

Only moments before, Tanja had been handing out flyers promoting Dylan's book, but she seemed to have disappeared. Gracie cracked open the book the reader handed to her then glanced around. Interestingly enough, Rick had vanished, as well.

Curiouser and curiouser.

Another reader, another sale made under Dylan's glowering glare.

He got up from his chair. "That's it. I'm going back to check out what's going on."

Gracie held out the signed book to the reader then rose just as quickly. "I'm coming, too."

Dylan pulled up short. She nearly rammed into him from behind. "What for?"

She straightened her skirt. "Why, to help, of course." She flashed him a smile. What she was really trying to prevent was him stumbling across Rick with the goods in hand. "I feel…bad, you know, about my having books and you none."

"Bad. Uh-huh. Tell me why I'm not buying that?"

"Because you're cheap?"

She loved it when his jaw twitched that way.

He turned back toward the stockroom and she followed, covertly looking around for Rick and where he might have stashed the boxes holding Dylan's books. She didn't see anything. Not that she expected to, but one never knew. Before she could blink, she and Dylan were standing in the back room amid stacks upon stacks of towering boxes.

"I have my staff on it right now," Dylan mocked. He looked at her. "Do you see a single staff member?"

She pretended to look when what she was really doing was scoping out Rick. "Um, nope?"

"That sounds more like a question than an answer."

She crossed her arms. "Well, Dylan, the truth is it's hard to tell. The entire Houston Oilers could be hiding out back here and we would be none the wiser."

He grimaced. "Good point." He began weaving through the maze of boxes, nearly toppling a mountain on Gracie where she was on his heels.

"I hope you're insured," she said, awkwardly moving to still them.

He glanced at her over his shoulder. "I am. I think it's under the heading 'in cases of intentional maiming.'"

"Very funny."

"I thought so."

He stopped. This time she was so busy dodging teetering boxes she did walk straight into him. He turned around to steady her when she would have fallen back into a stack of old magazines.

She stared at him, appalled at the gulping sound she made at finding herself so unexpectedly close to him. She could handle anything so long as there was distance between them. But this...

He grinned at her. "A thank-you would be nice."

Gracie stared up into his face, unable to do anything but wonder at the heat of his hands through her jacket. She tried like hell to remind herself that the cad was engaged. Instead, she was curious about why he hadn't let her go yet.

She licked suddenly parched lips, recognizing the sign of anticipation for what it was, and knowing he did, too, if his smoldering gaze was anything to go by. The tightening of his fingers against her flesh told her it was.

He cleared his throat. "We really need to be looking for my books."

She nodded, then blurted, "Why *did* you have sex with me?"

Had she really just said that? Judging by the shocked expression on Dylan's face, she had.

She watched his magnificent throat work and squelched the desire to swallow the hot moisture gathering in her mouth.

If ever there was a time when one was given license to babble, this was definitely it. She licked her lips again and plunged straight in. "It's something I've been meaning to ask you, you know, why you had sex with me when it's obvious you hadn't wanted to, but, gee, it seemed I never got the chance. I mean with you being engaged and all—"

The remainder of her words were sealed off with the same type of breath-stealing, thigh-quivering kiss that had landed them in so much trouble the last time they were alone together. Gracie registered this, but she was helpless to do anything more than welcome it.

Making a low sound in her throat, she melded against him…crushing her chest to his…molding her hands against his tight little rear…butting her pelvis against his…and attacking his mouth with repeated open-lipped kisses like he was a buffet and his mouth the main course. She felt his erection grow between them and hummed in spiraling agreement, at that moment not caring that they were in a public bookstore, that anyone could walk in at any minute, or that the world would judge her a fool for giving herself to an engaged man…again. All she could think about was that she wanted him deep inside her, her slick, hot flesh surrounding him…*now*.

Dylan murmured something against her mouth. She couldn't be sure, but she thought it was something along the lines of "This is crazy. Absolutely, stark, raving mad." Even as he said it, his hands palmed her breasts through the material of her jacket and blouse, kneading the sensitive flesh almost roughly, and his leg found its way between hers, drawing it up until her skirt lifted and the course material of his wool pants rubbed provocatively against her damp silk panties.

Seeking firmer ground, he backed her through an aisle of boxes, his mouth never breaking contact with hers as she restlessly laved him with her tongue. Finally, a wall. But when Gracie reached back to brace herself against a quaking shudder, she knocked over a pile of boxes. Ignoring them and the racket they made, she fumbled for the front of Dylan's slacks to get at the thick erection swelling inside. At the same time, his fingers found the damp center of her panties. She collapsed against him as he dipped those same hot fingers inside and pressed them against her throbbing core.

Somewhere in the back of her mind, she thought that she'd always wanted to do it in a library. Well, okay, this wasn't exactly a library, but it did smell of books, and when you closed your eyes tight enough, it was easy to imagine it was a library. And her eyes were definitely closed.

"Help…me," she whispered, unable to get his belt undone.

When he pulled slightly back, she discovered why she'd had such a hard time. He had a double-locking belt. A double-locking belt, for God's sake. She gave a breathless laugh as he pressed against her, his head against hers as he apparently fought for air.

She'd just about figured out the complicated contraption that was the male equivalent of a chastity belt when he caught her hand firmly in his. She froze, realizing at the same instant that he wasn't pressed against her anymore.

"There they are."

Her heart nearly stopped. "Wh…what?"

He pulled away, staring at a box sandwiched in the middle of others. "My books."

Gracie collapsed against the wall, trying desperately to make sense of his words. When they finally registered, she curled her hands into fists, swearing she'd never go near another engaged man again if he would just forget the damn books and finish what he'd started.

He began levering the box out. She dragged in deep, heaving gasps of air and closed her eyes. Obviously, God wasn't taking special requests today.

"Heads up."

Gracie moved just in time to prevent herself from getting beaned by the boxes that had been resting on Dylan's books. She was just about to open her mouth and make an official demand for either his head or his...erection, when movement on the other side of the cleared half-stack stopped her from uttering a word.

"Tanja," Dylan said.

"Rick," she said.

The couple looked like a mirror image of what she and Dylan had been doing just moments earlier. Rick had a hand up Tanja's trendy black sweater, while Tanja's fingers were tunneled in his hair. You couldn't have wedged a magazine between their hips if you'd used a crowbar.

Gracie supposed she should be thankful the couple hadn't been caught doing it on the box of Dylan's books. But she was more concerned with being caught herself.

She hastened to push herself from the wall, trying to put herself back in order even as Dylan and the young couple did the same. The situation was so absurd, she might have laughed. If only she wasn't feeling so damn horny she could scream.

Rick's quiet chuckle broke the awkward silence. "Looks like we all had the same thing in mind."

Dylan's back snapped upright. "*We* were looking for my books."

Rick's grin appeared not affected at all. "So were we."

Gracie rolled her eyes to stare at the ceiling. "Okay, just so we're all straight on what happened back here, we're all in agreement that we were looking for the books, right?"

"Oh, good, you found them," a fifth voice said.

Gracie nearly hit the ceiling she was staring at when the manager's voice sounded around the corner.

Dylan hoisted up the box. He glanced at Gracie, his usual grimace firmly in place, his dark hair still adorably, sexily tousled. "Yes, we did."

The manager motioned at him. "Dr. Dylan, I'll have to ask you to put that down. It's against company policy for you to handle stock."

"They're my books."

She smiled at him patronizingly. "And I paid for them. Now put them back. I'll have one of my staff come back and collect them for you."

Clearing her throat, Gracie navigated her way around Dylan, being extra careful not to touch him. "I'd suggest you do as she asks. She doesn't look like someone you'd like to mess with."

"She wouldn't be the first."

Gracie caught his meaning and gaped at him. The way he was acting, you'd think she'd been the one who'd molested *him*. Oh, but wasn't that special?

She made a none-too-elegant face at him and left the room.

TEN MINUTES LATER, GRACIE was no closer to getting a handle on what had happened back in the storeroom than she had while it was happening. She checked her reflection in her compact again, then slid a covert glance toward Dylan, who was sitting closed-faced, tight-mouthed and still bookless next to her.

She snapped the compact closed. "Good thing you found your books when you did, huh? No telling what might have happened otherwise."

He tugged at his tie. "Nothing would have happened." He met her gaze squarely. "I would have stopped it before it went too far."

Oh, but he was smug now that all was said and done, wasn't he? "Ah, so that's the reason for the double-locking belt."

She didn't miss his glance at the area in question. "It was a gift," he said.

Gracie let her gaze travel the path his had taken. Her eyes widened at the bulge she saw behind his zipper. Was she crazy, or did he still have a hard-on? Talk about gifts…

She immediately snatched her attention away from dangerous territory. "A gift, huh?" she said, keeping her voice from showing her own state of distraction. "From your fiancée?"

He winced. She took the response as an unqualified yes.

He looked over his shoulder toward the stockroom door. "What's taking so damn long?"

Gracie couldn't stop herself from leaning closer and lowering her voice suggestively. "I don't know. Do you want to go find out?"

He jumped and she withdrew to her own side of the table with a satisfied smile. Oh, Dr. Dylan might pretend he wasn't as on edge as she was, but his giveaway reactions said differently. High and mighty and impervious to her in public, put them in a room alone together—or in a room they thought they were alone in together—and the truth was revealed in all its tongue panting, slacks-bulging glory. It was reassuring to know that the uptight guy had no more control over his hormones than she did.

Gracie accepted a book for signing from a reader, catching a glimpse of a woman approaching Dylan's side of the table.

A well-dressed young professional woman around Gracie's age who was blonde, built and obviously on the prowl. It was more than just the way her gaze seemed attached to Dylan. It was the way that gaze honed in on him like a starving man at a good old Texas BBQ.

Gracie handed the book to the reader and thanked her, taking more interest than necessary in the woman who sashayed up to Dylan's side of the table as if he wore a sign that said Open for Business.

"Oh, dear, don't tell me you've sold out of your book already?" she said in a slow, measured Southern drawl Gracie openly envied.

Given the ridiculousness of the situation so soon after the stockroom, Gracie laughed. Dylan slid her a scathing look. She held her hands palms up and made a "what?" sign.

The woman seemed not at all affected by Gracie and her reaction. The woman cooed. "I was so looking forward to buying it."

Gracie itched with the desire to grill the woman on the contents of the book and exactly why she was interested in buying it, but she held her tongue. Her own book definitely wouldn't be able to offer the woman anything. She probably not only appeared to know every trick in any book, she presumably thought she had invented them.

Dylan grinned, flashing a wickedly sexy dimple at the woman. He leaned forward and said, "I'm assured more copies will be available in a few moments if you'd care to wait."

More copies? He'd yet to sell one.

Gracie's face heated. Of course no one had to know that the reason for his poor sales rested solely in her lap.

"I'd love to," the woman drawled.

Gracie was thankful that there wasn't another chair in sight. She was convinced the woman would have pulled it up right next to Dylan's.

She accepted a copy of her book from an older gentleman who requested she sign it for his wife. Gracie scolded herself for paying too much attention to the conversation taking place not two feet from her right ear and smiled up at him. She normally asked for the name of the person for whom the gift was intended, but this time said, "Actually, I think it might be a good idea if you read the book yourself. In my experience, I've discovered that women tend to be affronted when given a gift of this nature. You know, as if you're making personal comment on their need for sexual tutelage."

The Southern belle put her hands on the signing table—something she would never have been able to do had Dylan's books been there—and practically leaned across the expanse toward him.

The gentleman she addressed reddened. "My wife is over there. She requested I come over here and get it signed for her."

"Oh." Gracie's smile widened. "Then my apologies, sir." She asked the name, signed the book, then handed it to him. "Still, you might want to give a section or two a look. Chapter Four, I think, might provide a bit of entertainment." She winked at him.

He looked at her as if she were insane. Either that or an oversexed sex therapist. Neither prospect seemed particularly appealing to Gracie as he walked away.

She sighed and flopped back in the chair, nearly groaning when she realized Miss Texas was still chatting up Dylan next to her.

Just look at him. He was lapping up every sugarcoated word like a love-starved puppy. Which got her to thinking...

Seeing as Dylan's latest book was his second, it meant he was a veteran to the promotional trail. She tapped her unpainted fingernail against her lips, thinking, thinking. If that was the case, had the other night been the first time he'd been tempted by the sexual wares of another? Or was he used to being molested by horny women in stockrooms?

Oh, he'd said he was celibate, but was that really the case? Or did he mean he'd only been celibate with his fiancée?

Gracie crossed her arms, suddenly deciding she didn't like the direction of her thoughts. She also decided she didn't like being left out.

She sat up and folded her hands on the table. "Oh, pardon me," she said, interrupting the far too quiet conversation next to her and smiling solicitously at the woman, "but I just adore that necklace you're wearing. Where ever did you find it?"

The woman turned to her and beamed. Gracie's smile turned genuine.

There was only one thing women enjoyed more than staking out a sexual conquest, and that was talking about shopping.

As Gracie listened to the long explanation on how the woman had come across the piece in a little out-of-the-way antique shop in Austin—not a difficult task considering she really did like the necklace—she noticed Dylan's grin had left and he now sat glowering at her instead of the other way around.

Five minutes into the conversation, in which Dylan was relegated to making noncommittal grunts of agreement and smiling congenially, the manager finally rushed to the table followed by two stock boys who immediately spread Dylan's books out in front of him.

His resulting grin made Gracie's tongue swell, threatening to choke off air. God, but he was devastating when he smiled. Completely irresistible.

The woman ended up buying both of their books, then with a little wave, bid them adieu.

Finally Gracie found herself alone with Dylan again. Well, alone as two people could be in a public store, minus a sexually active PR rep and an assistant. This was as good a time as any to find out just how serious his engagement was. And whether or not he routinely climbed on and off the celibacy wagon during promotional junkets like these.

"So," Gracie began, straightening her books. "How's your wife?"

Well, that was certainly one way to open the conversation. She began to question her own faculties until she caught his wince. While not entirely judicious, her query produced the response she was after.

He slanted her a wary glance. "I'm not married. Yet."

"Yes, but you're as good as, right?" she prompted.

He tugged at his collar in a way that made her want to do some tugging of her own. "And what would you know about committed relationships?"

She smiled, deciding to ignore the jab at her principles. "You mean given what happened in Chicago? Or what just happened in the storeroom? Given both incidents, I'd say I know at least as much as you."

"That was a low blow."

"And you deserved it."

"True."

She looked at him a little more closely. He really did feel bad about all this, didn't he? It wasn't a source of minor agitation. It truly bothered him that he'd been unfaithful. So what did that say about the reason he'd done it? Not just the other night, but a few minutes ago?

Her stomach dipped, then bounced right back up into her throat. Was it possible that he had been so incredibly attracted to her he hadn't been able to help himself? Or had time away from his fiancée and circumstances weakened him to fundamental urges?

She wasn't sure she liked either choice, but still couldn't quite squelch her curiosity to find out. She felt as she had when she was fifteen and in her freshman year of high school. Her parents had insisted on sending her to an exclusive private school away from home and away from her friends. Of course, she'd felt out of place and developed a crush on the first male she crossed paths with. In an all-girl institution, it happened to be her English Lit teacher. There had been something…*dreamy* was the word she used then, about the way he quoted Shakespeare.

By midterm, she had convinced herself that he felt the same way about her. But when she approached him after class one Friday afternoon, she abruptly found out that wasn't the case. She'd felt so humiliated.

She'd been transferred immediately to another classroom and had persuaded herself that the entire school knew of the incident.

Remembering it all now made her shudder. Well, that little visit to the past had certainly helped, hadn't it?

She restacked her books, then moved them again. "You know, seeing as you are engaged, you might consider being a little more…conservative with prowling females from here on out. Just a bit of advice."

"I wouldn't say you are a prowler."

She glared at him. "Not me, Einstein. You're just as much to blame as I am in our case. I'm talking about Miss Texas."

"Miss Tex…oh." His dark brows drew together, making him that much more attractive. Then his brows lifted and he sat back. "Oh. You mean…what you're referring to…are you saying that nice young woman at the table just now was coming on to me?"

"Like a steam wrap."

He looked at her. "I beg to differ. She was just indulging in conversation until my books were available."

Gracie glanced at the books in question, hoping she wasn't as flushed as she felt. "Conversation…right."

"Is it so hard to believe that she was just interested in my book?"

"Yes," she said bluntly. "It is."

His laugh was unexpected and sent a shiver skidding down her spine. "Spoken like a true competitor."

"I'm speaking as a woman. If it's one thing we know how to do, it's spot another woman on the make. And her dance card definitely had your name written all over it."

"Dance card?"

She waved her hand. "You know what I mean."

"Uh-huh." He sat back and crossed his arms, pulling her gaze to his flat, tight midsection. God, how he had felt squeezed between her thighs. Much better than a pillow any day. "So now you're speaking for all women."

Gracie made a face at him. "Ask your fiancée. I'm sure she'll tell you the same thing." She tucked her hair behind her ear. "Men are always a little slow on the uptake when it comes to women, on the make or otherwise."

"Is that so?"

She nodded. "It's a known fact."

"Documented?"

"Very funny."

He clicked his Mont Blanc pen closed then tossed it to the table. "You know, if I didn't know better I'd think you were the jealous one."

"Jealous? Me? I don't have an envious bone in my body."

"Everyone has a jealous bone or two, Gracie. It's what makes us human."

"Then I'm an alien."

The glimmer of amusement in his green eyes made it impossible to turn away from him.

She cleared her throat, fighting against the heat wave of attraction that swept over her. He was practically a married man, for God's sake. And so long as they weren't alone in a storeroom or anywhere else, she could handle that. Right? "Anyway, you can't tell me you haven't had your share of come-ons during events like these."

"I could say the same of you."

"I've experienced one or two. Not always from males, either. And you avoided my question."

He finally glanced away, releasing her from whatever magical spell he'd put her under with his gaze. "Like you said, I've had my share. Females have come on to you?"

"Uh-huh. And how does your fiancée feel about females coming on to you when you're on the road?"

He winced again.

In fact, she thought, looking at him a little more closely, he winced whenever she referred to the woman he planned to marry. Because he had yet to tell her about the other night? Or were there other reasons responsible for his interesting behavior?

"What's her name?"

"Pardon me?"

"Your fiancée. What's her name? She does have a name, doesn't she? Or does she go around referring to herself as the future Mrs. Dylan Fairbanks?"

There it was again. That wince.

"Okay, you're giving off enough signals here to choke a Texas cow, Dr. Dylan. What gives?" At his look of surprise, she held up her hand. "Wait, don't tell me—you're already married." The prospect made her sit back in her chair and groan aloud. God, she thought the guilt was bad when she found out he was engaged. The idea that she had slept with a married man made her want to throw up.

"Her name is Diana. And no, we're not married," he said.

Gracie whooshed a deep breath, immediately relieved.

"In fact, we're not even officially engaged yet. I, um, was planning on asking her next week."

She stared at him as if he'd just grown another head. "What?"

Her voice raised to a decibel level she hadn't known she could reach. Somewhere between a shout and shriek, it earned them the attention of not only passersby, but also some of the outside mall patrons.

"What what?" Dylan said, startled. "Even you said that I'm as good as married."

"That's when I thought you were already engaged." She stuck her head in his direction. "Do you know what kind of hell I've put myself through these past few days?" She waved her hand to indicate the area behind them. "How...upset I was about what happened back there? Aside from calling myself every name in the trucker's handbook, I considered having the words *home wrecker* embroidered on my underwear just so I would remember the next time I decided to give in to my baser instincts."

"Come on, Gracie, what's the difference? Engaged...practically engaged...the only difference is a word."

"A very significant word." She started ticking items off on her fingers. "And a wedding date. And a guest list. And a down payment on a house with a white picket fence." She balled her hands into fists and made a strangled sound of frustration.

Gracie barely noticed when Rick came hurrying up from some hidden location in the stacks, concern marring his face. She was too busy trying to reduce Dylan to the puddle of slime that he was.

But Rick would not be ignored. "All right, Gracie, what gives?"

She snapped open her mouth to tell him.

"No, forget about that for a minute. There's something I want to tell you first."

She stared at her assistant, out of the corner of her eye noticing Tanja slink up to stand next to Dylan. She didn't like the looks of this.

Rick cleared his throat. "Um, we all know how both of you reacted when you showed up to find the other here."

Gracie's eyelids narrowed by millimeters. "Uh-huh."

Tanja said, "But after seeing the chemistry we both just witnessed we have to question the sincerity behind that response."

Gracie wished it *were* possible to shoot glare daggers.

"What Tanja means is…" Rick straightened. "Well, after considering the exceptional success of your joint appearances, and consulting with your publishers, we've all decided that it's in everyone's best interest if you are scheduled together for the duration of your tour."

Gracie stared at him for long moments, mouth agape, seconds away from spittle drooling out of the side, convinced her assistant had just gone completely, utterly, loony-bin-material insane. It was all she could do to stop herself from falling off her chair. She turned her head to stare in the same openmouthed way at Dylan and found him making a choking sound and grasping desperately at his tie.

8

DEAR LORD, HOW WAS HE going to make it through ten more days of this godforsaken promotional tour?

Seven hours had passed since he'd learned he and Gracie would be working together, side by side, for the remainder of the tour. But somehow the news had yet to completely seep through his skull. He hadn't succeeded in getting a grasp on the situation through dinner with Tanja, Gracie and Rick at a Houston steak house that touted traditional barbecue. Gracie had unabashedly licked each of her fingers after clearing a plate full of ribs, making him want to groan with longing. And now sitting in his hotel room, trying to meet the deadline of his weekly newspaper column, he was still grappling with the knowledge that Dr. Hottie would be by his side for days. Even the frustrating questions he chose to respond to—the worst being whether or not oral sex was really sex at all or just foreplay—could not distract him.

All he could think about was Gracie's response to finding out he wasn't engaged. *Yet,* he reminded himself. He wasn't engaged yet. Gracie's response kept getting pushed aside by the wicked image of her gazing at him provocatively as in turn she slipped each of her sauce-covered fingers into her mouth at the restaurant. Neither the picture nor the thought was conducive to getting a good night's sleep or working up a game plan that would see him safely through the next week and a half.

Dylan repositioned the too-soft pillows for the third time, then sat back in the bed again, clutching Gracie's book in his hands. Chapter Five—Sexual Safaris. He cringed, then leafed through the other chapters before coming back to five. Cracking the hardcover to hold it open, he glanced at the clock to find it after midnight. He really wished Tanja could have gotten them out to Baltimore tonight rather than having to wait until morning. When he completed an event, spending the night in the city in question seemed…anticlimactic somehow.

"Haven't you had enough climaxes in the past week?" he grumbled under his breath. He winced when his body gave him an unequivocal no.

But his body was completely unreliable without his head guiding his actions. Look at the mess it had gotten him into already. He'd better get a handle on his libido quickly if he held out any hope of making it through the next ten days.

Baltimore was next on the list, Memphis the day after that, then Los Angeles and he would be home in San Francisco for two short days before hitting the road again.

Ticking off his immediate schedule wasn't working. An obvious understatement when an image of Gracie's flushed face filled his mind again. Rather than fighting it this time, though, he settled back against the pillows a little more comfortably and sighed. So long as the thoughts weren't of a sexual nature, he'd be fine. And, oh, boy, did she give him loads to think about in other departments.

Had she really given herself that hard a time when she'd thought he was engaged? All indicators pointed that way. Which flew in the face of everything he thought he knew about the outspoken, sexually uninhibited woman.

Maybe she was right. Perhaps men were slow on the uptake when it came to women, despite all the input since the sixties' sexual and cultural revolution. He certainly had not thought the woman he'd been talking to was coming on to him. Then again, he'd missed the signals Gracie had been sending him, as well, perhaps even as far back as the shower scene.

He'd never be able to think, see, or discuss the movie *Psycho* again without seeing Gracie naked in that shower, her supple skin lathered up and inviting.

He grimaced. *Stick to the nonsexual.*

Since the beginning his estimations of Gracie, and his attraction for her, had been way off the mark. Off the mark? Who was he kidding? Hell, they'd landed clear off the charts. It began with overrating his ability to sway her to his way of thinking, and had taken a serious downward spiral when he'd taken her like a wild man on that kitchen counter.

A knock sounded on the wall behind him, followed by a low, unmistakably female moan. On the heels of his previous thought, the sounds were not a good omen.

God, no. Not tonight.

Well, he supposed he should be thankful of at least one thing. He was in no danger of succumbing to his attraction for Gracie tonight. Rick had managed to get Gracie a seat on a flight out to Baltimore tonight. In fact, she'd left for the airport right after dinner. He'd thought it a little odd that Rick had stayed behind, until he explained that Gracie was from Baltimore.

Good. That meant he wouldn't be sleeping under the same roof with her in Maryland, either. Very good.

He cracked open the book in his lap again, though he had never closed it, and tried to concentrate on the words written there.

He did have to give Gracie credit. In his cursory examination of the book, he couldn't help noticing that she'd put together a cohesive piece on her philosophies. Too often psychologists were so wrapped up in their own self-importance they didn't give thought to things like consistency and structure. But from the titling of Gracie's chapters to the bibliography and credits listed in the back of the book, he found hers didn't appear that way at all. In that department, she passed with flying colors.

Another knock on the wall...another moan, this time more pronounced.

Dylan swallowed hard and reached out and switched on the television. CNN. He pressed the volume control, but it refused to go up high enough to drown out the undeniable evidence of a couple having sex coming from the next room. He switched it off and instead turned on the radio. He found a broadcast of National Public Radio's nightly news. There. That was better.

He looked down at the book again, at the chapter dedicated to sexual safaris. And found himself immediately engrossed...and appalled. He quickly finished the section, then paged back to the beginning, unable to believe what he'd just read. Arbitrarily, he took back the points he'd given Gracie for organizational abilities. When combined with the minus points earned on content, one very sexy Dr. Grace Mattias was seriously in the hole.

He clapped the book closed, clutching it tightly with both hands. She certainly wasn't suggesting that the only way a person could find themselves sexually, to learn to be comfortable with their bodies and voicing their wants and their needs, was through anonymous sex, was she? She alluded to the fact that attraction stemmed from emotion, and emotion led to consideration of the other's feelings. But she encouraged the reader to put all that aside and enjoy sex for sex's sake alone.

He also recognized that she had followed her own advice the other night, right before they...well, adjourned their activities to the kitchen.

She'd avoided conversation of a personal nature, keeping

questions limited to the professional. After all, as she pointed out in the chapter, the less you know someone, the better.

Of course, he'd veered away from the personal as well, but for survival purposes.

The next giveaway was no discussion of her intentions. Her intent to let things play out naturally and not box herself in should she decide to change her mind at the last minute.

Oh, if only she had changed her mind, he wouldn't be having trouble sleeping now.

Next was the total lack of inhibition.

He knocked the back of his head lightly but effectively against the wall behind him. He could have done without that particular reminder. It brought back not only the memory of her luscious mouth, but the feel of her hands on his erection, her lips poised mere millimeters away. He was convinced that one flick of that naughty tongue would have done him in then and there. Then there was the vision of her with her skirt hiked up around her waist, her panties history, her bare bottom resting on top of that counter, her thighs spread in invitation. Or the way she'd leaned back, shamelessly tilting her hips upward to allow him deeper, mind-blowing penetration, her breasts rocking with each thrust into her slick wetness.

He swallowed hard, agitated to discover that a certain part of his body was growing firmer.

He really had to stop this…this fantasizing. Only it wasn't a fantasy, was it? It was a memory. One he needed to erase but quick before he could even think about moving on in life with Diana.

For long moments he concentrated on the radio broadcast until news on the current situation in the Middle East evened out his breathing and brought him back to a semimanageable state.

What had he been thinking before he'd been so thoroughly interrupted? Oh, yes. Gracie's sexual safari advice.

Step one had been no personal questions. Two, surrendering to the call of nature. Three, complete inhibition. And four...

Four was no postcoital mention of any future contact with the sexual conquest.

He slapped the book closed. Well, that certainly hadn't gone as planned, had it? Not only had they had future contact, but they would continue to see each other throughout the days ahead.

While the prospect both excited and scared the hell out of him, it wasn't what bothered him most about Chapter Five. Oh, no, not by a long shot. What got under his skin and refused to budge were her names for the couple involved in the safari. Words like *hunter* and *prey* were sprinkled deliberately throughout, further lending a wild quality to the advice, as well as encouraging anonymity.

And he knew without a doubt that he had ultimately played willing prey to Gracie's very skillful hunter.

Tossing the book to the second double bed, he shut off the light and slid down under the covers. Why did he get the impression his dreams would be filled with jungle images, big guns and soft flesh? He pummeled the pillows into place. And why didn't the prospect bother him more?

As he lay back and closed his eyes, he decided he'd done enough self-analyzing for one night. After all, there was always tomorrow to beat himself up.

THERE WAS NOTHING QUITE like a crisp autumn sunset on the banks of the Chesapeake to clear a tired mind. And if Gracie's mind was anything, it was definitely tired. Overrun. Plagued with questions that robbed her of appetite and held sleep hostage.

Not that she would starve—she'd never enjoyed a meal more than when devouring those ribs in front of Dylan's hungry stare last night—or die from exhaustion, but the brisk breeze did allow for a new perspective on things. Especially out from under her parents' roof.

She turned toward the mammoth wood-and-glass structure behind her, pushing her ponytail from her face when the wind blew it there. She tucked her chin into the neck of her Irish cable-knit sweater and tucked her hands into her jeans' pockets. She swore she could make out her mother watching her from an upstairs window. But whether it was Priscilla returned from her outing, or the reflection of the wispy clouds dotting the darkening blue sky, she couldn't be sure. She did know that after the strangely normal drink she'd shared with her parents last night in her father's stuffy library, she was waiting for the other shoe to drop.

Never one to do things by halves, with her first advance check from the publisher, she'd bought a condo not too far from her parents' house and decided to completely renovate it. Which made it unlivable during the three weeks the contractor would take. No problem, she'd told herself at the time. She'd be on tour anyway, and during the two days she would be back in Baltimore, she'd stay in her old room at her parents' house.

What she hadn't factored into that little plan was her mother calling her in Houston wanting to share her sex life.

She clamped her eyes shut. The price one paid for built-in bookshelves.

Not that her mother had said anything to her last night during that drink. Oh, no. Priscilla was more sophisticated than to even let evidence of their personal discussion show in the presence of her husband. But those few minutes Gracie had spent on the phone with her mother proved fateful. Gracie could no longer look at her parents together without thinking about her mother's comment.

Had her parents really not had sex for three months?

Not that you could tell. They seemed the same as ever to her. Her father sat in his chair. Priscilla perched on the arm of that same chair in the beginning, then moved to sit in the chair next to him. They talked of the same old things. Work, weather, politics, not an inflection or hesitation hinting at the concern her mother expressed to her yesterday. Of course, she didn't know their complete sexual history, either. For all she knew, a normal sex life to her mother was a once-in-a-while go at it.

Or her parents very well might have set the sheets on fire every night.

She sighed. Her mother hadn't breathed one word while they were with her father in the library. She'd waited until Gracie was in bed, sheet pulled up to her chin and just nodding off to sleep, to sneak in and startle her.

"Gracie? Gracie? Are you awake?"

For a long moment, Gracie had pretended to be sleeping, but that hadn't stopped her mother. She'd sat on the edge of Gracie's bed, determined to wake her. Then she'd had to listen to the story all over again.

After figuring out that her mother wasn't going to leave her alone until she responded in some definitive way to the quest for advice, she'd said, "Mom, have you ever considered just talking to him?"

Priscilla's appalled expression had been priceless. "Women of my generation don't initiate conversations of that…delicate nature."

Gracie had sighed and said, "Well, maybe it's time you did."

She knew her mother hadn't been happy with her suggestion. And probably discarded it the moment she finally left the room.

At least that's what Gracie preferred to think her mother had done. Imagining her parents discussing the problems that plagued their sex life was not the way to get a good night's sleep.

She cringed and turned back toward the Chesapeake, not

liking the direction of her thoughts. In all honesty, she wasn't enjoying much of what she thought about lately. What had life been like before? Before her book and Dylan and her mother's new bizarre attempt at bonding with her? She couldn't remember. But she was sure that it had been…great.

No matter how hard she tried, there was no returning to that idyllic period anytime soon.

A jogger passed her, shouting a hello. She smiled and waved, then walked backward watching the fifty-something man run in the other direction. Oh, what she wouldn't give for a nice refreshing jog right now.

What was she talking about? She couldn't run twenty feet before doubling over in pain with a god-awful stitch in her side. She'd accepted long ago that walking was about as close to jogging as she was going to get.

She'd also learned that occupying her mind with mundane thoughts would not solve anything. Before long she'd be right back where she started.

She couldn't stay out here forever. It would be getting dark soon and she would have to return to the house, no matter how much she yearned to check in to a local hotel.

Of course the thought would have to occur to her now, after she'd already essentially checked in to her parents' place until tomorrow.

She pushed her hair back again and sighed. Right about now Consuela would be setting the table for dinner, her last chore for the day. Considering that she hadn't eaten anything since the ribs in Houston last night, the prospect of a good meal should appeal to her. But it didn't. Her mind was far too busy turning details over and under, inside and out.

And with Rick in curious cahoots with Tanja, she suddenly had plenty of details to worry over.

Initially she'd been thankful when Rick had scheduled her for an appearance on a local news-entertainment show, simply because it meant she could avoid being alone again with her mother. Only Priscilla had already left the house when Gracie had finally rolled out of bed, running late, as usual. And with Rick meeting her at the television station, he hadn't been around to remind her that Dylan would be appearing with her.

Let's see, she thought, holding her hands out. On one side she weighed her mother…the other, Dylan. It was difficult to decide whom she wanted to be around less.

Of course, he'd appeared as pleased as she was about being together again so soon. Well, at least until he and the conservative male host quickly figured out that they were of the same mind and bonded. Between the two of them, they'd basically made her look like a sex addict. She made a face. Chalk one up for Dr. Dylan. She'd considered telling Dylan that she suspected the host probably hadn't gotten laid for a good ten years and pointing out the signs that he was latently homosexual but would never acknowledge the closet door much less walk through it.

But she figured she looked bad enough in his eyes without heaping that little bit more on top of it. She couldn't quite figure out why she cared what he thought about her one way or another. Still that teenager feeling abandoned at the private school longing for attention? Or was she stinging after his rejection of her after the kitchen encounter? She smiled at her pun. Encounter. Counter.

She sighed, not even finding her own attempts at humor amusing.

It didn't help matters to know that her mother and her cronies religiously watched the show. Probably made an extra effort today because she was on it. She could see ten perfectly coiffed women her mother's age seated in an elegant living room, sipping tea out of antique cups, gathered around a television set rolled into the room just for the event.

It was just as well that she'd opted out of attending the lecture scheduled for this afternoon at a nearby country club. If she thought the host and her mother's cronies were a tough audience, she could only imagine what she would have faced there.

Besides, Dylan was the one with the teaching background. Just his format. And so *not* hers.

Coward.

Yes, she was. And damned proud of it, too.

Rick hadn't been pleased, which, after his clandestine activities, cheered her. But she'd preferred to spend the afternoon bugging her contractor at her condo than facing a bunch of pinched-faced retirees any day.

In an instant, it seemed, day slid into night. Taking her hands from her pockets, she started trudging the fifty yards or so back to the house in the dark, hoping she wouldn't trip over something and break her neck.

Sneaking in the side door, she took off her shoes and tiptoed upstairs to her room to change. Aside from the sand on her jeans, she had sawdust in her sweater and a smear of something she didn't want to try to identify on her left pant leg. There was one thing her mother hated more than her being late to dinner and that was showing up at the table looking like a ragamuffin, as her mother used to call her when she was younger. Of course, her green mohawk deserved something far more severe than ragamuffin, but hey, it was the best her mother had been able to do.

In her bedroom she'd peeled off her clothes and headed for the connecting bath. A quick hot shower later, she rifled through her still-packed suitcase, frowning when she found nothing but dirty clothes. She had planned to put a load in the wash earlier, but had forgotten in her state of hopelessness. Giving up on the idea of the suitcase magically providing her with clean clothes, she turned toward her old closet. Certainly she'd left a few items in there. Whirling open the door, she stood in front of the dated selections. Yikes, had she really worn this stuff? She fingered a denim jacket with her name spelled out in pink sequins, evidence that these... things were indeed hers.

The least hideous item in the bunch was a denim dress she didn't think she'd ever worn simply because her mother had bought it for her. With short sleeves and V-neck, it stretched down to just above her knees. Not exactly seasonable, but beggars couldn't be choosers.

"Underwear," she murmured to herself, going through the bureau drawers. The drawers seemed to have every pair of pajamas she'd worn since birth but there was absolutely no sign of underwear.

"Gracie!"

Her hands froze on a pair of blue cloud-covered flannels and she rolled her eyes heavenward. God help her, but her mother's voice had the same impact on her now as it did when she was a kid caught going through her *mother's* underwear drawer. She hadn't found anything interesting then, and now she wasn't finding anything period.

She shoved the last drawer closed. Well. This was an interesting dilemma now wasn't it? She'd been concerned about showing up at dinner in inappropriate clothing. Now she was facing sitting at the table minus one important piece.

She considered the length of the skirt. Okay, this was doable. So long as she was careful when she sat down, made sure her chair was well under the table, no one would know she wasn't wearing any panties.

"Gracie!" her mother called out from downstairs again. Muttering under her breath, she filled a wicker basket full of her dirty laundry and hurried into the hall.

"Coming!" she yelled, though unnecessarily, because she could already see Priscilla standing at the bottom of the stairs.

Halfway down the stairs it struck Gracie that something was wrong with this picture. She slowed her steps and squinted at her mother's smiling face. Uh-oh. She was smiling. Priscilla never smiled when she had to call Gracie twice for anything.

Oh, no. Please don't make her bring up her little problem *now.* Not when the fresh air from her walk had made her appetite return for the first time since yesterday.

All too soon the steps ran out and she was face-to-face with her suspiciously happy mother. She moved the wicker basket from where she held it strategically in front of her and tucked it under her arm. "Um, Mom, I really don't think now is the greatest time for us to continue our little discussion. Dad's waiting—"

"Discussion?" Priscilla's perfectly arched brows drew together, then flew up high on her forehead as she apparently caught on. "Oh, heavens no! That's not why I was waiting for you."

"Okay," Gracie said, drawing out the word. She couldn't quite bring herself to ask what the reason was. She was too afraid of finding out the answer. Her mother had probably invited to dinner the whole crew of friends who'd likely watched this morning's show with her. No, no wait. She was chafing in her suit to tell her that in the two hours since she'd returned from peeking on the renovations being done at her condo that it had caught fire and burned down.

Gracie bounced slightly, repositioned the basket. Whatever it was, her mother had better spill it soon, because she was getting a wicked draft up her skirt from where the front door was still open.

Priscilla's smile widened. "I have a little surprise for you, Grace."

Gracie barely heard her as she slowly turned her head toward that ominously open door. It was November. Her mother didn't leave the door open in June, much less November.

"Oh, for Pete's sake," Priscilla said with a sigh. "What is taking him so long?"

· *Him?* What did she mean by *him?* Gracie started shaking her head, hoping against hope that her mother was talking about her father.

But as her mother dashed out the door, then reappeared moments later practically towing the man in question inside, Gracie knew her hopes were in vain.

The wicker basket slipped from her grip and thunked to the polished wood floor as she found herself staring at one very yummy Dr. Dylan Fairbanks.

9

DYLAN SAT STIFFLY AT the formal dining room table staring at where Gracie sat completely shell-shocked across from him. She looked as if he'd just appeared out of thin air. Which, of course, he had...with a little bit of Priscilla Mattias's persistence. Persistence? More like mother-handling. The woman had literally dragged him out of the country club, maneuvered him away from his waiting taxi and stuffed him into the front seat of her Lexus. She then proceeded to drive him here, to her house.

A clink of a serving spoon against a dish brought his attention back to the conversation. Gracie's mother said, "It's the funniest thing, really. After catching this morning's show at Adele's—" she slid a glance at Gracie that puzzled him "—Colleen invited us all to her country club for the seminar. Her reasoning, and my entire reason for going, of course, was in the hopes that you could somehow redeem yourself, Grace.

"Of course, I had no idea that you had decided to opt out." She took a sip of wine. "Very bad form, by the way. You could have feigned an illness in the family or something."

Gracie rolled her eyes. "A lie your presence would have certainly negated."

"I didn't mean for you to say I was ill."

"No, but you would have immediately made it clear that no one else was, either."

"Not if you had told me in advance." Priscilla frowned. "My, but you're in a mood tonight."

And Dylan didn't doubt that he was the cause of it. Even if he didn't think that way, he would have known the instant Gracie looked at him, turning the stare she had just bestowed on her mother on him.

"Anyway, where was I?" Priscilla continued. "Oh, yes, the country club..."

Dylan slowly spooned some sort of black rice onto his plate, then handed the serving bowl to the dark, tall, robust man who had been introduced as Dr. Richard Mattias, the most renowned reconstructive surgeon on the Eastern Seaboard. The movement placed Dylan's tie smack dab in the middle of whatever fish was on his plate. He cast a glance around to see if anyone had noticed, but Gracie was busy glaring at her own food, Priscilla was rattling on about it being her first time at the country club, and gee, they really should join and Richard was watching his wife with a bemused expression on his handsomely lined face.

Dylan discreetly dabbed at the stain with his linen napkin. He was astounded by the glimpse he was getting into Gracie's life and upbringing. Given her free-thinking philosophies, he'd figured she had come from a lower- to middle-class background, raised by parents that were by-products of the seventies disco scene. Instead he was surprised to find both Priscilla and Richard ultraconservatives who probably had never even seen *Saturday Night Fever* and had no idea who John Travolta was.

He really didn't know where he got off making assumptions about anyone, considering his own background. His parents, Moonbeam and Frank, often commented that they had no idea how they'd produced a kid so thoroughly uncool.

By the same token, he got the definite impression that

Gracie's parents thought she was somewhere between a quack and a loose woman.

Which put Gracie's parents and him on the same side, didn't it? Something he would never have imagined possible.

He glanced at her across the table as she said something to her mother, her tone more congenial than exasperated presumably now that the shock of his appearance had worn off a little. He supposed that part of his job was to be an expert on people. But that Gracie proved him wrong so many times... well, it was more than a blow to his ego, it made him rethink his entire approach.

He slowly tuned back in to Priscilla. "...so we all ended up sitting in the back, and it struck me that we were all acting like a bunch of schoolgirls—"

Richard's chuckle broke into her narrative. "Cilla, do you plan on getting to the point sometime soon?"

Dylan didn't miss Gracie's surprised glance at her father. Another subtle insight into the life and times of Grace Mattias? Did father and daughter disagree more than they agreed? Given surface appearances, he gathered that they did. Not surprising given Dr. Richard Mattias's traditional surgical position to his only child's determination to set the world free sexually.

That meant that mother had to be the mediator of the three of them. The one who kept the peace. Although Dylan wasn't sure what peace she was keeping, considering the clever verbal jabs she aimed in Gracie's direction every now and again.

He found himself liking all three of them. As far as dysfunctional families went, their differences seemed to bring them together rather than pull them apart. There was a connectedness between them that set off a tiny pang in his stomach.

He hadn't yet taken Diana to meet his parents, even though he'd shared dinner with hers on numerous occasions.

He wondered what Gracie would say on that topic, then reminded himself that he didn't want to know.

"Well," Priscilla said, sighing and draping her napkin across her lap. "The long and the short of it is that Dylan's visiting our fair and delightful city from out of town and when I discovered he didn't have any pressing plans for the night, I invited him here."

Dylan nearly choked on his wine. The room fell silent and he pardoned himself, claiming the liquid had gone down the wrong pipe.

He met Gracie's watchful gaze. "She really was quite persuasive."

Was that a playful light in her brown eyes? Yes, he believed it was.

Richard chuckled. "Trust me. Gracie and I understand just how persuasive Cilla can be."

Gracie smiled. "Oh, yes. When Mom gets her teeth into someone, er, something, she doesn't let go."

Dylan laughed, glad to see Priscilla was taking all this really well. More than likely she was used to the playful ribbing.

"Yes, well, not everyone has a daughter as stubbornly set against marriage as you, Grace. Someone has to watch out after you," Priscilla said.

For the second time in as many minutes, Dylan nearly choked again, this time without the aid of beverage or food. When the coughing fit went on, Richard rounded the table and gave him a hearty pat on the back. "Good God, boy, are you all right?"

Dylan nodded, then picked up his glass of water, making sure Gracie's dad didn't decide he was in need of another whack before taking a long sip. "I'm…fine," he said, drinking more.

Convinced he had finally regained control over himself, he waited until Richard had reseated himself, then turned his attention to Priscilla. The best course of action to take, he thought, was to ignore the reference she'd just made to his being potential husband material to Gracie. "So you saw the show this morning? You didn't tell me at the club." He looked for his napkin, but it was no longer on his lap. It must have fallen to the floor while he was coughing.

Priscilla waved her hand. "There really wasn't time, was there? I mean with so many people waiting afterward to meet you…well, I figured there would be time enough to discuss that later."

"So what did you think?" he asked, looking on either side of his chair and not seeing the napkin.

Priscilla's smile was awfully attractive and familiar. Then he realized it was because it was exactly like Gracie's. "I thought you did a marvelous job." Dylan looked at Gracie as if to say "See, she approves of you," when her mother continued. "You and the host seemed to get along famously, Dylan. The girls and I agreed that you were the definite winner."

Gracie sighed. "It wasn't a debate, Mother."

"It wasn't? Well, it certainly seemed that way to me." She straightened her jacket sleeves. "It was also clear that I'm not the only one who finds your thoughts on…reproductive science a little…out there, dear."

Since attention was no longer focused on him, Dylan leaned over to retrieve his napkin. He moved the tablecloth out of the way, and popped his head under the table. The first thing that caught his eye was the way Gracie was sitting with one leg tucked under her bottom, though from above she had perfect posture. He also noticed she was barefoot and bare legged, something that had escaped his attention before. Blindly groping around, he found his napkin, allowing his gaze to travel up the smooth, pale length of her long, long legs. God, but she had incredible legs.

He nearly swallowed his tongue. She also had an incredible vulva. A fact defined because she wasn't wearing any panties, either.

"The word is *sex,* Mother."

Heat rushing down to his own decently covered private area, Dylan couldn't help himself from staring at the red-gold thatch of fleecy curls edging the rim of her swollen flesh. He swallowed hard, filled with the overwhelming urge to reach out and claim the area with his palm, to seek out the pink bud even now peeking at him through the protective curtain.

All at once he was back at that hotel in New York gazing upon her in her shower in all her naked, lathered-up glory. And he'd never wanted her more.

He noticed that above him the table had gone silent. Then Gracie made a small sound and slapped her thighs together.

Dylan smacked his head against the table on his way back up.

"Oh, there you are, dear. Is everything all right?" Priscilla asked.

He waved the piece of linen in his hand, his words curiously gravelly. "I, um, must have dropped it earlier."

He didn't dare look at Gracie for fear of what he might see there in her face. Afraid of what his own face would give away.

Priscilla happily filled in the void. "Anyway, Dylan, after dinner I was hoping that you and I might have a talk. Privately. There's something Grace and I were discussing—"

Gracie's gasp brought all eyes to her, despite Dylan's vow not to look at her. But if she was thinking about the eyeful he'd just gotten of her under the table, her shocked expression wasn't revealing it. Rather, she seemed to be responding to what her mother had just said.

"What is it, Grace?" her father asked.

She hurriedly wiped her mouth on her own napkin. "Nothing. I just remembered I have clothes in the washer. In fact, I'd better go put them in the dryer now."

Richard frowned and Priscilla made a disapproving noise. "I'm sure it can wait until after we've finished," she said.

"I'm done."

"But we haven't had dessert yet. Consuela made your favorite. Cherry pie."

"I'll have some later." She catapulted from her chair, yanking on the hem of her skirt repeatedly. "If I don't get some clean clothes to put on soon, I'm going to freeze to death. Pardon me."

With that, she hurried from the room, taking tiny steps, presumably not to reveal more than she already had.

Dylan wanted to go after her, but he wasn't sure that was such a great idea.

"Richard!" Priscilla said, agitated.

Gracie's father sighed. "What would you have me do, Cilla? She's a grown woman. I can't order her to sit because you want her to."

She gestured toward Dylan. "But we have a guest."

Richard rested his forearms on the table. "Yes, that we do, dear. And don't you think it imperative that we not make him feel uncomfortable?"

Priscilla sat back, nonplussed. "She gets it from you, you know. That…that stubborn streak…"

Dylan slowly put his own napkin on the table and got up. "Excuse me. I seem to have gotten…something on my tie. I'm going to go see if Gracie has something to treat it with until I can take it to the cleaners."

He wasn't even certain the couple had heard him as they continued their lively debate on which of them, exactly, Gracie most resembled.

As he left the room, he resisted the urge to tell them she didn't resemble either one of them. As far as he was concerned, Gracie was a one-hundred-percent pure original.

And hotter than any one woman had a right to be.

GRACIE KNOCKED HER FOREHEAD several times against the laundry room door. Good Lord, had her mother really hinted that she was going to ask Dylan for sexual advice, just as she'd asked Gracie? She groaned. Wasn't it bad enough she'd asked her own daughter? Did she now have to go flinging the details of her personal life with her father—or lack thereof—at a total stranger?

She tugged at the hem of her dress in frustration and groaned again. The one and only time she forgoes underwear and Dylan has to lose his napkin. She clamped her eyelids closed. She could only imagine what he'd gotten an eyeful of down there. If the sound of his head banging against the table had been any indication, it was a whole precious lot.

A hot shiver ran over the surface of her cool skin. Okay, so her little peep show, no matter how unwitting, did seem a bit...risqué and excited her in retrospect. The thought of him skimming her exposed privates when she wasn't looking, right under the watchful, critical eye of her parents, held a certain naughty appeal.

What had he thought? she wondered. Really thought? That she'd done it on purpose? Did he find her hot and want to throw her onto the table right then and there?

She bit her lip. Not that his true feelings made any difference. He would never do anything. He'd also never admit that anything she did turned him on. At least not with words. His body, however, let her know exactly how it felt whenever it got the chance. Which wasn't often enough for her.

"God, what are you thinking, Grace?" she asked herself, adopting her mother's tone. She wrapped her fingers around the door handle. "That you want to be his beck-and-call girl?"

She grimaced. No, that's not what she wanted. That whole scenario had too much of a one-sided tone to it. And she wanted Dylan's side very much included, preferably squeezed between her thighs. For more than one night or two. She wanted him there until…well, until she no longer wanted him there.

There, she'd admitted it. She wanted Dr. Dylan Fairbanks for more than a one- or two-night stand. She wanted…more. A full-blown relationship. She wanted to debate their different viewpoints over dinner at a swanky French restaurant… or a rib joint. She wanted to crawl beneath the conservative veneer he wore like a suit—in fact it was a suit—and find out what really made him tick. She wanted to try out every single last impossible position outlined in the Kama Sutra, then when they finished, start all over again.

Was that too much to ask?

She nodded. Yep, it was.

She lifted the lid to the washing machine and sorted through the items that needed to drip dry from those that could go into the dryer, then she put a second load in.

"This place is larger than it looks."

At the sound of the familiar masculine voice Gracie nearly toppled straight into the wash basket. She swiveled around to stare at Dylan where he leaned on the doorjamb. And her mouth went dry at the teasing grin he wore.

He flicked his tie. "Do you have something to treat this with?"

"What did you do with my parents?" she asked.

He laughed. "I locked them in a closet. What do you think I did with them? They're in the dining room discussing the finer points of dinner etiquette. In fact, they probably haven't even realized I'm gone."

She turned toward the shelves behind the washer, fingering through the items there until she found a stick of stain pretreater. "Here. This should do the trick."

It was only after she had taken the lid off and was dabbing at the quarter-size stain on his tie that she realized the proper thing for a modern woman to do would have been to hand him the stick. If their roles were reversed, and she was at his place, he certainly wouldn't be applying a pretreater to a spot on her dress.

Then again, she recognized the move for the telling one it was. This was not succumbing to some hidden desire to mother Dylan; rather she was dabbing at his tie for the simple reason to be nearer to him.

She took a quiet breath. God, but he smelled good. He always smelled good. Like he had just come from a shower, his skin all squeaky clean and soap-scented.

And she was the naughty little girl responsible for soiling that image.

She reached for his hand and dropped the stick into it. "Here. I think I got it all, but you might want to double-check." She tugged on the silky material then released it. "Nice tie. That a gift, too?"

He applied more of the solution, his gaze on her rather than the spot. "No. Bought this myself."

Her attention drifted to his midsection. It was only when she got there that she realized she was looking to see if he had on his double-locking belt. He didn't.

She leaned her bottom against the washing machine and crossed her arms, considering him. "Tell me, Dylan. What's the real reason you're here?"

He grimaced and handed her back the stick. She recapped it and put it on the shelf behind her, then resumed her position.

"Your mother is a very hard person to say no to."

She took a deep, steadying breath, trying to ignore how tempting it was right now to slam the door shut and take him right here, right now, in the laundry room. "I don't mean here as in the house. I mean in this room."

"Oh."

She dropped her gaze to stare at the fine hairs on her forearm. "Yeah, oh."

She stood there for a long, silent moment, listening to the

sounds of the dryer whirling, the washer filling, and decided that now was as good a time as any to call a halt to whatever bizarre attraction pulled them together even when it was obvious his intentions lay elsewhere.

He cleared his throat. "You know, Gracie, I've been doing some thinking. Well, actually, it just occurred to me now, but that's besides the point. Considering what I have been thinking ever since we met…well, it's ridiculous it hasn't occurred to me before now."

She picked at her fingernails, thinking she needed a manicure. So long as she didn't look at him, ignored how damn good he looked and smelled and how much she wanted him, this could work. "Oh?"

"You're not going to make this easy on me, are you?"

She raised her brows but not her gaze. "Make what easy, Dylan?"

She heard him draw in a deep breath, then release it. "The fact that I'd like to stop fighting this…strange attraction I feel for you and just start going with the flow."

Heat swept low in her belly and, though she had vowed she wouldn't, she looked at him full in the face. "What?"

His half smile was both sexy and completely adorable, if that were even possible. "Are you going to make me say it again?"

She continued staring at him, wondering if he had really said the words, or whether she had imagined them. "I think you're going to have to because right now I can't quite bring myself to believe you."

"Believe what?" His voice lowered to a dangerously seductive tenor. "That I've been a jerk?"

He moved closer and she laughed a little breathlessly. "No, that I already know."

"Okay, I suppose I deserved that." She felt his fingers on her bare knee before she saw him reach there. He slowly drew his fingertips up, bringing the hem with him. "So what

is it you're having a tough time believing then, Gracie?"
He was close enough that his breath heated her cheeks. His
fingers continued their upward trek, circling to follow her
inner thigh. "That I don't want to…fight whatever this thing
is that's going on between us anymore? That I, Dr. Dylan,
am willing to admit that not even I completely understand
what's happening, but that it's time I stopped trying to control it and let nature take its course?"

His fingers reached the V of her legs and pressed against
the hair there. Hair that was already dripping with need for
him. She fought to keep her knees from buckling. "Yes. I
guess that would be the concept I'm having a hard time with."

She moved to kiss him, but he caught her chin in his other
hand, holding her still, his gaze sliding to her lips. Under
cover of her dress, he drew a finger the length of her opening, making her shudder from her head to her toes.

"Well, then," he murmured, his gaze lifting back to her
eyes. His pupils were so dilated they threatened to take over
the green of his irises. "I guess I'm just going to have to prove
it to you then, aren't I?"

She nodded and quickly licked her lips, trembling at the
prospect of him determined to prove anything to her. Using
his thumb and forefinger, he parted her swollen, throbbing
flesh, seeking and finding her sensitive core. Air gushed
from her lungs and she collapsed back against the washing
machine for much needed support.

He groaned and rested his temple against hers. "God, you
are so hot…so wet."

Gracie turned her face into his, needing to kiss him, to
thrust her tongue deep into the warm recesses of his mouth,
swallow his breath. He pulled back, again holding her chin
still.

"Uh-uh," he whispered, running the pad of his thumb
across her upper lip then following the line of her lower. "I

want to see you achieve orgasm. Watch the rapture on your face…hear your cry."

Under her skirt, he thrust a finger deep into her dripping wetness. Gracie went completely boneless. Who knew strait-laced Dr. Dylan could be oh, so deliciously wicked?

He slowly withdrew his finger but, before she could draw a breath, thrust back in, this time with two. Gracie's nipples under the coarse denim tightened to the point of pain as she fought not to close her eyes and surrender to the phenomenal pleasure rippling through her. She steadfastly held his gaze, pulling her bottom lip between her teeth and biting hard.

His thumb found her clit at the apex of her damp curls. She twitched involuntarily, moaning when he began rubbing the sensitive fold of flesh in small circles even as he withdrew his fingers again, this time twisting them so that her muscles clutched the digits even more tightly.

Then she was hurtling over some unseen precipice, roughly clutching his shoulders and riding out a wave of pleasure so incredible she was afraid her parents would hear her cry of release.

As her climax ebbed, Dylan slowly withdrew his fingers and pressed his lips against her damp temple. "God, do you know how beautiful you are?"

Then he finally kissed her.

Drawing his mouth along the length of hers, he dipped out his tongue and traced the edge of her lips. Gracie recognized the raw need in his eyes, but he appeared to be allowing her the time she needed to recover. Which happened sooner than she anticipated simply because the pleasure, while incredible, had been achieved without him.

Thrusting her hands into his hair, she pulled him closer, allowing for a more pronounced meeting of their mouths. She tugged hungrily on his lips, delved her tongue madly into his mouth, desperately wanting to unleash the animal she saw lurking in the depths of his eyes, in the heat coiling his muscles beneath his jacket. Impatiently she tugged his jacket down, his shirt open, then reached for his slacks. It wasn't until she held every glorious inch of him in her palms that she convinced herself that this was really happening. Dylan wasn't going to change his mind. Pull away. He wanted her as much as she wanted him, and the effects of that knowledge were dizzying.

Then she realized she didn't have any protection.

Oh, God, no....

She bit hard on her bottom lip, then hungrily kissed him again. "You're not going to believe this, but I don't have... anything."

He gazed from one of her eyes to the other, then held up a foil package between them.

The significance of him having a condom hit her full in the stomach.

He caught her earlobe between his teeth as he sheathed himself. "Even when I was too stupid to know what I wanted, my body always knew."

Behind her, the washer stopped its jerky movements, distracting her enough for her to be confused when he grasped her hips and gently turned her away from him toward the machine. Her breath caught as he pushed her dress up around her waist then directed her to lie chest first across the length of the surface. Cool air touched her bare bottom, leaving her feeling exposed...and oh, so horny as she thought of him looking at her, exploring her bottom with both his gaze and his hands.

Beneath her, the machine began the spin cycle. She caught her breath, bracing her hands against the back to steady herself, the swollen flesh between her legs quivering as Dylan parted her thighs and placed the tip of his erection against her opening. Gracie closed her eyes tightly, wanting him, needing him to fill her so badly she could scream, but he just stood there, perched on the brink.

Restlessly she tried to push back against him, but his hands on her hips prevented the move.

Then slowly he breached the threshold.

Gracie cried out, arching her back as he sank into her inch by torturous inch, then just as slowly withdrew.

Her breasts throbbed, her stomach quaked, her hands itched to touch something other than the cold metal of the washing machine…but she was completely at his mercy. And loving every minute even as she fought against it.

Thrust by delicious thrust, he incrementally increased the pace, but was still very obviously in control of himself and, by extension, her.

Gracie thought she would die from the frustration of it all.

She felt his hands on her bottom, kneading, caressing, then he drew his thumbs along the length of her crevice, parting the flesh there and thrust into her to the hilt.

The speed of her second climax caught her completely unaware, snatching away her breath, swirling through her like a roaring tornado until it had touched every muscle, every inch, contracting her muscles around his erection, and robbing her of every bit of control she had.

A deep sound of need emanated from Dylan and suddenly he grasped her hips, holding her in place as he thrust deeply into her again…and again…and blessedly again, until she felt him go rigid, every inch of him filling her, his fingers digging into her soft flesh, her name on his lips…and toppling her right over the edge again with him.

The spin cycle ended with a quiet thunk. Dylan lay against her, his breathless pants matching hers as she lay against the cool surface. What they had just shared far surpassed anything she had thought herself capable of. It definitely left their first time far in the dust. And she thought that had been mind-blowing.

This…this…

Well, this was something that transcended even her

professional ability and was outside her personal experience to even try to categorize.

"Grace?"

Gracie blinked, the fact that Dylan hadn't said her name slowly seeping through the warm, sated haze blanketing her along with Dylan's hard, damp body.

"Grace?"

More clearly now…closer. *Her mother,* she realized with an aftershock of terror.

Dylan seemed to catch on at the same instant she did. But it wasn't until the doorknob jiggled that the true gravity of the situation hit home.

Gracie shot her leg out from between Dylan's and slammed the door where it had begun to open. A surprised gasp sounded from the kitchen.

"Oh, God," Dylan said, quickly withdrawing from her.

Despite her awkward positioning, Gracie made a sound of disappointment. Not only because he'd left her, but because he'd still been erect while doing so.

Damn her mother and her awful sense of timing.

The door bucked under her foot. "Gracie…I insist you open the door this instant."

"Here," Dylan said, rumpled and sexy and fully dressed. "Let me."

Gracie saw where he had wedged his own shoe-clad foot at the bottom of the door and dropped her leg. She straightened and turned as her mother knocked insistently. Dylan jumped. Gracie had to stifle a laugh at the ridiculousness of the situation.

She felt as if she was sixteen again, when she'd sneaked an eighteen-year-old neighborhood boy up into her room where they stole a few kisses. As now, Priscilla had seemed to sense something amiss and had barged in on her.

It was after that episode that Gracie learned the value of door locks.

She grimaced. Of course, she and Dylan would have to pick probably the only door in the entire house that *didn't* have a lock. Think about it. Who really needed to lock themselves into the laundry room?

A pronounced sigh came from the other side of the wood. "Grace, I won't have you pouting in there like a child when we have a guest present. Where are your manners?"

Dylan met her gaze and she had to clamp her hand over her mouth to keep from laughing.

It took her a moment to realize that Dylan was about to move his foot and open the door. She grabbed his arm. "No... no, not yet."

She gathered the articles of her clothing she planned to hang in her bathroom and put them into the empty wicker basket, then carefully checked her hair. She looked up to find Dylan grinning at her in a way that made her stomach turn around as animatedly as the dryer basket.

"Are you ready?" he murmured.

She reached out and picked a piece of lint from his silky dark hair, then nodded. "Yep."

Priscilla was in the middle of another assault on the door when Dylan tugged it open. "Oh!" She quickly righted herself, then looked at the two of them. It took a few seconds, but she finally appeared to register that Gracie hadn't been neglecting their dinner guest at all. That in fact she had been providing her own naughty brand of entertainment behind that closed door.

Dylan jabbed a thumb over his shoulder. "We were, um...I was just..."

Gracie quietly cleared her throat. "Dylan was keeping me company while I waited for the, um, washer to finish." She smiled widely. "So where's that dessert? Suddenly cherry pie sounds mighty good."

10

San Francisco

THREE DAYS HAD PASSED since their tumble in the Mattias family laundry room during the spin cycle. Three days of plane trips, radio interviews, internet chats, newspaper journalists...and white-hot sex with Gracie.

Dylan thought his lungs were going to explode as he lay naked across the San Francisco hotel room bed. He loosened his grip on Gracie's slender hips and cracked open his eyes. He nearly groaned at the sight of her sitting gloriously astride him, her breasts heaving as she fought to steady her own ragged breathing. Her head was thrown back, her long, artful neck arched, her silken red hair tickling his knees behind her, her nipples engorged and blushed from the attention he had just laved on them. His gaze dropped to where the red-gold fleece between her legs meshed with his darker hair and an aftershock that could have easily registered on the Richter scale quaked through him.

He swallowed hard, thinking it incredible that the sex between him and Gracie had only gotten better and better. In the past seventy-two hours he'd seen more bathrooms than he could count...and his muscles ached from the inventive positions they had to come up with in order to have sex in enclosed places. The airplane bathroom, especially, had proved a challenge, but one they'd risen to…twice.

Damn, but he just couldn't seem to get enough of her. Not when he sat across a table from her in a crowded restaurant and reached under the tablecloth to see whether or not she wore panties. Not during joint book signings where he swore he would bust if he couldn't touch her just once. And certainly not at night when they tumbled into whoever's room was the closest, half the time not even making it to the bed before they were going at it, hot and heavy.

Staring at the contrast of his darker hands against her pale skin, he budged his thumbs inward until he pressed against what he had come to call her magic button. Touch it and bam, he was given access to the slick, wet enclave just beyond and all the magical secrets that lurked there.

Gracie gasped and caught his wrists. He chuckled, watching as she lifted her head to stare down at him. He wondered if there was a sexier sight in the world than Gracie's face after they'd just had sex. She smiled. Absolutely not.

"You're going to be late for your lecture," she murmured, running her fingertips down his chest and to his lower abdomen, causing a quick intake of breath.

"Screw the lecture."

She laughed. "Hmm…that could be interesting."

She slowly lifted herself from the length of him, her eyes widening at his still-aroused state. "Why, Dr. Dylan, I'm beginning to think nothing's capable of satisfying your little friend."

He hiked a brow. "Little?"

She pinched off the end of the condom, then removed it. But rather than leave him in peace, she wrapped her fingers around his width. "Figuratively speaking…of course." She tightened her grip and moved her hand ever so slightly, causing his hips to buck into her touch.

This time he caught her wrist before he could throw her

back down to the bed and thrust into her sweet hot flesh like nobody's business…as if he hadn't just spent the past three hours since breakfast with Tanja and Rick doing just that.

She laughed and got up, wrapping the spent prophylactic in tissue and throwing it into the garbage.

Dylan closed his eyes and swallowed. This was crazy. He couldn't even remember the guy he'd been just a short time ago. And he couldn't seem to get a handle on the new, bizarre, sex-hazed reality that was currently his life. Morning, noon and night, all he could think of was being between Gracie's tight thighs. The minute he'd finally decided to give in to his hunger for her, he'd fully expected the forbidden edge that was drawing him to her to abate. Instead, his stomach-tightening, penis-hardening reaction to her had only grown more acute.

He blindly finger-combed his hair back. He'd counseled a self-proclaimed sex addict once, years ago when he was first starting out. The patient had been a professor at the university where he was teaching at the time. It was rumored that he'd slept with at least five percent of his female students annually, and that percentage rate was rising. The professor's meeting with him hadn't been voluntarily, rather the board of trustees thought it would be a good idea if he sought some counseling. It seemed that one of the girls he'd been with claimed the sex hadn't been completely consensual.

It eventually came out that it had been, that the nineteen-year-old had been upset that the sex hadn't led to more than sex.

Of course, it didn't help matters any that the patient was married. To another faculty member at that.

Gracie sat down on the mattress next to him. "So what happened?"

Dylan blinked his eyes open, not realizing he had spoken his thoughts aloud until that moment. It took him a moment to adjust to the fact that Gracie had not only heard, she was responding to him. She had put on a robe and was watching him with weighty expectation. Dylan considered the string of events from her viewpoint, then answered, "I don't know."

She frowned. "Do you think you helped him?"

He fingered the hem of her robe, tugging on it just a tad so he could peek at her swollen womanhood. "It's just so hard to tell with these things, you know? Here I was, this greenhorn fresh from having written my doctorate thesis on human sexual behavior, when…this guy, old enough to be my father, completely chucked all of my beliefs out the window."

Just like you're doing now.

She lay her hand against his chest. "I'm sure you're exaggerating."

"Am I?" He absently caught her hand in his. "He transferred out the next semester. And all I kept thinking was 'Thank, God.' Our sessions…they were filled with my believing that his promiscuity was age related. You know, middle-age crisis, seven-year itch—though he and his wife had been married for twenty years, a daughter away at college. I'd convinced myself that he was no sooner a sex addict than I was. But all he kept telling me was that he couldn't help himself. An attractive girl smiled at him and it was a foregone conclusion that he would sleep with her." He grimaced. "He swore he didn't feel euphoric afterward, as though he'd carved a notch in his belt. But he would leave the room in which he had just bedded a coed, another student would smile at him and the whole cycle would start over again.

"He was…*insatiable* is the word he used. If sex was there to be had, then he would have it."

Gracie's hand had stilled beneath his. "Any root problems that you could uncover? A childhood incident? Sexual or mental abuse? Religiously fanatical parents? Or the opposite, sexually liberated?"

He was surprised to find himself grinning at her. "This question from Dr. Hottie? I would have thought you'd say something along the lines of 'Maybe the guy just liked having sex.'"

She drew her hand away from his. "Very funny, Dr. Dylan. I guess I'm curious because I haven't come across an honest-to-God sex addict yet, that's all." She tightened the belt to her robe. "I've had patients profess to love it and label themselves as such, but no one truly addicted."

He curved his forearm under his head, propping himself up so he could look at her more closely. "What type of patients do you get?"

She twisted her lips. "I get all kinds. Frustrated housewives, complaining husbands, the single career woman who thinks men can't handle a woman who's both successful and has a healthy sexual appetite, male professionals who are finding their sexual identities." She smiled. "You know, all the normal wackos who just really need to get laid properly by the right person. And by right, I'm not necessarily talking about the opposite sex, either."

He laughed. "Hmm…wackos. Is that a certified term?"

Her face went serious and her eyes took on a faraway look. "But I think the ones with histories of sexual abuse who are just trying to undo the damage done to them so they can enjoy a seminormal sex life are the most difficult."

The shrill ring of the phone seemed to jar them both out of their thoughtful clouds and they looked at each other.

Gracie laughed. "I can't remember whose room we're in. Yours or mine."

"Yours."

She twisted toward the nightstand and snatched up the receiver. "Hello?"

Dylan turned his head away, ignoring the fact that by some sort of silent mutual agreement, they'd decided to keep their relationship a secret. Oh, yes, her mother might suspect, and they already knew Rick and Tanja did, but in public they acted like two professional, unpersonal colleagues.

He smiled. Well, at least when no one they knew was around, anyway.

Gracie hung up the phone. "That was Tanja. I told her you weren't here, but she said that on the off chance that I happened to see you, to remind you that your lecture is in half an hour."

Dylan couldn't have gotten off the bed faster had he been shot from a gun. A quick shower and a fresh suit later, he came out of the bathroom to find Gracie still sitting on the bed wearing the hotel robe, her nose buried in a psychology journal, her laptop on and perched in front of her and a notepad, filled with scribbling, on her leg.

"You sure you don't want to come?" he asked. "You might learn something."

She peeked at him without raising her head. "Ha-ha." She closed the journal. "No, you go on ahead. It's your alma mater and definitely your forum, and so not mine. There's something about ratty tweed jackets that makes me break out in hives."

He chuckled and tossed a towel she'd left lying on the side of the bed at her. "Those are my esteemed colleagues you're talking about."

"Better yours than mine."

He was coming to like these little verbal sparring matches with her. She kept him on his toes in a way that was energizing and amusing.

"Look, I'm driving out to my parents' place in the valley later this afternoon. Do you want to come?"

He wasn't sure who was more surprised by the impromptu invitation—him or her.

Earlier he'd told her that he'd be busy for the rest of the day, but hadn't explained why. It was one of the reasons they'd ended up in bed together so early, knowing they wouldn't be together that night. Now he'd not only revealed his true plans, he'd asked her to join him.

He never asked anyone to visit with his parents. Not even Diana.

It was the first time he'd thought of Diana's name in more than just passing since making the decision to put his life on hold. Now he cringed.

He hadn't tried to contact Diana, and she hadn't called him. But he knew he'd soon have to reach some sort of decision about her, about their relationship. The logical conclusion would be to break his plans to propose to her. To break off with her, period. But nothing much in his life seemed motivated by logic lately.

Gracie's gaze seemed to rake his face, apparently trying to read the myriad emotions he was probably displaying.

"Thanks, but no." She smiled, but he noticed there was something decidedly…thoughtful about the response. "I think I've had enough of parents in general for at least a month." She picked up her notepad. "Besides, I have my weekly radio call-in show the day after tomorrow and I haven't even begun to think about what I'm going to say."

Dylan hadn't realized he was holding his breath until it came out in a loud rush. "Okay." He considered kissing her goodbye, then thought better of it. Aside from it making it tougher to leave her, the action would seem so…normal in what was a very abnormal relationship. At least for him. "I'll see you in the morning then."

She nodded, having already reopened the journal. "Bye."

Six hours, a long lecture, a tedious luncheon and a cigar with his colleagues later, Dylan thought of how easy it would be to turn south back to the San Francisco hotel and Gracie.

He drove his late-model Jaguar through the winding roads of Napa Valley, the late-afternoon sun highlighting the different shades of verdant green. Despite the beauty of the area, he really didn't want to make this trek out to his parents' compound. But it had been a month since he'd last seen them, and he knew from experience that if he didn't make the effort, they would. And without a doubt at the most inappropriate time in his schedule.

He rubbed the back of his neck, marveling at the tension there. He recalled the first time Moonbeam and Frank had popped up on his doorstep. He'd been living away from home for the first time in his life in a frat house just off campus. A month into the semester, the senior frat brothers threw a bash to celebrate the end of hell week and to officially welcome the junior members into the group. In a word, he'd been sloshed, happily indulging in all the juvenile behavior he'd never gotten a chance to while growing up.

It was while he had his head positioned under the nozzle of a beer keg, a fellow frat brother next to him doing the same in a race to see who could down the most draft without puking, that the door opened and there stood his parents.

He hadn't been ashamed of his behavior. No, he knew Moonbeam and Frank would probably hail the event as part of his coming-of-age, let him sleep it off, then try to ply him with their holistic hangover remedies the following day. Rather he'd been ashamed of them.

Dylan shifted uncomfortably in the driver's seat, tapping down the sun visor to cut off the sun's reflection.

Absently he pondered if he would have felt as…out of place had his paternal grandfather not told him that he'd been born to a higher station in life. During that Sunday afternoon visit to his grandfather's wealthy, sprawling estate, his grandfather had detailed how his parents had given away his birthright to various charities, using the last of the money to start their own self-sufficient ranch—basically a modern-day commune—before he was even born.

Strange, he'd never considered why his grandfather had not given him more if he truly thought Dylan deserved it.

Not that it mattered anymore. Grandfather had died ten years ago ironically leaving the bulk of his estate to institutions that would carry his name. He remembered thinking at the time that in the end his grandfather's behavior hadn't been much different from his parents'. Except his parents had done it while they were still alive and had made no ironclad stipulations that their names be connected to the donations.

He grimaced and caught himself scratching his left arm through his suit jacket. He stopped himself, thinking of the mudlike concoction his mother would cake all over him if she noticed. Then thinking what Gracie might do to help alleviate the pain…

Ah, Gracie. He caught a glimpse of his smile in the rearview mirror and stared at his reflection, amazed. Why, he didn't know. He wanted to have sex with her all the time, so it only stood to reason that thinking of her would bring a smile to his face.

Still, it did amaze him.

What also bowled him over was how much he missed her, though they had only been apart a few hours.

He reached out and switched on the radio, thinking that it was already beginning to happen. He was questioning the validity of the relationship and its dubious future. How long had it been since he'd given up the fight? Three days? While the sex had only gotten better instead of worse, he was a little surprised at the rapidity of his probing of their…curious union. The instant he was away from her, he began absently noting their differences and calculating what they would add up to in the long run. Ignoring their philosophical differences for the time being, he thought of the others.

He was a morning person who jumped out of bed, liked to get in a jog and saw that he had a big, balanced breakfast before starting the day. She slept till ten, dragged herself out of bed, hated exercise of any kind, took at least an hour before she was coherent and coffee—lots of it—made up her breakfast.

He sent his things out to the laundry the instant after he'd taken them off while she allowed nearly every item she owned to pile up before she even thought of seeing to laundry. He tugged at his tie, remembering proof of that at her mother's house when she'd been minus one pair of panties.

Browsing through shops after a book signing in Seattle, he'd learned that her taste in decor was funky, trendy and contemporary, while he preferred heavy pieces with a history and dark, dramatic colors.

He planned out everything in advance down to the last detail, allowing for little surprise and budgeting everything down to the penny. She was a procrastinator who freely admitted she worked best under deadline, hated balancing her checkbook, and gave at least a fiver to every beggar she came across. Which, in San Francisco, was every street corner.

He caught a glimpse of himself in the mirror again, but rather than the frown he expected, he found a half smile still firmly in place.

"Yes, Dr. Fairbanks, you have officially joined the ranks of the lustfully insane."

Oh, he'd figured out sometime yesterday that that's what he was suffering from. An extreme case of lust. An adult version of a really bad crush. And until he saw it through to its natural conclusion, he wouldn't be able to concentrate on anything else.

Of course, he didn't allow himself to think beyond that. Not now. There would be plenty of time for analyzing his behavior and how it impacted his own personal belief system later.

He realized that later was a time down the road when Gracie was no longer a part of his life and felt a leaden sensation in his stomach.

"You're just thinking of all that great sex you'll be missing out on," he told himself.

Up ahead was the turnoff for his parents' place. The words

El Rancho had been branded into a large piece of redwood and nailed to a sign at the end of the road. He turned onto the gravel driveway, looking around as he drove at a speed that wouldn't put a million gravel dings in his Jag. To the right, between neatly tended fields, were tiny houses, cottages really, that served as quarters for the newer or transient residents, those on their way to other places or in need of a little help until they got back on their feet. A little farther in and to the left were larger places. Houses that had their own mailboxes, running water, and looked exactly like they had been taken from the pages of middle suburbia…except that they had all been built by ranch residents and there were no locks on any of the doors.

He continued on down the two miles leading to his parents' house, never before considering how much the land would bring should they decide to sell. In the heart of Napa Valley the considerable acreage would undoubtedly restore the entire inheritance they'd voluntarily given to charity.

The prospect was astounding.

It also made him feel guilty as hell just thinking about it.

No. He'd never ask his parents to sacrifice anything on his account. Not anymore. Even if the thought had occurred to him before now, he highly doubted he would have seriously considered it even then. Everywhere he looked, everything he smelled, from the rich soil, the cool damp air, the hearty vegetation was where his parents lived. What they were. They were as much a part of the earth as the crops they planted.

Unfortunately, he'd never thought much of getting his hands dirty.

He pulled up in front of the low-slung, Spanish-style hacienda he had grown up in and felt an interesting pang deep in his stomach. Somewhat like that of being home. Which was odd, because all he'd ever felt before when returning to the place was dread. Wariness over what his parents had planned this time. What bombshell they would drop. A few years ago it had been their announcement that they were putting aside a portion of their land to grow marijuana for distribution to the terminally ill. The year before last, hemp was all the rage. He still had a scratchy, hideous shirt tucked in a bottom drawer at home, a gift from his mother last Christmas.

Getting out of the car, he supposed he should be thankful that they'd never displayed any interest in the paranormal or any cultlike behavior.

A car was parked off the side of the driveway. A newer one, which immediately set it apart from any vehicles that might normally be on the property at any given time. Frank still drove an old Ford truck, justifying the gas expense by saying that none of his money had gone to the sky-choking, environment-destroying automobile industry in the past thirty years. Besides, he rarely drove it. Dylan didn't even want to speculate on the date on his father's driver's license.

He got out of his car, leaving his overnight bag in the back just in case the opportunity for a quick getaway arose and he could drive back into the city for the night. Entering the house, he knew better than to call out. No one would answer anyway. He'd tried it a few times when he was in the third grade, only to find his parents along with myriad other "family" members in the living room. He'd once asked his mother why no one had responded. She'd said that it was up to him to want to be part of the group. They'd decided the day they'd found out she was pregnant with him that they would never pressure him into doing anything. It was up to him to find his own path in life.

He still thought that was a little too much freedom to put on any one child's shoulders. By going out of their way to never pressure him, they had created a whole type of other pressure. The pressure to make the right decision.

He closed the door behind himself, his eyesight needing no adjustment because it was just as bright inside the house as outside. Painted in airy white, the entryway was as he always remembered. As was the living room with nary a chair leg in sight, but rather various-size pillows that encouraged "sharing" as his mother said. The kitchen still smelled of cinnamon and various homegrown herbs. No preservatives allowed on this ranch.

He drummed his hands on the hand-painted ceramic countertop and frowned. Where was everyone? He couldn't remember a time when it had been so quiet here. What he wouldn't have done for a little quiet while growing up.

But right now he'd prefer a little noise.

It wasn't as though they didn't know he was coming. He'd called the other day to tell them of his visit. His mother had dismissed the entire notion of calling ahead, as she always did. The house was always open to him, she said. To live, to visit, to do with as he wished.

He preferred to call.

The sound of laughter came from beyond the open back door. Okay, there it was. The familiar sound. He'd probably go back there and find the pond his father had personally dug out years ago teeming with ranch residents.

But when he opened the door he saw only three people and a dog.

His mother. Completely nude.

His father. Completely nude.

Gracie. Who, shock of shockers, was wearing a bathing suit.

And his dog, Killer, who was in the pond and swimming his way.

He winced.

What were his parents doing naked? They had never been nudists. At least not in front of strangers. Was nudism this year's surprise?

His father's jackknife dive into the water told him that, yes, it undoubtedly was.

Then there was Gracie.

Damn if his libido didn't blaze to life at the mere sight of her sitting swinging her legs off the edge of the handmade pier at the west end of the fifty-yard pond. He knew she looked delectable naked, but in a swimsuit she was an out-and-out knockout. Just looking at the way her breasts pressed against the red-and-white striped bikini top, her nipples plainly erect, and thinking of the way the springy V of hair cushioned the decadently brief bottoms, made him go rock-hard. And forget the way the sinking sun set her red hair ablaze, making her look like Circe, the ultimate of Greek witches, and just as impossible to resist.

"Just call me Odysseus," he said under his breath.

At that moment, Killer climbed from the side of the pond and bolted for him, stopping only a foot away and giving a mighty shake that soaked Dylan from head to toe. He had the sneaking suspicion the mutt had done it on purpose.

"Dylan!" his mother called out from where she was getting into the pond nearer Gracie. He looked at her. And wished he hadn't. He didn't want to see that the years of healthy eating and countless hours spent working in the fields had gifted her with an attractive body. He didn't want to notice his mother's body at all. She *was* his mother, for God's sake.

"Maid's day off?" he commented, stopping where he was and crossing his arms over his chest.

His father's chuckle reached him where he was scooping water from his face. "Just trying to go back to nature, and improve our way of life."

"Well, you could improve my chances of not having a heart attack by putting something on. A fig leaf, I don't care. Just so long as I don't have to see your…family jewels flapping in the wind."

Gracie's bark of laughter drew his gaze to her. Funnily enough, he felt like laughing right along with her.

If only he could figure out what she was doing here.

His father swam to the side of the pond nearest Dylan and

hauled himself out of the water, letting it stream down him unhindered. Dylan cringed. "Jeez, Dad, did you really have to do that?"

"Yes, I did." He smiled. "You've always been a little too stodgy for your own good. Gives me nightmares some nights thinking about how much you resemble my old man."

"Yeah, well, you're *my* old man, and I could go for you resembling someone who is a little less wacko."

He caught the amusement in Gracie's eyes at the mention of the term she'd used earlier that morning.

Was it only six hours ago when that had happened? It seemed a lifetime ago.

He shifted his gaze back to his parents. Thankfully his mother was a little less…free. She wrapped a towel around herself when she came out of the water to give him a hug and a sloppy kiss. He was surprised how genuine his own hug and kiss back was.

"So," he said, clearing his throat. He tried not to watch his father walk across the grass to where a pitcher of what was likely herb tea waited, but failed. It wasn't every day you saw your own father walking around naked as the day he was born. "What gives with the nudist bit? Not thinking of changing the format of the ranch?"

His mother laughed and walked toward the pier. "No, we're not. Just something your father and I like to do when we're alone together. There are other nicer places we go when we want to hang out with other closet nudists."

He followed her. "Um, Mom, I hate to point this out but… you and Dad? You're not alone."

"Are you talking about Gracie? Because if you are, she said she didn't mind when she got here about an hour ago."

An hour? His mind swam with the things his parents could have told her about him. "I was talking about me."

"Dylan, it's not like we don't have anything you haven't seen before."

She was right there. His parents weren't really big on closing the bathroom door during showers or other…events. "Yes, but if it's all the same, I prefer if life has some mysteries. Especially when it comes to my own parents."

They finally reached the pier where Gracie was sitting. In deference to the warmness of the afternoon, and the soaking he'd taken from Killer, Dylan shrugged out of his suit jacket and loosened his tie as he looked down at her.

"Hi," she said simply, Killer taking a possessive seat next to her.

"Hi, yourself." He hung his jacket on top of a piling. "I thought you said you had work to do."

"I finished."

"Oh."

A shadow of something swam through her eyes, then was gone. She patted the wet, smelly dog. "Anyway, I thought after you got the inside scoop on my family life, it was only fair I get a gander at yours."

"Got more of an eyeful than you bargained for, didn't you?" He crouched down next to her, clamping his hands together between his knees instead of reaching out to tug on the strings at the back of her bikini. See how much she really approved of this nudity thing.

Only he was half afraid she'd leave the top off.

"So what's the verdict?" he asked, interested in her thoughts on his parents.

She tucked her hair behind her ear. "I'm curious to know why you don't mention your parents in either of your books." She motioned to where his mother had entered the pond again on the other side. "Why you let the reader assume you're from a conservative background when…well, you're so obviously not."

"So you managed to get your hands on a copy of my first book, huh?" He grinned. "That must have taken some doing. I personally bought all two hundred copies."

She smiled. "You didn't answer my question."

"I know." He reached out and twirled a curl around his index finger. "I could ask the same of you. While you never come out and say it, you lead the reader to believe that your parents are a by-product of the seventies disco era."

"I do not."

His grin widened and he tugged on the hair, nearly groaning when it forced her head back, exposing her delectable neck to his line of vision. "Not in so many words, but that's the impression I came away with."

"Then I'm disappointed that you didn't read the entire book."

He lifted his brows. "Oh?"

"In Chapter Eight I talk about the strong patriarchal roles that are apparent in even my own family."

"Do you give examples?"

"Of course."

"Are you going to tell me what they are?"

"Nope."

He caught himself laughing. "I knew you were going to say that."

She rubbed Killer playfully behind the ears. "I didn't know you were a dog kind of guy, Dylan."

He grimaced. "I'm not." He rose to a standing position, wondering just how much his parents had told Gracie about him. And at what point she would use the information as ammunition.

"All right, everybody," his father called out. "It's dinnertime. Any special requests?"

Dylan cupped his hands over his mouth. "Clothes."

Gracie's sexy laugh made him smile.

11

SHIRTSLEEVES ROLLED UP, Dylan stood side by side with his mother at the sink washing and drying the dishes.

He slanted her a covert look, glad she had decided to dress for the event. He'd never much cared for her long, flowing dresses, but he'd take them over her nudity any day.

"I like her."

He handed her a clean plate for drying, pretending he didn't know who she was talking about. "Who?"

She nudged his arm. "You know who."

Yeah, he knew who all right. She was talking about Gracie.

All throughout dinner he'd felt awkward somehow. He figured it was because this was the first time since his ex-wife that he'd brought a woman to his parents' house. Well, he hadn't exactly brought Gracie, but that was neither here nor there at this point. Still, that explanation hadn't seemed to pan out. As he'd watched the three of them laugh and joke over what seemed like a lifetime of his misdeeds and growing pains, he'd finally hit on it. She was more at home with his parents than he had ever been.

"I like her, too," he murmured to himself.

He grimaced, afraid of what he'd just revealed, and said almost defensively, "Of course you like her. She's just like you two."

"Oh, I didn't say Frank liked her. He can speak for himself. I said I did."

"Point made."

She smiled at him and he found himself smiling back. "So whatever happened to the other woman you said you were dating? Diana, wasn't it?"

Sometimes he wished his mother couldn't read him so well. Especially since he couldn't figure either of his parents out to save his life. He was sure she'd seen his wince. "What do you mean what happened to her?"

"Why did you stop seeing her?"

He cleared his throat. "I haven't."

Few were the times he'd been capable of shocking his mother. But her slack-jawed response meant he had. "What do you mean you haven't?"

He shrugged. "Exactly what it sounds like."

She lowered her voice. Another characteristic that went against her nature. She was always free about her opinions, seemingly uncaring of who heard what. "Do you mean you're…dating both of them?"

He shifted uncomfortably from foot to foot. "In a manner of speaking…yes. I suppose you could say that."

Dylan handed her another plate. She put it down on the counter without drying it. "Well, either you are or you aren't, Dylan. Which is it?"

He plunged his hands into the dishwater, searching for the silverware hiding out somewhere in there. "It's more complicated than that." Fork prongs stabbed him. He withdrew his hand and stared at it to make sure no serious scarring would occur. "Let's just say that Diana and I were very much a couple when I began the tour. Then I met Gracie. And she and I also became a couple.…"

"Dylan, I'm shocked."

He grimaced. "Trust me, so am I."

The kitchen fell silent. After a few moments, she resumed

drying the plates, and he finished washing. From the living room drifted the sound of Frank's hearty chuckle. He could only imagine what Gracie was telling his father. Why did the prospect make him…well, not so upset?

"What are you going to do?" his mother finally asked.

He shrugged. "I really don't know, Mom."

"So you're just going to leave both women hanging until you do know?"

"I wouldn't call what I'm doing letting them hang, but…yes."

She narrowed her gaze on his face. For the first time he saw disapproval in her eyes and it was a powerful thing. She'd never disapproved of anything he'd done before. He found it strange—and unsettling—that she'd chosen now to start.

"Do they know about each other?" she asked.

"What does that have—"

"Do they?"

"Gracie does."

"But Diana doesn't."

"Right."

She put the clean plates in the cupboard then smoothed the damp towel out on the counter to dry next to a bowl of granola. "No wonder."

"No wonder what?"

She looked at him full in the face. "No wonder that girl in there doesn't know if she should stay or go."

He laughed. "Gracie? Trust me, she doesn't have a hesitant bone in her body. You could put a sign around your neck that says she's not welcome here and she'd probably set out to change your mind."

His mother shook her head. "Is that what you really think?"

"Yes, it is. Why?"

"Because you have it all wrong, that's why."

He looked at her for a long moment, trying to put together

what she was saying with Gracie's behavior tonight. Could his mother be right? It seemed incredible, but after the 180-degree turn his own life had taken recently, he wasn't quite so ready to rule anything out, as he might have done before. At least not yet.

It was then he realized that Gracie had been a little…distant from him during dinner. Oh, she smiled. She joked. But most of it had been directed at his parents, not him.

Could it be that she was also questioning exactly where they stood? That she needed something beyond the great sex they shared?

He leaned against the counter, the prospect mind-boggling. He'd been so wrapped up in his own thoughts, trying to sort out his own feelings, or rather purposely blocking them, he hadn't stopped to factor in Gracie's.

Of course, she'd never given him cause to, either.

His mother touched his shoulder, making him jump. "Are you ever wound up. When we go into the other room, I'll light a eucalyptus candle to help calm you."

"Just what I need," he said drily.

She laughed. "You know, if you stopped being such a smart-ass all the time, determined to find differences between us, I think you'd discover that we have a lot more in common than you believe."

"Tough sell."

"Oh, I don't think so." She tilted her head. "There's something…different about you this visit. You don't seem so anal. Oh, you say the words you always say. Make cracks at Frank and me. But the bite's missing somehow."

Dylan began rolling his shirtsleeves down. He'd noticed the same thing. Though what had brought about the changes was anyone's guess. And what impact the change would have on his relationship with his parents…well, that remained to be seen.

"You know, I was just remembering when you first brought Julie to meet us."

Dylan grimaced at the mention of his ex-wife. "Talk about someone you didn't like."

"What makes you think that?"

He shrugged. "Oh, I don't know. Maybe the way you went out of your way to shock her. Point out what life on the ranch meant. And underscored that you fully expected me to move back here, and oh, wouldn't it be nice if it were soon, so that Julie and I could raise our kids here."

His mother laughed. "You have to admit, it was effective."

"Did you ever stop to think that I just might have wanted to spend the rest of my life with her?"

"Yes, despite what you believe, I did. Unfortunately, I had a feeling Julie didn't feel quite the same way. I got the impression that no matter what you did, she would eventually end up leaving you. I guess I thought the sooner the better for both of you." She sighed. "How is she doing lately, anyway?"

He rubbed the back of his neck. "In the middle of divorce number three."

"I'm not surprised."

He grinned. "No, I guess I'm not, either."

The twang of guitar strings sounded from the direction of the living room. Dylan grimaced, suspecting Frank was now going through his collection of original albums.

This was going to be a long night.

Then something occurred to him. "Is that why you and Frank decided to indulge in a little exhibitionism? For Gracie's sake? To test her?"

She looked at him. "I wish I was as devious as that, but no." She smiled. "But if we had, I'd have to say she passed with flying colors. Barely even blinked an eye."

"That's probably because they were ready to fall out of her head." He crossed his arms, sorting through everything that had just passed between his mother and him. Funny, he'd never really thought of their relationship in the typical mother-son way. But considering things now, wasn't the time they had just shared exactly what a normal family would do? Her gently prodding. Him responding. Their comments giving them both things to think about?

"I don't suppose you'd care to give me any advice on my current situation, would you?" he asked.

Moonbeam adamantly shook her head. "Nope." She grasped his shirtfront. "This is something you're going to have to figure out all on your lonesome."

"Now there's a concept."

She tugged him in the direction of the living room. "Better to have you curse me for giving you too much freedom, than have you blame me for bad decisions that may or may not have come as a result of my advice. Come on. Let's go join the kids. They're playing my song." She hesitated. "However…if I were to decide to offer advice or anything, it would be that I think Gracie's perfect for you." She smiled. "But, of course, I wouldn't do that."

"Of course not." He caught her hand for a moment. "Mom?"

She looked at him automatically.

"Have you ever done anything conventional in your entire life?"

"Sure. I had you."

Oh, THIS WAS SO VERY, very good…and so very, very bad.

Gracie lazily ran her fingers across Dylan's sweat-coated chest, finding something surreal about the thick hemp-stuffed tick they lay on top of in the middle of the bare wooden floor of his old bedroom, the fiery light from dozens of flickering candles dimming the thousands of stars visible beyond the balcony doors.

"I can't believe I had sex under my parents' roof," he murmured, twirling a strand of her hair around his finger in that way that made something in her chest go thunk. "And that I enjoyed it."

She halfheartedly thwapped him. "Very funny."

He chuckled quietly. "I didn't mean it that way."

"I know."

She stretched her leg along the length of his, shivering at the crisp hair against her smooth skin. "Actually, I've come to an interesting conclusion. Promise you won't laugh."

He raised his free hand and swore.

"I'm convinced we were switched at birth."

His chuckle vibrated his chest beneath her hand. She smiled and rubbed her nose against his bare shoulder.

"I like your parents."

He tugged on her hair. "Then we have something in common." She looked at him. "I like your parents."

She smiled. "What's the matter with yours?"

"Aside from the fact that they're in a suspended state of childhood and like to parade around in front of visitors completely nude?" He shrugged. "Absolutely nothing."

"I think they're refreshing."

"I think they're demented."

She slid her foot down to the top of his. "Is that your professional diagnosis?"

"Nope. Completely personal. Besides, Frank agrees with my assessment."

"He used to be a child psychologist," she said rather than asked. She'd found out a lot of surprising information about the modern-day flower children over dinner, then afterward as they listened to what she suspected was Frank's entire record collection over a couple of bottles of homemade wine.

"Shocker, isn't it, considering they raised such a screwed-up kid."

"You're not screwed-up," she disagreed, wondering if he really felt that way. "Just a little…uptight."

"Oh, you think so, do you?"

"Uh-huh."

"And what do you prescribe to…treat this illness of mine?"

She made a U-turn with her hand and sloped down to his erection. Incredible as it seemed, he was hard again. She wrapped her fingers around the silken width then rubbed the pad of her thumb over the bead of moisture at the tip. "Hmm…I don't know. But give me a minute. I'm sure I'll come up with something."

For long, quiet minutes they lay like that. Him rubbing his hand down her back and caressing her bottom, her lazily stroking him. Gracie determined that she should have been exhausted. But oddly enough, she wasn't, even though it was four in the morning and she'd been up since six the previous morning.

She supposed that part of the reason was because her mind refused her peace. Though she told herself she was happy with things just the way they were, she was beginning to suspect that wasn't entirely true.

Oh, the sex was spectacular. That wasn't the problem. In fact, if anything, the heights Dylan took her to every time he slipped between her thighs grew more and more dizzying.

But, somewhere over the past couple of days the dynamics of her relationship with him had begun to transform. Which wasn't surprising in and of itself, since it was only natural that the more time they spent together, the more intimate they would become.

It became more obvious that while she willingly gave herself over to the burgeoning emotions, he was holding back. Oh, not in obvious ways. He was too smart for that. It was the little details that began to add up that gave her pause.

Like the fact that she knew his apartment was in San Francisco and he hadn't said one word about going there. She had begun to suspect he hadn't even gone himself until she saw the Jaguar parked in the driveway. While it wasn't beyond the realm of possibility that he'd rented it, chances were pretty slim, meaning he had gone to his place and purposely not mentioned it to her.

Another bit of information he hadn't revealed—and she hadn't asked about—was the woman he had supposedly been on the verge of proposing to. Was that why he hadn't taken her to his place? Was he living a double life, and going to extraordinary measures to make sure they didn't overlap?

Then there was this morning when he'd accidentally invited her to his parents' house. He looked like someone had dumped the contents of an ice bucket down the front of his pants when he'd realized what he'd done.

Of course, she'd turned him down. But over a late lunch with Rick and Tanja, she must have come off as a little too needy, asking them what they had planned for the day when it was obvious they wanted to be left alone. That's when Tanja had passed her the address to Dylan's parents' and suggested the drive would be the perfect way to see the area.

What was a woman to do? Go to a show by herself? Walk the piers? Go to Chinatown? Or go see exactly what Dylan was trying to hide from her?

She thought his attitude toward his parents was quaint. But she also saw that there was more behind his behavior than probably even he realized. Rather than the shame he hinted at, she suspected he was actually trying to protect his parents and their way of life from others.

"You got awfully quiet all of the sudden," Dylan said, breaking into her thoughts.

"Yeah."

"Is that all you have to say?"

"For now? Yeah."

"Well, that's illuminating."

At this point, Gracie didn't particularly like the direction of her thoughts. And since the only time she could shut off her mind was when she was having sex with Dylan, she raised herself up on her elbows and smiled down at him suggestively.

He chuckled. "Uh-oh. What's going on in that beautiful head of yours?"

"I've just come up with a prescription plan."

"Uh-huh."

She drew her tongue along one flat nipple, then moved over and did the same to the other. He threaded his fingers through her hair and gently tried to tug her to his mouth.

She caught his hands. "Oh, no. Not part of the game plan." She moved his wrists until his arms lay at his sides.

As she ran her tongue along the middle of his stomach, dipped lower, then came back up again, she relished his quick intake of breath.

"Do you, um, mind telling me what is?"

She laughed against his skin. "Are you always this bossy?"

"Always."

"Then remind me to invest in a gag tomorrow."

She dipped lower again, flicking her tongue along the edge of the crisp, curly hair between his legs. "Does a gag normally play a role in your treatments?"

"Depends on the patient." She caught the head of his erection between her lips and sucked deeply. His answering groan and the bucking of his hips from the tick set fire to her own limbs. She released him. "Now be quiet. The doctor is in session."

Curving her hand around the base of his erection, she drew the very tip of her tongue down one side, then back up the other, repeating the movement until nearly her entire tongue made contact with him.

She'd positioned herself so that she was straddling his left leg. When the rough hair of his knee began rubbing against her swollen womanhood, she shuddered. Gripping him more tightly, she slowly slid her mouth down over the rigid shaft, applying light suction and curving her tongue around him so she could pull him deeper. Then she withdrew, following her lips with the upward thrust of her hand.

He groaned and reached for her hair. She looked up to find his half-lidded, passion-filled eyes watching her. She tilted her head and placed tiny little flicks down the length of his erection while holding his gaze, then fastened her mouth from the side, beginning a slow torturous rhythm with her hand.

"Good Lord, you're going to be the death of me, woman."

She pulled the tip of his arousal into her mouth, then released it. "Maybe. But you're proving to be the life of me."

Then she gave her full attention to the task at hand, her own desire rising with his, rubbing her pelvis against his leg as she increased the tempo of her mouth and hand.

She sensed his climax in the sudden stiffening of his legs, the straining of his pelvis against her hand, the locking of his jaw. He tightened his fingers in her hair to give her warning, to pull her away, but she merely took more of him in her mouth, knowing that what she was about to do was possible but having never tried it before.

"Gracie...please."

She grasped his closest hand in her free one and held him still as she continued her up and downward motion, then positioned the head of his erection against the back of her throat. Unable to hold back any longer, his hips bucked up off the mattress and she felt the hot stream of his sweetly bitter seed in the back of her mouth.

Finally he lay back against the makeshift mattress, out of breath and spent. She slowly took her mouth from him, thoroughly licking the remaining dampness from his skin.

"I've never... No one's... God, I didn't even know..." He gazed down at where she had rested her cheek against his lower abdomen. "That was incredible."

She smiled at him. "So I take it you're happy with my prescription?"

"Oh, baby, I'm more than happy. You've just earned a patient for life."

12

Miami

"GREETINGS AND SALUTATIONS, listeners. This is Dr. Gracie Mattias. Thank you for joining me tonight for a very special edition of 'Sex Talk Live.'" Gracie leaned into the mic at the affiliate radio station in Miami, Florida, one hand readjusting her headphones as she gave the toll-free numbers listeners could call nationwide with their questions or comments. She said all this by rote, having hosted the weekly two-hour program for the past year and a half and comfortable with the format and protocol, only needing an update on who the sponsors were of the show before she went on.

Normally she used her local Baltimore radio station to handle the broadcast, along with their engineers and producers. But since she was on the road, Rick had made the necessary arrangements to have a sister station and its staff host the show. Last week they'd run a series of clips of some of her more interesting conversations with listeners to cover her absence.

"Now, I don't know how closely you've been following my schedule over the past two weeks but if you haven't caught one of my appearances coast to coast, then you've likely heard of them. If neither applies, well, then, I want to know what rock you've been hiding under and whether or not there's room there for me.

"For those who are familiar with my goings-on, then you've probably also become familiar with another doctor who specializes in the same area I practice…and that, of course, is sex." She purposely drew the word out, then smiled at Dylan while he grimaced next to her at a small round table usually used for guests. "The dashing and delectable Dr. Dylan Fairbanks is who I'm talking about, and he's generously agreed to join me for tonight's show, so you'll actually be getting two heads for the price of one." Under the table she slipped out of one of her heels then slid her toe up the back of Dylan's pant leg. "So I'm sure you'll join me in welcoming Dr. Dylan to our lively forum."

Dylan cleared his throat. "Thank you for having me, Dr. Mattias."

Thank you for having me, indeed, she thought, the tension that had begun to plague her in recent days rearing its ugly little head.

That day in San Francisco, the visit to his parents' ranch, had thrust her onto an emotional roller coaster she was searching for the end to. When they were alone together, she could no sooner deny him or her own needs than she could the earth's gravitational pull. When they had sex, her body sang with exquisite pleasure, reassuring her that there could be nothing intrinsically wrong or bad in being with Dylan in this elemental way.

Afterward, she caught herself examining his comments, looking for the true meaning behind them, or worse, reading a significance into them that probably wasn't there.

She didn't like not having control over her careening thoughts…or her body.

The strange thing was, she sensed Dylan was thinking along the same lines. She'd catch him staring off into space with a grim look on his face that said he was mentally pulling something apart. And she knew that that something was her.

Forcing herself to focus on the matter at hand, she glanced down at the touch-sensitive computer screen set up between them that outlined callers and briefly described the nature of their questions. She looked at Dylan and indicated she wanted to go with Wendy from Wichita who had a question on feminine suppositories. Dylan shook his head and pointed to Don from Denver who wanted to talk about being an eighteen-year-old virgin.

Gracie made a face then touched a selection somewhere in the middle. "In honor of our host state, the first caller is Fran from Fort Lauderdale. Hi, Fran. What's on your mind tonight?"

"Um, hi, Gracie. Am I on the air?"

"Yes, Fran, if you're talking to me then you're on the air."

"Oh! Okay, um, I just wanted to say how much I enjoyed watching you on TV last week. I mean I've been a fan of your radio show for like six months now, and it was great finally seeing what you look like."

"Thank you, Fran. I'm glad I got the chance to put a face to the name for you. I take it you haven't visited the home station's website, then? Because there's more information up there than you've ever wanted to know about me."

"No, I'm sorry, I haven't seen the site. I don't have a computer yet. But I'm hoping Santa will think I've been a good little girl and buy me one for Christmas."

Gracie laughed. "I'll bet someone's a happy camper right now."

Fran's sigh came across the line loud and clear. "Well, that's just it. *One* of us is happy."

Dylan cleared his throat again, obviously awkward as he positioned the microphone closer to his mouth. "Are we talking about your husband, Fran?"

Gracie rolled her eyes. He would ask that question. Before

she'd given herself over to her attraction for Dr. Dylan, she would have found his question amusing, perhaps even offered to indulge in a playful debate on the subject. But now that their own behind-closed-doors activities proved you didn't have to be married to enjoy mind-blowing sex, his conservative attitude pricked at her patience.

Thankfully the topic was moot. Fran answered yes, that she and her husband had been married for eight years.

"The problem is this," Fran said. "While I'm happy to, you know, give him blow jobs—"

Gracie hit the delay button, cutting the words *blow job* from the broadcast and replacing them with a prerecorded "oops, I said a bad word," then interrupted Fran.

She smiled at Dylan. "I think the description the censors prefer is that you don't mind performing oral sex on him, Fran."

"Oh. Sorry."

"No apologies necessary. So, we've established that you're happy to perform oral sex on your husband. Sounds good so far. What's the problem?"

"Yes, well, you see…he's not into returning the favor. In other words, he won't go down on me."

Gracie glanced at the on-site producer on the other side of the glass divider to see if the expression would send up any censor flags. He shrugged and she let it slide.

"I see. And obviously you're a little upset by his oversight."

Oversight? Dylan mouthed. She smiled.

"Yes, I am."

"And have you told him of your feelings, Fran?"

"Oh, yes. I mean, no, not in the beginning, but a couple years ago I commented on it."

"And what was his response?"

"That he didn't like it."

Dylan cleared his throat in that way that signaled Gracie that he was about to speak. She wrote a brief note, telling him to give her another signal, like touch her on the arm, or just jump right in lest listeners get the impression he was hesitant. Either that, or ill.

"I think you'll be happy to know that your husband's response is not all that unusual, Fran. Statistics show that a good percentage of men are uncomfortable performing oral sex on their wives."

A brief silence. Gracie bit her lip to keep from filling the dead air, deciding to give Dylan the benefit of the doubt.

Finally Fran said, "Yes, but how do I change that?"

Gracie hiked a brow at Dylan, curious to hear what he had to say.

"Well, my advice," he said slowly, "is that you don't."

"Pardon me?" Gracie couldn't help putting in, trumping her own decision to let him run with the caller.

"I said that I don't think she should try to change his behavior. I mean, if the guy's uncomfortable, then he shouldn't force himself to do it. And neither should his wife."

Fran's tinny voice came back. "And do you think it's comfortable for me to give him…er, perform oral sex on him? If you ask me, he has it much easier."

Gracie gave a quiet laugh. "You touch on an interesting point, Fran. So let me ask Dr. Dylan this. What's the sole purpose of performing oral sex?"

"Well I think 'sole' is a little too constricting."

"You're right. I'll amend that to overriding reason. What is the overriding reason for performing fellatio on your mate?"

He cleared his throat again, but this time she recognized that it was because he was uncomfortable. "To give your partner pleasure."

"Uh-huh. That being the case, do you think it's fair that Fran's husband is denying *her* that pleasure?"

"To the contrary, I believe Fran's being unfair by suggesting her husband force himself to do it. Look, let's set up the scenario. Her husband, giving in to her demands, decides to give it a shot. He's uncomfortable, awkward and doesn't have a clue what he's doing to begin with. Tell me, what are the odds that she'll end up getting any pleasure out of the exercise?"

"None," she agreed. "Because you've basically just suggested he give it a shot. As in one time. Implying that hey, if it doesn't work out, well, he'll never have to do it again." She smiled. "Of course it's not going to work out. Because the guy will just be going through the motions. In fact, he may set out with the intention of failing."

"Which just emphasizes my advice that he not be asked to do it."

"Okay, Dr. Dylan, answer me this. Do you believe giving good…fellatio is an inherent skill, or is it something that has to be learned?"

"What are you getting at?"

"The quality of oral sex you give depends on the amount of time and attention you put into it. It's an art, if you will. Like the old saying, 'How do you get to Carnegie Hall? Practice, practice, practice.' Well, in this case, how do you give exquisite pleasure to your partner? Do it again…and again… and again. Sooner or later you're bound to get it right."

"So you're saying that Fran should make him do it not only once, she should insist on him doing it several times."

"I'm saying that Fran's husband needs to try to approach all this from a different angle. His wife is not asking him for this because she wants to make his life hell. She simply wants to be pleasured. Desires equal time. Something that, as her husband, he should be interested in doing."

"I disagree."

"Obviously." She laughed. "Okay, Fran, you've heard Dr. Dylan's advice. Mine is this—tell him to get down there or else you're cutting him off. He won't go down on you, you're not going down on him. Got it?"

Fran's voice was much happier. "Got it. Thanks, Gracie."

"Oh, and you might want to think about saving up for your own computer, because I don't think Santa's going to be very happy this Christmas. Good luck."

From the looks of it, Fran's "Santa" wasn't the only unhappy one. She glanced at Dylan to find him gaping at her. She squinted at him. He'd known going into this that their perspectives on human sexual behavior were polar opposites. She couldn't understand what would surprise him at her response.

She gestured toward the monitor. "Why don't you decide which call we take next, Dr. Dylan?"

On went the eighteen-year-old virgin from Denver, and out faded Gracie's attention.

Not that what the caller had to say wasn't interesting or comment-worthy. She suspected that had he come on with a comment like "I'm a virgin—at least I think I am. Do space aliens count?" she still would have zoned out. No, her distraction had to do with the similarities that emerged between their conversation with Fran, and the blocks she was currently stumbling over in her sizzling, definition-bucking relationship with Dylan.

At that moment five days ago, in her mother's laundry room, had Dylan felt he'd been forced to do something he'd rather not do? A prisoner of his hormones, so to speak? Like Fran's husband and his dislike of performing oral sex on his wife, did Dylan view their relationship as a one-shot deal? A case of temporary insanity that a little—okay, a lot—of sex would help him get over?

Had he gone into all this expecting that it would fail?

She absently bit her bottom lip, at once knowing that what she feared was true. He hadn't had any intention of truly cutting loose and seeing where things went. He'd only partially done so, all the while holding on tightly to his belief that there was no future for them. By doing so, he was essentially guaranteeing that there wouldn't be.

"Thanks for calling, Don." The significance of Dylan's words sank through the thoughtful cloud threatening to explode in her head. "And good luck controlling that libido. Remember, it's just a matter of mind over matter."

Gracie picked up on her cue to say something, anything. The only problem was, she hadn't heard a single thing the caller had said.

Dylan thankfully took up the slack. "You were awfully quiet during that call, Gracie. What, no bones to pick about my advice?"

She shook her head. "Not right now, Dr. Dylan. After all, virginity is your specialty, not mine." She repositioned her headphones and said, "Okay, who should we go with next?"

She glanced down at the monitor to find it ablaze with callers. She couldn't help her surprise. While she always had a steady stream of calls, she'd never garnered this type of a response.

Touching a button without prejudice, she sat back, settling in for the next hour of nonstop call-ins, nearly all of them weighing in on where they stood on the contrary advice they'd given Fran. Which was usually the way Gracie liked to have things work. Start off with a controversial topic or caller, and bam, the show was off and running. She'd had some shows that dragged nearly the whole two hours and it had been trying just to get through them. But tonight she didn't have to worry about coming up with items to fill the gaps, or reword advice she'd basically given the caller before.

The only problem was, she'd never realized how much of her listening base had been silent up until now. But, oh, boy, were they making their opinions known tonight. Dylan and his conservative take on affairs had been the one to wake them up.

She twisted her lips, listening as Dylan wished a twenty-year-old who wanted to wait for her wedding night good luck, then she disconnected the caller. She didn't think this new slant was such a good thing. Especially since she suspected that the root of her concerns about her relationship with Dylan lay in the advice he gave consistently, straightforwardly and without a tinge of remorse.

"Wow, you guys are really hot tonight," Gracie said, having to page down in order to see the entire caller queue. "Tell you what. For those of you just wanting to put your vote in on the Fran fellatio issue, I'm going to have my home station's webmaster put up a poll on our website so you can add your two cents. But for the second hour of the show, I'd like to continue on to other issues."

Dylan leaned over and budged her right earphone aside. "What's the matter, Gracie? Can't handle the heat?"

She turned away from her mic. "Just trying to remind you whose show this is." She flashed him a bright smile, then pushed the button for the next caller. "Hello, Josh from Jasper. What's your question tonight?"

There was a long pause.

"Josh?" she repeated, dead air a four-letter word in the radio world.

"Uh, yeah, hi."

"Hi, Josh. You're going to have to speak into the receiver a little louder so we can hear your question." Talk-show tactics to get the caller to talk, period.

"Okay. First, I just want to say that I agree with Dr. Dylan on the oral sex issue."

Gracie frowned and Dylan grinned.

Refusing to rise to the bait, and resigned that the majority of callers would continue to weigh in despite her request they not, she said, "My screen says here that we've spoken before, Josh?"

"Oh." Obviously he'd been hoping to restart the Fran debate. "Yes. We have. I've spoken to both of you, in fact."

"You mean you called earlier tonight?" Dylan looked at her and she shrugged, not recalling a Josh from Jasper, although the engineer changed names and cities when callers indicated they preferred anonymity.

"No. A couple of weeks ago. When you were on that New York morning radio show."

"You caught that, did you, Josh?" Gracie motioned to Dylan, who thoughtfully rubbed his brows. "Gotta tell you, that was a new experience for me and one I'm not anxious to repeat again anytime soon, if you know what I mean."

"Do you remember me?" Josh asked.

Dylan's eyes brightened and he touched her arm. "Of course we remember you, Josh. Although I think the name you were going by then was John, right?"

"Right."

Gracie nodded. Okay, now she remembered. "For the listeners who may not have heard that conversation, John was having some problems interesting his wife in having sex more often. Is that right, Josh?"

"Right."

"So," Gracie said, stretching back and taking her mic with her. "Did you take my advice? Talk to your wife about her secret fantasy then turn your house into a replica of it?"

A pause, then. "She told me she doesn't have a secret fantasy."

"I see," Gracie said slowly. "So did you improvise, then?"

"Yes," he said with relief. "I wasn't sure if I should have done that, you know, until you just said something. I'm glad you approve."

Gracie smiled. "Just so long as it worked."

The pauses between the caller's responses caused dread to begin building up in her stomach. Normal hesitancy she'd come to expect. After all, it usually hit the caller during the actual call that they were on national radio in front of God and everyone.

But there was something more at work here. And Gracie wasn't sure she wanted to find out what.

After another moment, Dylan asked, "What did you do, Josh?"

"Well, since she'd told me that she didn't really have any secret fantasies, I decided to try to guess what she might like. I arranged for all that romantic stuff—you know, that you see in the movies—to be sent to our house, then I set it all up before she got home from work. You know, flowers, wine, candles, soft music. And since I can't cook, and I didn't want her to have anything to clean up anyway, I ordered in from our favorite restaurant."

"Sounds good so far," Gracie said. "Was she surprised?"

"Oh, yes. She was surprised all right."

Dylan looked at her. "Doesn't sound like it was a nice surprise, though, was it?"

"No. She accused me of putting too much pressure on her. Then she told me she'd eaten at the office and went to bed. Without me."

Gracie leaned forward. "Sounds to me like you two might lead pretty stressful lives, is that right, Josh?"

"You could say that."

She thought she just had. She'd been hoping he would say a little more. "Let me know if this hits home. You both work full-time jobs. Money's a little tight. You're still relatively young and would like to have more than you have right now and are pretty much working for the future. Does that sound about right?"

"Yes."

"So on this particular night your wife was probably pretty tired, wasn't she? Sometimes stress and exhaustion can make people do or say some things they really don't mean. Have you thought about trying this again, say on the weekend? On a night when neither of you haven't worked during the day, and don't have to go to work the next? Say a Saturday?"

"That was a Saturday."

"I see. And your wife worked that day?"

"She works every day."

Not good.

Dylan touched her arm, sending tiny little shivers dancing along her skin. "Josh, sometimes grand gestures aren't really what's needed. You know the saying. Sometimes the best things in life are free. So I'm going to suggest this. Next time your wife comes home, have dinner ready and the kitchen cleaned. Nothing fancy. No candles that indicate you're interested in anything more than doing your part. Then when you're just sitting around say the television, or reading the newspaper, offer to give her a back massage. Better yet, a foot massage. Make it look like sex is the last thing on your mind."

Gracie cleared her throat, then cringed as she recognized herself making Dylan's mistake. "Actually, Josh, I think, on that night, sex really should be the last thing on your mind. You should tell yourself from the beginning that it's not in the cards so there are no underlying intentions she might pick up on that may set her off. It also guarantees that you won't be upset if nothing does happen." She warmed to her topic. "In fact, if she indicates she wants to get intimate, you should refuse her. Tell her that's not what you're after and just offer to hold her."

"But how does that solve my problem?"

"It doesn't. Not that night. But it's a step in the right direction that will hopefully lead you down the full path to renewed sexual intimacy between you and your wife."

"Nicely said." Dylan's voice sounded in her ears.

"Why thank you, Dr. Dylan. I think that's the first time we've agreed tonight. On that note, I think it's time we took a brief commercial break." She glanced at the monitor. "Make sure you don't touch that dial, because Monica from Missoula is on the line and wants to talk about bondage. Personally, I can't wait to hear where Dr. Dylan stands on this issue."

DYLAN STOOD ON THE marble-tiled balcony outside one of the best hotel suites Miami had to offer and stared out at the sun-sparkling surface of the Atlantic Ocean. He drew in a deep breath of the thick salt air, allowing the sea breeze to tug at his unbuttoned white shirt and shoot through his hair. It seemed odd that a thousand miles north, one of the first snowstorms of the season was battering New England.

He shook his head. Surreal.

As was just about everything else in his life right now.

He remembered last night's showdown with Gracie on nationwide radio and couldn't help a grin. It wasn't so long ago that he would have choked on any response he'd made to his professional and sexual counterpart's words of wisdom. But over the past few days he'd learned to give just as good as he got. And it felt damn good.

Of course, he admitted that wasn't the only reason he felt good. He'd come to some sort of decision last night on the way back to the hotel after torturous days of indecision since they'd left San Francisco. That determination had gelled into reality this morning when he'd woken to find her still sleeping, her rounded little bottom and slender back curled against his side, the smell of her sex, their sex, filling his nose.

His mother was right. Gracie was perfect for him.

He stood still for long moments, waiting for objections to present themselves, for fear to begin gnawing away at the new roots, for lifelong convictions to quickly erect a wall against what he'd come to see was inevitable from the instant he'd first laid eyes on savvy, sexy Gracie Mattias in the shower on that fateful autumn day in New York.

Nothing.

Nothing but a sense of rightness so profound that for an instant it was easy to imagine himself one with the sea and sand sprinkled out like precious jewels just beyond the balcony railing.

He grinned again and slid his hands into his pants pockets.

He supposed the suddenness of the realization should be cause for some concern. Told himself that caution might be the better part of valor. That time was the ultimate test of any relationship's durability. Especially given his history. One failed marriage. An almost-engagement derailed. But much in the same way urgency filled him whenever he was in the same room with Gracie, so was the desire to claim her as his, completely, the next time he saw her.

He absently rubbed his stubble-covered chin. Of course, he was overlooking the little detail that she might not want to be claimed. By him or anyone else. During the past few days, she'd seemed to grow more and more distant from him. Her contagious laughter was slower in coming. Her lovemaking more intense, serious even, as though she were searching for an elusive something she couldn't find and he didn't know how to give her. He'd been so wrapped up in himself, he hadn't even considered how she felt about all of this beyond Moonbeam pointing out that she felt something more.

What if he and his mother had it wrong and Gracie didn't want anything beyond fantastic sex?

The thought numbed him. Was it possible that she didn't want anything beyond today? This moment? Was she still living out her own personal extended sexual safari and he was the prey she would cast aside when lust waned?

He slowly finger-combed his hair, the breeze instantly undoing his efforts though he couldn't bring himself to care. He tried looking at the situation from her side, tried to gain insight into her point of view, but found it difficult without tainting it with his own. He could come up with at least a half-dozen reasons why she shouldn't want him for the long haul. Hell, that part was easy for him because he'd hung on to the same reasons for so long himself.

He withdrew his hand from his pants pocket, taking out the antique engagement ring along with it. Clicking the velvet box open, he looked down at it and frowned. The platinum band with three large diamonds shone dully in the bright light. Not Gracie at all. She needed something that was her. Something that took the light in the room then reflected it, increasing its strength tenfold.

He needed to find a way to break down any final barriers that she might have erected between them. And he was sure there were a shitload that he'd only given her the freedom to fortify over the past few days. While he sensed a somewhat desperate longing in her lovemaking lately, he also sensed that she had yet to give him everything. And it was exactly that everything that he needed. Not only to appease his ego. But to prove that what they shared was more than just great sex. That his philosophy that great sex came as a result of a deeper connection, a greater understanding still held true for him. The reason why they were so good together was that they were made for each other. Complete opposites in every way. She was the yin to his yang. Well, if you went in for that kind of thing, anyway. He normally didn't, but right now, standing on that beachfront balcony, staring out over the vast Atlantic as if he was gazing out upon the uncertainty of the future, he couldn't come up with anything better.

And he couldn't help thinking that the key to convincing her of the same lay in what had brought them together: sex.

He shoved the ring box back into his pocket. But first he needed to arm himself....

13

JUGGLING WHAT ADDED UP TO a month's budget in shopping bags, Gracie stepped into the slot that opened up in the hotel's automatic revolving door. Comfort buying, she thought, though for some reason she didn't feel all that comforted. As if to prove her point, she nearly toppled right off her high heels, a virtual death sentence in the enclosed space. She was forced to choose: her dignity or the bags. Dignity won hands down and she released at least three of the half-dozen bags in order to steady herself against the revolving glass. Before she could regain her equilibrium, the contraption spit her out into the lobby. She swung around, watching her lost bags make another go-around.

Dropping the remainder of her bags to the floor, she sighed. Well, better the bags be stuck in the apparatus being propelled in circles than her, right? Although she really didn't need a revolving door to accomplish that for her. She was doing quite all right by herself in that department.

"Ma'am, can I help you?"

Ma'am? Gracie scowled at the bellboy in a hat similar to those worn by minstrel monkeys and motioned to where her bags were coming up in the revolving door.

She didn't think it possible, but her day was rapidly going from bad to worse. She squinted against the late-afternoon sunlight reflecting off a chrome bumper of an approaching limo, then hurried to rescue her other belongings, nearly colliding with the bellboy who had the same thing in mind. She stumbled back, motioning for him to go ahead. He presented her with his rear end. She fought the temptation to give him a propelling push, sending him sprawling along with her bags. She figured it was no less than he deserved for calling her "ma'am."

She caught herself smiling. Well, as close to smiling as she'd been all day. She'd take it. Even if it meant her amusement had come as a result of maiming someone else.

The small smile vanished completely when he reached out and punched a button that stopped the revolving door from... well, revolving.

A moment later, the world was set back on its axis and he stood in front of her holding all of her packages, the door moving on to terrorize its next unwitting victim.

"Why don't I see to these for you. What room are you in?"

She told him, then fished a tip out of her purse and gave it to him. She bit her tongue to keep from asking if he'd be around later when she inevitably decided she didn't need a lick of the clothing she had just bought and wanted to return the items. Instead, she smiled.

The bags and the bellboy gone, she slid off her shoes, then sighed as her bare feet cooled against the smooth marble floor. An older couple, reminding her just a little too much of her parents, walked by, frowning at her. Ignoring them, she padded toward the house phones. She plucked up one of the receivers and dialed the number for Rick's room. After seven rings, the line automatically switched over to voice mail. She pressed Disconnect then tried Tanja's room. Nothing there, either.

Earlier, Rick was supposed to meet her for a late lunch with reps from the regional distribution center. He'd been a no-show. She and the three Floridians had waited two hours, then headed on over for a tour of the warehouse, after which she signed five hundred copies of her book. Her feet ached, her fingers had permanent pen indentations, and she just wanted this tour done and over with.

She realized the significance of what she'd just thought as she left a message for Rick on Tanja's voice mail then slowly replaced the receiver. It went without saying that once the tour was over with, so was her fun little tryst with Dylan. She didn't want to use the word *affair*. Despite her modern take on life and sexuality, she hated to think of herself as "the other woman."

But no matter how much she argued the point, that's what she was, wasn't it? While Dylan wasn't married, she had no reason to believe he didn't still plan on becoming engaged. And at least until the tour ended tomorrow and they inevitably went their separate ways, she was openly cheating with a guy who planned to spend the rest of his life with someone else.

That was a bitter pill to swallow.

Making a beeline for the concierge's station, she stood in the line three people deep, peering over shoulders to try to gauge how long the wait would be. It might just be more convenient if she went on up to her room and checked her voice mail. If she had been thinking, she might have scribbled down the code to remotely access the system. Then again, she hadn't expected Rick to disappear off the face of the earth.

The line shortened by one as a tall blond woman stepped up to the desk. Good, maybe—

"Dr. Dylan Fairbanks…"

Gracie's stomach plunged to her feet as she overheard the name. She leaned to the other side of the guy in front of her, trying to listen in.

"Tell him Diana Evans is waiting for him in the lounge, please. I'll be there for the next hour."

The guy in front of her shrugged his shoulder. It wasn't

until that moment that Gracie realized she'd had her cheek smashed against his back in her effort to eavesdrop. She mumbled an apology, then moved completely next to him, moving up when he did as one Miss Diana Evans finally turned and stepped away from the desk. She hesitated, looking around the spacious lobby, then began walking toward the small lounge.

Gracie felt as if someone had wrapped their hands around her lungs, denying her air as she watched the woman walk away. There was no doubt in her mind the woman was, in fact, Dylan's Diana. And she was here to see Dylan.

Neat, short, honey-blond hair. Pretty blue eyes. A body to kill for. A stylish suit and low heels. Even the guy next to her nearly pulled a neck muscle trying to get a look. Gracie irrationally felt like thwapping him in the arm from where she still stood in her bare feet on the other side of him, her hair frizzy and mussed from the past two hours hoofing it through trendy little shops in the humid air, her impractical high-heeled shoes, nearly touching the floor, dangling from her fingers.

She swallowed hard, watching as the striking woman disappeared into the dim interior of the lounge. Well, it wasn't difficult to figure out what Dylan saw in her. Diana Evans was the quintessential woman that all men looked for. In fact, if she weren't happily heterosexual, she might just have wanted to marry her herself.

"Ma'am?"

As if in slow motion, she turned to find the guy in front of her had left and that she was standing a desk away from the concierge.

"May I help you, ma'am?"

She fought the urge to bean him with one of her shoes. Bet he hadn't called Diana Evans "ma'am."

"Um, yes. Are there any messages for Gracie Mattias?"

She caught the flash of impatience on his face.

"*Dr.* Grace Mattias?"

He made a show of looking around his counter space. "And you might be?"

"Dr. Grace Mattias," she repeated evenly, thinking she might just have to bean him with both shoes.

Impatience turning to flirtation, he smiled at her. "Sorry, ma'am, but I don't see anything here."

"It's *miss,* you nimrod. Oh, and thanks."

She stepped away from the counter, her gaze drifting again to the lounge, then scanned the nearby area. A grouping of couches and chairs was positioned not too far away from the lounge entrance, as were a couple of leafy plants. If she could pull one of the plants over to the chair...

She caught herself. What was she thinking? Was she seriously considering hiding behind a palm and staking out Dylan? If he went into that lounge, hugged the pretty, blonde Diana and proposed to her on the spot, what would she do then? Congratulate him?

"Excuse me, ma'am—"

Gracie whipped around to face the concierge again. Her glare must have told him not to dare call her ma'am again. Instead, he said, "Dr. Mattias, I'm sorry, but I do have a message for you."

She sighed in relief and leaned again the counter. Thank God. She really needed to talk to someone, and it looked like Rick was going to be her man.

She accepted the brief, handwritten note, realizing immediately that it wasn't from Rick. "Meet me in Suite 1001. Six o'clock." Signed, simply "D."

Glancing back toward the lounge in case he had somehow gotten by her, she turned the note over, thinking that maybe he'd made a mistake. That the note was for Diana, not for her. After all, they already had rooms. Separate, of course. It didn't occur to her until now that Dylan's motivation for keeping separate quarters might not be the secrecy he proclaimed, but was more likely because of the woman waiting for him just off the lobby.

No. The note was for her. Her name was written on the outside in the same, sprawling handwriting.

She murmured a thank-you to the concierge and began walking toward the elevators. Well, if this was going to be the kiss-off meeting, damned if she was going to look like something the cat threw up during it. She punched the elevator button, then shoved the crumpled note into her skirt pocket. She wouldn't think of standing him up. To do so would be to make herself out as a spineless coward. And she wasn't about to be a coward now. Spineless or otherwise.

Besides, given Dylan's anal tendencies, he'd probably track her down. To make sure that she knew exactly where things stood between them.

And where did they stand?

After spending so many days not standing, she supposed that standing itself would be a first.

The elevator finally dinged and she stepped inside the empty claustrophobia-attack-waiting-to-happen and pressed the button for her floor.

She toyed with the face of her watch. She'd find out in just a little under an hour, so why give herself a headache now?

She sighed and gave in to the urge to lean against the wall. What did one wear to such an event?

DYLAN CHECKED HIS WATCH for the third time, but it didn't read much later than the last time he'd looked at it. It was a quarter past six. And still no Gracie.

He paced the length of the suite, past the four-poster bed with its filmy white curtains, the champagne chilling in a shiny silver bucket, the half-dozen flower arrangements, all roses in varying vivid colors, then stopped in front of the special table set for two, complete with food that was delivered at promptly two minutes till six. The lighted candles were already dripping wax. He glanced at his watch again, sighed and considering dousing the flames.

He'd called the concierge the instant he'd returned to the room a half hour ago. Yes, he was told, Dr. Grace Mattias had picked up the note. And no, it wouldn't be a problem to have a privacy block placed on the phone for the remainder of the evening.

So where was she?

A low knock sounded at the door. Swallowing thickly, he began to rush toward it, then told himself to slow down. Pausing briefly to erase any panic that might show on his face, he curved his fingers around the doorknob and pulled the door open.

Only to find Tanja standing there.

"Can I come in?"

He didn't have a chance to answer that no, she couldn't, before she was breezing on by him.

Dylan grimaced and peeked out the door into the hallway. Empty.

He closed the door and turned to see Tanja sitting on the edge of one of the armchairs, completely oblivious to the seduction scene laid out in the suite.

"Rick left me."

His brows shot up on his forehead. He amended his guess to distracted.

For a long moment he stood rooted to the spot near the door, not knowing what he should do. To say he and Tanja had never been...personal with each other was a major understatement. The confident PR rep was always in control of herself and his agenda, even when she manipulated that agenda to serve her own needs.

He cleared his throat. "How did you know I was here?"

She rolled her eyes then looked at him, but said nothing.

He didn't have to ask again. She'd probably threatened the concierge with bodily harm to get the room number. He had no doubt wiry Tanja could best anyone twice her weight just with sheer determination.

He glanced at his watch again. Twenty after. Stepping to the table, he blew out the candles, then went to sit on the sofa opposite Tanja.

She made a low, mewling type of sound. "Oh, God, how was I supposed to know that his surprise was for us to get married at the county courthouse?"

For the second time, Dylan's brows shot up. "Married?"

Sure, after the incident in the Houston bookstore stockroom, he'd guessed that Tanja and Rick were…intimate. But, married?

She nodded and sniffed, producing a wadded-up tissue from the side pocket of her cargo pants. "Yeah. Married. Can you believe it?"

Given the changes wrought in his own life over the past week or so, he was ready to believe just about anything.

"I take it you turned him down?"

She looked at him for the first time, her dark eyes red-rimmed. "Of course I turned him down. What do I look like, some sort of idiot?" She blew her nose loudly then sighed heavily. "Sorry. You didn't deserve that." She waved the hand holding the tissue. "It's just…why can't he accept that I can't even think about getting married right now? I've just gotten promoted. Moved into my own apartment in New York after rooming forever with two other girls. Then there's the little problem of his living in Baltimore, over two hundred miles away."

Dylan was still trying to work out the scene at the courthouse. "He had a ring?"

"Yeah." She held her left hand out, flashing him a modest-size pearl engagement ring. Even as he looked at it, he noticed she didn't. "Isn't it the greatest thing you ever saw?"

He nodded, thinking it was the appropriate thing to do.

She dropped her hand back into her lap. "Do you want to

know why I know exactly how far Baltimore is from New York? I'll tell you. Because that's where I used to live. Where I grew up. In fact, it's where Rick and I first met. In high school. But we were both going out with others at the time. After high school we dated a bit. Then I moved to New York and…well, we just kind of drifted apart." She frowned. "At least until we bumped into each other again on this god-forsaken tour."

"You're from Baltimore?" So this thing between Tanja and Rick had been going on for a lot longer than he and Gracie had ever suspected.

She didn't hear him. Or at least she acted as if she didn't. "When I asked him how we'd go about solving the little distance problem, do you know what he said? He told me that he'd automatically assumed that I would return to Baltimore. That I'd…proved whatever I set out to in New York and that it was time to come home." She stared at him. "I love New York." Her eyes teared up all over again. "And I love Rick."

Uncomfortable and not at all sure what he should say, he asked, "So…what happened when you told him no?"

She rolled her eyes, as if running out of patience with a slow child. "We argued. Of course. Right in front of a jury pool. Then he…left." Her voice broke. "And I haven't been able to find him since." Tears streamed down her face and she tried unsuccessfully to mop them up. "He's not answering his cell phone…he hasn't been back to his room. I…just don't know what to do."

Dylan didn't know what to do, either. Worse yet, he couldn't come up with another question to ask her.

What was standing out clearly in his mind was that Rick and Tanja's situation wasn't all that different from his and Gracie's. His gaze snapped to the intimate little table for two, the provocative bed and the flowers everywhere, and he felt panic rise in his throat.

If Tanja was currently career-minded, with any thought

of marriage or kids far on the back burner, then Gracie was doubly so.

And he may have been about to make one of the biggest mistakes of his life.

Tanja suddenly appeared uncomfortable, as if the act of unloading had cleared her mind, allowing her to understand exactly what she had just done. Which was share a huge hunk of her personal life with him.

Her gaze darted around, then retraced the path more slowly. When she looked back at him, her eyes wide, her purple-tinted hair sticking up at odd angles from where she'd been running her hands through it, Dylan had to look away.

"Oh…I'm like totally interrupting something, aren't I?" She shot from the chair. "I'm so sorry."

Dylan got up after her. "There's no reason to apologize."

She tried for a shaky smile. "God, I can't believe I just said all that to you."

Dylan grimaced. "Why?"

"Well, because, like, you're my boss. Well, not my boss, really, but you know what I mean. And besides, even though I don't know what's going on with you and Gracie, I know you don't approve of…well, promiscuous behavior." She stuffed her tissue back into her pocket. "You probably think I should have married him, huh?"

Dylan followed her to the door. "I think you need to do whatever you feel you have to, Tanja."

She turned back toward him and he cringed, because she looked on the verge of tears again. "Thanks," she said, throwing her slender arms around him.

Dylan stood awkwardly, nearly knocked backward by the surprise onslaught. He held his arms out, not quite knowing what to do with them. Then he managed to clumsily pat her on the back a couple times before dropping his hands to his sides.

"Thank you," she said again, then gave him a peck on the cheek.

"Um, don't mention it."

She opened the door…to find Gracie standing, hand in the air poised to knock.

"Oh!" she said, clearly startled.

Dylan was so glad to see her, it was all he could do not to yank her in, shove Tanja out and then slam the door. Especially given the hopeful expression on Tanja's face, as if again forgetting the scene of seduction mapped out behind him and assuming Gracie was there for her and not him. Either that, or she was so wrung out she was desperate for another ear. A fresh ear. A woman's ear to hear her story of woe.

Afraid she was about to latch onto Gracie like some long-lost relative, he cleared his throat. "Tanja was just leaving," he said.

His gaze slid back to Gracie. He finally registered exactly how she looked. And felt the bottom drop out of his stomach.

Where he had dressed down for the evening in a pair of white string-drawn cotton pants and matching shirt, she had dressed up. He'd never seen her look so damn good. The black dress she had on stretched down to her freckled little feet, the neckline dipping enticingly, as if the edge of the fabric itself wanted to touch the delectable mounds of flesh, and the stringiest of straps disappeared over her sculpted shoulders, left bare by the upswept style of her hair. She could easily have gone to a museum event, the opera, or been at home in one of those jazz joints Tanja had gone to in Chicago. All that he could think about was how damn much he wanted her.

At the thought of Tanja, he turned to find her beginning to open her mouth, her gaze seeking Gracie's, her expression hopeful.

Dylan none too gently guided her out into the hall. "I'm sure it will be all right, Tanja. Why don't you just go back to your room and get some rest. Things of this nature have a way of working themselves out."

He cringed at the obvious lie and at the fresh welling of tears in her dark eyes.

"Wait," Gracie said, fishing through a tiny black, beaded purse. Dylan wanted to groan, thinking that if she were about to hand Tanja a tissue, he wouldn't be alone with Gracie for at least another hour. Instead, she held out a room key. "Rick came by my room about a half hour ago." She smiled. "I'm guessing for the same reason you came to Dylan's." When Tanja merely stared at the hole-punched piece of white plastic, Gracie pressed it into her hand and told her the room number. "You decide what you want to do."

Tanja nodded almost imperceptibly and began to turn away. Then once again she was launching herself into someone's arms. This time Gracie's.

Dylan stared at his shoes, deciding not to watch the display of feminine bonding, not looking up again until Tanja had murmured her last thank-you. Gracie stood speechless as the waiflike PR rep hurried down the hall toward the elevators.

"So that's why you were late," he said in relief.

She looked at him with a blank look on her fascinating face, apparently taking her a minute to make the mental transition. "Oh! Yes."

She came inside and he closed the door and locked it, then checked the locks again. "You could have called." He thought he detected a hint of tension around her lips.

"I tried. Someone put a privacy block on the phone."

"Oh. Yes." He grinned. "That, um, would have been me."

He stood back as she slowly wandered around, touching a rose petal here, caressing the gauzy curtains on the canopy bed there. As she explored the room, he allowed his gaze to openly explore her.

She looked absolutely...beautiful. Exquisite. And as she

moved, he saw that the dress wasn't entirely conservative. He caught his breath at the sight of the nearly hip-high slit up the left side of the black material that revealed not only a decadent amount of leg, but the fact that she wore thigh-high black stockings and a lacy black garter.

He instantly grew rock-hard, prepared to abandon all his carefully laid-out plans, forget about dinner getting cold on the table and just throw her to the bed and plunge into her wet, hot flesh, dress and all.

Even as she examined the romantic trappings, he sensed that she was ultra-aware of him. His impression was confirmed when her gaze swept him from eyes to feet, then lingered at the thick ridge he was sure stood out cleanly under his white cotton pants. Her knuckles turned white where she grasped one of the iron bed posts, then her pink, pink tongue darted out to lick her lips.

She laughed quietly. "Looks like I'm not the only one who did some, um, shopping today."

While she played for normalcy, he noticed the sudden shallowness of her breathing, and the way her nipples pressed tantalizingly against the black fabric. He swore he could make out her heartbeat there. At the base of her graceful neck, just beneath her pale skin.

Dylan swallowed hard and silently counted to ten, afraid that if he didn't rein himself in, his slow, night-long seduction would be over in less than fifteen minutes.

"I...ordered dinner." He motioned toward the table, then forced himself to step to it where he relighted the candles.

She came to stand on the other side, her brown eyes black in the flickering light. "I'm not...hungry."

His hand froze where he was about to uncover the warming tray. He chuckled. "Funny...suddenly, neither am I."

At least not for food. Gracie, on the other hand, he wanted to devour from the tip of her curly head to the arch of her high-heel-clad feet.

Her gaze darted away from his in a way that was uncharacteristic for Gracie. She'd never played coy with him before, so it was inconceivable that she would start now. He noticed the way she practically mangled her evening purse and knew something was up. Something other than an insatiable body part of his.

"Uh-oh. What's the matter?" he asked.

Her surprise was evident as she looked at him. Still she said nothing.

He started to slowly round the table to stand nearer to her. She rounded it the other way, making sure distance was maintained. Dylan wanted to groan, feeling like a starving man having prime rib dangled just out of his range.

"Well, gee, if I was unsure something was wrong before, I'm sure now," he said. The absence of any playfulness in her movements told him that tenfold.

She seemed to realize what she was doing to her purse and stuck it under her arm. She didn't put it down. Didn't make a move to sit. And everything that was Dylan began to worry. "Tell me," he continued.

Her small smile gave him cause for hope. "God, this is just so damned awkward."

He slipped his hands into his pants pockets, trying to ignore how much her words sounded like she was on the verge of giving him the brush-off.

"You know I've always been honest with you, Dylan. And I'm not going to stop now. All I ask is that you…be honest with me." She tucked a curly strand of hair that teased her right shoulder behind her ear. "I saw Diana."

At first he didn't understand the significance behind the words. Then it finally began to seep through his concern. *She'd seen Diana.* This is what all this was about. Her choice of attire. Her distance. Still, despite everything, there was no denying that she was just as drawn to him as ever. He could tell by the way she stood rigidly still, the high color in her cheeks and her moist eyes unable to disguise her feelings for him.

He prowled around the table, this time without her making a move. God, but she smelled good. And her skin radiated a heat that reached him the mere inches he stood away from her.

He slowly circled her, then came to stand just behind her. He caught her quick intake of breath. Her shallow swallow. With the lightest of touches, he drew the tip of his index finger along the fine column of her neck down to where her pulse pounded out an erratic rhythm.

He knew at that moment that he could tell her anything. Play it off, pretend he didn't know what she was talking about. Or admit that yes, Diana was there at the hotel but offer no more. Whatever he told her, he knew one thing for sure: she was his.

He only had to make her admit it.

"Where?" he murmured against her neck, absorbing her shiver though he still stood away from her.

He felt her pulse leap beneath his fingertip. "In the lobby. An hour and a half ago."

"I see." He nodded, moving his finger along her beautifully defined collarbone then dipped it down to rest between her breasts. It was damp and warm there, not unlike other, more inviting parts of her body. "That probably would have been right before I met her there then."

He felt her stiffen and immediately curved his other hand around her rib cage, drawing her back along his hard length. She didn't fight. Didn't argue. She merely stood stiffly, her ragged breathing telling him that despite what his words implied, he could still have her. The prospect fascinated him.

He pressed his lips against that same pulse point at the base of her neck, feeling it leap for an altogether different reason. "Along with her new boyfriend."

"What?" her voice was barely above a whisper.

He moved his head to the other side of her neck, pressing another kiss to her sweet-smelling skin. "Funny, but while I was away having my world turned upside down by a certain redhead, Diana met someone else, as well. A colleague, as irony would have it. A man who swept her off her feet. Much as someone else swept me off mine."

A small sound escaped her throat and she collapsed against him, all the tension leaving her body like a sigh. He tightened his arm under her breasts to keep her from crumpling to the floor.

He brushed his nose against her hair, wondering how many pins were in there, and how much fun he was going to have taking every one of them out. "So, tell me, Gracie. If you thought Diana and I were still a couple…what are you doing here?"

He cupped one of her breasts through the thin fabric, relishing her strangled sigh. "To show you what you'd be missing." She slid her hand over his, then shifted until his skin lay against hers just inside the neckline of her dress. She wore nothing underneath, the hot sphere of flesh fitting perfectly in his palm. Then she moved his fingers so that he was pinching her distended nipple.

Her shiver made him want to groan.

He traced a wet trail down the length of her neck, then back again. "Well, then it's a good thing I don't plan on missing anything, isn't it?"

She wantonly pressed her lush bottom against his arousal then sought his other hand. "Uh-huh."

Somewhere in the back of his mind he realized this wasn't going at all as planned. He was the one who was supposed to be in control. To seduce her senseless, until nothing remained but the love that he knew she felt for him. But he was helpless to do anything, fascinated by her own unfolding plan for seduction.

Her hand on top of his, she pulled it across the fabric

around her waist, then bent slightly forward, sliding it inside the slit at her side. His fingers hit silky stocking, then they were moved beyond that to the creamy bit of flesh that was softer still. Then his fingers were being burrowed under the soaked crotch of her panties and he felt how much she really wanted him when her body shook in an undeniable series of shudders. Enthralled with the rapturous display, he pressed his hand against her engorged flesh, feeling her juices drip down through her curls and around his fingers.

His own pulse hammered out a need so intense it took every ounce of restraint he had not to take her right now.

Had he ever wanted a woman so desperately? Had he ever had a woman want him so much that she should come at the faintest touch?

Her shudders subsided and she leaned even more heavily against him, relying solely on him to hold her upright. Support he was only too willing to provide as he parted the swollen folds of her womanhood and delved his fingers into the hot wetness awaiting him inside.

Her hands remained on his, both at her breasts, and between her legs, encouraging him…guiding him.

God, but she felt so damn good. So ready for him. He rubbed the pad of his thumb against her enlarged hood, absorbing her shudder, then slowly slid two fingers into her dripping flesh. Instantly, she rocked against his hand, her hips jolting forward then back again, betraying a need that went beyond that of conscious want, transcended inhibition, reducing her to one hundred percent hot-blooded female to his one hundred percent willing male.

Feeling her on the verge of another climax, he groaned and withdrew his fingers, knowing that this time she wouldn't come alone. She uttered a protest and he turned her so he could pick her up. She grasped his shoulders to steady herself, then all too soon he was laying her across the soft white bed then following her up. His gaze slammed into hers, seeing in the depths of her eyes a desire so consuming, he nearly shoved her dress up right then. Instead, he lowered his mouth to hers, finally claiming her lips.

She pulled him against her length, his erection fitting perfectly between her spread thighs, her hands ripping at his shirt, tugging at the drawstring to his pants. He caught the marauding limbs and held them still at her sides, plundering her mouth with his tongue, drinking in her low whimpers, nipping at her swollen lips until she sighed against the mattress, giving in to his demands to be in control.

Continuing his assault on her mouth, he reached behind her and slowly unzipped the dress, restraining himself from the overwhelming desire to rip it off. Soon enough, he tugged his mouth away from hers so he could draw the thin straps down the length of her arms, then drag the fabric down over distended nipples. Nipples that he immediately pulled deep into his mouth, one by one, leaving them pink and wet. She arched her back and he grabbed the opportunity to haul the dress the rest of the way down then tossed it to the floor beside the bed.

This time when she reached to undress him, he let her, too distracted by all the wondrous curves and shadows and valleys of her body. All too soon his pants and shirt rested next to her dress and she was sliding down the mattress to position herself under his hard arousal, jutting her hips up until her soaked panties were all that separated them. When she reached down to do away with even that barrier, he caught her gently by the wrists again. His pulse pounded in his ears, blood roared through his straining erection, and he knew he was one second away from breaking every last detail of the plan he'd so carefully laid out since this morning.

"Uh-uh," he said, twining his fingers with hers, then bringing her hands to his mouth where he languidly kissed them, fighting to regain some of the precious ground he had lost in the past few minutes. "Please...indulge me."

The width of her pupils had nearly obliterated the brown of her eyes as she watched him. A long minute later, she swallowed, then nodded ever so slightly. He smiled and slowly began lifting her arms above her head where he'd fastened two gauzy ties around the bedposts. Keeping his gaze locked with hers, he loosely circled the fabric around each of her wrists, then closed her fingers over the leads. Without telling her, he communicated that her bondage was completely voluntary. All she needed to do was let go, and she'd be free.

The sight of her stretched out beneath him, voluntarily, completely at his mercy, did crazy things to his libido. He slid down until he was crouched between her thighs, then hooked both his index fingers under the waist of her red-and-black lace panties. Slowly, torturously, he drew them down... lower, and lower, until the top of her red-gold curls sprang from their imprisonment. Groaning, he fastened his mouth around the wet spot in the silk and softly blew. She gasped and her hips bucked from the mattress. He smiled, realizing she'd put her panties on over the garters, guaranteeing that he wouldn't have to unfasten them in order to bare her. He continued the downward movement until she'd lifted her legs, allowing him to toss the indecent scrap of silk aside along with the rest of their clothing.

Spreading her legs out on either side of him, he gazed down at her engorged womanhood longingly. Oh, how he wanted to bend down there, lave her, drink from her, until she screamed out his name in orgasm. But what he was working toward...well, it was more important than any one climax. When she reached climax again, he wanted to be there right with her. He wanted to coax her to look into his eyes. And he couldn't do that if he was lost in the soft, damp curls between her legs.

Sitting back on his haunches, he curved his hands between her legs and under her hips then tugged her until her bottom was elevated off the mattress, her swollen flesh resting against his hard, throbbing length.

Go slow, he ordered himself, resisting the overpowering urge to plunge into her hot flesh, thrust into her, his plan be damned. But there was too much riding on this. Too much at stake to risk for a quick release.

Instead, still clutching her bottom, he drew his hips so that the inflamed tip of his arousal rested between her swollen folds. But rather than thrusting in, he thrust up, through her flesh, not stopping until his head rested against her engorged hood, all the while holding her gaze captive with his. Her white teeth flashed as she bit on her bottom lip and he slowly drew his erection back through the silken valley, only to quickly thrust upward again.

Her eyelids fluttered closed and she arched her neck. "Please...oh, God, please."

He swallowed past the thick need in his throat. "Tell me, Gracie. Tell me what you're feeling."

Her eyes cracked open, the dark passion in them setting him on fire as he repeated the move.

She cried out. "I want you to take me, Dylan. I'm so hot I feel like I'm burning up."

Good. Good. That's where he wanted her to be at this point. Where he needed her to be.

He drew his hips back, preparing her for another almost penetrating thrust, but rather than move upward, he propelled downward, burying himself in her to the hilt. She gasped and arched clean off the bed, her hands grasping the ties loosely binding her wrists, her breasts quivering from the unexpected move.

Everything that was hot and wet and wonderful and Gracie surrounded him, squeezed him, pulled at him, tempting to give himself over to release. He fought against it, gritting his teeth in determination. He ignored her soft pleas, battling to regain some of his all too precious control.

Finally he slowly withdrew from her.

"Look at me, Gracie," he softly commanded.

Her eyelids fluttered open and she restlessly wet her lips.

"That's it. No matter what, I want you to keep looking at me. Okay?"

After a long pause, she nodded.

And he plunged into her hot flesh again. This time half-way. Then pulled out again, her soft protest and upward thrust of her hips telling of her disappointment. Moving one of his hands from her bottom, he grasped her hip, holding her in place as he slowly entered her again, again halfway, then withdrew. He didn't know how long he could go on. Didn't know how long she would let him. But he needed to see this through to the last of his endurance. Needed to coax her toward a destination they had merely glimpsed before. Wanted to show her that great sex was great sex but making love...well, that was the ultimate utopia. And the only way he could do that was by making her admit that she loved him.

Again he thrust into her, this time a little farther, his gaze holding hers, his skin coated with sweat from the effort. Nearly his entire body shook from the price he was paying. But still he fought on. Thrusting and withdrawing, slowing when she appeared too close to climax, plunging when she least expected it. Purposely taking her breath away. And in the process losing just a little bit more of himself to her.

He leaned forward, resting his damp temple against hers. He tried to slow the pounding of his heart, his jaw clenched tight. "God," he whispered. "I love you, Gracie."

Beneath him, she stilled.

He tightly closed his eyes, praying she wouldn't pull away. She didn't.

He plunged into her deeply. Only when she was once again panting for release did he pull back to his knees.

Then he plunged again, entering her just a little more shallowly.

"Dylan!" she cried.

He thrust into her until he could thrust no more. "Tell me, Gracie."

He withdrew.

She closed her eyes and began restlessly moving her head back and forth. He caught her chin in his free hand and captured her mouth with his. "Tell me."

Every inch of him inside every inch of her, he began rubbing against her swollen bud, the friction caused by their mingling eliciting even more heat.

"Tell me, baby."

Her breath caught, her eyes held an intensity he'd never seen before, telling him that she knew exactly what he wanted from her. And that he would get it. Although not without some cost.

Still, he thrust hard again, bringing her legs up off the mattress. He grasped her knees, trapping them between them.

"Tell me," he ground out.

Holding his gaze, she freed her hands from the makeshift ties and thrust her fingers through the hair at either side of his face. "I..." She bit her lower lip and cried out as he thrust again. "I...love...you."

The world crashed around him, then under him, lifting him to a place he hadn't even dared imagine existed before, and pulling her right along with him.

14

SOMEWHERE BETWEEN DUSK and dawn, Gracie awakened with a start, her breathing raggedly painful, her skin coated with sweat. In her dream, she'd been skillfully, unwittingly stripped of her most fundamental defenses. Laid bare, her greatest fear held out for her like a bullfighter tempting a bull with his red cape. Daring her to tell him she wasn't a fraud.

It took her long, quiet moments filled with only the ir-regular sound of her breathing to figure out where she was. Sense Dylan's heat reaching out from where he slept next to her.

She lay silently, the night before drifting back to her much like the song of the early birds floated in on the pungent sea air. She turned her head away from where Dylan slept, tucking her chin against her shoulder and swallowing hard. Her body was blissfully sore, every muscle aching and raw. It seemed as if her very soul was foreign to her somehow... as if Dylan had expertly, cunningly reached inside her and claimed it as his own.

Worse, she didn't know how she felt about it. Had she willingly given Dylan what he'd asked for...or had he stolen it from her?

She closed her eyes, the sweet smell of their mingled sex calming her in a way a thousand breaths couldn't, and, between her thighs, rekindling the fire she was beginning to fear would never go out. A fire that burned for Dylan and Dylan alone. Almost of its own accord, her body shifted to the side and sought a more direct contact with his heat. She shivered in renewed awareness as he unconsciously hummed and turned into her, pressing his growing arousal against her bottom, his hand sliding down her quivering belly and pressing against her sex.

Then the white, gauzy mist of sleep reached out wispy fingers and claimed her once again.

She couldn't be sure how long she'd slept. It could have been an hour. It may have been ten. But this time when she awakened, it was to the sound of the surf through the balcony doors, and the warmth of what could only be the sun streaming across her sheet-covered body. She smiled and stretched her arms out languidly above her, blindly reaching for the makeshift bonds that had effectively held her captive the night before.

God, talk about your fantasies. She'd certainly indulged in her share from the instant she'd hit puberty and grew aware that she wasn't one of the guys. But this…a delicious shiver rippled over her skin and she arched her back.

"Good morning."

Dylan's voice was low and very, very near. Keeping her eyes closed, she smiled. "Is it morning already?"

The feel of something on her chest drew her brows together. It wasn't Dylan's hand. It wasn't the sheet. The object was slightly heavier. But small.

Thinking it might be food, she hummed and slowly cracked open her eyelids.

"Marry me, Gracie."

Her breath balling in her throat, she stared at the ring box resting between her breasts and watched as Dylan clicked it open then lay it against her skin again. The marquise-cut diamond, flanked on either side by two other diamonds,

embedded in the dark blue velvet, caught the morning light...
and sent her heart racing from zero to sixty in a nanosecond
flat.

She bolted to an upright position, catapulting the box and
the object within across the bed where it landed upside down.
She dragged her gaze from it to Dylan, where he sat on the
side of the bed in his white drawstring pants. He smiled at
her and smoothed her red hair back from her face.

"What...what did you just say?" she asked, resisting the
urge to bat his arms away from her. She felt the urgent need
to think. And she couldn't do that when he was touching her.
A fact she suspected he knew all too well.

He dipped his finger into his mouth, then drew the damp
tip along her collarbone to her right breast, where he circled
the nipple. She shivered, everything that was her responding to him.

She swallowed hard and caught his wrist. Not...entirely...
everything. Her brain was still working. And it wanted answers.

His chuckle was low and slid along her spine like a touch.
"I said, marry me, Gracie."

He leaned over and kissed her. But she could do little more
than stare at him in shock, her lips frozen, her eyes wide. He
ran his tongue along the rim of her bottom lip, then her top,
dipping inside to coax a more welcoming response.

She shot from the bed, dragging the top sheet along with
her and shakily pulling it against her bare chest. She stared
at him, convinced he'd gone insane.

His grin never wavered. "Not exactly the response I was
looking for."

"No? Well, that makes two of us. Because you couldn't
have shocked me more had you told me you were a twin and
I slept with both of you last night." The sheet refused to co-
operate and she realized she was standing on it. Stepping to
the side, she jerkily circled the silky material around herself

twice then tried three times to fasten it at the top. It wasn't until she tried to move that she discovered she'd wrapped herself as tight as a mummy. She kicked at the bottom until she'd earned enough room to walk.

"God, Dylan, have you completely lost it?" She paced frantically one way, then the next, not knowing where she was going, or if she should be going anywhere. "Marry you?" She stumbled over one of her shoes from last night, then kicked it out of the way, her heart beating a million miles a minute. "I…can't…marry you!"

She was vaguely aware of him getting up from the opposite side of the bed, then rounding it. "Why not?"

His steadfast grin only made her…more confused. And just a little angry. "Because…because just last night I thought you were going to break things off, that's why not." She stopped in front of him, holding on to the front of the sheet for dear life. "Because not even ten days ago, you had planned… were convinced you wanted to marry somebody else, that's why not."

She resumed pacing, needing to put some distance between them and make some sort of sense out of her thoughts. Near the table, she swung back around. "Is that…the same ring?"

The grin finally vanished.

She groaned. "Oh, my God! It is, isn't it? You were going to propose to me using the same stinkin' ring."

"Correction. I did propose to you."

"With the same ring!" she shouted. She resumed pacing, this time in a different direction. "What am I talking about? Who cares about the damn ring? I still can't figure out why in the hell you would even offer it to me."

"Because I love you."

She winced, her heart giving such a tremendous squeeze she had to stop pacing. She clamped her eyes shut and swallowed hard.

"Listen to me, Gracie," he said, his voice sounding just over her shoulder, his hot breath caressing her bare shoulder. "That ring was the one my grandfather used to propose to my grandmother. It holds a special significance for me."

When she spoke, her voice came out a whisper. "Did you give it to your first wife, too?"

The telltale anxious clearing of his throat told her that he, indeed, had.

She shot off again, in yet another direction, nearly covering every square foot of the large suite. The sheet caught on the coffee table and she gave it a yank, ignoring the ominous tearing sound.

"Look, Gracie…I knew the ring wasn't…hell, it just wasn't you. But when it comes down to it, it's just a piece of metal and rock, isn't it? Isn't it a little ridiculous that you're making such a big deal about it?"

She glared at him and kept pacing.

He heaved a sigh. "If it makes any difference, I placed an order for another ring, a different ring, one that had your name written all over it, yesterday while I was shopping. It… it just wasn't ready in time, that's all."

She tripped over something that toppled her onto the bed. Making a sound of frustration, she righted herself and glared at the offending object. It was her new dress. The one she'd purposely worn last night to show Dylan what he would be missing out on. Way back when she'd convinced herself he'd meant to end things between them.

Instead, he'd asked her to marry him.

He came to stand at the foot of the bed, leaning against the iron post. She busied herself picking up the dress and trying hopelessly to smooth the wrinkles out.

"What's really the matter, Gracie? Both you and I know it's not the ring."

She plucked up her shoes, tempted to throw one of them

at him—heel first. "Though we both know that offering me the same one is in extremely bad taste."

His grin made a comeback. She did lob the shoe at him. He easily caught it, staring at it as if it were her foot, then running his long, tapered thumb along the arch of it. "Granted."

She rearranged the sheet across her breasts, then held her arms stiffly at her sides to prevent it from falling down. "God, you're serious, aren't you?"

She discerned his nod from the corner of her eye but refused to look at him.

She didn't say anything for long moments, couldn't think of a single thing that would accurately describe the panic she felt bunched up in her chest. She was so wrapped up in her own thoughts, or lack of them—that she jumped when he sat down next to her. She automatically shifted to put some much needed distance between them.

"Listen, Gracie...I know all of this is sudden."

She made a sound of agreement.

He reached for her hand. She pulled it away. "But I've been doing a lot of thinking over the past couple of days and... well, I came to the conclusion that this is the next step in the natural progression of things."

She jerked to stare at him. "Maybe in your book, Dylan," she cringed, realizing it *was* in his book. Literally. "In mine... well, there are lots of things that come before the 'M' word. Like career. Financial success. An understanding of self."

He chuckled quietly. "I've never known a woman more comfortable in her own skin than you."

She restlessly ran her hands through her hair, trying to undo the bedroom tangles, then gave up. "Well, that's just a perfect example of how little you do know about me, then, isn't it?"

She moved the dress in her lap to the bed between them, absently smoothing the cool, dark material. "Don't you see? You've...screwed everything up. You've screwed me up. It was bad enough that I didn't have the puzzle in my head quite put together when I met you. Then you had to go and mess the pieces all up again." She caught herself balling the dress in her hands and forced herself to stop. "And the damnable thing about it is that none of them fit anymore."

He slowly placed his hand over hers. "That's only natural."

A gargled sound of irritation escaped her throat and she got up from the bed again, no easy feat while wrapped in the sheet. "Don't you dare try to psychoanalyze me, Dylan."

"I'm no—"

She pointed a finger at him, stopping him in his tracks. "It's my turn."

He grimaced. "I wasn't aware that I'd had mine yet."

"Tough."

She picked up the dress, then tried to find the corner of the sheet she had tucked against her chest. "So you're interested in psychoanalyzing me, are you, Dylan? Well, then, why don't you try this one on for size?" She finally found the corner, then after several struggles, determined that the only way she could get out of the damn sheet was to turn out of it. She did, catching herself when she would have fallen over. "I…don't…want to…be…my mother."

She threw the sheet over him, preventing him from looking at her in that heated way she knew would set her blood to boiling with desire instead of anger. He pulled it down, his gaze strictly limited to her face even as she tugged on her panties. "Explain yourself."

She picked up the garter and silk stockings then threw them across the bed, abandoning them. "If you had read my book, I wouldn't have to."

He winced. She almost felt sorry for him. Almost. If only his reaction and his behavior up until that point didn't emphasize every last belief, or lack of belief, she had about the institution of marriage and man-woman relationships.

"Okay," she began. "Marriage, as a whole, is supposed to be based on mutual respect, trust and one hundred percent effort from each partner, right?"

"Right," he said slowly, obviously trying to follow her argument.

"It doesn't exist."

"What doesn't? Marriage?"

She picked up her dress, turned it front to back, then tugged the zipper the rest of the way down. "The ideal of marriage. Of course marriage exists. So does a fifty percent divorce rate." She raised a finger, almost ignoring the fact that she was lecturing him in nothing more than her panties. "Do you know why those marriages fail, Dylan? Because those couples act strictly on emotion, not respect, not trust."

His smile made her heart trip in her chest. "Sounds like something out of my book."

"No way. Because in my book I go on to say that even when couples think they have it, many don't. Not really. The fact remains that to this day, ninety-nine percent of the marriages succeed or fail solely based upon the actions of the female." She shimmied into her dress, pulling up the spaghetti straps over her shoulders one by one. "She's the one who's expected, no, must, put her own interests aside, all her career ambitions, anything and everything that was important to her before the marriage in order to make it work. Oh, she may still work. Appear to go about her life in the same way she did before. But she really isn't. She's the one who has to make all the sacrifices, while the man makes none. In fact, he's the one who reaps all the benefits. Tell me, Dylan, what do statistics prove when it comes to the running of the shared household? Don't know? Let me tell you. In one hundred percent of the cases, the woman is mostly in charge. And why not? Because somebody has to be, right? So where she might have just let the laundry go until, say—" she waved her hand, reaching for an example, then a perfect one occurred to her "—until she didn't even have a clean pair of panties left, now she not only has to see to her own, she has to take care of the man's."

His grin nearly derailed her. "I think we've already established that I don't have a problem with you going without panties, Gracie." She glared at him and he held up his hands. "And I'm certainly not asking you to wash my underwear."

She had to do the equivalent of a Harry Houdini trick to get up the dress's zipper, but she did it. "Aren't you? Then tell me, Dylan. Why is it that I've read both your books, not once, but twice. And you…you haven't even read my book once?"

She bent over, searching under the bed for her shoes. She found one. Then realized she had thrown the other at him earlier. Leaning over him, she lifted it from the mattress. Then her gaze snagged on another object, very near to where the second shoe was. The ring box.

He cleared his throat. "I simply haven't had the time to read it yet."

She drew back and sighed. "Wrong answer. You haven't read my book yet simply because you don't respect my opinion enough to even learn it. And that lack of respect will ultimately lead to the infringement upon everything I feel is important. Your lack of interest in understanding me, the way my mind works, learning what moves me beyond sex… well, that disinterest will inevitably turn into you discarding what's important to me. And that leads to divorce." She laughed humorlessly and slipped on her shoes. "Because hey, let's face it, one day you both wake up and you find you're not the same people. Instead, you're the people you've made each other and guess what? You just don't like each other very much anymore."

Leaving her hair a massive tangle around her face, she planted her hands on her hips and stared at him. He looked as if she had just jerked the sheet he was sitting on right out from under him, his eyes round and somewhat unseeing. "So?" she said.

He seemed to shake himself out of his reverie. "Well…that was certainly an interesting little scenario you just painted, wasn't it?"

She swallowed hard. "And one I'm not interested in living." She pretended to smooth the wrinkles out of the waist of her dress. "You know, you could have just let things continue on the way they were. Had you considered that?"

He blinked several times. "That would have been better?"

She nodded. "Yes, because when a couple is dating, neither partner is in a position to put the other out. The scales, if the woman is determined enough, can remain balanced."

He nodded, as if still in shock. Then his eyes cleared and he shook his head. "Then you're not sharing, either. Not really. Not where it counts." He ran his hands through his sleep-tousled hair several times in anxious jerks, looking more handsome than he had a right to at that moment. "The fact remains that I…" He searched her eyes. "That I believe in marriage, Gracie. It's what I'm about. Who I am. And I can't continue a relationship without knowing the end result. Or at least predicting it." She watched his throat contract around a swallow. "I love you. I want to marry you. I want to have kids with you. Is that so bad?"

Emotion welled up in her chest, threatening to choke off air. She nodded nearly imperceptibly, her voice coming out in a raspy whisper. "Yes…it is."

She stood there for long moments, almost wishing he would say something to try to change her mind. Or change his own. Throw his hands up in the air and say "Okay, we'll do it your way."

But he didn't. He sat there as stubborn as ever. And, she realized, she was also too stubborn to give an inch.

She slowly reached around him, grasping the ring box. Popping it open again, she took one long, last look at the bit of metal and rock, as he had called it, then snapped it back closed. Taking his hand, she carefully placed it in the middle of his palm. "Thanks, but...no."

Sliding her hands from contact with his, she turned and gathered her hair clasps from the bedside table, then her purse from the untouched dinner table, and headed for the door.

It was only when she realized that he wasn't coming after her, wouldn't be coming after her, that she felt the first big, fat, sloppy tear splash from her eye and onto her cheek. She told herself she wasn't crying because she'd just turned down Dylan's heartfelt proposal. No. She was mourning a relationship that had been the best thing she'd ever had in her life.

She bit determinedly on her bottom lip then quickly pulled the door open and bolted through it.

IT SEEMED TO TAKE AN eternity for Gracie to get back to her room. She ended up riding the elevator up and down twice before finally getting off on her floor, completely immune to the curious looks she received from fellow guests. They were in tennis whites and casual day wear; she was still dressed to the nines and feeling more exposed than ever in her life. Not just physically. Emotionally she felt as if she wore her throbbing heart on her sleeve. That is if she'd had a sleeve.

Even when she finally reached her floor, it took her three complete circuits around the triangular hall to figure out which room was hers. Mostly because the number refused to emerge from her pain-clogged mind and the damn thing wasn't written on her card key for security purposes.

Security purposes. She tearfully wondered if there was some sort of security one could purchase to guard the most precious of objects...her heart.

Not that it mattered now. It was far too late for any of that.

She slid her card key in several times before the little green light finally flashed. Not taking any chances that the mechanism would change its mind, she quickly opened the door and rushed inside.

And became instantly aware that she wasn't alone in the room.

Gracie went very still. She wasn't sure how she knew there was someone else there, but she did. Call it human instinct, the basic desire to survive. The tiny hairs on the back of her neck stood straight out and an ominous shiver swept across her exposed skin.

Before her, the room was cloaked in shadows, the heavy curtains blotting out even a sliver of light. Her first thought was that Dylan had changed his mind. That he had decided to accept her on her terms and had come to tell her that. But she was sure that she would have sensed his presence rather than feel threatened.

She turned and immediately tried to leave the room.

"Don't."

Her leaden fingers hesitated over the door handle at the one-word command. Definitely not Dylan. Not even a voice she recognized. She supposed it was too much to hope that the man behind her was a male maid upset she was going to get fingerprints on the freshly cleaned door.

She slowly turned to face the intruder, her heart thump-thumping in her chest. She rubbed the heels of her hands against her damp cheeks then looked at him. She was pretty sure she'd never seen him before. But he was looking at her as if they knew each other very well.

"Pardon me," she said, "but I, um, think one of us has the wrong room."

He moved his hand, revealing the gun he held. "You don't know who I am, do you?"

She looked at him again, her heart rate accelerating beyond normal range. She fought to hold on to reason and battled to be calm, when she felt anything but. "No. I'm sorry...I don't know who you are. Have we—"

There was a light pounding on the door behind her back, making her realize that she'd unconsciously leaned against it for support. "Gracie? Gracie, are you there? Open up, please...we are nowhere near finished with this conversation."

Dylan.

Gracie felt dizzy, her gaze darting from the gun to the man's face, then back again. She swallowed against the bile rising in her throat.

"Is that Dr. Dylan?" the man asked quietly, the gun wavering then righting again.

Gracie nodded almost absently, wondering how he knew her...knew Dylan...and wishing she could remember him.

"Invite him in. He needs to take responsibility for his actions as much as you do."

Responsibility for his actions? As much as she did? What was he talking about? She knew for a fact that she'd never counseled the man. She never forgot a face. And she knew for certain that the odds were stacked against her and Dylan having shared a patient, seeing as they were located on opposite coasts.

"I said invite him in!" the man shouted.

Gracie jumped, then turned around to do as he ordered. Her hands shook as she turned the handle. The door opened, but only a scant couple of inches. She met Dylan's confused gaze through the opening and tried to shake her head.

A cold, hard hand encircled her arm then she found herself being yanked back from the door, helpless as the man opened it and aimed his gun at Dylan's chest. "Come in, Dr. Dylan."

Gracie stumbled backward, the back of her knees hitting the bed. The way the man kept saying Dr. Dylan began to zoom through her brain cells, but she couldn't seem to find the information she sought.

"What's going on here?" Dylan asked darkly, looking from her to the man.

The intruder fastened all the locks, then motioned for Dylan to step farther into the room. He did, coming to stand stiffly next to Gracie.

"Good, it's better this way. With you both here."

Dylan's eyes narrowed. "I'm sorry, sir, but do I know you?"

"We," Gracie corrected, clearing her throat. "Do we know you?"

Dylan frowned at her and Gracie shrugged, indicating she had no idea who the man was, either.

The man smirked. "Oh, I think you should know me. Considering that you both ruined my life."

Gracie's stomach dropped to somewhere in the vicinity of her feet. She'd heard of stalkers, and had learned early on the necessity of having an answering service field calls from the general public, but she'd never actually met one up close and personal before.

After what had just gone on between her and Dylan, she could have gone without this experience.

"I'm John from New York," he said. "Or Josh from Jasper. Whichever you prefer. But my real name is Jerry Presser and I'm from Orlando."

Realization dawned on Gracie. The guy who had called them during the radio show in New York, then again the day before yesterday, seeking advice on how to put his and his wife's sex life back together.

"My wife left me. I...did what you said. Twice. And she packed up all our stuff, our three kids and slapped a restraining order on me."

Gracie stared at him. The rims of his eyes were red, he looked like he hadn't shaved recently, and his clothes smelled as if he hadn't changed them in days. He was somewhere in his late twenties or early thirties, and it struck her how close in age they all were.

She glanced at Dylan for guidance and found him looking at the stranger in deep contemplation.

"Sir...Jerry...I'm sorry to hear that. But if that's the case, then it's my guess there was much more wrong with you and your wife's relationship than lack of sex."

Gracie glanced from the shaken man, to Dylan, then back again, unable to believe that they were so similar, yet so apart. Jerry used the back of the hand that held the gun to wipe away beads of sweat collecting on his brow.

Her mind whirled. The terrifying situation, on top of everything else that had just happened, threatened to overwhelm her. She bit hard on her bottom lip, feeling hot tears prick the backs of her eyelids anew. Air. She needed air. She turned, rushing for the balcony door.

"Stop!" Jerry ordered.

She did so immediately, her fingers still clutching the curtains, her lungs refusing to pull in the oxygen she needed as she tried to gain control over her emotions. The light cast an eye-blinking glare on the man holding them hostage, giving his skin a greenish tint. She glanced back at the doors and her breathing stopped altogether as she remembered another set of balcony doors at another hotel room in another city. Her mind began to race. The Miami hotel was owned by the same chain as the Houston one had been. And this time her room was located on the second floor. Easily accessible from the ground level. Did she dare hope...?

She snatched her hands from the curtains, trying to feign nonchalance. "I...I just thought we could all use some air, you know? I can't seem to catch a breath."

"Leave it closed."

Gracie looked to Dylan, who frowned again. She licked her lips. "You're sweating. Maybe it will help cool the temperature in here."

She cringed the moment she said the words. They were in Miami, for God's sake. It was always hotter outside than it was in.

"Oh, for crying out loud, let her open the door," Dylan said, clearly exasperated. "What do you think she's going to do, jump?"

The man named Jerry looked from him to Gracie then at the gun in his hand.

"May I?" she asked hopefully, her heart beating a thunderous rhythm against her rib cage.

Jerry finally waved the gun. "But then I want—"

Gracie grasped the balcony door with both hands, sending up a silent prayer as she yanked the door open.

Instantly the room filled with the piercing sound of the same siren she'd encountered in Houston.

Of course, she hadn't worked out what to do from here....

Jerry swung around, staring at the wall speaker in the corner, his hands clamped over his ears.

"Do something!" Gracie said to Dylan, grabbing for the phone as the prerecorded voice spoke over the speaker, apologizing for the interruption.

Dylan finally sprang into action, grabbing Jerry's gun arm as she dialed 911. Jerry fought for control and an elbow to his midsection sent both men barreling into Gracie. As the 911 operator's voice came on the line, Gracie pulled the receiver from her ear and brought the plastic receiver down hard on Jerry's head.

A HALF HOUR LATER, AFTER Miami police officers had led Jerry Presser from the room in handcuffs, and after Gracie and Dylan had both given their statements, Gracie closed her hotel-room door against the last of the officers. She shuddered at the locks there, not feeling reassured that the police suspected Presser had likely gained access while housekeeping had been cleaning her room.

Hugging herself, she turned to face Dylan where he stood in the open balcony doorway.

As it always did when she saw him, her heart dipped low in her stomach than bounced back up again, filling her throat.

As if sensing her attention, he turned from the view outside, his face drawn into long lines, his eyes watchful and... full of determination somehow.

"Are you okay?" he asked.

She nodded. "I'm fine. Or at least I will be when my rattled nerves realize the threat has been removed." She rubbed her arms, cold despite the blast of thick, steamy air flooding through the open balcony door. "And you? How are you doing?"

He shrugged, as if his condition was of no concern to him. "I'm okay."

Considering they both had had a gun pulled on them and had been held hostage—even if it was for only a few minutes—she supposed that they had fared far better than they might have. Gracie told herself she should be grateful. If not for Dylan's somber, significant stance, she might have.

She managed to summon up a halfhearted smile. "So... you, um, wanted to talk to me?"

Confusion flicked over his features then he frowned, looking down at his shoes. "Yeah. I guess I did."

"Did?" she said, finding her voice little more than a whisper.

He nodded then curved his hand around the back of his neck. "After what happened I...well, I don't know what to say."

Gracie caught herself wringing her hands in front of her and forced herself to stop. "I know what you mean."

He glanced at her as if to ask if she truly did understand. "Something like that, someone like Jerry...well, they have a way of making you wonder about yourself, don't they?

Compel you to rethink your profession and the impact you have on others' lives."

"We're not to blame for his problems, Dylan."

"Yeah, I know…but still." He sighed. "Look, Gracie. I'm not really sure why I did come to your room. Clearly you're not going to change your mind…."

His words trailed off and she realized he was asking her if she had rather than stating it. She shook her head. "No…I'm not."

He dropped his hand to his side. "That's what I figured." He glanced toward the open balcony door then back at her. "And I'm not going to change mine. So that brings me back to what I'm doing here."

Gracie bit hard on her bottom lip. "Um…maybe you wanted to say goodbye?"

He stood there for a long moment, saying nothing.

"Yeah," he finally murmured. "Maybe that's it. I came to say goodbye."

He moved toward the door, then hesitated a moment when he drew even with her. Then he bent to place a soft, torturously sweet kiss against her temple. "Goodbye, Gracie."

She closed her eyes and moved to lean into him, but he had already moved away. Moments later, she heard the door clap shut behind him, leaving her completely, utterly, totally alone with her broken heart.

15

THE DRAPES WERE DRAWN TIGHT, the air in the room was stale, and the television silently flickered images across where Gracie lay on the bed, the bedspread half on, half off a portion of her bare legs. Two days had passed since she'd left Dylan behind in that sumptuous suite, balked at his proposal, but it could very well have been two years, the way she felt.

She aimed the remote in the general direction of the TV and absently surfed through the channels, the untouched lunch tray she'd forced herself to order not tempting her from where it sat on the nearby ottoman, beside the ignored tray from the day before.

She distantly knew she should eat something. Then she reminded herself that she had. She had choked down half a muffin that very morning. And the tasteless sucker still sat like a rock in the middle of her stomach.

She rolled over onto her back to stare at the ceiling, the sound of crinkling paper barely catching her attention. Lethargically, she dislodged the offending piece of literature, holding it above her and staring at it. Chapter eight of her book. A book from which she'd torn each and every page the previous morning, grouping each into chapters, the empty hardcover sporting her picture on the back sitting spine up near the door.

She moved each page behind the last as she scanned the words, the once familiar text and ideas now reading like a foreign language.

Sighing, she put the chapter down right where she'd found it, then lay back against it. She'd come up with a reason for the placement of each small stack of papers, but was now unable to remember what it was.

She stuck her thumbnail between her teeth and glanced at the silent phone. Everyone was gone. She was the only one who remained in steamy Miami. Not that the temperature mattered to her. She kept the unit in her room at the same level and hadn't stepped foot outside for two days.

Rick had called her the morning of her...breakup with Dylan, telling her he was heading back to Baltimore if she didn't need anything more. She told him to go ahead, and while he was at it, take a few days off. Both because he deserved it and she needed some major time alone to work her way through her thoughts and feelings.

Then there was Dylan.

She hadn't tried to contact him. What she had done was call the concierge, threatening him with a personal visit if he didn't tell her what she wanted to know. And he had. Dylan had left the fateful suite only a short time after she had and a hotel limo had taken him to the airport where he presumably caught the next flight out to San Fran. On the complete opposite coast.

She absently wondered why she hadn't gone home. Oh, yeah. Because she temporarily didn't have a home to go back to. Good reason. Her condo was still being renovated, the contractor having left a message with her answering service saying he needed another week. That meant that if she went back to Baltimore, she'd either have to stay with her parents or check into a hotel. Since she was already in a hotel, she'd decided to stay put, placing a standing request with the same concierge to tell housecleaning she'd call if she needed anything, but until then they were to stay away. He began to tell her it was hotel policy that the maid at least check the room, but her torrent of curse words had stopped him in his tracks and he agreed to see to her request.

She turned her head and stared at the piles of paper laid out purposefully all over the floor, chair, desk and even the bathroom counter and the side of the tub, some covered with notes, others hardly touched, then rolled over again, kicking at the covers that held her captive. Despite her stationary state, she'd gotten very little sleep. Every time she closed her eyes, snippets from her last showdown with Dylan mingled with Jerry Presser's phone-ins, oftentimes rewinding like a videotape and replaying again, freeze-framing on certain images. Dylan opening the ring box and laying it against her chest, his grin devastating. Jerry Presser emerging from the shadows of her room, holding a gun on her and looking like a man on the edge, beaten and desperate. Then there was the vivid memory of Dylan sitting on the edge of that decadent bed looking at her as if she'd just snatched away his last dream and stomped all over it in her high-heeled shoes.

She groaned. God, she didn't even have to close her eyes anymore for the images and words to haunt her.

She picked up the remote again, staring sightlessly at the screen. It took a full five chirps of the phone for her to realize it was actually ringing. Changing the channel again, she blindly reached for the receiver. Probably the concierge calling to tell her her credit card limit had been reached.

"Yeah…hello?"

"Grace? Is that you?" Her mother's voice. Definitely her mother's voice. "Are you sure you got the right room number, Consuela?"

Gracie cleared her throat. "Yes, Mom, she got the right room number."

There was a sigh that she almost interpreted as relief. "Thank God. Where are you, Grace? I expected you home the day before yesterday. I can't even reach your assistant, what's his name—"

"Rick."

"Yes, that's it. I couldn't even get him on the line. Is everything all right? You're not sick or anything are you?"

Just in the head, she thought.

"Pardon me?"

Gracie realized she'd said the words aloud and fought to get her act together. She could barely handle Priscilla Mattias when she was at her sharpest. Pushing herself up from the bed, she sat and gathered her tangled hair on the side of her head. She grimaced at the white camisole and cotton panties she wore and fought to straighten them. "I'm fine, Mom. I just needed a couple days to myself." She tried to inject some enthusiasm into her voice. "Where better to do that in November than sunny Miami, right?"

She cringed. Even *she* didn't believe her tone. Fat chance her mother would buy it.

"Grace…would you like me to come down there?"

Wrapping her free hand around her midsection, she closed her watering eyes, finding it hard to believe that she had any tears left to shed. The day she'd walked out on Dylan and his proposal, she'd spent five straight hours soaking every pillow in her room. But now…well, now she could have done without the reminder that while she needled and teased and basically ran from her mother, Priscilla was always there for her when it counted. When she had her first period during seventh-grade gym glass, there her mother was, taking her out of school for the day and making all right with the world by taking her shopping in the women's department of every store they came across. When she was sick during her first year at university, her mother was on the next flight out, pouring chicken soup down her throat and sleeping on a cot in her dorm room until the bug finally fled. After a boyfriend had broken her heart, Priscilla had helped her make a dartboard out of his picture and had thrown darts at it right alongside her.

She had no doubt her mother would also be at her hotel room door faster than she could blink if she only said the word.

Yes. "No," she murmured instead, not sure what she hated more—her inability to snap out of her current state, or the desire to run into her mother's arms, tuck her head against her chest and pretend the world didn't exist. She bit hard on her bottom lip. "It's…nice of you to offer, but I'll be fine. Really, I will. I just need a little time, that's all."

Silence. "Is this about that nice Dr. Dylan?"

She nodded. "No."

"Grace, you don't have to hide anything from me. Even though we like to pretend that we don't, you and I…well, we know each other better than anyone else on earth."

"I know," she whispered, grabbing for the last roll of toilet paper she'd taken from the bathroom after she'd run out of tissue. She tore off a section and blew her nose, not caring that her mother would hear. "I'm telling you the truth. It's not about Dr.…Dylan. It's about me."

"Okay," Priscilla said slowly.

Gracie ran the heel of her hand against her nose. "Anyway, I'm sick of thinking about my own problems," she said, meaning it. "Tell me…how are you doing. And Dad?"

"We're fine."

She moved the phone to her other ear. "Fine? Define fine, Mom. Did you talk to him?"

Priscilla's voice lowered, making Gracie realize that Consuela was probably still in the same room. "As a matter of fact, I did."

Shock pushed through her malaise. "You did?"

"Yes."

Her heart skipped a beat, dread mixing with hope in her belly. What if she'd been wrong? What if she'd been way off base in advising Priscilla to confront her father? What if two minutes of hastily voiced advice meant the end of her parents' marriage, much as it had Jerry Presser's?

She hardly dared ask. But she couldn't not ask, either. "And?"

"Grace, this is hardly a discussion to have over the phone."

"Right now it's the only place we can have it." Her knuckles hurt from where she was gripping the receiver too tightly. "What happened? Tell me, or else I'm going to ask that you put Consuela on the phone. I'm sure she'll tell me."

Her mother's gasp told her she'd made her point. "Okay, just wait a minute. I'm going to switch phones."

Gracie pushed from the bed and began pacing, mindless of the papers she stepped on, uncaring if she pulled the body of the phone from the bedside table. All she could think about was how readily she had dished out advice, even to her own mother, pretending that a degree in psychology qualified her to interfere in others' lives. Tell them what to do, when she didn't have a clue what to do with her own life.

Some expert she was. If she ever wrote another book, she would title it *How to Royally Mess up Your Life and Everyone's Around You.*

She didn't realize she was holding her breath until her mother finally told Consuela to hang up the extension. "All right. I'm back."

Gracie froze on the top of Chapter Four. "So?"

Priscilla laughed. "I'm in the bedroom. Appropriate place for this conversation, don't you think?"

"Mom," Gracie said.

"Are you sure you're all right, Grace? You sound... stressed."

"Don't change the subject."

"All right then..." she said slowly. "I don't know how to say this but to, well, just say it. Your father and I...we're back to normal."

Gracie's legs gave out from underneath her and she plopped down in the middle of the floor, relief flowing through her so profoundly she could have cried for a reason that had nothing to do with Dylan. "Really?"

"Actually, no," Priscilla said. "I wasn't entirely truthful with you. Things are better than normal. They're…great."

"Oh, God, Mom, you don't know how happy I am to hear that." She crossed her legs under her, ignoring that she'd just mangled another chapter of her book. "So tell me…what did he say? What did you say? I want you to share everything."

Priscilla's laugh made her blood surge through her veins in a way it hadn't for days. "I'm not so sure I should be sharing this with you."

Gracie rolled her eyes toward the ceiling. "Oh, fine. Tell me the problem but don't tell me the solution." She caught a shadow of a smile pulling at her mouth and offered up a silent prayer of thanksgiving to whomever might be listening. "Spill it."

And her mother did.

It turned out that three months ago during a normal checkup, her father had been diagnosed with a prostate problem. A blockage of some sort that his physician was concerned may or may not have been cancer. Of course with some outdated, gallant notion, or perhaps out of sheer fear, he hadn't shared the news with his own wife. Rather, he'd sweated out the three months of tests and examinations until Priscilla confronted him with his distance. As luck would have it, the latest prescription had cleared up the problem and he'd just been given a medical thumbs-up. Which also turned out to be all he needed to try to make up for lost time with his wife.

Priscilla wound down her story and the line finally went silent for the first time in fifteen minutes. Gracie leaned back against the bed, her eyes closed.

Her mother cleared her throat. "So I guess I have you

to thank, Gracie. If you hadn't...told me to confront him, I might never have known what happened. He probably just would have come home one day and taken up right where he'd left off and that three months would have been between us forever."

She smiled into the phone, thinking for the first time in days that maybe, just maybe, she wasn't a fraud. Perhaps there was still some good she could do. "I'll send you the bill in the morning."

"You wouldn't dare," her mother exclaimed.

"Don't bet on it."

She got to her feet again, sitting on the edge of the bed. Not lying across it, not listing to the side, but sitting, as if on the verge of doing something else. And it felt good. She began wrapping up the call, telling her mom she didn't know when she would be home, but that it would probably be soon, and that she'd call her the instant she arrived.

She was just about to hang up when her mother said, "Oh, by the way. I read your book."

Gracie nearly dropped the telephone receiver. "What?"

"You heard me, Grace. I read your book."

She glanced around the room where her copy was scattered about the floor in bits and pieces. "And...?"

"And I can't tell you how proud I am of you."

Her heart filled to almost bursting. "Thanks," she whispered. "You have no idea how much I needed to hear that right now."

"Oh, I don't know. Mother's intuition told me it's exactly what you needed to hear. Now come home so we can discuss those areas I disagree with."

Gracie smiled. "Soon, Mom. Very soon."

She slowly replaced the receiver, then got up, standing still for a long moment, contemplating the room around her. She knew she still had a long way to go before the world started making complete sense, if it ever did again. And she suspected the ache in her heart for Dylan would never go away. But at least she felt capable of breathing again. Truly breathing.

She picked up the phone again, putting a call in to Rick's answering service for him to contact her as soon as he was able, then placing another order with room service. Suddenly she was starving. Then she hung up, yanked open the curtains and the balcony door beyond. When it didn't emit a loud screeching alarm, she smiled, took a shower and started putting back together the pieces of her book. This time in a different order. And minus a couple of chapters. And as she did so, she couldn't help feeling as if she was reconfiguring the puzzle that she had told Dylan about. That one she had accused him of screwing up.

She paused, holding the papers tightly to her chest as she stared at the phone. For the briefest of moments, she thought about calling him. Letting him know that she'd been wrong. He hadn't screwed up her life at all. He had merely forced her to take a better, closer look at it. It wasn't his fault that she hadn't liked what she saw.

Her throat grew tight, her heart pounded an erratic rhythm in her chest, and she felt that almost overwhelming physical need for him surge through her veins.

She picked up the phone. But rather than calling San Francisco, she pushed the button for the concierge. "This is Gracie Mattias. Send housekeeping up, please."

Then she turned from the nightstand and the telephone, knowing it wouldn't be fair to call Dylan now. Not to herself, or to him. Because facts were facts, and the overriding fact was she wasn't anywhere near the place she needed to be before she started figuring out more than the immediate future for her personal life.

As for her professional life…well, it was time to start putting the pieces back together. And she would begin that process by having Rick track down Jerry Presser in Orlando and get him some professional counseling. On her dime.

Next, she planned to come up with a proposal for her next book. A book that would nearly completely go against the advice she had given in her last....

16

THIS WAS JUST TOO WEIRD for words. Six weeks had passed since Gracie's last visit to the Big Apple, but the snow-covered streets and bitter cold made it seem like months. She had changed just as much as the weather since that time she'd stumbled on those high heels into that radio station where she officially met Dylan for the first time. Now, dressed in more casual flat-soled boots, ankle-length black leather skirt and warm black turtleneck, she felt…older somehow. Correction, much more mature. And much, much wiser.

Her publisher had gone for her new book proposal with a considerable increase in advance monies. But that wasn't the reason she was in New York. She climbed the steep steps to the midtown church. No. Visiting her publisher and signing her new contract was something her being there allowed her to do. She was really there to stand up for her now ex-assistant Rick Mahoney in his wedding to one spunky PR rep Tanja Berry. She opened the door to the church and stepped inside, shivering as she shrugged out of her black leather coat. She told herself she really wasn't losing an assistant in Rick, she was gaining a new friend in the shape of Tanja. But she knew how much she would miss him when he moved to New York to be with his new wife right after their honeymoon.

She had begun to move down the long aisle, her footsteps sounding against the smooth marble, when she caught sight of a familiar someone standing in front of the altar. Her steps slowed.

Dylan.

Rick had told her he'd be there. That just as she was going to be Rick's best woman, Dylan had agreed to be Tanja's man of honor. Still, no amount of preappearance pep talk could have prepared her for her immediate physical response to him. Despite what had happened in Miami and the time that had passed, she felt desire for him so swift and sure she nearly tripped over her own feet.

He turned, spotting her, and the grin he'd been giving Rick froze.

Oh, God, but he looked better than even her memory of him.

She forced herself to walk the remainder of the way, giving first Rick a hug, then Tanja. Finally she faced Dylan. "Hi," she said, unable to help a smile she feared might swallow her face.

"Hi, yourself." His grin was just as wide. And made her throat go dry.

She forced herself to look at Tanja. "What, no long walk down the aisle? No flower girl? No long, lacy white dress?"

Tanja made a face, nervously smoothing down her trendy champagne-colored suit and shiny vinyl jacket. "It's called compromise."

Rick slid his arms around his wife-to-be's waist. "It's the price I had to pay to get her to agree to marry me in a church."

Tanja playfully elbowed him in the ribs and he feigned injury. "Just wait until you see the price tag on that doozy." She leaned back into him and tilted her dark head back for his kiss.

"Oh, no! Where are the purple spikes?" Gracie asked, staring at the other woman.

Tanja fingered her stylishly short, black hair. "I let them grow out." Her dark eyes twinkled. "Don't tell me you miss them?"

Gracie smiled. "As a matter of fact, I do."

Rick withdrew his arms. "I do, too. But she insists that if she's going to get this new promotion she's up for, the purple streaks had to go." His grin took on a decidedly wicked quality. "So I had to settle for coloring other areas purple."

Gracie stared at him, mouth agape. "Um, Rick, that comment definitely falls into the 'a little too much information' category."

His chuckle was familiar, reminding her how much she was going to miss hearing it on a daily basis. "What? This from the preeminent Dr. Hottie? I'm disappointed."

Gracie stuck her finger into his chest. "Well, don't be. You never really did catch on that the only one allowed to tell off-color jokes was me."

She realized that during her conversation with the couple, Dylan had taken a noticeable step back. But it didn't stop her from being aware of him with every cell of her body. Or wanting him more than she ever had.

He cleared his throat. "Um, guys?"

They turned around to find the priest had joined them.

They immediately quieted down and settled into position, Gracie next to Rick, Dylan next to Tanja.

While the couple exchanged vows, Gracie couldn't help but feel thankful that at least one of the relationships started during the PR tour had withstood the test of time. She looked at the bride and the groom, smiling at the love in their eyes, the passion evident in the way they touched. Her gaze moved past them to Dylan, and an inexplicable lump bunched up in her throat. Too bad another relationship couldn't have weathered the storm.

DYLAN CAUGHT GRACIE STARING at him, her heart so fully in her eyes that he nearly groaned.

There was little consolation in knowing that he'd been right. Knowing that what he'd felt for Gracie then, he still felt for her now. Nor did suspecting she still loved him help matters any, either. The fact remained that she was too stubborn, too scared to take it to the next logical step.

And he was too much of a coward to give her the room she needed to grow into the relationship.

He stopped himself from tugging at his tie, the only one of the foursome dressed properly for a wedding. Then again, it depended on your idea of a wedding. While the vows were as binding as any he'd ever witnessed, he didn't think he'd been to a ceremony where neither the bride nor groom's family were present. And Tanja's casual attire, and Rick's tweed sports jacket and jeans, made them look more ready for a day at the mall. Then there was the fact that immediately following the ceremony there was to be no reception, no celebratory meal. No. The couple planned to lock themselves into a suite at Trump Plaza for the weekend, for what basically would constitute their honeymoon.

Dylan rubbed the back of his neck, thinking that Moonbeam and Frank would approve of the unconventional marriage ceremony. The complete opposite of the disapproval he'd suffered through when he'd returned to San Francisco alone and refused to talk about what had happened with Gracie. Not that it mattered. His mother had figured everything out, anyway. She called him one hundred kinds of stupid for being such a slave to convention. And for always needing the type of control over life that no one could ever get.

Not for the first time, he wondered if she was right, if he had been stupid. He'd caught himself pondering that very issue often over the past few weeks. Then he'd remembered the way Gracie had placed the engagement ring back in his hand and told him no and to banish any such thoughts from his mind.

He straightened his suit jacket. Of course, that was easy to do when he was three thousand miles away from her. Standing so close now he could smell her perfume, it was impossible.

Lord, how he wanted her. She looked different, somehow. More sober, composed, and even more unbearably beautiful. He allowed his gaze to devour her from head to flat heel. Despite the obvious external changes, he sensed that under all that clothing, and pulled-back hairstyle, she was still the same passionate, responsive woman who had once driven him nuts between the sheets. And probably would still be doing so had he not essentially given her the ultimatum of marriage or nothing.

Maybe his mother was right. He was a fool.

The priest pronounced the couple husband and wife. But it wasn't that which caught his attention so much as Gracie's burst of clapping, followed by a loud, rafters-echoing whistle as Rick and Tanja kissed. He couldn't help a chuckle.

They all thanked the priest, then hugged, and finally he and Gracie were standing on the front steps of the church alone, watching after the limo he'd hired as part of his wedding gift to the couple.

Gracie tucked her chin into the front of her leather jacket. "Nice touch, the limo."

"Thanks."

After six weeks and countless nights lying wide awake imagining what he might say to her if he had the chance, was that the best he could do? *Thanks?*

He cleared his throat. "Would you like to get some coffee?"

Her expression told of her surprise as her white breath filled the distance separating them. "Coffee?"

He grinned, gesturing to his right. "There's a place just down the street. Tanja says they have great pastry."

Her smile made him feel like someone had just sucker-punched him in the stomach. "I'd love to...but I can't."

"Oh."

"No. It's not what you're thinking. I have an appointment to meet with my publisher this afternoon."

He should have felt relieved, but he didn't. "That's okay."

"How about later?" she said. "I'm at the Marriott Marquis again. Are you?"

"No. I'm not staying. I'm on the red-eye back to San Francisco."

"Oh."

A taxi pulled up to the curb to let someone out. Dylan looked at Gracie. "Go ahead. I can get the next."

"Are you sure?"

No. He wasn't sure about anything except the almost overwhelming desire to yank her into his arms and find out if she tasted as good as he remembered. To see if she would still melt under one carefully placed touch. To discover if she still wanted him as much as he wanted her.

The taxi driver pressed on the horn, then cracked his window open. "You guys coming, or what?"

Gracie held up a hand to indicate he wait then turned back toward Dylan. "It was...um, great seeing you again."

He nodded, shoving his hands deep into his coat pockets. "You, too."

She began to walk toward the taxi, then moved back to him, giving him a quick kiss on the cheek. She drew back and gave him a more lingering kiss on the cheek. "See you," she said, walking backward and smiling.

He nodded and watched her get into the back of the taxi, standing stiff as a pole as the car pulled away from the curb.

He couldn't be sure how long he stood there, wondering if he would relive this moment for the rest of his life. Pondering what might have happened had he canceled that flight. Told her he still wanted her. Turned his head into her kiss.

Cursing under his breath, he turned in the other direction and began walking away.

GRACIE BLEW INTO THE LOBBY of the Marriott Marquis in Times Square along with a fiendish gust of winter wind. She should be feeling pretty pleased with herself right now. The meeting with her publisher and agent had far surpassed her expectations, the bonuses built into her contract enough to keep her in Victoria's Secret for the rest of her natural life. But throughout the meeting, and the drinks afterward at a swanky restaurant, all she could think about was how Dylan had looked standing outside the church. And how good it had felt to press her lips to his flesh. Even if it was just his cheek.

She looked around the lobby, questioning her decision to stay in the same hotel she'd been at last time merely because she was familiar with it. That was the problem. It was *too* familiar. Everywhere she looked, everywhere she stepped, another memory of Dylan sprang forth to claim her mind and play havoc with her senses.

Shivering off the chill that remained from outside and heading for the elevators, she wondered if it was too late to catch a flight out to Baltimore. She'd stayed overnight so she could shop in the city for the coming holidays, but right now the thought didn't appeal to her in the least.

An elevator dinged open and she stepped into it, smiling at a young couple that hurried in behind her. As she pressed the button for her floor, she couldn't help remembering the time when she and Dylan had been standing in this very elevator. And another young couple, not unlike the one that had entered, had indulged in some very risqué behavior behind them. She recalled the way he had looked, his eyes about ready to pop out of his head. The thought made her smile.

As did the memory of telling him he needed a wild turn in the sack.

The smile faded away. She realized now that she'd been playing a wicked game of seduction even then, before she'd made the conscious decision to sleep with him in Chicago. A game that had seriously backfired on her. She'd be well served to remember that.

The elevator opened on her floor and she got out, her leather coat billowing behind her as she made her way down the hallway to her room. She thought about ordering room service, then grimaced, suddenly regretting having turned her agent down for dinner. But all she could think about was escaping any sort of company that would detract from her thoughts of the past. The mistakes she had made. And how seeing Dylan again had moved her to the bottom of her soul.

She fished her card key out from her handbag, wondering how much finagling it would take for Rick to get her on that flight to San Francisco tonight. What was she thinking? Rick was no longer her assistant. Right now he and his new wife were doing all those wonderful things that couples do on their honeymoon.

She worried her bottom lip between her teeth, surprised by how quickly the idea was taking root and how eagerly her mind raced forward with the details. She could pack up her stuff in no time flat, make it out to the airport and do what she had to do to get on that flight with Dylan.

And after that? What would she do if he rejected her company?

Well, she'd have to do whatever it took to win him over. Because if one thing was becoming abundantly clear, it was that life was oh, so much better with him in it.

She fit the card key into the door slot and tried the knob. Nothing. She stared at the little red blinking light and sighed. She would not take this as a sign that she wasn't meant to go to San Francisco. She wouldn't.

And if, when Dylan finally caved in, he asked her to marry him again? What would she do then?

Her palms went instantly sweaty as she tried the card again. This time it worked and she pushed the door inward.

And became instantly aware that she wasn't alone in the room.

Clouds of steam billowed out from the open bathroom doorway directly to her left. Her heart giving a hard triple beat, she stepped a little farther into the room while still managing to hold the door open. It hadn't been so long ago that she didn't remember the fear she'd felt when Jerry Presser had held a gun on her in her room in Miami. It also hadn't been so long ago that she didn't recall how concerned she'd been when Dylan had walked into her room while she was taking a shower on that fateful day. She wasn't about to impede any possible quick escape she needed to make.

But as she peeked around the corner into the misty bathroom, her grip slipped on the door and it slowly slapped shut behind her. Not that she noticed. She was too busy gaping at the man standing buck naked and grinning at her from her shower.

Dylan.

She blinked. Then blinked again, her gaze shifting from his marvelously defined abs, back to his face, then dipped lower again to where lather slid down his stomach, over the soft V of hair leading to other, more interesting, and completely aroused places.

"Hi," he said, running the soap over his upper arm.

"Hi, yourself," she virtually croaked.

It was then she realized that there were worse things than coming home every night to find this fine, super-sexy specimen hanging out in your shower. To wearing his ring, and occasionally picking up his socks, and perhaps buying him extra pairs of underwear so he wouldn't have to worry about running out.

To hell with underwear...she wanted to keep him exactly like this.

She swallowed hard and allowed her purse to slide from her arm to the floor, her coat following after it. Hopping on first one foot, then the next, she yanked off her boots, and only had her leather skirt half off when she climbed into that tub and launched a full-scale assault on his mouth and body, hungrily trying to make up for the past six weeks in two minutes flat.

His telltale groan merely fed the flames licking at her. She lifted her arms, helping him take off her soaked sweater and grasping his head when he lowered his mouth to her nipples, pulling at each like they were the answer to world hunger.

"God, I've missed you," he whispered huskily, grinding his erection against her soft flesh.

"Have you?" she murmured between openmouthed kisses and insatiable flicks of her tongue.

He slid his hand to her bare bottom and pressed her farther against his steel-hard arousal. "Can't you tell?"

She moaned, wanting him, needing to feel him inside her this instant. Now. Her every muscle crying for a release she now knew only he could give her. She reached for his erection, intent on driving it home in her tight, wet and waiting flesh. He gently caught her wrist, holding her there, his other hand sliding up the line of her jaw and into her damp hair. She blinked to stare at him through the droplets falling from the showerhead. The weighty shadow in his eyes made her catch her breath. She braced herself. Ready for him to propose again. Ready for him to make at least a token argument so she could tell him yes.

"Gracie...I've been a fool. An idiot. So utterly stupid I don't know how I lived with myself without you."

She eagerly licked the moisture from her lips. She needed to hear the words. But right now she needed to make love to him more.

He tightened his grip, holding her in place.

"We don't have to get married in order for us to be together. I'll accept any conditions you lay down…just so long as you agree to reenter my life…my bed."

She squinted at him, surprised at the smile tugging at her lips. "Really?"

He kissed her deeply. "Really." He ran his thumb over her bottom lip. "I do have to warn you, however, that I probably will never give up trying to talk you into marrying me. It's just something I have to do—"

She clamped her free hand over his mouth. "I know. It's who you are." She slowly slid her fingers over his jaw, down the side of his neck, then entangled them in the wet hair sprinkling his chest. How easy it would be to leave things at that. Her body was screaming for release. Her heart was pumping an erratic rhythm in her chest. But as desperately as she wanted him physically, she needed to set things straight between them. Needed to tell him of the decision she'd come to.

When she wasn't looking, he'd dropped his hands to her thighs and begun parting her. She caught her breath…and his wrists. "Wait."

He looked at her, confusion clearly written across his striking face.

She briefly bit her bottom lip, then said softly, "I, um, just wanted to tell you that I've been just as big a fool as you've been. Bigger, even." She kissed him, then forced herself to pull away again. "That speech I gave in Miami…I was wrong."

She felt his heartbeat speed up beneath her hand.

"I…blamed you for screwing up my life. When the truth is…you gave me life. You opened my eyes, challenged my beliefs, made me see that just because you don't know the outcome, what will happen years, perhaps decades down the road, that you can't rule out doing something now."

His brows drew together, as if trying to work out what she was saying but not trusting himself to believe it.

She laughed nervously, focusing her gaze on his chest and the water that streamed down the tantalizing muscles outlined there.

"So…you know that question that you asked…and that I answered?" Her breath hitched. "Well, if the question still stands, I'm changing my answer. To yes."

His groan and ardent kisses was all the answer she needed. She finally gave herself over to the torrent of emotion and need whipping through her, allowing him to back her against the wall of the shower, not relaxing until he thrust into her to the hilt. Then a whole different type of tension began to spiral within her. She grasped his face in her hands and kissed him, and kissed him, and kissed him again.

He met her kiss for kiss, the passion on his face undeniable, the love in his eyes overwhelming. "Say it. Say 'I love you,' Gracie."

She smiled against his mouth. "I love you…Gracie." She laughed at his surprised expression. Then she opened herself to the power surging through her, and willingly and wholeheartedly whispered, "I love you, Dr. Dylan Fairbanks. I love you…I love you…I love you."

Epilogue

"YOU CAN'T TELL HER to do that!"

Gracie snapped upright from where she had the back of Dylan's head cradled between her unfortunately clothed thighs in their shared home office. But neither one of them were at their desks. Instead, her contemporary corner of the room with its yellow walls and purple furniture stood abandoned, as did his corner with its dark green walls and heavy antique desk and bookcases. An hour before, they'd both wandered to the neutral territory carefully mapped out between the two spaces, Gracie sitting on the couch, Dylan on the floor in front of her with his laptop open on the coffee table.

He stopped typing in the middle of his weekly column. This week's question came from a woman in Oklahoma who was "seriously attracted"—her words—to a guy who worked at the same company she did, but in a different department, and wanted advice on how to approach him.

Dylan had just told her to seek out Dr. Gracie Mattias-Fairbanks's first book and check out Chapter Five on sexual safaris.

"Why can't I tell her to do that?" he asked, rubbing his

head against where her right thigh was left bare by her cargo shorts.

"Because in my second book, I tell readers to disregard that advice."

He frowned up at her. "You do?"

She thwapped his shoulder. "You know I do."

His grin touched her in places his hands could not. And that was saying a whole hell of a lot, because he touched her everywhere. All the time. Even with both sets of their parents in the house.

Realizing she'd forgotten about Priscilla and Richard and Moonbeam and Frank, she glanced toward the double balcony doors overlooking the garden of their suburban Chicago ranch-style home, the location a compromise that put them more or less equally apart from their families. Besides, there was something…right about ending up in the place where they had first made love.

Gracie bit her lip, wondering how the two couples were faring. It was the first time in five days that they'd left them alone together. This morning she and Dylan had come to the mutual conclusion that they couldn't just go on playing mediators forever. And secretly shared their regret at having invited the couples to stay at their place for a full two weeks. Next time, they agreed, no longer than three days. Aside from their constantly having to be inventive in order to find a few important, hot moments alone together, they were afraid that if the couples didn't kill each other, they would give in and kill them all.

Dylan looked up at her. "What's the matter?"

She slowly shook her head. "I don't know. It's…too quiet out there." She ran her fingers through his hair. "You don't think they've drowned each other in the pool, do you?"

He ran his tongue along her upper thigh and dipped it under her cargo pants, causing her to gasp. She pulled his head away with a shaky jerk. "I'm serious."

He grinned wickedly up at her. "So am I."

Removing her hands from his hair, she got up from the couch and stepped toward the balcony doors. And nearly fell on her bottom from the shock of what she saw. "Oh, God, no!"

Dylan grimaced at her from where he'd resumed typing. "What is it?"

She urgently motioned for him to get over there. "Oh, Dylan, you've got to stop them before my parents go into cardiac arrest."

He was at her side in a blink. They stared out, wide-eyed, at Moonbeam and Frank, who had decided that their nice, modest neighborhood needed to be instructed in the finer points of nudism.

Gracie moved to yank open the balcony door, but Dylan caught her hand.

"What are you doing? I've got to stop them before somebody calls the cops."

"That's what the privacy fence is for, Gracie." He placed her hand against his growing erection. "Remember?"

"But my parents—"

"Are fine," he interrupted, groaning when she curved her fingers **as** far as she could around his hardening shaft. "Look."

Gracie did and thought she was the one at risk of having a heart attack. While her father sat at the patio table reading the *Wall Street Journal,* her mother was…oh, my God, she wasn't!

A few hard blinks and a swallow later told her she was.

Priscilla Mattias had just dropped her robe, indulging in a bit of "when in Rome" behavior.

Gracie cringed and turned to press her face into the front of Dylan's oxford shirt. "Please tell me she just didn't—"

"Get naked? Sorry, I can't."

His chuckle vibrated her face.

"You know what this means, don't you?" he murmured, running his hands down her back to her bottom and pressing her boldly against him.

"That we'll probably have to have all our parents committed?"

"No. It means we have the house to ourselves for a few precious minutes."

She jerked to look up at him, flashing him a wicked smile. "How stupid of me...."

He swept her up into her arms and threw her to the couch, then followed after her. Pushing her shirt up and claiming a straining nipple through her bra, he asked huskily, "So... where, exactly, were we on that debate on children?"

She hummed, absently making sure they couldn't be seen over the side of the couch from outside, then undoing his zipper. "Let's see...one child, I think. In five years."

He sank deeply into her hungry flesh. She caught her breath and grasped his tight rear end, pulling him closer. When she felt him hesitate, she blinked up at him. "What?"

He grinned and thrust again. "Oh, I don't know. I was just—" he slowly pulled out and thrust again, sending her senses spiraling "—wondering what it would take to change that to two kids in three years."

She wrapped her legs around his hips, arching her back when he blessedly thrust into her again. "A miracle," she said.

He worked a hand between them and pressed his thumb against her hypersensitive bud, nearly toppling her over the edge even as he thrust again. "Let's see what I can do...."

* * * * *

COMING NEXT MONTH

Available August 30, 2011

You can find more information on upcoming
Harlequin® titles, free excerpts and more at
www.HarlequinInsideRomance.com.

HBCNM0811

New York Times *and* USA TODAY *bestselling author*
Maya Banks presents a brand-new miniseries

PREGNANCY & PASSION

When four irresistible tycoons face
the consequences of temptation.

Book 1—*ENTICED BY HIS FORGOTTEN LOVER*

Available September 2011 from Harlequin® Desire®!

Rafael de Luca had been in bad situations before. A crowded ballroom could never make him sweat.

These people would never know that he had no memory of any of them.

He surveyed the party with grim tolerance, searching for the source of his unease.

At first his gaze flickered past her, but he yanked his attention back to a woman across the room. Her stare bored holes through him. Unflinching and steady, even when his eyes locked with hers.

Petite, even in heels, she had a creamy olive complexion. A wealth of inky-black curls cascaded over her shoulders and her eyes were equally dark.

She looked at him as if she'd already judged him and found him lacking. He'd never seen her before in his life. Or had he?

He cursed the gaping hole in his memory. He'd been diagnosed with selective amnesia after his accident four months ago. Which seemed like complete and utter bull. No one got amnesia except hysterical women in bad soap operas.

With a smile, he disengaged himself from the group

around him and made his way to the mystery woman.

She wasn't coy. She stared straight at him as he approached, her chin thrust upward in defiance.

"Excuse me, but have we met?" he asked in his smoothest voice.

His gaze moved over the generous swell of her breasts pushed up by the empire waist of her black cocktail dress.

When he glanced back up at her face, he saw fury in her eyes.

"Have we *met?*" Her voice was barely a whisper, but he felt each word like the crack of a whip.

Before he could process her response, she nailed him with a right hook. He stumbled back, holding his nose.

One of his guards stepped between Rafe and the woman, accidentally sending her to one knee. Her hand flew to the folds of her dress.

It was then, as she cupped her belly, that the realization hit him. She was pregnant.

Her eyes flashing, she turned and ran down the marble hallway.

Rafael ran after her. He burst from the hotel lobby, and saw two shoes sparkling in the moonlight, twinkling at him.

He blew out his breath in frustration and then shoved the pair of sparkly, ultrafeminine heels at his head of security.

"Find the woman who wore these shoes."

Will Rafael find his mystery woman?
Find out in Maya Banks's passionate new novel
ENTICED BY HIS FORGOTTEN LOVER
Available September 2011 from Harlequin® Desire®!

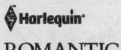

ROMANTIC
SUSPENSE

NEW YORK TIMES BESTSELLING AUTHOR

RACHEL LEE

The Rescue Pilot

Time is running out…

Desperate to help her ailing sister, Rory is determined
to get Cait the necessary treatment to help her fight
a devastating disease. A cross-country trip turns into
a fight for survival in more ways than one when their plane
encounters trouble. Can Rory trust pilot Chase Dakota
with their lives, and possibly her heart?

**Look for this heart-stopping romance in September
from *New York Times* bestselling author Rachel Lee
and Harlequin Romantic Suspense!**

THE NEXT GENERATION

Available in September wherever books are sold!

www.Harlequin.com.